KILLER GOLD

A Bedard Adventure

BY

Garet Anderson

Killer Gold
Copyright © 2019 by Garet Anderson

Tellwell Talent
www.tellwell.ca

ISBN
978-0-2288-1486-3 (Hardcover)
978-0-2288-1485-6 (Paperback)
978-0-2288-1487-0 (eBook)

To Georgina Harrison for her many thoughtful
contributions to this story.

KILLER GOLD

Introduction

1858 was a remarkable year for the Lower Fraser River Valley. This valley is part of a very large area that was then called New Caledonia. New Caledonia is now known as the Canadian Province of British Columbia. One of the world's most beautiful large cities, Vancouver, is located at the mouth of the Fraser River as it runs into the Pacific Ocean. The Lower Fraser River Valley currently has a population of about three million people.

On January 1, 1858, there were fewer than fifty white men living at the Hudson's Bay Company's Fort Langley, located about thirty miles upstream from the mouth of the Fraser River. Another ten white men lived at Fort Hope, sixty miles farther upstream, and none were recorded living anywhere else in the Lower Fraser River Valley. It is probable that there were more than 5,000 natives living in this area; there is no written record of this.

It has been estimated that 20,000 to 30,000 miners came to New Caledonia in 1858 to mine for gold on the Lower Fraser River. When the river rose in July, curtailing all mining operations, many of those who first arrived returned south very disappointed. A small number of the men moved on to the Upper Fraser River past steep canyon walls and tortuous rapids. Some also used the long water and wagon road route that was created in the summer of 1858 and opened in September that went from Lake Harrison to Cayoosh Flat, now known as Lillooet. Food and supplies were difficult to obtain there in 1858, and all but a few returned south again.

The weather at the mouth of the Fraser River has always been mild. Snow is rare, but it rains almost all winter. In 1858, spring came early and the rain was intermittent. The winter of 1858–'59 was very cold, and most of the remaining miners travelled south to warmer climes in November and December.

At this time, the Hudson's Bay Company held a fur-trade monopoly over a large part of what is now known as Canada. Fort Langley was a key fur depot and the western area was administered from Fort Victoria on Vancouver Island just off the coast.

On August 2, 1858, the British government passed an act proclaiming the mainland a Crown colony, and it was named British Columbia by Queen Victoria.

Gold was found by the natives on the Thompson River near the Upper Fraser River as early as 1856 and was traded to the Hudson's Bay Company, which decided to keep this information secret. Small amounts of gold continued to be mined in this isolated area, mostly by natives. Eventually, in January 1858, the Hudson's Bay Company sent a gold sample to the U.S. Mint in San Francisco for assessment. The cat was then out of the bag.

There are unconfirmed reports that a few gold miners managed to make their way to the Upper Fraser River in the winter of 1857 and in the early spring of 1858. But the majority of miners started arriving on April 25, 1858, when the *Commodore* docked at Fort Victoria with four hundred and fifty men on board. This almost doubled the population of non-natives in all of New Caledonia and Vancouver Island.

Many of these men perished on the treacherous ocean trip from Fort Victoria to the mouth of the Fraser River. They travelled in canoes and very small vessels, including some log rafts.

Later in the year, small steam-powered ships arrived. These ships travelled from Fort Victoria to Fort Langley and Fort Hope, transporting the miners in relative safety.

Many miners were killed by hostile natives who wanted to beat back the invading white men, who they felt were taking something that belonged to them.

Yet more miners had limited wilderness experience and succumbed to a lack of food or appropriate cold-weather clothing. Others failed because of a lack of funds to support themselves and returned to the United States greatly discouraged.

Some of these miners came from all over the world to make their fortunes on the Fraser River, but most of them came from the San Francisco area in the United States, where the gold rush that started in 1849 was petering out.

Most of the gold miners travelled through Fort Victoria, but some travelled overland from the south to Fort Langley and more came north up the Okanagan River to the Thompson River, a tributary of the Upper Fraser River.

The most accurate record of the numbers of miners travelling to Fort Victoria has been extracted from the Port of San Francisco's list of sailings in 1858. This list does not include the unauthorised overloads on these ships, nor does it include any of the decrepit sailing ships that were illegally resurrected from abandoned hulks that lined the local rivers. The huge demand for passage northward made all of these ventures very profitable, but unfortunately some of these ships were lost at sea with all of their passengers and crew.

The miners from the San Francisco area had previous experience in dealing with natives: They just killed them all! The natives in British Columbia had been trading furs with white men for years and, in some cases, for several generations. In the areas where gold had been found, the natives knew the value of the gold and had the weapons and the fighting skills to protect themselves from the onrush of white men. Many natives and white men died as a result. The historic records of these events are few.

The detailed recorded history of this short period of time, 1858, relies for the most part on accounts written by well-educated travellers and journalists as well as the journals created at various Hudson's Bay Company forts. Most of the written accounts have been shown to be second-hand reports at best, and in some instances have been found to be incorrect or fictional. This recorded history is entirely from a white man's perspective and does not include anything from the natives' viewpoint. The history of the region is not the main focus of this story, but it is referred to from time to time to support the events described.

The Musqueam Nation's language is Hunguminum, a dialect of the Halkomelem language. All of the nations on the Lower Fraser River and on a southern portion of Vancouver Island speak a Halkomelem dialect.

In this story, the Songhees village at Fort Victoria was also included in the Halkomelem language group. The Songhees are actually Straits Salish and speak a dialect of the Salishan language.

The nations located on the Lower Fraser River have often co-operated as a group under the name Sto:lo: *People of the River*. To simplify this story, some villages near Fort Hope are identified as part of a Sto:lo nation. In the story, Sto:lo will be represented by the more outdated (thus historically correct) spelling: Staulo.

The small Musqueam village of Tsusnahm probably existed in 1858, but the English spelling of the name and the location of this village was chosen by me.

Several other actual villages on the coast and on the Fraser River Valley are identified. The English spelling of all of these villages, including the large Musqueam villages of Mahli and Stsulawh, was chosen by me.

Bedard, the hero of this story, has been personally requested by Queen Victoria to deal with a list of villainous people whom the British Government feels will be attracted to the goldfields, not as miners but as criminals and killers feeding off the miners' successes. Most of the people on Bedard's list are well known to him from his previous adventures in San Francisco and other parts of the world. Many on the list have been evicted from San Francisco recently as undesirables and are therefore thought to be amongst the first wave of miners to reach the Lower Fraser River.

This story is a work of fiction. Bedard—or Copco, as he wishes to be known in this adventure—is adopted into a small Musqueam Village near the mouth of the Fraser River. I hope that you enjoy the story.

Garet Anderson

Historical Characters

Only four real historical characters appear in these pages: James Douglas, Amelia Connolly Douglas, Matthew Baillie Begbie and Captain Tagore.

Several others are identified, such as Captain Jeremiah Nagle, the captain of the sailing vessel *Commodore* and the Hudson's Bay Company's chief factor, Murray Yale at Fort Langley, but they do not become a part of the story.

James Douglas was the head of the Hudson's Bay Company's fur trading operations in New Caledonia based at Fort Victoria. He was also the governor of Vancouver Island and the Queen Charlotte Islands now known as Haida Gwaii. He became the first governor of British Columbia on November 19, 1858.

He was born in British Guiana, the son of a Scottish merchant and a Creole mother. He married sixteen-year-old Amelia Connolly in 1828. She was the daughter of a Cree mother and William Connolly, who was James's boss at that time.

Matthew Baillie Begbie was an English barrister who became the first chief magistrate of British Columbia, and Captain Tagore was the long-time captain of the four-masted sailing ship *Cobalt*.

In some cases, such as when Begbie was sworn in as chief magistrate and Douglas was sworn in as governor, my fictional characters are witnessing an event that really happened.

When any of these four people have conversations with my fictional characters, the complete conversation was created by myself.

Other than the four persons identified above, the names, characters, places and incidents in this work of fiction are either the product of my imagination or are used fictitiously; any resemblance to actual persons living or dead, events or locales is entirely coincidental.

One
January 1, 1858

The flash of light surprised him. Bedard brought the binoculars up without moving his eyes from the distant shoreline to the north where the light had emerged. The ship, a beautiful two-masted schooner, the *Lady Bell*, was running before the wind in a light swell, so he did not have to steady himself against the rigging. The tide was on the rise and the shoreline that they had been passing varied from dull brown tidal flats of silt and small stones to brown or white sand or rocky cliff rubble. The schooner would soon turn into the well-demarked Middle Fraser River channel coming up about half a mile to the east. The foreshore of the north bank of the northern arm of the Fraser River, about five miles away, was light green—probably a grass meadow. Behind this was thick forest. The trees seemed much taller in this estuary than in similar areas they had passed farther south.

Bedard was impressed with his first view of New Caledonia. It was definitely a wilderness area with only a few white men at two fur-trading forts and several thousand natives living in the river valley. He had met the head of the Hudson's Bay Company's fur-trading operations, James Douglas, several times in the past but had never crossed over from Fort Victoria on Vancouver Island to visit the Fraser River.

Bedard slowly moved the glasses along the shoreline but saw nothing. He removed the glasses and immediately saw the flash again. This time he found an indication of some presence beyond, in the trees. He guessed that someone in one of those bloody tall trees was looking at the schooner with a telescope. He dropped the binoculars, which were fastened around his neck with a braided cord, and reached over his shoulder for his telescope. He extended it to its full length of two and a half feet and moved over to the shrouds so he could stabilize the looking device. The shoreline sprang to life—what a difference twelve power made! He could see a small long wharf poking out from the grass and smoke in the trees beyond from what could be a cooking stove. Sweeping the glass slowly to the east, he saw structures in the grassland: A local native village similar to the many others they had seen when the schooner passed close to land.

He put the glass away and brought out a greasy hand-drawn map from inside his jerkin. There was the village, actually two villages close together, and the house just back from the shoreline in the forest that could be Julius Voight's. The map was created for him in a tavern in San Francisco. He allowed himself to smile. He had not seen Julius for more than twenty years. He was still not certain what kind of a reception he would receive when, or if, they met again. Surely Julius had mellowed over the years. *Well, we'll see,* he thought.

Bedard was determined to visit Julius as soon as possible. But he needed to explore the land first. Life was too precious. Bedard, who was now sixty, had always tried to minimize his exposure to potential danger, and Julius was very dangerous. He was one of twenty-eight unsavory men and two aggressive women who were thought to be headed to this river, attracted by a gold rush about to start here. Bedard's assignment from the British government was to dispatch them. Many he knew as criminals from previous adventures.

The schooner changed direction suddenly amidst the usual bedlam, in response to the shouted orders and the shifting of sails. On her maiden voyage, this incredible sailing ship was also a powerful coal-fired double-screw vessel designed for travel inland up coastal rivers where the wind was fickle and unreliable. They were going very slowly toward the shoreline, still under sail. The river mouth had been obvious for some time. The captain planned to anchor several miles up the river for the night and arrive at Fort Langley the next day. He had agreed to slow down just before the junction of the north and middle arms of the river so that Bedard could disembark.

Bedard was ready. At the last land stop, he had obtained two light canoes—one for his gear and another for himself. When they entered the river, he planned to go ashore with a minimum of fuss. He would put the boats over the starboard side on a line, load them up and then cast off at an appropriate spot so he could make his way to the shore partly shielded by the schooner.

He would then stash the boats with the gear, and in due course, after ensuring that his canine family was fit, make his way through the estuary toward the area where Voight's house was located.

The local natives could present a problem. White men were no longer unusual. The fur trade had been going on for eighty years, and the pending gold rush might have already brought more men. But Bedard did not know how the local natives in this specific area had been treated by the newcomers, so he would be as careful as he could.

The rest of his family was ready, too. All the dogs were very excited. Being cooped up on the ship for ten days with a minimum of exercise was a major problem. This would delay his exploring by at least a few days until he could determine that they were able to shoulder their responsibilities. JoJo and Haus were mastiffs. They were about three feet to the shoulder with huge heads and incredibly strong bodies. Although they looked like twins, JoJo was about six years older than Haus and was the first dog of this family that Bedard had adopted nine years ago.

Because of their massive size, their job was protection. You would not want to take them on at any time. They were extremely bush-smart and able to move through thick forests rapidly and quietly. Most of the bears they had met so far had turned tail immediately. The mastiffs were not very bright, but they were well trained and instantly responded to many commands. They were, however, a target for cruel humans with guns, but both of them had managed to survive several gunshot wounds. As a result, they were particularly unhappy for the last ten days, having been caged and in close proximity to over thirty humans on the ship.

The other two dogs were collies: Hy and Liz. They were incredibly intelligent and very sly and personally trained by Bedard. He worked them twice daily on the ship, to the complete amazement of the passengers and crew who never tired of their antics—swerving and crouching at Bedard's whistle and word commands.

Because they were so much smaller than the mastiffs, their job was security. Their highly developed sense of smell and of hearing was very useful to Bedard. Both JoJo and Haus worked very well with their small friends and responded to their leadership. A very unusual family, to say the least.

Bedard left the ship with his family and navigated the short distance to the shore with ease. The shore was covered with small stones and cobbles. He immediately sent

Hi and Liz out to secure the immediate area and left JoJo and Haus to guard the canoes. Bedard went inland and found a trail parallel to the shore. He noticed that it had not been recently used. The vegetation in this area was thick but the trees were not tall. His first task was to hide his canoes. He soon found a reasonable animal track leading inland and determined that the main trail to the southwest ended abruptly at a landing area close to where they had arrived.

Returning to the canoes, he found the pull-and-lift harnesses for JoJo and Haus and attached them to the first canoe. They were experts at this, and Bedard and the dogs soon had both canoes well hidden. He then inspected their landing spot to remove any traces of their arrival.

His next task was to investigate the area and find a secure temporary campsite. With all the dogs in a normal security diamond around him, he walked carefully to the northeast. He carried only his rifle, a small backpack and a utility belt. The trail started off fairly close to the water and then moved back from the water onto higher land. Here, although the vegetation continued to be thick, the trees were much larger and taller. He was certain that he could find a perfect lookout tree. An island presented itself as a possible campsite and the family moved down to investigate.

Two
January 2, 1858

Thud!

The arrow buried itself in the root three feet from Bedard's head. He was instantly awake. He did not move. Bedard always slept well, but over the years he had developed a high degree of survival-based sensitivities; he instinctively knew that none of the dogs had signalled.

The arrow had come from across the water to the northwest. Slowly, he moved his head up from the tree-bough bed and cautiously looked across the water. It was still night, but the moon was bright. He could see three points of light six hundred feet away on the far shore—fires, very small. The lights went out suddenly. He could feel the hairs on the back of his neck rise.

Dammit, he thought.

A warning, but who sent it? Was it for him? There was no time to think. He must move.

He made three low, sharp whistles. At the same time he gathered up his gear, hastily stuffing his bedroll into his backpack and abandoning his makeshift bed under the deadfall roots. He turned and moved toward the shallow waterway on the east side of the long, thin, overgrown sand-bar island. The four dogs had responded quietly to his signal and were already silently across the water and off into the forest to their emergency positions.

Bedard ran carefully toward the fallen tree trunk that extended from the grass over the sand and into the water. Using this tree bridge in order to not leave footprints in the soft island sand, he entered the waist-high water and strode noiselessly to the cobble shore a hundred feet away. He then melded into the forest fringe.

Less than five minutes had passed. He had been putting on his gear as he moved. The backpack and small front pack were in place. The rifle, bow and quiver were over his shoulders, and his compact utility belt was clipped in place.

Bedard was very comfortable travelling in the dark forest with his heavy gear. He continued to move purposefully toward his target: a tall tree that he had chosen the day before and had prepared as a temporary base. It was about six feet in diameter with no branches for the first twenty feet, and then a profusion of growth leading more than two hundred feet above the forest floor. This treetop had been hit by many lightning bolts. From this perch, he was slightly above the other treetops in this part of the thick forest, well protected from being spotted from below and with a clear view of the land and river delta for many miles around.

At his usual rambling trot, he detached his climbing rope from his belt as he reached the tree. Whipping the rope around the tree, he was up it in a flash. Reaching the first protected level, he removed his heavy gear. Less than twenty minutes had passed when he reached the lookout. It was still dark and partially overcast with high scattered clouds, but no rain and no sign of the moon. He looked to the east—the first light of the day was still several minutes away.

A dog barked twice—unknown danger pending! It was definitely Liz. Her responsibility was the far northern point, actually a small sandy beach about half a mile away. Bedard strained his eyes looking west and north from his perch. He thought he saw a small flash of light on the water. Yes, there it was again, about two hundred feet off the shore in the blackness of the night: a small canoe with one or two people.

A sliver of sun popped over the mountains in the east under the high cloud cover. Bedard now saw the light outline of the canoe clearly against the black water—two men. In the distance, supposedly hidden from his view around the point, he could also make out six other canoes holding against the outgoing tide and the river current.

It was clear that the arrow had come from the small native village on the island across the middle arm of the river. The three fires had been purposeful. But why had these strangers come to his aid? Bedard mused over this point as he watched the two men beach their canoe and then move carefully and stealthily along the cobble beach on the west side of the small island.

From his perch, Bedard could see the whole island. One man moved across it and waited near the water in an aggressive warlike stance. He had a short bow in his left hand with an arrow in place and he searched the shoreline carefully while his partner moved through the undergrowth behind him. The remains of Bedard's hastily abandoned bed were soon found, and the two men moved back and out of sight into the small island's sparse undergrowth toward the west side.

It was still very dark on the ground. Bedard abruptly decided that the men were not native people but were probably white men and that they represented a serious danger to him.

What's happening here? Did the lookout see me yesterday? Surely they wouldn't come with so large a group unless they had additional information, but how'd they get it so fast? Who's in charge of this group? Julius?

He surveyed the six canoes that remained at the point. There were more than ten men and at least four of them could be white. They were too far away for Bedard to make out any of their features.

The two men below had to be dealt with in a hurry or they would signal to the other canoes. In the darkness, the men had four options: yell to attract attention, but this would also alert the stranger; wait for twenty minutes until it was light enough for a silent visual signal from ground level; build a small signal fire; or climb a tree to signal. Bedard decided that they would climb a tree.

He moved silently down from his perch, taking only his bow and arrows, his climbing rope and his knives. A soft coo brought JoJo up from his station near the water. Bedard sent him northeast to start a diversion. They had used this tactic many times.

JoJo moved away silently in the undergrowth, very pleased that he had been chosen for this action. Bedard moved in a running crouch toward the water. He stopped and waited in the tall grass until JoJo signalled that he was in position. A distinctive bark from JoJo was acknowledged with a high-pitched whistle from Bedard. A bear-like bark and a thrashing of trees to the northeast followed by splashing would distract the attention of his two enemies. Bedard, assured that the two men were concentrating their attention to the north, moved confidently into the water toward the tree bridge.

He passed through the undergrowth over the island to the cobble beach. It was still quite dark but he could see a form ahead near the base of one of the few trees on the island. This person was looking northeast. Placing an arrow in his bow, Bedard moved closer. The second man was about thirty feet up the tree. The first arrow caught the man on the ground in the middle of the back. The second arrow hit the leg of the tree climber and he fell to the ground with a thud. JoJo arrived on the scene and stood over the wounded man. Bedard reached the tree and determined quickly that the first man was dead, and that his companion was only slightly wounded with his wind knocked out from the fall.

Bedard looked carefully at the dead man's face. He decided that this was Woolsome Taylor, a mixed-race knife killer, who was also an expert archer and was high on Bedard's list.

He grabbed the shirt of the wounded man. "Well, Martin, we meet again!"

Martin's face showed pure hatred. "The Wolverine will be here shortly and then we'll see what's what."

Old Tommy Hunter, otherwise known as the Wolverine.

Well, what do you know about that! Top of my list!

Martin lunged at Bedard with his knife, but JoJo caught Martin's arm in his mouth. Bone crunched; Martin screamed and fainted. Bedard wanted Martin to tell him some more information about the Wolverine but the scream would surely carry over the water in the quietness of the morning and the other canoes would move forward. Bedard planted an arrow in Martin's chest. He then removed the arrows from both men.

Bedard and the dogs moved back over the island, across the water and into the forest with Bedard moving rapidly toward his base tree. The four dogs were again directed to their emergency positions.

Two more canoes arrived shortly with four men. Bedard could not tell if the Wolverine was one of them. The new arrivals found Bedard's bed and began a search of the shoreline that was soon abandoned. They loaded the bodies of their companions into the canoes and moved back toward the waiting group. After a short pause, all of the canoes turned around and moved off to the west.

From his perch high in the tree, Bedard watched them depart.

Julius Voight would not have anything to do with the Wolverine.

Where is Julius now? Is he still alive?

Three
January 12, 1858

Hy heard it first. Incredible hearing sensitivity. He stopped and rose slightly on his rear legs so that his head was just above the tall grass bordering the narrow path that they were travelling. The sound was momentary, and Bedard noticed Hy's movement in the darkness but the family had a major project underway and was in a hurry.

Over the past ten days, Bedard had worked his dogs effectively. They were now very much into their flexible security responsibilities and Bedard was pleased and looking forward to this new adventure. It was certainly a beautiful part of the world and it was obvious that the four dogs agreed. The weather had been initially cold with occasional flurries but it had started to warm up three days ago.

It was about two hours before sun-up and they were proceeding east along the south bank of the middle arm of the Fraser River toward the junction of the river's middle and north arms. They intended to cross over the north arm to the north shore in the darkness. Hy was on point with Haus. Bedard was carrying a light pack on his chest and a medium-sized mountain pack on his back. JoJo was pulling the canoe, and Liz was somewhere behind.

Hope it's nothing. We do not need complications today.

It was black as hell. No moon. The trail markers could only be seen when he was right on top of them. The shoreline appeared suddenly, and Hy came to greet them. He was excited, which didn't bode well. It meant something, or someone, was out there.

They stopped behind the rubble and waited for Liz. Soon she appeared, and then all four dogs stopped dead and rose up on their back legs to listen to the sound. Bedard could not hear anything, of course. He found that it was very frustrating not to be able to hear the sound that the dogs were hearing in situations like this. But that was what the training was all about.

Is there danger? What is it?

Hy moved forward again. This was a good sign. At least there was no immediate danger.

Bedard removed his packs and untied the pull harness from JoJo. He told Liz to move back down the trail and JoJo to guard the canoe and packs. He went forward softly in search of Hy and Haus. They were lying down on the sandy beach by the water at the end of the trail wagging their tails. They both looked around as if to say *isn't life grand.* The sound was not menacing.

Bedard sat with them surveying the far bank of the river. No movement. Nothing. Then he heard a faint sound from across the water and to the east. *Well, it could be anything.* It was the direction that they were heading, so in due course they would find out what it was—if it was still there.

After about half an hour of waiting, he heard the faint sound several times but could not identify it. He then moved back and refitted the pull and lift harness on Haus, put the packs in the canoe and lifted the other end. Off they went right to the water's edge. It was just before high tide. Off with the harness. Low whistle, and the three dogs jumped into the boat. Bedard pushed it out and turned to see Liz break from the shoreline and dash toward them.

Off they went across the river. Very exposed. No protection. No current, fortunately. The force of the tide matched the outward flow of the river. It was very easy to cross the thousand feet or so to the far side. The family had previously made two practice runs to establish a good landing place, to hide their other canoe and gear and reconnoiter the three villages they planned to pass on the way to the objective.

The sound came again. Clearer this time.

A plaintive wail is what it sounded like. Possibly two thousand feet to the east upstream. They were about two miles from the first village, so the villagers there would not hear anything.

As soon as the canoe touched the far bank, Hy was off like a flash. All of the family had jobs to do, and as soon as the canoe was in its hiding place Bedard settled in for his planned snooze. Just before he dozed off, Hy returned, licked his face, and was off again. Oh well, Bedard said to himself, and moved off into the gloom to follow him.

Soon he was aware of the sound, clearer now, definitely a wail, not unlike a baby's cry for food. Hy returned several times to ensure that Bedard was coming. He was now wagging his tail madly.

Bedard was near now. Definitely a baby's cry. Hy came back again and Bedard grabbed his tail to slow him down so that he could follow him closely in the darkness. They came upon a small clearing. Bedard made a sign to Hy to circle the area for danger. He didn't move. He had already done that. Bedard signalled again, and off he went. The sound was fainter now, running out of energy. In about ten minutes Hy returned. Still nothing. Bedard followed him to the sound.

We definitely do not need this! A small baby wrapped in blankets and encased in a front-pack that the local women used to carry their young. Very small. Bedard stuck a little finger in its mouth and the crying stopped. The baby sucked the finger madly. It was very hungry.

What now? No choice. He scooped up the bundle and went off at a run westward to the landing area. The baby continued whimpering but not very loudly. The baby needed food, but there was no milk. Water with berry juice would be good for a start.

When Bedard arrived back at the landing, the sun was just starting to come up. He poured some water from one of the water bags into a bowl and crushed a mixture of berries in the water. The resulting liquid was sweet and not bad-tasting.

Well, what the heck. A fingertip of the juice was well received. He cut a leaf of grass with a small knife and poured a bit of juice down the leaf into the open mouth. This worked, more or less. A couple of sputters from time to time and then a good burp on his shoulder. He had to smile in spite of himself.

The dogs had kept away, but now Liz passed by and gave them a sniff. Bedard realized that the baby was quite smelly. *Shit! Literally.* He smiled again, *In for a pound...* He unlaced the pack and unwrapped the blankets from the boy (he could now tell). The last wrapping was made of leaves, which he removed. He collected some similar leaves, wiped him off a bit and wrapped him up again. Liz was ahead of him. She had dug a hole and was in the process of burying the old leaves—Bedard helped her complete the job. The baby was now asleep.

Now what? The original plan was to walk through the first smaller village with one dog and then pass around the next village, the very large one. The first village was probably already aware of his existence whereas the second village probably was not.

The situation had now changed. *Why had this baby been abandoned? Very unusual!* He could not leave the baby behind. On the other hand, it was not possible to look after him. *So, now what?*

The new plan was not a good one. He was too exposed and knew next to nothing about the people here.

Hy and Haus would take to the edge of the forest beyond the grasses on the high land and remain about two hundred feet inland—out of sight but within hearing—Bedard would signal all clear from time to time. When he did not signal, Hy would come down for visual contact with Haus remaining undetectable in the forest. Their other call signals would be used when appropriate.

JoJo would carry the special pack and follow him closely with Liz out in point. Every mile or so Bedard planned to have Hy circle back behind them for a security check.

Bedard decided to name the boy Noua, a name he would have called his son but for the fact that the child had been born a daughter and named Dorthea instead.

Noua seemed content, especially when the walk began. He went to sleep again. The sun was now up and there were no clouds, so it would become warmer as the day progressed.

They plodded on at a medium pace through the grassland beside the river on a well-defined walking trail that he had never used before. No wheel marks. He had previously determined that the main east–west trail was located up on the ridge to the north some distance back from the river.

The Musqueam village that they were approaching was called Tsusnahm. The Fort Victoria letter to Bedard in San Francisco had indicated that this village was small, composed of three groups of five or six longhouses with one very large family or a number of families sharing each one. Bedard had seen the village from a distance and had thought that there might be close to four hundred people living there if all the longhouses were occupied.

These groups of longhouses were separated from each other by streams and small soft ground ponds. Their arrangement did not seem to indicate a placement for defence or protection but more a haphazard choice. They were all facing the water, and a few were distinctively decorated.

Their previous scouting trips had identified one of the longhouses to be a special place, incredibly ornate—probably the chief's home, but it also could be an activity place.

The information obtained from Fort Victoria was more extensive on the next village, which was actually two large Musqueam villages, Mahli and Stsulawh, located on either side of a small river flowing from the north into the north arm of the Fraser River. The only clear point Fort Victoria had made was that the Musqueam in this area had very little direct contact with the white man in recent times. The few white miners who had already arrived used the south bank trails of the Fraser River to move up the river in search of gold and did not use the north bank trails past these villages.

The Tsusnahm villagers were primarily fishermen, with some hunting and gathering, and were not particularly wealthy. They did not do much fur trading.

Minimum information. Not a good plan.

First contact brought Liz racing back for instructions. The village dogs had picked up her scent and were howling. Bedard shortened her point lead to about three hundred feet, fed Noua who was awakened by the sounds, and moved out again.

The village dogs, sensing strength, kept out of the way. A group of six circled around behind them but made no move to investigate. One wiggler, as Bedard called this type of dog, tried to befriend Liz, but Liz bared her fangs briefly and the mongrel scurried away.

The first longhouses were in sight when a vanguard of women and children, who were probably out collecting berries, saw them. Bedard and his entourage stopped to let the foragers look them over and then moved on at a slower pace. They were some distance away, and he did not think that they noticed Noua strapped to his chest.

Within five hundred feet of the first group of longhouses, Liz stopped and sat down, the signal for non-dangerous contact.

A young boy stepped out of the grass, saw Liz, and then the whole group appeared. Accidental contact, obviously. Probably not a sentry. A very innocent village, on the surface. Bedard called Liz back to him and she came, head low, tail between her legs—a trick that she had used many times when faced with non-threatening contact.

Bedard and the two dogs moved forward slowly until they were about three hundred feet from the boy. There was no doubt that JoJo was a formidable sight: huge head, three-foot-high to the shoulder. In the harness and pack, he looked non-threatening— almost like a small deer. Bedard was wearing his usual loose, open-neck jerkin, long hair in a gathered tie at the back. His skin was as dark as the boy's, and there were no weapons showing.

Noua cried, and Bedard instinctively knelt on to the ground to check him. The youth was off in a flash toward the village. Liz jumped up in an action stance and Bedard signalled no. It might be best to have the village warned of the family's approach.

Liz was sent out again to about two hundred feet and Bedard followed her rapidly. He wanted to get to the middle group of the longhouses where the main one was located before being seriously confronted. The forest had come closer to the grasslands and he now suspected that Hy and Haus were both within visual contact.

The first group of longhouses looked abandoned and were not in good condition, but there were people inside the last longhouse, which seemed to be in better condition—but no children to be seen. *Unusual.* Man, dogs and baby passed by at a fast walk.

The first two longhouses of the centre group were not in good condition either, but they were definitely occupied. He could see children being pulled in through doorways. Notice of their approach was not particularly fast.

The next building, the ornate longhouse, was out of sight around a small bluff of small trees. When they turned the corner, they were confronted with a group of about thirty men and women. No children! They had obviously interrupted something—a meeting in front of the main longhouse underneath a huge tree by the water.

None of the men had weapons, some wore belt-mounted knife sheaves and there were some smaller dogs on leads—probably young hunting dogs. Their clothing was not remarkable except for one man, considerably older than the group, who seemed to be a senior elder or chief. The group was sitting on the ground in a circle and the youth who had first spotted them was standing next to the chief, having obviously told him and the group about the stranger and his dogs.

Bedard stopped immediately. About one hundred feet separated the two groups. JoJo came up behind him; he turned and pulled the quick release and his pack slid to the ground. JoJo did not sit.

"Stay!" he said.

He removed his own backpack and walked slowly forward with Liz, who was doing her slouch thing again. Nearing the group, Bedard signalled Liz to stay. She lay down, watching intently.

In the meantime, the villagers had spread apart, leaving a pathway to approach the chief, who sat down. Some sort of command was made and the others also sat. A particularly non-confrontational stance. *What is happening?*

Noua cried out. Essentially ignoring the group, Bedard dropped to the ground and pulled out his pouch of berry water, stuck a finger in the juice and then to Noua's mouth—it worked like magic. Some of the women smiled. The chief almost did too.

Then Bedard noticed a young woman lying on the ground nearby with her arms tied to a tall stake. She was either unconscious or dead.

He whistled for Liz. In a flash, she went near the woman and came back to sit beside her master with her tail wagging madly. Bedard motioned her away. Mystery solved—Noua's mother. Bedard wondered what to do next.

He unfolded himself from the ground, moved over to the woman and cut the twine on her arms. She was breathing. The sound of Noua's second cry caused the woman's eyes to open. Startled, she gathered the baby into her arms and started to sob. She had not seen Bedard yet. He moved slowly away and, still standing outside of the group, smiled at the chief. Amazingly, no one had moved.

A drum sounded once, and very softly a melodic song started in the group. Almost a chant or a prayer. Bedard and Liz had moved back from the group to where JoJo was still standing by the packs, tail swinging. He sensed that there was some potential for a happy ending here.

A well-dressed older woman got up and approached Bedard. There were tears in her eyes. *Oh, oh, the grandmother.* She came right up to him and hugged him. Flustered, he mumbled something. Liz was beside herself and did one of her happy upside-down backward flips. Then others, men and women, came forward and touched him.

No more hugs, please, he said to himself, smiling.

Bedard felt a bit uncomfortable, not knowing exactly what had happened. Noua's mother had disappeared behind the longhouse, walking unsteadily with Noua crushed against her chest and another woman running to follow her. The group returned to the tree and sat down again, so Bedard gathered up his belongings and moved off quietly to the west along the same trail past the village.

The other three longhouses in the centre group were also not in good condition but seemed to be occupied. The third group of five longhouses was definitely abandoned. Bedard thought about this and decided that his estimate of the village population was significantly incorrect. He now felt that there might be fewer than one hundred people living here, including the children, and not the four hundred he had originally estimated. He wondered why Victoria had not known this.

The trail that they were following ended, as did the grassland. He had not travelled this way before. In front of them was a mucky rubble-strewn inter-tidal land. Bedard decided to turn north and walk back behind the village, where he soon found a trail that climbed the bluff following a small fast-flowing small stream that eventually intersected the main east–west trail. He noted that the undergrowth was incredibly thick on either side of the path up the bluff. They met up with Hy and Haus again and had a few minutes of hellos, and moved off to the west on the main trail. No one had followed them.

Bedard sent Liz forward and directed Hy to the rear. He kept JoJo and Haus with him.

He went slowly, searching the forest to the north for an old hunting or animal trail that they could initially use. What he wanted to do was find a reasonably secure campsite for the evening and then look for a better one the next day. He needed a base from which to work. The almost impenetrable thickness of the rainforest was not as evident from the main trail as it was on the one up from the village, so he had missed this problem when they came through before. The main trail showed evidence of recent maintenance. Deadfalls were cut away with axes. No saw cuts in evidence, which was strange—but maybe not. He had just identified what appeared to be a faint trail to the north when Liz came storming back down the main trail, her tail held high. *Danger. Not good!*

Bedard whistled to Hy and carefully took the three dogs into the underbrush. Within twenty feet they were completely hidden. He had no concern for Hy—he would move off the trail and hide quite easily. In about ten minutes they heard voices on the trail. Natives for sure. Soon a large group of about fifteen men and women came past. Bedard was surprised. They could be seen through the leaves, but they could not see Bedard. They were all carrying small packs and they looked weary. *A very strange group, indeed.*

In about twenty minutes, Hy came sniffing along and found his family immediately. They had entered a side trail carefully, so Bedard decided to continue farther and investigate the land. Hy was left on guard at their first hiding place near the main trail and the others moved farther inland to the north. It was probably a hunting trail. Not used very often.

They soon ran into a massive tangle. The trail seemed to go straight into the middle. Liz was sent forward to find the path of least resistance. After two false starts, she gave a low woof, and they followed her. Bedard carefully inched himself along on his stomach through the tangled brush using his elbows while JoJo and Haus squirmed along close behind. They soon found themselves at the edge of a very long swamp, sixty feet wide with a stream snaking through the middle.

At one end was a large beaver lodge and dam. The path that they were on was probably designed to capture any beavers who came here to repair their structures. It would be clever if he could get across the swamp leaving only a minimal trail. The dogs could cross over with no problem because their trails were typical animal trails. The area there had the potential to be an ideal campsite. The ground between was wet and looked typically mucky. The dogs had not given any indication of animals nearby, so Bedard assumed that the beavers had left or had been taken. On the far side, a large tree had started to fall over. That would make an ideal bridge if they could force it to fall more, or if another could be found on this side to fall toward it.

He called over Haus and JoJo and tied packs to their backs. The three dogs were told to stay but not to move or sit. The longer they stayed in one spot, the lower the risk of leaving an unusual trail. Bedard moved carefully to the left until he was opposite the leaning tree. The ground in front of him was definitely soggy and would show footprints. He had a number of light ropes with him, but the task of lassoing the leaning tree seemed impossible.

Bedard sank to his heels and thought for a while. He then stood up and called for Liz. He tied the end of the rope around her neck and pointed north. She immediately entered the water and swam to the far side. She picked her way carefully onto the dry land. After a big shake, she looked back with her tail wagging furiously. This is fun, she seemed to say.

He motioned her toward the leaning tree. After several false starts, she arrived at the bottom of the tree with the rope clear of snags. The next step was simple because the tree had brought up a huge tangle of roots and vegetation when it toppled. Liz jumped up on the tree and proceeded under Bedard's direction up the trunk. The rope got tangled a few times, but they managed to free it. Now he had her weave her way around the branches until she was thoroughly tangled. Because she did not like this, it was difficult to keep her calm.

Bedard carefully tied the rope to a nearby tree with a slip knot, tied another rope to the free end of the main rope and the other end to his belt. He climbed the rope, hand over hand, to the tree, dragging the second rope behind him. Very easy. The tree did not move very much under his weight. He then untangled Liz and sent her down the tree. He jerked the second rope to undo the slip knot and reeled in the two ropes. He moved down the tree after her and then called the other three dogs. They swam over to greet him.

The ground on this side was solid, the forest undergrowth that surrounded them was not as entangled, and the trees here were in transition, probably due to a recent fire. Most of the fast-growing new trees were not evergreens. Bedard sent Liz on an exploratory run. She came back in twenty minutes wagging her tail. Everything seemed safe for now.

Looked good. Bedard found another tree uprooted with a natural cave underneath. It had also fallen toward the marsh. He climbed up and found that he now had a protected view of the long marsh in both directions. Good deal.

The next step was food. It was nearly noon, and they'd had a long day already—with no food. Typically, Bedard only ate twice a day and the dogs once. They now needed to kill a fair-sized animal for the dogs. The hunting trip would allow him to carefully explore the surrounding land. This spot by the swamp might turn out to be the secure area that they needed as a base for the next phase in their journey.

The hunting trip was successful. Not only did they bag a small deer, but they found a berry patch in a small meadow not far from the camp. The first tour of the area was very favourable.

A well-used north–south trail was encountered about two and a half miles to the west, skirting around a huge cranberry marsh. This marsh was inland of Mahli and Stsulawh. This trail would stop people from moving into the relatively thick rainforest to the east of the trail toward their campsite.

The current campsite was still fairly close to the main east–west trail, but it was protected from it by the long, narrow marsh and the stream. This stream continued east about a mile and then turned south. Another stream running north–south was found just farther east. These streams acted as a small barrier to discourage access to what Bedard was now calling "our area." He also found a well-used path some distance east of this north–south stream that he thought led down toward Tsusnahm.

The immediate area near the swamp was lightly forested with fairly clear underbrush. The rainforest thickened considerably in all directions beyond this area. It looked good. If they were careful not to scare them off, game animals would come for water.

In the heavy forest, darkness came early at this time of year, but it was still relatively warm. Bedard estimated that it was only five o'clock and it was pitch black. By this time, the dogs were well fed and already set up in a defensive pattern. Liz was to the west; Hy was to the east. JoJo was not too far away to the south and Haus was ranging to the north.

This was like the good old times when the dogs would snooze lightly through the night, moving about twice an hour. Bedard doused the small smoke-free cooking fire and had supper. The cold fresh water tasted particularly good. He then stowed the packs for a fast getaway—a standard precaution—and was asleep as soon as he closed his eyes.

Four
January 13, 1858 (Morning)

Liz licked his face. Bedard awoke quickly, all his senses alert. Someone was coming but there was no danger. Not yet. He unwound to his haunches and saw, sitting under a tree not thirty feet away from him, a young native man about twenty-five years old. He remembered seeing him at Tsusnahm in the background with the village dogs. The young man was grinning from ear to ear.

The young man made a come-here gesture to Liz and she went over to have her ears scratched. Bedard clapped his hands softly and Liz tore off with her tail between her legs. *Dereliction of duty,* he thought to himself. The young man must be a really gifted animal person to have come through his defenses so easily. At that moment, Haus came into the clearing for a quick check and then swung away abruptly back to his station. He didn't want to test Bedard's patience just yet.

It was early, the sunlight was just starting to filter through the trees. Bedard decided to ignore the young man for the time being, since he did not seem to be a threat, and went about his morning routine of washing his upper body by the stream, making a small campfire, brewing some coffee and cooking some ground-up grain meal. The young man turned down the porridge but took a cup of steaming coffee.

Bedard inspected his guest during this time. He had a walking stick and was dressed a little differently from the others in his village. In fact, his clothes were not too dissimilar from Bedard's: simple but durable with no beadwork or leather decorations. He was very pleased with himself and smiled constantly.

They heard a sound to the north and the young man raised himself in a crouch as if to flee. JoJo arrived a few moments later for a check out and immediately fled like Haus had.

"Four dogs. You have four dogs," the visitor said relaxing on the ground again.

Bedard's jaw must have dropped four inches. *He speaks English, yet.*

"You are surprised that I speak English. When I was quite young, only four years old, I became very sick and my family took me south to the hospital at Fort Edensfield where I stayed for seven years. I learnt Spanish from the monks there. I was then moved to a farm they owned, and I stayed with an English family for ten more years. When I came back, I had to learn my native language all over again."

He had put his mug of coffee down on the ground and was feeling around with his hand for it. Bedard looked carefully at his face and came to the startling conclusion that he was blind.

Extraordinary! He found me and came through my defenses blind. He shook his head. *Unbelievable! Speaks English too.*

The young man went on, not noticing, of course, Bedard's astonishment.

"I have a keen sense of smell and hearing due, of course, to the partial loss of my eyesight. The villagers let me tend the dogs, and that is perhaps why your dogs are friendly to me. What are their names?"

Bedard ignored the question. "How did you find us?"

"I know the area very well, as I often go for long slow walks in the woods. My walking stick helps with that. Although my vision is blurred, I thought I found the place where you went off the main trail and decided to circle around behind the swamp and pick up your trail there. One of the small dogs found me and actually brought me here—she is very clever. What is her name?"

"Liz. She and Hy are collies. The other two dogs are JoJo and Haus, who are mastiffs. What is your name?"

"My name is Mothway, but I am usually called Mot."

"Why did you want to find me, Mot?"

Mot shrugged. "I wanted to meet you. I thought that I might be of some use to you. I want to do something more with my life than look after the village dogs. The fact that you are travelling with dogs interests me because I like animals." He paused, a little embarrassed. "And I think animals like me."

"Did any of the dogs come with you today?"

"Oh, no. They do not like the darkness of the forest, too many animal enemies. They only venture anywhere in daylight in a pack or with their master hunting."

Bedard had not thought of that. A skilful native hunter with a dog could give them quite a bit of grief.

"Have you ever come to this place before?"

"Not really. I am more interested in the larger meadows, ponds, and swamps farther inland and to the east."

Bedard sat there for a time thinking; there was something nagging at the back of his mind.

"Who is your father?" he asked. Bedard watched Mot's face closely. Mot did not answer for several minutes.

Mot mumbled something.

"What?"

"My father is the chief, Chief Sparrow," Mot said with downcast eyes.

Bedard waited. Mot was smart enough to know that this needed some explanation.

He looked up. "My mother asked me to find you and invite you to come back to the village."

"Why did your mother pick you?"

"I don't know. Perhaps she sensed that I could convince you to come back, that I could communicate with you, my affinity with the animals, I don't know."

He sat motionless for a long time. Neither of them spoke. Then he rose, nodded at Bedard and strode off to the east. Bedard whistled for Liz. When she appeared, he waved her off. She turned abruptly and went after Mot.

Mot soon appeared with Liz holding onto the end of his sleeve in her mouth.

"She was persuasive," he said.

"I would like to stay for a while if you don't mind."

Mot laughed and sat down at his place by the tree.

"What is your name?" said Mot.

"I call myself Copco."

Bedard smiled. But the plan needed to be reviewed and changed again. A simple camp in the woods would not work out. Perhaps hiding in the village would be better.

He could even learn the language and pass himself off as a local native, an intriguing concept.

"Mot, would you like to work for me? I need help to learn your language."

Mot said, "Yes, that would be wonderful! All of the nations on the Lower Fraser River and on the southern portion of Vancouver Island speak a dialect of Halkomelem. We all fish together in the river at various times of the year and have been doing so for thousands of years. This plus intermarriage has caused our languages to become similar. Our older elders, who are responsible for bringing forward our history, believe that this evolution of our languages was a very important and beneficial thing. We often call our language Musqueam because it is easier to say, but it is really a dialect of Halkomelem."

Suddenly Mot stood up and faced east. Then Bedard heard Liz give a short bark in the distance. Enemy coming—Mot had obviously heard something too. Bedard gave three whistles, each slightly different: contain, disarm and retrieve. All four dogs would be involved to some extent depending on the difficulty of each task and what else was happening in the forest.

Mot sank to the ground and buried his head in his arms. Bedard guessed that he had been followed and that he had not thought of that possibility.

"Mot! Sit up straight! You work for me now. As my assistant and translator, you are under my *amparo!*"

Mot looked up, surprised that Bedard knew the Spanish word for protection.

"The person will come into my camp. You will not speak to him or to me until I tell you. You will translate for me what he says when I ask you. You will translate what I say to him when I ask you."

Liz came steaming into the clearing with a short hunting bow in her mouth. No bowstring. She dropped the bow and roared off again. Obviously, she was trying to get back into her master's good books. Five minutes later, Liz rushed back with a knife in her jaws, dropped it, gave a small woof and raced off again at full speed. The woof meant that all was secure. Bedard relaxed a little. Although he did not anticipate a problem, you never know.

He then realized that Mot did not know what was happening.

"The dogs have been successful in containing the person. They have disarmed him and are now bringing him into our camp."

In about ten minutes, Liz came into the clearing followed by a middle-aged man with his right hand holding up his pants. He was very lithe, obviously a fisherman or a hunter. He had a quiver of arrows but no pack and both the belt that had secured his pants and his bowstring were in his left hand. Otherwise there was no apparent damage.

Neither Bedard nor Mot moved from their seated position. Mot stared straight ahead and Bedard watched the newcomer with interest. He stopped about forty feet away and said something to Mot. Mot turned his head toward the man but said nothing.

"I'm sorry, he is my uncle," said Mot.

Bedard slowly stood up, and the man turned his attention to him. Liz was sitting patiently in the small clearing and the other dogs were out of sight. Bedard waved his hand and Liz went off in a rush, giving the man a wide berth. Then he whistled once: back to stations.

He motioned the man to sit beside Mot and then sat down himself. The man shrugged and went over to Mot, put on his belt and sat down.

"I am going to ask our visitor some questions. You will translate the words just as I say them. He will answer. You will translate the words just as he says them. If you have a problem with a word or a phrase that I say, you will tell me, and we will choose another word or phrase. If you have a problem with a word or a phrase that he says, you will tell me and we will decide on the translation or on a question that I will ask him to clarify the translation. You will not talk to him otherwise. This will be a difficult task. Can you do this? Answer yes or no."

"Yes."

Bedard turned his attention to the man. He looked into his eyes and was silent for a few minutes.

"What is your name?"

Mot translated the answer. "Komuhhallu. I am called Kom."

"Why have you followed Mothway?"

Mot hesitated, but Bedard did not look at him—it was going to get very difficult for Mot very soon.

Mot sat up straighter and translated. "I felt that his mother was wrong in sending him to find you. I was afraid that Mot was in danger."

Bedard smiled. "You have found him. Is he in danger?"

"I don't know."

"How can you determine if he is in danger?"

"Is he free to go?"

"Yes."

Kom said to Mot, "I want you to come back to the village with me, now."

"Answer him," Bedard directed Mot.

Mot spoke for some time. He then turned to Bedard and said that he had told Kom that he was employed by the Englishman and that he did not wish to return to the village just yet.

Kom looked at Bedard and there was silence for some time. Bedard whistled for Liz, and she came in a rush and sat down in front of him. Mot whistled, and Liz squirmed. Bedard flicked his little finger and she swirled over to Mot for a scratch and a lick. After a few moments, Bedard whistled again and a much happier Liz sped away to her post.

Bedard whistled, and in a few minutes JoJo came silently into the camp. Bedard didn't have the large dogs sit. Their body geometry was such that they looked awkward and vulnerable when they sat. Kom had seen JoJo from a distance. Up close, the dog was a substantial animal. Bedard gave a sign and JoJo went over to Kom for a good sniff. He then went to Mot and traded licks for scratches. Mot was very pleased with this turn of events and almost said something. Bedard gave a low whistle, and JoJo turned and disappeared silently into the forest.

Kom and Bedard looked at each other and once again there was silence.

"Do you think that you are in danger?" he asked Kom. Mot translated.

Kom smiled. "Probably not, if I do not do anything to anger you."

"Do you think Mot is in danger?" Bedard asked him again.

He thought for a while, looked at Mot and then back at Bedard. "No, I think that he is probably in good hands."

Mot looked relieved and seemed more relaxed, so Bedard assumed that this was the truth.

Kom then asked, "What is your name?"

"I call myself Copco."

After another long silence Kom looked at Bedard. "Why are you here?"

"I am searching for some very evil white men."

"Why are these men evil?"

"They have killed good people, and that is against our laws."

"Why do you think they are here?"

"My people believe that they will have come to this area to prey on the gold seekers," Bedard replied.

Kom had a problem with the phrase "gold seekers" so Bedard changed it to "bright metal seekers."

Kom was silent for a long time and then turned to Mot and asked him something. Mot started to respond directly, and then he remembered that he had to translate to Copco first.

"Kom asked me if I had talked to you about the white man's camp to the west."

Bedard said to Mot, "Answer not yet, then say that I want Kom to tell me about the camp."

Kom was again silent for a while. He was obviously someone who thought before he spoke. This was a trait that Bedard admired.

"There are others who can speak with more knowledge than I," Kom said.

"I will be very interested to speak with others, but I am most interested to hear what you know about the camp. I know the location of the camp because I saw a flash of sunlight off their spyglass when I arrived by boat some thirteen days ago," Mot translated.

"Then the next morning I met two men from the camp who were sent to kill me. Unfortunately, they made mistakes and died. They had come with others by canoe.

"Others landed, four of them, and made a short search for me. I think that two of them were local natives. They did not have the skills to find me and left taking the two bodies with them." Mot translated and both he and Kom smiled.

"Kom says that the people who help the white men are very young and do not have many skills. He also says that the elders from the village these young men come from are using them to monitor the white men. These young men are volunteers, and this work is probably quite dangerous. In fact, they are very brave," Mot said.

Bedard nodded his head. "The white men are not stupid. I found out from one of the men who tried to kill me that their leader is Tommy Hunter, otherwise known as the Wolverine. He is very sly and very dangerous. He probably knows what the young people are doing and will be using these young people as hostages against any action toward them by the villagers."

Kom nodded his head after Mot translated. He then spoke for some time with Mot, interrupting from time to time to translate.

"A small group of these white men first came about one year ago. They landed near the rock point to the far west of these lands. After making a preliminary camp, three of them carefully investigated the river shoreline as far as Fort Langley. This took about three weeks. They did not visit the villages but met some of our people to trade for food.

"The three villages discussed these people, and it was agreed that they were up to no good. They chose to make a more permanent camp near an old abandoned village called Kullukhun near the point and farther west than any of our own villages. They built three cabins within a small area that they then fortified and guarded. A few of us helped in the construction, cutting trees and finding food, but no one has been in their fortified area.

"The number of people there has varied somewhat but never more than thirteen nor less than about ten at any time. Every two or three months, a small group of men arrive, stay for a day or two, and then travel by boat across the river to a good walking trail on the south side. Then they move up the river beyond Fort Langley. We estimate that about ten white men have passed through their camp in this way."

Bedard asked Kom about the village on the island and about the very tall person he'd seen there.

Both Mot and Kom smiled. Kom said that the village is called Skwisahthun and that it is very small. Only twenty-five people including children and women. Only six men including Chief Bonchicallea. Chief Big Bon is more than seven feet tall and is very strong.

Kom stood up. "May I return to the village now?"

"Yes, of course," Bedard said.

Then Bedard said to Mot, "You have had a challenging day."

"I have had an extraordinary day," Mot said, taking the opportunity to show off his knowledge of English.

"I now want you to go back to the village with Kom," Bedard said. Mot's face fell. "I want you to take him to your father and mother, and I want you to report to them all that has happened here today. Having Kom with you will give strength to your new position as my"—and here Bedard paused for a moment, smiling—"new assistant."

Mot smiled, feeling a bit better.

Then Bedard turned toward Kom and, with Mot translating, said, "Mot will accompany you back to the village. It may be useful for both of you to immediately see Chief Sparrow and Mot's mother. I have asked Mot to report to them everything that he has seen and heard here this morning, everything."

Kom nodded and looked at Mot. After a moment of silence, he said to Mot, "You have had another adventure today."

Bedard then said to both of them, "I have decided to ask Chief Sparrow if I can make a small temporary home, a shelter from the rain, somewhere in the village where my family and I will be out of the way, perhaps even hidden. I will follow you down to the village later this afternoon. I plan to do some hunting for family food."

Mot and Kom then set off to the east toward the trail that headed down to the village.

Five
January 13, 1858 (Afternoon)

After Mot and Kom had left, Bedard sat down and planned his next moves.

It was meal time, and they still had some deer and berries. He retrieved the food pack from the tree stash and cut the meat into dog portions. He had some meat from yesterday that was partially cooked, so he built a small fire to continue cooking his own meal. The small berry hoard looked so good he could not resist eating directly from the bags.

Bedard found many berries frozen by winter's early frost and he took the time to collect them as an important supplement to the basic meat and fish diet that he was forced to adopt in this area at this time of the year.

In particular, what he believed were cranberries grew in profusion in the bog lands near the river and soon became Bedard's favourite fruit. The cranberry bush grew very close to the ground, and the small round berries turned a deep red when fully ripe. Now frozen, the berries remained edible and were easily picked from the bush, but he found over the past week that they were even better when crushed and dried.

Hy and Haus were called in for their meal, and Bedard had Liz and JoJo range around the area twice before calling them in for their turn.

Bedard cleaned up and rearranged the area a bit, including sweeping away the footprints and sprinkling some needles and fine dirt and ground cover around. He then reorganized JoJo's pack so that more berries could be added. They were so good! He wanted to have a good reserve to eat for the next few days. Bedard set up JoJo with his pack and then slipped into his own backpack, converting one of the two carry packs into a front pack so that he could more easily carry the small deer that he wanted to find before they went south to the village.

Liz, JoJo, and Bedard moved out of the temporary camp toward the east and the trail that led down to the village. Before leaving, he surveyed the area and was pleased that his occupancy left only minimum traces. A good hunter would have no problem deducing that they had been there if he knew what to look for, but a casual hunter would not.

Just before coming to the village trail, Bedard took all but two of the packs and hid them carefully. He then headed northward at a medium run, directing the dogs to their positions for the hunt. The dogs enjoyed these hunting trips and often could find a deer and surround it without it knowing that it was in mortal danger.

To his great pleasure, he found a cranberry patch on the edge of a small inland fresh-water pond where it was simple and safe to collect them.

Two hours later, a deer that they had easily found was dressed and tied to Bedard's backpack. A very good selection of berries was stashed away in JoJo's pack, and they were on the way south to Tsusnahm.

He had decided to take only Liz and JoJo into the village at this time, leaving Hy and Haus to range around the area until nightfall. At that time, he would send all the dogs out on security detail until he was comfortable with the village situation.

The trail came down the cliff following the small fast-flowing stream. Bedard was very impressed with the size of the trees at the top of the bluff. Some were more than twenty feet in diameter and seemed to stretch all the way up to the sky.

As he approached the village, another small boy darted out of the bushes in front of Liz and went scurrying past the longhouses toward the river.

Mmm. Do they have a security system, or was the youngster sent specifically out to warn the village of his pending arrival?

As he came to the first longhouse, Bedard called Liz in to about thirty feet from her usual security range distance. He noticed that the space between the longhouses, about fifty feet, was covered by a very coarse gravel rather than grass and vegetation. There were many things about this village and its occupants that he did not understand.

When he turned the corner at the front of this longhouse, he saw a similar gathering of villagers sitting in a circle down near the water underneath the huge tree. Yesterday there were about thirty adults, but today there were many more and about fifty or sixty children scurrying around playing.

The young boy that he had just seen on the trail was standing near Chief Sparrow, and several others who were wearing what appeared to be ceremonial cloaks or blankets. Bedard could also see Mot and Kom sitting near the chief.

Liz had turned around and came back to Bedard who had stopped in his tracks, not knowing what to do next. This was perhaps some sort of welcoming ceremony for him, and he did not like that very much. He just wanted to disappear into the village without anyone noticing. This was, however, not the way it was going to be.

Someone had apparently told Mot that Bedard and the dogs had arrived, and he was running toward them. He arrived a bit breathless from his exertion.

"I am sorry. I know that you would prefer to come here and live in some obscurity, but my father and mother will have none of that, and as you can see, they are going to make this a big event. They believe that your arrival with the baby was a miracle of some sort. Many of the people in the village had been out looking for him without success for more than two days. That is why there were only a few villagers in the circle when you came here yesterday morning. Now almost everyone is here."

Bedard said, "Are you still working for me?"

"Oh, yes, yes!"

"Do you know everyone here?"

"Yes, I think so."

"We need a close security net around the village immediately. Can you set that up?"

"Yes. We have a group of youngsters trained to do that. I can get them into position right now." And Mot went off running toward the circle of people.

Bedard stepped back onto the gravel and removed his packs, the deer carcass and JoJo's pack and sent both Liz and JoJo out to join the other two dogs on a security net around the village.

Thinking furiously, Bedard ran to the north end of the longhouse. He whistled to the dogs, instructing them to alert him of any out-going travellers. This was going to be tricky. They had previously set up these special signals but had not used them for several years. Hy and Liz would get it immediately, but he did not know if JoJo and Haus would understand. He watched Liz and JoJo scurry up the trail. JoJo stopped and turned around to look at him. Liz also stopped and barked at JoJo, who then turned and continued running after her. He wondered if they really could communicate that sort of thing to each other.

He then moved back to the front of the longhouse and took out one of the ropes from his backpack. The roof of this longhouse was ornate enough for him to toss the end of the rope up and over a projection and haul the deer carcass up out of reach of the local dogs.

By this time, Mot was back with a breathless report that the security system was being set up and that Bedard was to accompany him down to the gathering.

Mot said, "I have asked one of my older sisters to inventory all of the people and children here now. I have also asked both of my brothers, who are the ones who set up and trained the young people, to further search the village area for people not in attendance."

Bedard stood with Mot and looked down on the large group by the tree. Not many teenagers, he noticed, about three that he could see, all boys. A very curious and fascinating village from a number of points of view.

They started down the slope toward the tree together. Bedard turned to Mot. "What is the name of the mother of the baby that I found."

"Adrona, and she is my cousin." Then he waved his hands. "Almost all of the people in the village are some part of my family." He smiled. "Do you have a big family?"

"No, I was an only child, but I think that I have a daughter."

"You think you have a daughter?"

"Yes," he replied, surprised that he had said this to Mot. He had never said this to anyone else before. "I have not met her yet."

"How old is she?"

Bedard thought for a moment. "She will be twenty-two this year. Her name is Dorthea, and she is probably with her mother, Donna, and I do not know where they are. They were not in England when I left there early last year. They could be anywhere in the world." He spread his hands in a way to emphasize what he was saying.

Bedard then gestured toward the group. "How does this work? What should I do? I do not want to insult anyone."

"I will take you to Chief Sparrow and my mother. My mother has a very long and complicated name. Almost everyone calls her Mother. My father will probably shake your hand. That is what I have suggested that he do. Mother will probably hug you," Mot said, almost laughing. "She told us that she lived with an English sailor for about two years when she was young, and he liked hugging."

Bedard looked at him and laughed lightly. "I guess I will survive that."

"Then Chief Sparrow and Mother will take you around the circle and introduce you to everyone including some of the older children. The chief is very old, and he does not speak clearly now. Two of his granddaughters will be with him tonight and will help him communicate. This works fairly well. Adrona and the baby are here somewhere."

"What is the baby's name?" asked Bedard.

"He does not have a name yet. He is only about ten weeks old. In our culture, the names of babies occur in some sort of mysterious manner that I admit that I do not understand. We have a ceremony for that."

Bedard saw that most of the children had noticed that he and Mot were approaching the tree and had moved closer to the circle, probably to be nearer their parents. The children's clamour was also noticeably less.

As he approached the pathway through the seated group, Mot hung back a step or two and, quite incredibly, a drum sounded. Chief Sparrow and his wife stood up and the circle of people started singing very softly. All of the children who were not already near the circle moved rapidly over to their parents. A number of other men and women near the chief also stood up. All of these people wore very ornate blankets. Chief Sparrow was the only one with a hat: curiously conical-shaped with a medium brim.

Bedard approached cautiously.

Mot said to Bedard's back, "I have asked them all to speak slowly and pause so that I can translate for you. Some of them will be greatly honoured if you would say something to them individually now and perhaps later at dinner as well." And Bedard glanced briefly back at Mot. "Ah yes," Mot said, "the whole ball of wax!" Mot almost giggled at his beautiful turn of phrase.

Bedard, who had been brought up with nobility in Spain and elsewhere in Europe before he moved to England, was very comfortable approaching Chief Sparrow and his wife and looking both of them in the eye. He shook the chief's very gnarled hand and suffered another hug from Mot's mother who was once more a bit wet-eyed.

Mot tugged at Bedard's shirt, and he turned to see Adrona with Noua almost at his side. Mot's mother reached over and took the baby from her, allowing Adrona to hug Bedard. *I may get to like hugs after all.* Then he bent his head down and kissed her on both cheeks and the gathering murmured. They were both smiling widely. Then it occurred to Bedard that this was the first time that Adrona had seen him.

Bedard glanced briefly at Mot and said to Adrona in English, "And how is your baby?" Mot translated.

"He is perfect," she said, "although he has a liking for berry juice to supplement the milk." Those nearby laughed at that. Bedard assumed that the berry-juice story had made the rounds.

He turned and held out his arms for the baby and then held it above his head as he had seen many of his friends who are fathers do. The baby giggled—well, gurgled, anyway.

The group liked this, and many were whispering to their neighbours. Adrona was very pleased. Bedard then turned and gave the baby to her.

He then squinted while contemplating Adrona and the baby. "You know that I am travelling with my family." Mot translated. "The dogs and I are very close. We have been together for more than nine years. They were, in fact, the ones who actually found your baby. They liked your baby very much. When my family meets your family again, they will easily recognize him and they will be very pleased to see him."

Adrona looked a bit confused so Mot added some information and then she nodded and smiled.

"When we found him, we did not know who he was. All we knew was that we had a new member of our family."

Adrona put her hand over her mouth. "You named him!"

No dummy this!

"Yes, we named him Noua."

Adrona continued to stare at Bedard and then looked down at the baby in her arms. "Noua," she said.

A murmur was moving around the circle and the soft singing started again.

Adrona sank to her knees, hugging the baby to her chest and saying Noua over and over again.

The chief did not know what to do, but Mother moved over and brought Adrona to her feet. She took the baby from Adrona, held it over her head and said, "Noua." Adrona hugged Bedard again.

With his arm around Adrona, Bedard moved over to Chief Sparrow and shook his hand again.

Mother was making her way around the circle, saying Noua time after time.

The Chief then moved to his right and, with the assistance of his granddaughters, introduced Bedard to the village elders with Mot translating.

Bedard shook each man's hand and allowed each woman to give him a half hug.

Bedard tried to say something intelligent to each person. He had done this many times in the past, starting as a youngster holding his father's hand.

This is interesting, I have not learned a completely new language for more than five years. Of all the many languages that I have learned over the past fifty odd years, I have only just realized that the language the Musqueam use is easily the most interesting and challenging.

Mother came back and gave Noua to Adrona and then participated in the introductions as Bedard moved slowly around the circle. He was also introduced to some of the children who were not too shy. Adrona stayed close by.

At about the mid-point in the circle, Mot moved in a little closer and introduced Bedard to the three teenagers that Bedard had seen previously.

The three boys were almost the same height as Bedard at six feet, and were thin and probably very fit. All three looked at him with great curiosity, prompting Bedard to address them through Mot.

"We should meet sometime soon, and I will share with you some of the adventures that I have experienced in other parts of the world."

They all nodded and Mot added something; they all smiled as they shook Bedard's hand.

Mot said, "I told them that perhaps they could ask you to show them some hand-to-hand fighting moves that they could learn. The three of them think that they are very tough, but in reality they are just undisciplined bullies and need to be introduced to a new level of skill, along with a measure of respect. The elders do not like them at all but the three of them together are already a formidable force."

"Why do you think that I have knowledge of hand-to-hand fighting?"

"I just know," Mot said. "You are one tough guy."

And then he again almost burst into laughter, which he stifled with his arm, at his casual memory of these neat English phrases dredged out of his past.

Bedard had almost completed the circle of introductions and returned to the tree where he had started. Bedard did not release the hand of the last person that he met in the circle and stared into the man's face. This man was also about six feet tall but slim and again probably very fit.

"Do I know you?" Bedard said.

"You are very kind to remember me," said the man in hesitant English. "My name is Roanyon. When we met in Hawaii, I was using the name Roy Kanyon. And yes, I speak some English, but I am out of practice, I apologize. I have just returned to my home here six months ago, and I am focusing on learning my native tongue all over again with the help of Mot, who is a very good teacher. I have been away for about twenty years and have spent the last seven years sailing on Spanish ships. Mot also speaks Spanish and that is, obviously, very useful for me at this time."

Bedard looked at Mot who was beaming.

"When do we start my language lessons?"

Six

January 13, 1858 (Evening)

Bedard heard a bark in the distance: Liz with a danger signal.

He said to Mot, "I must go and see what the problem is on the hillside, please make my apologies. I do not think that it will be very long. I will probably need the help of your brothers."

And he was off at a fast run. He could hear the group murmuring behind him in response to his sudden actions.

Just past the buildings, Bedard could see a youngster running down the trail ahead. The young boy stopped and turned around as soon as he caught sight of Bedard and started back up the hill again. Bedard soon caught up with him and decided to let him lead the way. Mot's brothers, Modan and Towaba, soon caught up with them. Ahead Bedard could see Liz and JoJo standing guard beside a woman who was on her knees and appeared to be crying. A pack was on the ground beside her.

The brothers passed Bedard and arrived at the scene just before him. They asked what she was doing there—Bedard could understand that much—but got no answer. He tried to catch her name but couldn't.

Then, Adrona arrived with Mot and knelt at the woman's side, repeating the woman's name. Dot.

The two women embraced, and Dot sobbed and shook with a great deal of emotion.

After some time, with Adrona whispering to her, Dot's distress subsided somewhat.

Adrona looked up at the four men and Mot translated what she said.

"She said that Dot was going to meet up with a white man from the corral."

This was a term that they used to describe the Wolverine's compound.

"Adrona knows the man. She says his name is Don. He is a womanizer. He wanted Dot to tell him if any new person showed up in our village. She was trying to get on his good side because he really knows how to make women happy. And she is not happy at this time because her husband died last year."

Dot again cried, with some great heaving and wailing.

Mot said, "It will be good for you to go with her back down to the village. We will talk to her later. Thank you, Adrona."

Bedard gave some silent signals to the two dogs, and they rushed off to continue their security routine. Then he and Mot turned around and returned to the festivities.

When they arrived at the front of Chief Sparrow's longhouse, the chief and his wife, along with the other village elders, were just coming up the slope from the tree, and everyone was pleased to see Bedard and Mot. One of Mother's daughters was carrying Noua.

"Just in time, I think," said Mot.

The elders passed by and entered the building.

Mot's mother asked Bedard, through her son, if everything was satisfactory. They spoke for a moment.

Mot said, "Towaba reported to them that Dot was not in the village, so Mother sent Adrona after you. I told her that was very wise of her."

Bedard had understood much of the conversation even before Mot's translation and said, in halting Musqueam, "We know why you are well respected in this village." She beamed at that and took his arm to guide him into the building.

Bedard had almost a full day with Mot translating conversations for him, and he was really focusing on the language and its unique sounds so that he could better fit in to this community. He looked like a villager. His tanned skin and his tall structure did not stand out as it did in other places that he had visited because here all the men were dark and many of them were tall. Learning the language was very important.

Chief Sparrow caught up with them and they entered the longhouse together, with Mot close behind.

The large building was arranged with what Bedard guessed were private rooms and storage areas at the rear and along part of the side walls. Some of these had wooden doors, but most of the rooms and areas were closed off with curtains of some type. The remaining portion of the room was now filled with adults and children milling about. In the centre was a huge complex fire area where the meals were being cooked.

Bedard counted twelve women, two older and ten young, along with two men actively involved in the area around the fire. *This is where the teenaged girls are.*

Mot's mother said to him, "You will meet the experts later." Mot translated only the word "experts" and when Bedard glanced at him he smiled widely. "You are indeed an incredibly fast student," Mot said.

Mot's mother and father guided Bedard through the crowd to a table set up at the back of the longhouse. Mot followed. There was a space in the middle of the table and the four of them passed through. Two men immediately came and placed a set of long boards over the space, covered the boards with an ornate cloth and added some flowers and eating implements. Again, immediately as they sat down on the bench behind the table there was the sound of a drum. Bedard quickly looked around but could not see the drummer. Mot laughed quietly at this but did not say anything.

The crowd then dispersed rapidly to a seating arrangement on the floor facing the table. Food started to arrive at the ends of the table to the elders and was smoothly passed to the middle. Bedard noted that the people seated on the floor facing him were being served in a similar fashion with the food passed down the rows to the centre.

Mot, standing behind him, said to Bedard, "Don't forget that this meal will last more than two hours, and all of the courses are going to be extremely good because this is a major event for us. I will be nearby, just raise your arm above your head and my eyes assistant and I will come and translate for you." Then he added, "Your humble assistant!" and moved off, laughing into his arm again.

Bedard decided that he was going to call Mot's mother *Mother* in Musqueam.

After Mot moved off, Mother pointed at the food in front of him and said something. The dish was clams, and there were three small dishes of dip which she also pointed out and described. Bedard repeated the words and then said, "Thank you, Mother," in Musqueam.

She did not catch this immediately, but three seconds later she grabbed his jerkin, kissed his cheek and said, "Thank you," in English.

Bedard kissed her back and the two of them looked at each other for a few seconds before diving into the amazingly good clams.

Bedard decided to make Mot work a bit and raised his arm over his head. Mot arrived rapidly with his eyes assistant. Bedard struck up a conversation with Chief Sparrow and Roanyon, who was seated beside the chief, about where the clams were obtained and whether they had tried cultivating clams. This was something that both Roanyon and Bedard were knowledgeable about from their experiences in Europe and Hawaii, and Chief Sparrow was very interested. The chief's granddaughters participated significantly as the chief had much to ask.

Bedard smiled when he saw that Mot had soon disappeared, so he had Roanyon help with some of the words.

Bedard finished his clams fairly rapidly, and before he could relax another serving of clams arrived. He turned to his left and said in Musqueam, "Mother, please help me. I do not have as big a stomach as"—he stopped and quickly looked around the room—"Bolloma, over there has."

Mother said nothing but took three of the twelve clams off Bedard's plate and looked up at him smiling. "There," she said in English.

Bedard did not know what to think of Mother's English, so he decided to tease her a bit. He shook his finger at her and said in Musqueam, "I need to learn Musqueam," and then he added in English, "Please." And the two of them laughed.

The next two courses were also shellfish: oysters and mussels. Bedard, remembering what Mot said, tried to be conservative but soon realized that this was going to be a very challenging evening.

He looked around at the other diners and found that some of them at the head table were passing plates to some youngsters behind them. He noted that, on the floor, people were passing some of the plates off to the other end of the row. He tried that, and Mother just smiled and either just passed the plate behind her somehow or passed it on to the elder beside her.

Right, well that works.

The next dish was a big platter of shrimp and other fish, so he decided to be conservative and only took a small serving. Mother smiled in approval. It turned out that the shrimp were an extraordinary delicacy for the village. They had apparently been sold to a coastal village from a boat that came up to the river delta area from the south earlier this week. This morning Tsusnahm had bartered with this village for them at great cost for this celebration. On the floor, several women were in heated discussion and that attracted Bedard's attention.

Mot spoke quietly in Bedard's ear, saying that the shrimp portions were evidently not equal and that some of the villagers did not appreciate this.

Bedard then turned toward Mother and she just shrugged as if to say, *C'est la vie.*

Fish dishes followed in uncounted numbers. Bedard, watching his neighbours and the floor, adopted the strategy of asking for more of his favourite two fish dishes.

One was salmon, of which there was several species offered, including fresh, dried and smoked salmon, and the other was a small river and lake trout which had an absolutely marvellous flavour. He was told that salmon was the basic food of the region and that it was available in abundance, but not always in the different varieties that were offered on this special night.

All the villagers were, of course, salmon experts and the floor hummed with conversation as they tasted the offerings. Having noted where the three ladies who had voiced their concern over the shrimp portions were seated, he noticed that the three of them had got over that and were talking amicably and generously sharing the fish.

He looked toward Mother who had seen him looking at the women. Bedard held his hand up. Mot came just as she said, "They are sisters and have had many disagreements over the past twenty years. Battles, in fact! But they are actually very caring people and strong supporters of each other and their immediate families and of Tsusnahm. You will surely meet them because, although they are married and have several children each, they like men!"

Mot disappeared again. Bedard smiled. *I hope that he is getting enough to eat.*

The next dishes were meats garnished with dried and cooked fresh mushrooms, roots and vegetables. He called for both Mot's and Roanyon's assistance many times over the next half hour to identify the various offerings. He decided to sample everything and then ask for slightly larger portions of those that he enjoyed most. It was a very difficult time for Bedard. He could feel his body filling up to overflowing.

Mot arrived at his side on two occasions during this period, offering condolences mixed with mirth, and saying to Bedard that guests often excused themselves to go outside. Bedard noted that Mother smiled several times during these interchanges, giving Bedard the notion that she knew more English than she had admitted so far.

Bedard thought about this for some time and decided that it would be fun to create a situation that would reveal her knowledge of English. He did not really want to insult her or embarrass her, so it would have to be cleverly created.

Bedard was almost the last one to leave the banquet. He was satisfied with his short thank-you speech and pleased with his ability to articulate it after only one day in this community.

Outside, he and Mot gathered up his packs and moved them to an enclosed corner of the building next door to the chief's building. Bedard checked the inside path to the front and back door and then Mot showed him two wall boards that were designed to be moved for exit from his corner.

They then butchered the small deer that had been hung outside and Bedard portioned four meals for the dogs. He called Liz and JoJo in to the village first and then Hy and Haus. During the night, the dogs would provide ample security for him. Mot said that in the morning the children would be, as usual, set up on a close security perimeter of the village.

The village was almost quiet by the time Bedard and Mot went out in search of Dot. They had been told that Dot's mother, an older sister, and Adrona were keeping her company and that Mot's two brothers were close by.

Dot was sitting with her sister's arm around her and two children sitting at her feet hugging her knees. Her mother was busy in the background. Dot looked composed and immediately apologized to him for the trouble she had almost caused him. Bedard had decided not to share with her the issues that he had with the men in the corral. Dot, glancing at Adrona and Noua, said that she now understood Don's true nature. Adrona did not look up. She also said that she was beginning to understand her own current situation and, with the help of her family and other members of the village, she was going to work hard to begin a new life. She went on to say that she had previously refused help because she was devastated with the loss of her husband and was angry at everything and everyone.

She started to cry again but stopped when Bedard spoke to her slowly in English, with Mot translating, saying that the journey of life had many turns and twists and that he was certain that her life would move forward into happiness. The two held hands for a moment, and then Bedard and Mot excused themselves and left.

Adrona came out and stopped Bedard. Mot moved on down the trail. Adrona was crying and she hugged Bedard.

"Thank you. We need to talk," she said in Musqueam.

Bedard smiled, moved back a bit and put both hands on his belly. "Yes, but tomorrow. I have had a long day."

Adrona, smiling through her tears, said, "Yes, tomorrow."

And she turned and went back into the building and Bedard went off down the trail following Mot.

Bedard awoke in the darkness and was startled to see a small flame near his bed. In the darkness beyond he saw Adrona carrying Noua and placing him on a small pile of leaves that had materialized nearby.

She then dragged a thick fur sleeping robe, not too dissimilar to his own cover, over toward him. She lifted a corner of his cover and arranged hers to her satisfaction, and snuggled her cold back and bottom into his warm body. She found his arm and placed his hand over her ample breast and then, to Bedard's complete amazement, went to sleep. He looked at the small flame and realized that it was just a few leaves in a small bowl. The flame went out, and the blackness descended once more. *I suppose that she now expects me to sleep!*

He was still awake two hours later when Noua made a small noise. Adrona awoke and twisted in his arms, kissed him, and got up with her cover around her. She lit some new leaves in the bowl. *I don't know how she did that.* She picked up Noua and turned to face him. She exposed both of her breasts and brought Noua up to one of them to nurse and smiled intensely at him. He smiled intensely back. Her breasts were beautiful indeed. Then she wrapped the cover completely over both her and Noua.

Bedard closed his eyes and was immediately asleep. He awoke briefly when she returned to his side. This time she faced him, snuggled up and put her head on his chest. Surprisingly, he went back to sleep only to awake briefly once more when she got up to feed the baby. He watched her but she offered no show this time, so he went back to sleep.

He didn't even awaken when she got up again later in the night, but briefly snuggled with her when she returned. He awoke fully rested but still feeling very full in the early morning. When she again got up for a feeding, he also got up and prepared for his morning run. It was still dark. He saw that she lit the dried grass and leaves in her clever little bowl with a small sliver of hot wood from the fireplace. He kissed her on the top of her head, said nothing, and left the building through one of the wall boards.

Seven
January 14, 1858 (Morning)

The morning was crisp, and the air was heavy with mist. Bedard noted in the very early sun's rays that the snowline had crept farther down the mountains to the south.

He still felt heavy from the previous day's meal and decided not to push his run that morning. He went through his usual stretching program and then moved out of the village in a light jog to the north, up the bluff trail and into the forest. He had brought a small strap pack for JoJo because he could always use more berries—they were so good—and they needed another small deer for dog food. He called in the dogs from their night stations and dispatched them in their usual tight security net around him.

This left the village a bit unprotected, but he had talked to Mot's two brothers the day before and they were aware of Bedard's priorities. They had talked of training some of the village dogs to be used in village security, especially at night when the dogs' eyesight, sense of smell and awareness of movement in the distance was significantly better than humans.

He then jogged eastward along the main east–west trail at the top of the bluff. The village dog pack gave only a few ruffs, for they were already used to the movement of his dogs. It was still dark as Hades in the forest, and Bedard decided to take the trail to the northeast for his run. He had investigated part of this trail yesterday morning on the hunting trip. It was a very remarkable route starting at the riverside trail near the village and then continuing beside a streambed up the bluff above the river to the main trail. It then jutted off to the northeast to a large swamp area surrounding a shallow lake. Another trail branching off to the west at the swamp seemed to be as well travelled as the original trail continuing northeast.

The family group moved onward. Bedard could occasionally see Hy running ahead of him in the gloom. Liz was guarding the rear this morning and she soon gave a very soft bark and came up closer, wagging her tail before moving off into the heavy brush to the west of the trail. Bedard slowed down and soon heard a figure running on the trail behind him. The person soon materialized from the mist and Bedard recognized Roanyon.

"I hope that you do not mind if I join you," Roanyon said.

Picking up the pace a bit to match Roanyon's, Bedard said, "Of course not. You are a morning ghost, too, are you?"

"After a feast like that something must be done," he said, and they both laughed.

"I chose this route today because I have only travelled a short distance this way, and I am curious to see where it leads," said Bedard.

"The trail ends at small village on a beautiful long inlet. The mountains that we see occasionally through the trees are on the other side of this water. It is an exceptionally beautiful area. I like it very much," said Roanyon.

"There is also another path to the west near the lake that leads toward several Squamish villages, including Khwaykhway. Wh'mullutsthun is located directly across the water from it," Roanyon said. "These are large communities that you should perhaps visit sometime soon. The early English, Spanish and Russian sailing ships all stopped there. I would be pleased to accompany you, as I speak their language. Some of those villagers actually speak a little English, too."

"We will try to skirt any villages that we see today. I do not want to expose myself any more than I have already," said Bedard, and they both laughed again.

"You have met Mot's two brothers, Modan and Towaba," Roanyon said, and Bedard nodded. "We are a small village, as you know. These two clever and resourceful men are involved in almost everything here, including food and firewood distribution, our simple security system using the older children, solving problems and supporting all the other needs of our community. You might call them our *managers*." They both smiled. "If you need anything, they are the ones to approach."

"Thanks. I will remember that."

"We have two other individuals, Inchesca and Bella, who are our shamans. They actually live on the island just across the water from our village in a small village called Skwisahthun. Their mother was also a shaman and very well-known up and down the coast. These two wonderful sisters mediate with the spirit world on behalf of our community and give guidance and support to everyone. They are traditional healers and medicine people who enjoy teaching our children to sing and dance."

"They sound very interesting. I look forward to meeting them."

Bedard decided that this village's leadership and management was strong and more than adequate. He knew that he had a forceful personality and therefore he had to be careful to maintain his visitor presence and approach this new world softly.

"Why are you visiting us?"

"Our government believes that there will be a gold rush on your river this year. Perhaps more than twenty thousand miners may come, mostly from California. I have been asked by my government to deal with thirty criminals who are thought to be amongst the first to arrive. Many on this list are also astute leaders and politically shrewd. With many Americans in this valley, perhaps the U.S. would try to claim this area. My government wants to stop that."

Roanyon was thoughtful.

It was about eight miles across to the water and Bedard had changed the team, with Liz now in the lead followed by Hy, with Haus behind Bedard and Roanyon and JoJo with the empty pack bringing up the rear. The trail was clear and dry, and even in the darkness they made good time.

They had run for more than an hour at a medium pace and had skirted only one small village of two buildings on the inlet. It was indeed a very beautiful area. Bedard noted that Roanyon did not seem tired, and he was impressed.

Bedard again tried to remember Roanyon in Hawaii and then suddenly realized where they had actually first met.

"I have just remembered that we met in China and eventually took a junk over from Hong Kong to Hawaii together with a small group of men that I had asked to join me to solve a problem in Hawaii caused by some Japanese."

Roanyon nodded. "What a memory you have! I remember that now! China was a lot of fun, although I was there for less than three years. I really enjoyed trying to learn the Shaolin hand-to-hand kung fu combat, but I did not become as proficient at it as you did."

"Yes," Bedard said, "that adventure is all coming back to me now. I was most impressed with your ferociousness. I also remember that you became a leader of one of the teams that I assembled in Hawaii to contend with some Japanese intruders."

Roanyon said, "I certainly remember that. I was most impressed at how a mixture of people, Americans, Australians, British, Chinese and Hawaiians, could work together. That was one of the great pleasures of my life."

The ocean water was mirror-still and the two men and four dogs, continuing to move to the east, made a wide circle around another small village. The forest was dense but the game trails were numerous, and they moved smoothly parallel to the waterline, crossing over several small creeks and encountering nothing but a few animals moving in the early morning.

The sky was gradually growing light and the sun was set to rise when Liz gave a short bark, and everyone stopped to listen. Hy came into sight and then moved inland. Bedard, Roanyon and the team went into the forest to hide.

After about ten minutes Bedard could hear the passage of a boat manned by what he judged to be several paddlers. He and Roanyon moved quietly toward the water's edge and soon could see a large canoe of local conventional design moving toward the west—four paddlers plus six passengers, baggage and two dogs. They were well out from the shore, and the dogs on board had not smelled them. Visitors, they guessed.

Proceeding farther eastward, they came to an escarpment. He and Roanyon again went down to the water for a look. Across the water, at a little over half a mile, Bedard could see the start of another arm of the steep ocean inlet leading toward the north around the towering mountains. The east–west arm of the inlet continued on to the east. No sign of any more villages yet.

Roanyon said, "There is a small village called Tsleil'waututh directly across from us, back in the forest. It has a unique language that is said to be very old, but I understand that not many of the villagers speak it now, which is very sad."

Bedard nodded and decided that this would be a fascinating village to visit.

The sun was now rising, and they had been out for over two hours. Bedard called Liz and Hy and sent them back toward the villages. He would need a canoe to further investigate this attractive area.

Circling the small villages again, they came back onto the trail and moved off at a brisk pace. Bedard was mentally reviewing the security of the current arrangements. It would be easy to become complacent and he could not allow himself to do that.

The corral farther to the west on the north side of the river had been identified and needed to be investigated further. Bedard had an uncanny feeling that there was something else. He could not understand his feelings. It was almost as if he was being watched.

This feeling was strongest when he was at Tsusnahm.

They were approaching the lake when Bedard slowed down and turned to Roanyon. "We are going to stop here and hunt for food."

"I will continue on to Tsusnahm. Thank you for the company."

Bedard and his family were familiar with the area and they soon killed a small deer, which Bedard dressed and attached to JoJo's pack. They went farther east to a meadow that was bursting with various kinds of berries. Bedard filled the pack and started back.

The family had passed the swamp and was proceeding to the south. He slowed and looked with awe at the tall trees. It still fascinated him how tall some of them were—over three hundred feet and projecting above the general forest by at least fifty feet. It was such a tree that he sighted on the day he arrived with the reflection of light off a spyglass. A spy tree, he mused with a smile. Then he stopped so abruptly that Haus came into view behind him and scurried into the brush to hide. He whistled and Hy came back leaving Liz in the front guard position.

There must be a spy tree near the village. But which one, and how to identify it, and what danger does it pose?

More secrets that his new friends had not yet seen fit to share with him. It was also probable that those in Tsusnahm, including Mot, were well aware of the spy tree and had decided, or were directed, not to tell him about it.

Firstly, the spy tree was probably located near one of the trails. The spies would not leave a track through the bush to the tree. Secondly, the tree had to be reasonably tall. If it was only manned in daylight, then the spy had to climb it in darkness. It might be possible to actually live in the tree, coming down occasionally for food, water and fuel. Cooking would not be a problem at early daybreak and dusk, with a shielded fire and the smoke invisible in the semi darkness.

Bedard examined a typical tree nearby. There were hundreds of them. This tree was massive. He paced around it—close to sixty feet in circumference! Looking up, he saw that the lowest branches were at least one hundred feet above the ground. In his pack he carried a thin cord that was super strong but only fifty feet long. His reserve of cords and rope, over two thousand feet in all, was still hidden with his canoes.

To climb such a tree was impossible. A team of three or four might be able to do it using a wrap rope as he had seen demonstrated in California, but that would be very difficult. To snake a rope up over a lower branch, one hundred feet up, was not feasible. A light cord on an arrow might work. This suggested local residents rather than white men.

After initial access up the tree had been established, this entrance had to be maintained. *Was there always someone in the spy tree? Unlikely.* Leaving a rope hanging down for next ascent was not reasonable.

Therefore, there must be some other access method. Puzzling.

He remembered that close to the bluff above the village there was a real monster tree. The trail actually curved around it. A likely target, but there were many others, too.

It was now mid-morning, and Bedard and his family moved off at a brisk pace toward Tsusnahm to finish the morning run. At the top of the bluff, Bedard dispersed the family to their village perimeter roaming security assignments and then followed the path down and into the village. He found a tree and hung the deer carcass up out of the reach of the village dogs and passing animals.

Entering his new home from the front of the building, he found Adrona and Noua at the central cooking area stirring a pot of something that smelled good. He went into his sleeping area to drop off JoJo's packs with the berries and then returned and sat down at the end of a bench some distance from Adrona. They smiled at each other.

"We have many things to talk about," Adrona said.

"Yes," said Bedard, and he looked around, seeing no one nearby. "Should we start now?"

"No. The walls have ears. We all need to eat." They both smiled greatly. "I will give Noua to my sister who also has a new baby, and we will visit a private place that I know to talk."

Bedard shrugged. "I do not need much food." And they both laughed.

Just then Mother, Mot and Roanyon entered the building.

"I have invited them to join us for the early meal," Adrona said.

Bedard nodded. "Good to eat with friends." And they all smiled.

Roanyon said, "You mentioned earlier this morning that you needed be at Fort Victoria tomorrow. I know the owner of a small sailboat that is available tomorrow. He told me that it will make the trip over to the island in about six or seven hours. The weather tomorrow will be favourable for this trip. I would like to come with you if that is agreeable. I have some business that I have been wanting to do over there for some time, and this would be perfect for that."

He and Mother exchanged looks.

"Perfect," said Bedard. "Will it be possible to leave here early in the morning?"

Roanyon said, "Yes, the boat is anchored at a small inlet to the east of here. It is owned by my cousin Tomara. He is a very experienced small-boat sailor. When I told him that you had some experience, he was very excited. He said that with a crew of three it might be possible to allow the boat to really perform and he does not have that opportunity very often."

Bedard said that he was meeting with James Douglas in Victoria who they all had heard of but had never met. Bedard went on to say that he had met Douglas several times in the past, and shared some anecdotes. Mot and Roanyon provided some of the translations for Adrona's benefit. Then the conversation turned to Bedard's obvious skill in languages.

Adrona had noted, of course, that Bedard's knowledge of her language was improving, but she did not realize that he had only been speaking the language for one day. She was stunned.

Mot also had the advantage over the others by having the opportunity to actually witness Bedard's astounding language proficiency.

Mother asked Bedard, "Just how many languages do you know?"

Bedard had played this game many times, so he gave her the simple answer, "I do not know exactly. About ten fluently and about thirty proficiently. But languages are complex and there are many dialects."

Mother said, "Our own language actually has many dialects and is, in fact, a dialect of a language group known as Halkomelem or even Hunguminum."

Roanyon, whose father was also a chief, knew this and nodded his head. Bedard remembered that Mot had mentioned some of this when they first met. *As usual, the world is more complex than one realizes.*

Then he smiled. "My current favourite is your language, and I thank you all for your contributions."

Adrona then said, "But you learn a new language so fast. How can that be?"

Bedard turned to her. "I have a unique mind. I remember everything that I hear. Mot has been translating your language into English for me, and so I have built up a fairly large vocabulary, but I am still learning how the words and the sentences go together. As well as a strong memory for languages, I also have a good idea of language structures and how thoughts and communications can be expressed. Languages are complex, and I enjoy learning them."

The translation of all of this took some time, but Mot and Roanyon were becoming an excellent translation team.

Adrona shook her head. "Amazing."

Then Bedard turned to Mot and Roanyon. "For most of my life, I have been threatened by my enemies and I have tried several ways to combat this. In this part of the world, the best protection is to be essentially invisible combined with the unique protection my dogs provide for me. The dogs are very good and have been doing exactly this for more than nine years. There were others before them."

Bedard stopped for a moment and looked at each one of the four. "Being invisible has always been difficult, because I am six feet tall and many people are much shorter, so I stand out like a sore thumb." He smiled.

Roanyon said, "In Hawaii, you were not so tall most of the time."

Bedard said, "Yes, I have had some very clever teachers who have passed on to me many secrets of disguise."

Adrona had trouble with the word "disguise" and when she finally understood she put her hand to her mouth.

Bedard continued. "Here my height is not noticeable. Many of the villagers are tall. My skin is also similar in colour, and my clothes are, or can be, similar. The only things that makes me stand out here are my use of the language, the way I walk and use my body to support my communications and the manner in which the villagers treat me."

The three thought about this for a while.

Mot said, "The celebration yesterday was not particularly useful for you."

Bedard said, "No, it was not useful for me, but it was a spontaneous event, and I tried to be as invisible as I could." The four smiled, remembering his travel around the room and his position at the head table.

"My enemies may be hard-pressed to find me now," Bedard said.

Roanyon just shook his head again.

Adrona then said very carefully, "Then your name is not Copco. You have adopted that name in order to blend into our community. Your enemies know you under a different name or under different names."

Bedard nodded.

"Roanyon," Adrona said. "You knew him in Hawaii." Roanyon nodded. "Do you remember his name there?"

"He had several names. I could remember one or two if I really tried, but we were all using different names at that time and subscribed to the same philosophy. Only, at that time"—he smiled at the memory—"the most feared people were from Japan, another large island many miles away. None of the Japanese spoke English, and only a few spoke Hawaiian. Our names then would be meaningless to anyone now."

Bedard said, "I have always tried to use a different name, or names, in each place that I have visited. This is a part of the basic concept of disguise."

Eight
January 14, 1858

They had managed to finish all of the large early morning meal—a delicious fish stew that Adrona had created from some of the leftover food from yesterday's feast. The leftovers had been distributed around the village and would no doubt be the basic meal ingredient for everyone for several days. Bedard wondered where the shrimp had gone, and he smiled.

Roanyon noted the smile and said in a very good English falsetto, "A penny for your thoughts, young man."

Then, as Mot translated for Adrona's benefit, Roanyon said, "That was what my mother always said," and everyone laughed. "My mother spoke English quite well and tried to teach it to all of us in the family, and to many others in Tsusnahm. My memory of that part of my childhood is very pleasurable." He looked at Mother.

"I was actually wondering where the delicious shrimp and lake fish dish went," Bedard said. And at that all five of them burst into laughter, and Adrona had tears in her eyes.

Mot, Mother and Roanyon left.

Noua had been awakened by the laughter and Adrona moved over to deal with him. Bedard watched closely but no show happened, so he went into his room and examined the berries that he had picked.

He then returned and again sat down at the end of a bench an appreciable distance from Adrona, who was now cleaning up after the meal. They smiled at each other.

When she was finished, she beckoned Bedard to come with her. She led the way out the back door and started up the path to the north. About halfway up, she turned to the east and found a stepping-stone path across the stream that the main path followed down the hill. They soon found themselves in a delightful meadow with a light sprinkling of very small early-blooming flowers. Adrona took his hand and led him to a spot in the middle of the meadow. It was at least five hundred feet from the brush and forest that surrounded them.

She sat down on a log and motioned for Bedard to sit opposite her on another one.

Before he did that he whistled, and Liz came racing across the field from the north, skidding to a stop in front of him. He whisked his hand and Liz, tail wagging furiously, went over to meet Adrona and get some scratches. Another hand signal and off she went to her station.

Adrona said, "What is her name?"

"Liz."

"She is really beautiful."

Bedard whistled again and JoJo came steaming across the field from the east, brushed by Bedard and went immediately to Adrona for scratches. Bedard could see that she didn't know what to make of this huge animal, so he called him over and had him give her his award-winning head-high legs-stiff pose. She got up, went to him and gave him a hug.

That was perfect, said JoJo, and gave her a big lick. Off JoJo went, and Bedard put his arm around Adrona.

"That was JoJo. I have two very large dogs called mastiffs and two collies in my family."

She looked up at him and then returned to her log. Bedard sat down opposite her.

"Who are you," she said, "and why are you here?"

Bedard thought for a moment, not certain how to respond. His Musqueam was still very basic and Adrona understood only a little English, but he decided to try to respond using a mix of both languages as best he could.

"I live very far away in England. It took me almost a year to travel to your village from there. I was asked to come here by our supreme leader, our nation's chief, to protect the English people who already live in these lands at, or near, the forts, and to protect the peaceful people that we think will travel here in the very near future looking for gold. I believe that these good people have already started to come here, and their numbers will increase over the next few years.

"We believe that some very bad people are already here, with more bad people coming soon. The group of men at the corral are bad people. They are led by a man who calls himself the Wolverine. I know him personally. I have met him many times. He is very smart and very evil. I also have Don on my list. I have not met him, but I know that he has previously worked for the Wolverine."

Bedard stopped talking. He was not certain that his rudimentary Musqueam augmented by a bit of English had been all that successful.

She continued to stare at him and tears came to her eyes.

"Don is Noua's father!" she said.

Bedard was not surprised because of the way she had acted several times yesterday. But he was very surprised that she felt the need to admit this to him in this abrupt way.

"I hate him; I hate him with all my heart. I will kill him! I will kill him! When the baby came, he was surprised and would not have anything to do with me. He told me that he did not want the baby. Then one day the baby disappeared, and I could do nothing. I was powerless. The baby was gone and it was all my fault. The baby could not be found. I tried to kill myself. Chief Sparrow had me tied up to stop me from doing that. I would not eat. I wanted to die." Tears were flowing down her cheeks, but she was still under control and this impressed Bedard.

"Then the miracle happened and my baby was back. I was so happy that I cried for a long time. Then I realized that nothing had changed. Don was still alive. Dot's story brought me to my senses, and then I decided that you were different and perhaps could help me, so I acted on that last night." They both smiled. "And now that I have more information from you, I feel that perhaps there will be a solution to my problem. And that is why I am telling you this story."

Then she broke down and sobbed. Bedard immediately crossed over and took her in his arms. She continued to sob. Telling her story had taken a great deal of effort, and now she was spent.

In half an hour or so Adrona stopped crying and smiled up at Bedard, but did not attempt to move from his embrace.

This is nice, he thought.

Bedard decided to try to move the conversation forward a bit.

"I hope to be able to solve your problem. If Don dies, then perhaps his friends will try to kill me and perhaps you and Noua as well. But we will try. I want to get rid of all of the men at the corral. It will not be useful for you to repeat that information to anyone. That is our secret. Do you agree?"

"Yes, I will not tell anyone."

"Not even Noua!"

"Not even Noua,' she said smiling, and kissed him.

"How old am I, Adrona?"

Adrona was not expecting this question and moved back from Bedard a bit so that she could look into his face.

"How old am I?" he repeated.

She moved even further back from him and said, "Why are you asking me this?"

"Because we are both enjoying being close, and we need to understand where this friendship will go."

She thought about this and then looked down. "I am thirty years old. My husband drowned while he was fishing. I have two other children, twins, they are now six years old. They are perfect!" She looked up into his face, smiling through the tears. "I missed my husband horribly, just like Dot. Both Dot and I made a huge mistake getting involved with Don."

She was now looking down and crying again.

"I am sixty, twice your age. I was married, but I have lived apart from my wife for over twenty years. I have a daughter that I have never met." Adrona looked up into his face again through the tears.

I have done it again! I have admitted that I have a daughter twice in in the last two days. I have never done that before! He looked away and shook his head.

"My daughter, Dorthea, is twenty-two, and she is probably with her mother, Donna, somewhere in the world. I do not know where. I will leave this area in about a year," he said, "and probably never return here again. During this year, I will not be in Tsusnahm very often because I have much to do elsewhere."

In the distance, Liz barked once. Bedard unfolded himself from the embrace, stood up and looked over toward the west along the path that they had taken to get here. He saw someone crossing the stream. It was Mother.

"We have a visitor," he said.

Adrona stood up and stretched. Bedard liked that. She saw him looking at her and laughed. She took him in a full body hug and kissed him. He also liked that.

Then she said, "I guess we should go and have our midday meal."

So they walked with their arms around each other toward Mother, who had stopped on this side of the stream.

"Oh, there you are. Food is ready." She moved on in front of them across the stream again. Along the path down the slope by the stream, Bedard put his other arm around Mother and they walked along.

As they approached the village, Mother said, "We are having the midday meal in our home. It is almost ready, so do not"—and then she added the English word—"*dawdle.*"

She broke out into an enormous giggle and ran the last little way to her building.

Bedard and Adrona entered their building, where she found some warm water in a big pot on the central fire embers. She dipped some into a bowl and washed her face. Looking in a mirror, she stuck out her tongue and laughed.

Mother's meal was for sixteen, including Mot, Roanyon, Bedard and Adrona. She could have easily fed thirty, the food was so plentiful. Bedard tried unsuccessfully to eat modestly. It was so good that refills, offered often with threats of crying fits if refused, were wolfed down. Noua arrived halfway through the midday feast and was passed around with great pleasure. To everyone's amusement, Noua had learned how to giggle.

Adrona's sister, Aurora, and her new baby, Basso, were introduced to Bedard. She had not been at the feast yesterday because she had taken on the support role of what Bedard knew as "kinder-homing" back in London, a phrase taken from the German society in Europe. Here they used a word that roughly translated into "empire-building," much to Bedard's and Roanyon's great amusement.

"That is a perfect word," said Bedard, "and you must be the empress!" This took a moment to translate, and everyone broke into laughter and clapped for Aurora, who was a bit embarrassed with all the attention.

"I have always enjoyed babies and young children. I am very happy in their presence. Little Noua is a great pleasure," Aurora said, looking at Adrona, who went over to her and gave her a big hug.

After eating, Bedard captured Adrona. They went to their home and snuggled and kissed a bit in their room. Adrona then left to undertake her afternoon assignments while Bedard decided to search for the spy tree.

He left Tsusnahm, followed the creek up to the top of the bluff and called in his family from their general stations, setting them out in their usual tight security net around him.

They turned eastward along the main east–west trail past the intersection with the northeast trail toward the big tree that he remembered from a previous exploratory trip. It was indeed a monster, at least seventy feet in circumference and incredibly tall, with many slightly smaller brothers in the near vicinity—a grove of monsters. He liked that. It was very dark and gloomy in this area as the sunlight was almost completely blocked out by the forest cover.

Bedard examined the ground at the base of the tree and decided that the ground cover had been meticulously created—it was just too perfect. If this was the spy tree and well known by the locals, they would probably stay away from it and keep their children away. The ground was as if the tree was in the middle of the deep forest—not a broken twig or bent blade of grass. Perhaps even the animals knew to keep away.

He sent the dogs into a special security diamond around him and stepped away from the tree while examining the upper reaches. The first branches were more than one hundred and fifty feet above the forest floor. Stubs of previous branches were numerous on the massive trunk below the existing branches, but from earlier experience Bedard knew that these stubs were typically old, rotten and not secure. On the east side of the tree, about forty feet up the trunk, Bedard saw an unusual dark stub perhaps ten inches long. He unwrapped one of his cords and prepared a slipknot loop on one end.

He launched the loop toward the dark stub. On the ninth try, the cord caught the stub and he moved closer to the tree, tightening the cord till the loop was tight.

He then carefully went up the cord, hand over hand. As he neared the dark stub, he saw two others to the side. Grabbing the first with his hand, he brought his right foot up and placed his weight on another stub. It was awkward. He reached out and grabbed the third one and examined them. They were made from a hardwood bush and still had most of the bark on them. They were definitely man-made and driven into a hole cut or drilled into the tree. The lower one was obviously designed as a foot hold and the other two as hand holds. *The spies are a little shorter than me!*

Looking up through the gloom he could see another set of three stubs. Using his waist strap, he tied his shoulders to one of the stubs so that he could use both hands.

He undid the cord and fashioned the slipknot loop again. Crouching down and using a long sidearm throw, he managed to catch a stub the first time. Testing the cord with his full weight, he released himself and moved upward smoothly with long overhand reaches. The cord was biting into his hands by the time he made it to the second stage.

He saw yet a third set of stubs and repeated the procedure again. He was now at least one hundred and twenty feet above the ground.

Looking up after first securing himself, he could not see any further stubs. The lowest branches were at least another thirty feet up. It was not easy to see in this light, and he feared that he may have to try another day. The branches and foliage above actually looked impregnable, perhaps even unnaturally so.

He leaned out to his right side first and then to his left, and finally spied something that looked promising—a hole in the foliage above with what looked like a large long stub immediately below it. This was off to his left about twenty feet around the tree and up about thirty feet from his current position. Bedard smiled. He always enjoyed being ambidextrous.

Twenty minutes later, he was trying to throw the loop with his left arm for the thirty-something time. It was mid-afternoon but very dark. Then the cord caught something. Again, testing it with all his weight and jiggling it back and forth, he decided that it was substantial.

He released himself and swung over slowly under the access. *Burning my bridges behind me.*

He then moved up the cord smoothly and reached the large stub that he had indeed snagged. It was much thicker than the others and about two feet long. He managed to get both hands around it, and with a quick twist brought his armpit over the stub. He then fashioned a foot sling with his waist strap so that he could climb up and sit straddling the large stub. Looking up, he saw a short-looped rope that looked like a convenient handhold and, using it, pulled himself up to a standing position.

For some time he had been aware that there was a person in the tree. Now he could smell him. He knew that if this was a potential enemy he was in grave danger.

The rifle barrel that came out of the darkness to rest against his forehead belonged to a flintlock muzzle-loading Kentucky Rifle, and Bedard could smell the powder in the barrel of this very old gun. *Looks in good shape. It will probably easily blow my head off.*

A small flame appeared by magic and instantly disappeared again. He could not see a thing. The gun barrel was withdrawn and a helping hand reached down to him.

He clambered up and followed the person up the branches. His guide stopped occasionally to indicate hand and foot holds. He appeared old but lithe, even thin—definitely native. Near the top, they came to an area where a platform had been fashioned. A small fire glowed and several pots and plates were neatly stacked nearby. Looking around, he guessed that the platform could hold about four people and perhaps more in other locations in other branches.

The view was spectacular. In fact, the mountains surrounding them in all directions were clearly visible. Those immediately behind them and to the immediate east and west dominated the view. Peaks far away to the west on Vancouver Island could easily be seen, as was the range many miles off to the south and a monster snow-covered mountain to the southeast. *That must be a volcano.*

The man uncocked the gun and placed it on the floor of the platform within easy reach. He smiled with a toothless grin and said something in Musqueam that Bedard didn't catch, so Bedard introduced himself. The old man said that he knew who Copco was and was not surprised to see him.

He introduced himself as Bob, implying that his Squamish name was difficult. In due course, Bedard learned that he was about forty-five years old, which he said was quite old for the local natives.

Bob said, "Some of my uncles lived well into their sixties so there is hope for me yet. I married a Musqueam woman many years ago and we lived in Tsusnahm. I was what you might call a *forester*"—he used the English word and smiled—"but it was really firewood, sometimes logs for the boat builders and for those building or repairing a longhouse. My wife died of smallpox and I now survive and contribute to my village as best I can."

Bedard asked why the village had a lookout tree.

The basic story was that a small group of Haida marauders looking for child slaves came up the middle branch of the Fraser River in the darkness on a stormy early-winter night four years ago. The last time such an attack on a Musqueam village had occurred many years ago, before Fort Langley had been constructed. At that time, it was relatively common for Haida, Yuculta and other ferocious war parties to come up the Fraser River looking for children and young females for slaves. The Musqueam villages on the lower Fraser River were then reasonably well equipped to battle these cruel warrior groups.

But after these many years and the reduction in native population everywhere by smallpox and other diseases, the need and the ability to maintain war-party defence had disappeared. This Haida group, numbering about forty, easily surprised and overpowered Tsusnahm in less than one day, killing twenty-five villagers and going off with all of the young children that they could catch, totalling thirty in all.

Most of the adult villagers were off fishing and hunting at the time. When they returned, some of them immediately went after the Haida, to no avail. Almost all of the adults that had remained in Tsusnahm had been killed.

The two large villages at the mouth of the north arm of the Fraser River, Mahli and Stsulawh, were bypassed by the Haida, possibly due to their relatively large populations and also because the narrowness of the river in that area would reduce the effectiveness of the Haida's surprise attack. These villagers did swarm the upstream area, but they were too late to be of help.

The result was that Tsusnahm was reduced to a small group of men and women, several older children and some very young children, many without their natural mothers and fathers. It was a difficult time. Some of the older men decided to create a lookout program as a basic defence against the possibility of another attack. Since that time, the lookout tree had been manned continuously from daylight to nightfall.

The villagers had often considered going north to recover their children, but found it complicated by a lack of information as to where the children were located and the high risk of retaliation by the Haida. Bob felt that it was, unfortunately, wishful thinking because of their lack of warrior skills.

Mahli and Stsulawh also created a lookout tree and manned it day and night. This was taken over by the white men at the corral. It was this lookout tree that Bedard had noticed on the first morning of his arrival. The fact that a small party had been dropped off near the mouth of the South Fraser would have been quickly passed on to the Wolverine, and this resulted in his rapid reaction and the scouting party that Bedard had encountered.

Climbing down the tree was not difficult, and Bedard arrived in the village without causing concern. After touching base with Adrona and doing some afternoon chores for her, he sought out Mot, whom he found talking with Roanyon.

Bedard reported his encounter with Bob and asked Mot to fill in some more details about the Haida attack four years ago.

"I was still at the monastery's farm at that time," said Mot, "and received a report of the attack from a trader about two months later. Against the wishes of the monks, and in hindsight at great risk to myself, I immediately took off north with the company of two of the tracking dogs that I had trained. After a period of sixty very eventful days, I arrived at Tsusnahm and found that my family had been significantly reduced. I was very fortunate to still have my father and mother and some of my brothers and sisters.

"In spite of the strong advice of my mother and father to stay home, I spent the next ten months visiting all the accessible villages up the northern coast trying to determine where the Haida had actually gone. I was upset because I could not convince any of the groups that I met up the coast to take me farther into the area that the Haida controlled. I did determine that they probably came from a southern Haida village called Skidegate.

"I returned to my village very angry and, for the first time in my life, really frustrated that my blindness had stopped me from accomplishing something.

"To my surprise, my quest, even in its failure, had brought me some measure of respect from the remaining villagers. I needed this respect not only to exist from day to day but also to help me try to make something of my miserable life."

Bedard thought that he now had most of the current history and secrets that the people of this village held closely—it now all made sense. There was no doubt that the purloined children were sorely missed.

Mot said, "My parents were present during this Haida invasion and you would find it interesting to hear what they remember of that day. We should find them and see whether they have time to talk to us tonight."

Chief Sparrow and Mother were relaxing in their very comfortable quarters after their late meal, and after hearing that Bedard had met Bob up in the lookout tree, agreed to talk to Bedard, Mot and Roanyon about the Haida attack and the kidnapping of the children four years ago.

Bedard was getting used to the chief's guttural speech, and Mother helped Mot and Roanyon with the translations.

Chief Sparrow said, "They arrived early in the morning with a great deal of yelling and screaming. Mother and I came out of our building and it was immediately obvious to us who they were and why they were here. We instantly saw that anyone who got in their way would be battered or killed. I tried to stop them and protect Mother, but I was not very successful." He looked at Mother. "We have talked about this day many times."

Mother said, "I tried to protect the children and was badly beaten for my efforts. I then tried to watch the ongoing activities from our doorway, but I was attacked there as well."

Chief Sparrow said, "It was obvious that I had neither the strength nor the skills to battle with these madmen. After some thought, I put on my best chief's blanket and my favourite hat, went out and sat on the grass under the tree and watched them. They could not hurt me without risking huge reprisals from the Musqueam Nation, and they apparently knew that as they left me alone. Forty years before I would have been able to memorize all of their faces—eighteen canoes with two men paddlers plus four women: forty Haida. I memorized the faces of four men and two women and noted that two other men had marked limps and four other men had distinctive facial scars."

Tears were starting to flow down their faces. This was obviously very difficult for them. Four small children from their family were taken. Mot, of course, and four of his sisters and his two older brothers were not there at that time. A great deal of anguish was being shown.

Mother said, "Most of the men and women and many of the older children of Tsusnahm were away fishing and hunting, otherwise a lot more villagers would have been killed. There have been very few warriors in our village for sixty years." She looked at Roanyon. "Since before your father's time." Roanyon nodded.

"People from Mahli and Stsulawh came to the rescue too late. The chiefs were enormously upset and set off in hot pursuit, unsuccessfully. Some of these villagers stayed with us for four or more weeks. Many of us were crying so hard we were unable to sleep, and we greatly appreciated the presence and assistance of these great friends. You have heard Mot's story. He was very brave. Artists were sent from Mahli and Stsulawh and spent two weeks with my husband. He still has the charcoal sketches."

The three men thanked Chief Sparrow and Mother and left the building.

They stood for a moment outside and Bedard said, "I wonder if it would be possible to create a plan to find and retrieve some of the children captured by the Haida."

Roanyon said, "You are very good at this type of planning. We need to train a specialized group of warriors for this. Perhaps this same group can then help you in your mission."

Bedard said, "The sketches may be very helpful in focusing our search."

That evening, Bedard sat at a table in the central-area darkness of his building for some time, thinking about the various strategies needed to execute a search and withdrawal plan. As Roanyon had said, he had planned and executed many of these types of sorties before and knew that the key to success was simplicity and training.

He needed to increase his knowledge of Musqueam, and he could use Mot as his teacher. Bedard knew that both he and Mot were very good with languages and that becoming reasonably fluent in the local dialect would not take much more time.

At the same time, he needed to create and train a small band of five or six warriors to lead into Haida territory to locate the children. Mot, in spite of his blindness, might be a great asset.

A medium-sized war canoe could easily carry this group, the four dogs, basic weapons and some food. More food could be obtained along the way from the sea and from the forests or from the villages that they would be passing.

An alternate plan to travel on land and portage on borrowed boats or rafts was easily discarded, due to security considerations and the definite possibility of a very difficult long open-water trip to reach the homeland of the Haida.

Bedard was certain that they would receive help and support from most of the villages to the north. But there was a risk that they would eventually encounter villages that were under the protective arm of the Haida, and they would have to determine this in advance in order to be able to sneak in and out of the Haida territory on the first trip.

The return trip to the Haida territory to actually recapture children would require a much larger group of warriors and would probably require a simultaneous attack on a number of villages where the slaves were kept.

Bedard wondered if it could be arranged to use a large ship like the *Beaver* to transport those men that he was now calling his warriors.

Adrona came in late and dragged him to bed with her. She did not give any shows that evening but she was extremely cuddly, and that suited Bedard very well as he continued to think through the Haida problem for several more hours. *A ship would be perfect! They definitely needed a Haida speaker.* He also wondered if there were any Haida families living in the area that might pass on information to other members of their families still living in the north.

Nine
January 15, 1858 (Fort Victoria Visit)

The next morning, Bedard did not go for a run. Roanyon joined Bedard and Adrona for an early morning meal. Bedard finally got to meet Adrona's twin daughters. Like their mother, they were very pretty, but they were shy and tended to stay in the background most of the time. After the quick meal, the two men got up to move on to their morning's adventure. They thanked Adrona for the food and said goodbye to the twins.

Bedard said to Adrona, "We will probably be away for at least three days. Remember our conversation. You should be cautious." They looked at each other carefully, touched hands and parted.

Bedard picked up a small pack from his room and joined Roanyon out near the big tree in front of the chief's building. Roanyon had a medium backpack and a small front-pack and was carrying a longbow and quiver.

Bedard called Liz and Hy down from their security duties to go with him on this trip.

"I need to stop where my canoes and gear are hidden to retrieve some of my clothing and equipment," said Bedard. The two of them moved off eastward from the village at a fast walk.

In about forty minutes, Bedard stopped and partially uncovered one of his boats and removed some bundles and two packs. He took a medium-length bow and a quiver, a long telescope and a set of throwing knives.

Roanyon shook his head. "This boat is very well hidden; I would never have found it even if I was looking for it."

Bedard spent some time recreating the boat-covering camouflage.

Roanyon was watching carefully and was impressed with the results. "You must teach me how to do that." Bedard smiled.

Roanyon then said, "I recognize the bow. It is a compound bow, is it not?"

Bedard was again impressed with his friend's knowledge.

"I would guess that you also have a crossbow in there somewhere."

Bedard just smiled.

"I also recognize the knives. They are Hawaiian throwing knives. I have a set like that too."

Bedard again just smiled.

The two men then moved off to the east with Liz in the lead and Hy following. In due course, Roanyon stopped and moved down a small trail toward the water to where the boat was moored offshore. Tomara was waiting for them with a small skiff.

"Wow!" Bedard said. "That looks American."

Tomara and Bedard shook hands. "Yes, this is my fourth boat. It was made in San Francisco. It is a twenty-five-foot single-masted sloop and, as you can see, it has a small covered centre area to protect us from the rain."

"Perfect," said Bedard. "Roanyon tells me that you have a ton of different sails."

Tomara laughed. Roanyon was pleased. It took them three trips out to the boat with the skiff to get all the gear and the two dogs on board. Bedard made a quick inspection of the vessel and then, with their gear and the two dogs stowed amidships, Tomara directed his crew to raise the mainsail and the sailboat moved out into the river.

"This is going to be fun. It has been a long time since I was on a sailboat this small," said Bedard.

The wind was light but the tide was ebbing, and with Roanyon and Bedard acting as experienced seamen, they hoisted a small jib and moved downstream at a reasonable rate.

"We are going to take the middle river channel," said Tomara with a laugh, "so that the enemy has a harder time seeing who we are."

Bedard smiled. "Good plan, Captain."

As they moved out past the extensive silt beds at the mouth of the river, the wind picked up from the southwest and the small boat started to skim across the water. They tried a number of sail combinations and decided on the mainsail and two medium-sized jibs.

Tomara had Roanyon take the helm and rigged two ropes from the mainmast. He then instructed Bedard, who recalled that he had done this many years ago, how to swing out beyond the side of the boat to produce some extra balance that enabled the boat to travel faster, closer to the southwest wind. In due course, Roanyon joined Bedard and the little vessel really skimmed along. Tomara, at the wheel, was grinning like a madman.

Their first tack was a long one almost due south. Roanyon proposed that they travel as if they were going farther south, as most of the vessels travelling out of the river would do. This would rapidly put them out of sight of the corral and would allow them to sit with their backs to the corral's lookout tree.

They then changed to a westward tack that Tomara said would allow them to travel between some islands to the small landing that he felt would work for Bedard's plan to go to Fort Victoria.

"The landing is about six miles from Victoria," said Tomara.

"That will be perfect for me," said Bedard.

They arrived at the landing just after midday, and Bedard with his two dogs and his packs and packages unloaded onto the shore.

"We are going farther north," Roanyon said, "but we will be back here, as agreed, probably late in afternoon two days from now."

Tomara nodded. "The trip north will not be a problem, but the trip back down here will be a trial. We may even arrive after dark."

"I will try to build a two-fire beacon," said Bedard. "Do you have a reasonable fog horn?"

Tomara reached down and produced a fog horn which he sounded with major intensity.

"That will work!" Bedard said, and they all laughed.

Bedard pushed the boat from shore and Tomara and Roanyon were soon off behind one of the offshore islands.

Bedard found a good hiding place high up in a tree for a small pack of clothes that he did not need. He was soon on his way with Liz in front and Hy behind.

A light rain was falling, with the sun breaking through from time to time. Mot had told him the previous day that the shamans were now predicting an early spring bringing warmish weather and a minimum of snow. He said that at this time of the year it occasionally snowed lightly, but it usually rained almost every day. *Sunshine is good,* Bedard thought.

He had been following a twisting road southwestward toward Fort Victoria for most of the afternoon, moving off into the forest whenever voices were heard. It was a well-used road but not well constructed. It was very slow going, and time after time he had to find his way through the heavy wet forest to pass around muddy quagmires and broken-down log bridges. *I should have stolen a horse* was a favourite thought that day.

After coming over the brow of a hill, the forest had given way to scattered groups of arbutus trees, light brush and grasslands with many stumps giving evidence of man's clearing of the forest land.

White man damages the land wherever he goes. I can't do much about that, I guess.

Liz had returned briefly for instructions. Bedard had finally seen water in the distance and so he directed her that way. They had been following a faint path for the past ten minutes or so. The sun was starting to set. He looked at his watch for the hundredth time and sighed with relief. On time, or as near as dammit. It was six o'clock and the meeting was at eight.

Reginald Edward Bedard the Third, now known as Copco to his native friends, stopped in the shadows near a large group of old arbutus trees and looked down on Fort Victoria and the small sprawling community around it.

I'm not impressed. It should be larger.

He dropped the bulky pack he had been carrying onto the ground under a big evergreen tree. He surveyed the tree and then removed a coil of light sideline from the pack. He twisted his body and sprang up to grasp one of the lower branches and hauled himself up into the higher reaches of the tree. Choosing a suitable branch, he looped the light rope over it, letting both ends fall to the earth below. On the ground again, he looped one end of the rope through the tie at the top of the backpack and secured it carefully. He then removed his walking boots and his travel clothes.

Hy came in for a look, and Bedard laughed at him. Bedard was a big man, six feet in height and weighing about a hundred and eighty pounds. He was in superb condition in spite of having spent a good part of his early life disregarding his health—now, of course, he exercised whenever he could.

From the pack, he carefully removed a suit of formal clothes, a light raincoat, a top-hat case and a pair of high boots polished to a shimmering gloss. Standing under the tree out of the rain, he carefully put on the suit and the coat, and then his walking boots again. With a wry smile, he put the high boots and the hat case in a small kit bag. He decided not to take the bow or knives that he had with him. With his travel clothes now in the backpack along with other clothing and gear, he hoisted the pack up into the tree. Again coiling himself, he leaped up to grab the low branch again and, hanging on with one hand, he tied the rope to a smaller branch and stuffed the trailing end up out of sight. Dropping to the ground, he surveyed his handiwork. *It will do.*

He called the two dogs in and positioned them in the brush near the tree. He then moved downhill toward the rear of the fort. There was definitely a smile on his face.

I haven't seen James for over six years. This is going to be very interesting. I hope he has something for me. I've come a long way to meet with him.

The letter that had reached him in San Francisco just before Christmas was very specific:

Fort Victoria, rear entry, January 15th, eight o'clock precisely, knock four times, come unobserved and wear a cummerbund and polished boots.

At eight o'clock precisely, Bedard's ham fist pounded on the small rough-wood rear door to Fort Victoria. It was actually a door within a larger double doorway obviously used for wagon entry. The door was opened immediately. Standing before him was a soldier about four feet six inches tall with sergeant's stripes on his arm. Bedard almost burst out laughing.

"Well, don't just stand there gawking, man, come in and let's get this show on the road. I'm Sergeant Bill Woodsworth. Sergeant Bill to you, and I have to get you to the big show on time." He turned on his heel and said over his shoulder, "Follow me."

Bedard sensed, in the shadows on either side, several other soldiers with muskets at the ready.

He followed the little sergeant, walking quickly in the darkness along the inside walls of the fort. The light rain continued to fall, and his feet made crunching sounds as he walked, indicating a sandy gravel surface. Looking around, he could see lights in windows showing signs of occupancy. Obviously, residences of the Company's management and staff.

Sergeant Bill climbed the stairs to a porch, stomped some of the dirt from his boots, and entered what seemed to be a rear door to a large three-storey building. Inside, Sergeant Bill took off his coat, hung it on a wooden peg by the door and used a chair to stand on to turn up two lanterns that were hanging from rods attached to the ceiling.

On the floor again, he put his hands on his hips and circled around Bedard.

"Open the bag, please," he demanded.

There was a table, a chair and a full-length mirror on the far wall, and Bedard removed his boots and the hat case from his bag and inspected himself in the mirror. A little mud on the pants, he noted, but other than that and a few wrinkles not too bad. He reached down and rubbed at the mud spots.

"Never mind that," said the sergeant. "Sit down and change your boots, or we'll be late."

A door opened and a woman bustled in, carrying a pail of water and a wash bowl with towels and assorted cloths draped over her shoulder.

"Well now, is this him?" she asked.

"What do you think now, you addled cow!" Sergeant Bill scoffed. "He has some mud on his trousers and tails. Get to work, woman!"

Bedard removed his boots and went to the table where the woman had filled the wash bowl.

"I'm Sue," she said. "You only have time to wash your hands and face. I'll see what I can do with your pants." As he washed his face with the wonderful warm water and real soap, she fussed with his pants. In a few moments, he dried himself and sat on the chair to put on the clean boots.

Bedard got up and Sergeant Bill, standing on a chair with Sue beside him, said, "Come over here and let's see what else we can do. Turn around! Again! Let me adjust that tie." Sergeant Bill stepped down and circled Bedard a few times. Sue bothered with the pants and coat again.

Bedard was greatly amused by the antics of these two, obviously man and wife. He hadn't been fussed over for many a year. In fact, it made him a bit homesick.

Interesting, I haven't thought of my wife in many years.

Sue led the way through a doorway and down a hall to a stairway.

"Mr. Douglas is in the study upstairs," she said. "The door is open."

Bedard, holding his hat carefully in the prescribed manner, mounted the stairs and entered the study.

James and another man were sitting in high-back chairs near the middle of a medium-sized room with Eastern carpets on the floor and well-filled bookcases set against the walls between several windows. Other chairs were scattered around the room. James got up in a rush, and the two men met in the full embrace of old friends.

James stood back, holding Bedard at arm's length. "What a pleasure it is to see you again. I have been waiting for this for many months."

"And you haven't changed a bit," said Bedard. "It has been a few years."

"Six years, four months and three days," James replied, and the three men laughed.

James turned toward his companion who was standing by his chair.

"I am sorry. How impolite of me. Will, may I present Reginald Bedard, the old friend I mentioned who would be joining us. Bedard, this is Wilbert Abercrombie, also an old friend, who is now helping me to solve several of my current problems. Have the two of you met before in some other life?" The three men laughed again.

"No," said Will.

"Yes," said Bedard. Will was quite startled and came forward a step to better see Bedard.

He squinted his eyes and pursed his lips. "I think that you must be mistaken, sir."

"You were living in the Hotel Royal in San Francisco in the early summer of 1849, and we met in a rather rough but very popular nearby bar called Small Albert's. We were introduced by your son David who had worked with me on several projects in Hawaii the previous year. As I recall, I was very tanned and rather roughly dressed, and using the name Alberto and speaking with a Spanish accent."

Bedard smiled as Wilbert obviously remembered the occasion.

"Oh my God!" he said, falling back into his chair. "I remember that! That was horrible!"

Bedard turned to James. "Yes, it was rather horrible. A man beside me at the bar with whom David and I had been in a heated discussion with earlier had drank most of his bottle of whisky and then tried to stab David with a rather dangerous-looking knife. Fortunately, I was keeping an eye on him and was able to disarm him. Whereupon the bouncer unceremoniously escorted him to the door. We were all a bit upset, and Mr. Abercrombie here insisted that we all move on to the bar at his hotel. Of course, the ruffian was still outside Small Albert's and made a further nuisance of himself."

"Nuisance of himself? He tried to kill David again!" said Wilbert.

"David is a bit bigger than his father and quite experienced with the rough crowd," said Bedard with a smile.

"David picked him up and slammed him down on the roadway. I though he had killed him. It was terrible!" said Wilbert.

"As I recall, we had several drinks and a delightful meal at your hotel that night," said Bedard, looking for a place to put his hat.

"Let me take that from you," said James.

"Yes, well, I was probably feeling no pain as the evening wore on," said Wilbert.

"I had a great time," said Bedard.

"Well, it is wonderful that you have met before," said James, and the three men laughed again.

"Please, come over and sit down and have a glass of wine. You must have had an eventful day. Where did you camp and where are your dogs?" James asked.

"I arrived at midday about six miles northeast of here on the ocean with two friends in a small sailboat. They went farther north in the boat and I walked southwest, keeping to an old road. I should have stolen a horse. The road is not very good." The three men laughed. "I left two of my dogs to guard my walking gear that I hid in a tree about half a mile west of here."

Willard was still staring at Bedard. "I still don't recognize you, but I certainly remember the day. It was the first day that I had seen my son in ten years, and I was amazed at the change in him. When I had last seen him, he had just graduated from Oxford with a first in languages and a second in something they called history in those days, but what David swore included a clever set of business courses. He was very pleased with the schooling adventure and was looking forward to joining his uncle in Hawaii, of all places!

"He had written to me saying that he would be in San Francisco and, of course, I immediately jumped on the next boat from England so that I could meet him. You, Mr. Bedard, are now a very different person than the person I met with my son."

"This is the real me, Mr. Abercrombie. Well, not completely," Bedard said, touching his formal jacket. They laughed again.

"This wine is very good," Bedard said.

James beamed. "I won't tell you, but you can guess."

"Must be one of Amelia's masterpieces," said Bedard. And there, right on cue, Amelia entered the room in a stunning floor-length rose gown with a small train, wearing a simple pearl necklace and earrings. It was a magnificent entrance.

The men rose. Amelia came directly to Bedard. "No, you can't hug me—save that for later." She turned slightly to glance at her husband with a sly smile. "But you can kiss my hand." She offered it with a short laugh. Bedard bowed in the prescribed European court tradition and complied. The other two men clapped in mock appreciation and the group laughed.

Bedard brought over a chair so that Amelia could join the men and James poured her a glass of wine.

Amelia offered her glass in toast. "Here's to old friends."

"Incredibly," said James, "Will and Bedard met in a previous life, just after Bedard had returned from Hawaii."

"Ha!" said Amelia. "One of the Spanish periods, as I remember."

Wilbert said to Bedard, "And what are you involved with these days in this wild and woolly part of the world?"

Bedard looked at James and raised his eyebrows.

James looked very serious. "Firstly, Wilbert is a major part of our team here. He is on loan to me, so to speak, from the Company. I believe he might be useful to us relative to your assignment. And Amelia, of course, knows everything that I know."

Amelia said, "More than what you know!"

The group laughed.

Bedard raised an eyebrow. "Is it time to talk about my assignment, as you call it?"

"Yes!" said James.

Bedard leaned forward and studied his boots for a moment. "Well, let me outline the story. I met with the Queen."

"Victoria!" The other three gasped.

"Her Royal Highness said her advisors had convinced her that there was a disaster developing in this region. She said that pressures from the United States were building and that Great Britain had to move forward and consolidate the land here but that governments always seem to move forward slowly.

"In the meantime, there was potential for a gold rush somewhere in this region and whether or not this came to fruition, it would attract a migration of miners and others from California and elsewhere to the area. This influx might form a small population that would allow the United States to claim the lands.

"She had convinced her government to take some action, but the biggest threat is that some of the first men to arrive will be men who have been evicted from San Francisco. These people are criminals, and some of them are, the Queen assured me, very sophisticated and politically aware. Her advisors said that this is a very dangerous situation that has to be solved immediately."

James passed Bedard an envelope. Bedard saw that it was sealed. The Queen's seal! He looked at it for a moment. "This, I assume, is an updated version of list that the Queen gave to me at our meeting a year ago." He opened the envelope and read its contents. "Yes, that's precisely what it is. Very interesting. Very valuable to me."

Still looking at the sheet of paper, Bedard said, "Two of these men are now dead and I have tracked and found more of them, including the most dangerous, in my opinion, Tommy Hunter, also known as the Wolverine. You see, I have already been working on my assignment."

He then looked up at the group. "Unfortunately, the Wolverine has gathered a number of men to him which makes him not only very powerful but also difficult to access. They have been on the mainland for about one year and have built a small fortress while waiting for the miners to arrive.

"I first met the Wolverine in the gold fields of Australia and then again in the gold mining area west of San Francisco. He is not a miner himself, but he feeds off the miners. I think they know someone is in the area and have started a soft search for me."

"How would they know of you?" asked Wilbert.

"I think probably because of my dogs," Bedard replied. "The dogs are very valuable to me, but occasionally they become a bit of a liability. On both of the previous occasions that I mentioned, I was working independently as a consultant to one of their many enemies and was using my dogs as a protective shield. One of the men that I killed, whom I knew as Woolsome Taylor, was probably working for the Wolverine on special assignment. It was he who actually tracked me down on my very first day in this area, which I found quite incredible and emphasized his value to the Wolverine. The Wolverine found the two bodies, but I had disappeared by then.

"I am now living in a small Musqueam village called Tsusnahm about six miles east of their fort. There are a lot of dogs in the area, so I am not very concerned. When I am not gussied up"—at this the group smiled—"I blend right in to the native group. I have been there two days, and I have focused on learning their language."

Wilbert was listening very intensely. "How many men are on the list?"

Without looking at the list, Bedard said, "Twenty-eight men and two women."

Wilbert asked, "And what about the others?"

Bedard smiled. "I don't think that many have arrived in the area yet, but I am planning a trip to Fort Langley and Fort Hope in the near future, where I will search for them."

Wilbert smiled sheepishly. "And what do you call yourself now?"

"Bedard is fine," he said. "On the mainland, I am known as Copco."

At that moment, another door opened and a woman in a white formal gown floated in and proceeded across the room. Bedard and Amelia were the first to see her. Bedard rose immediately, followed by the other two men as Amelia spoke.

"Oh, how wonderful that you could join us, Donna."

Bedard gasped and Donna went to him.

"I heard that you might be here tonight," she said, and gave him a peck on the cheek and took his arm, turning to Amelia and the others. "I have not seen my husband in several years, so I am pleased to join you."

Bedard was still in shock.

Amelia sat there like a smiling peacock, obviously knowing the story, but James and Wilbert were looking quite surprised. James rushed off for another chair and the group settled down again.

James turned to Bedard, who still had Donna clinging to his arm.

"Bedard," he said, "Donna is the headmistress of the new private school located a few miles to the west of here in Esquimalt."

Bedard finally turned his head to look at his wife and was rewarded with another kiss and a beaming smile. "My turn to surprise you, my pet!" she said.

"Bedard?" she said for the benefit of the entire group and paused theatrically, putting her hand to her mouth aghast. "Is that what you are calling yourself today?"

Bedard nodded.

Donna recovered her poise. "Bedard, as you know, has great skill in turning himself into someone else and then disappearing. It took me some time to become resigned to this and to treasure his returns." She turned to him. "Isn't that right, dear?"

Bedard remembered other returns and departures that were quite different, but he was not one to confront the tiger—for that was how he characterized her—in her den.

"Yes, eh, dear." He returned her smile.

Then Bedard saw another incredibly beautiful apparition float into the room, this one in very light pink. She stopped a few feet from the door. Donna got up and moved toward the newcomer.

"Dorthea, my dear, please come and join us."

Dorthea! When the two women turned to walk toward the group, Bedard almost fainted.

They moved directly toward Bedard and stopped. Donna was beaming like a Cheshire cat just like Amelia was a few moments before. The incredibly beautiful woman turned to Donna.

"Well, Mother, are you going to introduce me to my father?"

Bedard immediately stepped forward and gathered her up in his arms, and tears ran down his cheeks. Donna gathered both of them in her arms, and the trio swayed together for a few moments. Dorthea was the first to back off a bit. She immediately put her finger to her father's lips.

"You don't have to say anything."

Bedard needed to sit down and did so, sweeping his daughter into his lap and holding her tight. Donna also sat and continued to hold on to her husband's arm.

James and Wilbert were, of course, just a bit astonished at this turn of affairs. James hustled off again for a tray of more wine and glasses.

Amelia was beaming as she looked at the threesome. "Well, that was fairly successful, I must say."

James was back quickly. "Amelia, you are something else again!"

"Thank you, Amelia," said Dorthea. "This is the best day of my life!"

Then she turned to kiss her father.

Ten
January 16, 1858
(Morning at Fort Victoria)

At sunrise, barefoot and wearing borrowed pants and vest, Bedard ventured outside of Fort Victoria for a morning run. He had been advised to go to the northeast or northwest but not to the south because of the large native village located there. He of course turned south.

After a good stretch just outside Fort Victoria's front gate followed by a short warm-up jog, he moved into high gear and followed a well-worn path along the waterfront to the southwest, past many canoes and small cargo vessels of various sorts at the water's edge. There were many native longhouses, some very ornate and some very ordinary. Only a few natives were about at that time of day and these were not inclined to wave or show other signs of friendliness.

Bedard soon ran past the village and turned south and then east following the path along the shoreline. Occasionally he passed a smaller building that he assumed was the home of someone evicted from the larger village or someone who chose to live alone.

He saw another runner coming toward him in the distance. Bedard had been out almost an hour by then, and he decided to turn around before meeting up with the other runner. Sometime later, in spite of his brisk pace, he heard behind him the steady footfalls of the stranger. He slowed down a bit and soon a very fit-looking man came up beside him.

They nodded and Bedard spoke to him in the Musqueam that he had been learning. "You are a very fast runner."

The runner was obviously surprised at this and replied in a slightly different dialect. "You come from across the water." Then he added, "But you are not one of us, how is that?"

Bedard was very tanned and had often been mistaken for a native in many of the areas that he had visited over the years.

The two had slowed down somewhat. "I enjoy languages, and yours is very beautiful and rich with unique structures. I am very fortunate to be able to absorb some of this, and I also have some very patient teachers."

Smiling, his new friend said, "Mot no doubt, and perhaps Roanyon," he said. "I now remember hearing of you two nights ago, from my wife's cousin Tanis who came over from Tsusnahm the day after the big celebration. You are Copco. My name is Cowen." He was now almost laughing. "My wife is Adrona's twin sister. I am very pleased to hear your progress with our language."

Bedard was initially not too pleased to hear that Cowen knew of him. He would have to quiz Adrona when he returned to find out more about her family. He should have known that this might happen. Most of the native villages were now small and no doubt many people had left the Fraser River communities and married into other villages over the years.

Cowen then switched to English, and it was Bedard's turn to be surprised. "I speak English, and a little bit of Spanish, too. I also like languages." He smiled. "I have been a trader; therefore, I have a good working knowledge of many of the languages and dialects of villages up and down our coast."

The two continued to converse and when they entered the village near the fort, Cowen said, "I would like you to meet my wife, Aroga."

Bedard agreed, and they both went through a slowdown and cooling-down procedure following their run, and Bedard followed Cowen into one of the longhouses.

Switching to Bedard's dialect, Cowen said, "Aroga, I have a guest for our early meal."

The woman who turned around was the spitting image of Adrona, which briefly startled Bedard.

Smiling broadly, Cowen said to Bedard while continuing in Musqueam, "Yes, it is quite incredible how alike the two twin sisters are. I have to be very careful when the two of them are together."

"There is no doubt that you are Copco," Aroga said as she turned around and saw Bedard. She came forward and gave him a big hug. He was a bit embarrassed, but she said, "You are an extraordinary person to have saved my dear sister and her baby from death's door. Our family will remember this forever!"

Bedard started to say something but she interrupted, switching to English.

"Please sit down and we will speak of all this later. Now we must feed the hungry beasts."

She turned around and said something in a louder voice that Bedard could not catch. About eight people detached themselves from the shadows around the large room and came up to what was obviously a serving bench near the central cooking fire where Aroga was serving food. Cowen was first in line and carried back two platters of food to where Bedard had been asked to sit.

"Aroga is, among other things, an excellent cook and specializes in the early meal for our extended family." Several other people arrived, and the group looked like it numbered about twenty. Cowen continued in English. "We have thirty in our family including six babies and twelve young people." He smiled. "I am sure you understand how this works."

Bedard nodded. "I enjoy the extended family concept that you have. I think that it has the potential to solve some of what we call family problems."

It was Cowen's turn to nod. "I do not have much experience with white man's families, but from what I have seen I think that I would agree with you. Ours is not perfect, but it has the potential, as you say, to solve and correct most family issues. But the larger group also brings its own problems."

Aroga joined them. Bedard noted that another woman was now serving the stragglers.

Aroga looked intensely at Bedard for some time. Bedard was familiar with this process and returned the stare, smiling a bit, knowing that this was his best image. He then laughed.

"You win," he said.

The three laughed.

"She always wins," Cowen said.

"I do not," Aroga responded, frowning.

"I love it when you frown," Cowen replied, and they both laughed. Bedard did not know what to say.

"So, what brings you to our village today?" Aroga asked.

Cowen explained how they had met, and then Bedard responded in a mixture of Musqueam and English, "I came to meet with James Douglas." The two were quite surprised. "We are old friends and I had not seen him in over six years." He had decided not to mention his wife and daughter.

"As you might know, I am in the process of understanding the purpose and future plans of a number of white people who are camped near the villages at the mouth of the Fraser River. I thought that James would have some information for me, and he did, so my trip over here was worthwhile. Now I have met you two, this is an even better trip than I had expected."

Aroga, apparently the spokesperson for the family, asked, "Is there any way that we can help you?"

Cowen was now frowning. "Cousin Tanis mentioned that you might be planning an exploratory trip northward. We think that it may be more than that and, if so, several men in our village will want to join you. I speak some of the southern Haida dialects."

The conversation had turned faster than Bedard had anticipated. He stopped for a moment and stared at Cowen.

"Cowen," Aroga said, "is not very good at that game."

The three of them laughed, and the tense mood became more relaxed.

Bedard switched to English. "I think that Cowen's trader experience would be very valuable to us on an exploratory trip. He would provide a very valuable language and contact service that we are sorely lacking. As far as further action to solve obvious problems that all the families have, I feel that everyone in Tsusnahm will probably see success as the only acceptable outcome, and to have success we need accurate information on which to formulate a plan of action. As far as I know, this idea has not been discussed with all the families in Tsusnahm. So, we will first be working toward an exploratory plan with a very small group so as to minimize our exposure. This is very good food, by the way. I must come back to this eating house again!"

Both Cowen and Aroga laughed heartily at this. They spoke more about the pending trips and about when Cowen could come over to join the group training sessions.

After giving Aroga a hug, Bedard left them and returned to Fort Victoria.

He met Dorthea near the entrance to the fort, and she rushed over and gave him a big hug. She then sniffed.

"You have been down in the village. I can smell the wood smoke."

"Yes," Bedard said. "I met some very interesting people, and I learned more about this area and its history. I now need to go up the hill and visit briefly with my dogs and retrieve my pack. Do you want to come with me?"

"Yes, I will go upstairs and put on some walking shoes and get a lunch basket." She vanished in a flash.

Donna came across the entrance courtyard.

"Our daughter is very excited to have finally met you. I want you to promise me that you will tell her about your life and your current situation in London and elsewhere, the *truthful* version, if you please. I have not told her much. She is now twenty-two years old, well-educated and a very good person. She is also a very good teacher, much to my surprise and pleasure."

Bedard said, "She has had very good care and guidance over the years, I am sure. She is very beautiful. I will try to share with her what I can to help her understand me, and perhaps us."

They were looking at each other when Dorthea arrived back in a rush. She stopped abruptly.

"Oops, am I interrupting something?"

Donna stepped back from Bedard and turned toward her.

"We have been apart for some time and, as I told you, we may need to start a new dialogue. We have both changed somewhat." She turned back to Bedard and smiled.

Bedard was not too certain what was going on, but he decided to keep calm and go along until he understood more. He felt that Donna was still very much a tiger. She had already made several negative impacts on his life, and he was concerned that she could somehow have a similar impact on his current life.

Dorthea then bounced over and took Bedard's hand. "Very well, I am looking forward to meeting the dogs. What are their names?"

Bedard and Dorthea waved goodbye to Donna, made their way through the assortment of houses and buildings near the fort's front entrance and started across the meadow.

"The two dogs that are with me here are Liz and Hy who are very experienced and well-trained collies. I have left two other dogs in Tsusnahm, the native village where I am now living on the Fraser River. Their names are Haus and JoJo. They are very large mastiffs, fierce and aggressive, but they are also well trained." Bedard smiled. "These dogs are my family and keep me alive and well. They protect me from my enemies and have been doing so for about nine years. It is unusual for me to travel anywhere without at least one if not all four dogs with me."

"Mother told me that you travel throughout the world and that your home is London. Why are you here?"

"I have been asked by my government to deal with thirty criminals who are thought to be amongst the first of more than twenty thousand gold miners forecast to arrive here this year. Many on my list are also astute leaders and politically shrewd. With many Americans miners in the Fraser Valley, coming mostly from the gold fields of California, perhaps the U.S. would try to claim this area. My government wants to stop that."

They discussed this as they were approaching the tree containing the hidden pack, but the dogs were nowhere to be seen, and Dorthea was surprised.

"Don't they come rushing out to greet you?" she said.

"Not until I call them," he said, and gave a very low whistle. Liz emerged from a brush nearby and came forward very cautiously. "Please sit on this old tree trunk, and Liz will be able to meet you."

"She is very beautiful" said Dorthea. Liz brushed by Bedard's legs in greeting and then approached Dorthea, sitting down about three feet away, just out of reach. "The natives have a staring game. Does Liz do that?"

Liz looked back at Bedard and with his wave of encouragement moved forward to smell Dorthea's feet. Dorthea moved one hand toward Liz to scratch behind her ear, and then they were friends. After a few minutes Bedard whistled and Liz tore off. Moments later another collie arrived. Dorthea noted that he had very similar colouring but was just slightly larger. Dorthea sat fascinated and amazed as Hy went through the same drill. She apparently had two new friends.

Bedard sat down beside Dorthea and scratched Hy's ears too.

"They are simply incredible," said Dorthea.

Hy was waved off to his station. Bedard retrieved his pack from the tree then sat beside his daughter again.

"Well, should I just talk, or do you want to ask me questions?"

Dorthea turned toward her father and looked very serious. "Why don't you start talking, and I may interrupt with questions as I think of them." She smiled.

She is indeed a very beautiful woman, he thought.

So Bedard started his tale.

"I was born about sixty years ago in Spain, but unfortunately the records were lost. I am an only son. My mother and father were wealthy aristocrats, complete with a huge castle, extensive grounds, a town and a very large agricultural land holding in northeast Spain."

"I'm Spanish then," said Dorthea.

"Well, yes. But your mother and her very wealthy family are English, so you are English-Spanish, or, if you prefer, Spanish-English." Both Bedard and Dorthea smiled.

After a moment he continued.

"Both my father and my mother died when I was twelve, almost thirteen years old. The wars in Spain against Napoleon's France were continuous throughout my early life, and my family was very active in these wars. After my parents' death, I was sent to England to live with my mother's brother."

"My goodness, that was terrible."

"Well, yes. But my life in the castle was very lonely and restricted. My education was directed by my mother and supported by a long series of nannies and tutors. The tutors were usually specialists: languages, history, music and the like. They did not stay with us very long because my mother was not easy to get along with. She and I often disagreed and even argued. I had no friends my age.

"When I was young, I travelled with my father, but only in a very adult-oriented way with lots of servants. Not much fun for a small boy, or at least that is what I remember. When I was sent to England, a new world opened up for me. For a short time, I was put into a very sophisticated private school where I met many boys my age from all over the world.

"One of the first things that the teachers and I discovered was that I had more education than anyone else my age. That gave the school administrators a serious problem because they had not been forced to deal with this type of educational situation. I also had an almost perfect memory and could recall everything that I had read or heard. Word for word. And I could read very fast.

"After extensive testing, and in consultation with my new guardian and his wife, Oxford University accepted me as a student. As you can imagine, a thirteen-year-old at Oxford was a bit of a sensation. Fortunately, this was September and the start of a new semester, and after the initial excitement and confusion I was enrolled in several courses.

"The third thing that I discovered about myself was that I had a natural aptitude for languages. Not only that, but I was able to learn them very rapidly and to mimic the accents so well that some could not detect that I was speaking in an adopted language. When I entered Oxford I spoke Spanish, of course, but in about six dialects. When I spoke Spanish with someone I would naturally adopt his or her accent. When I adopted a different accent, just for fun—after all, I was only thirteen years old—they would be amazed.

"English was a challenge in that I spoke it very well, but I discovered to my complete amazement and pleasure that there were an unbelievable number of accents and dialects. I found Cockney and the rhyming phrases to be exceptionally fascinating. I would hear someone speaking and I would ask where they were from. Over the years, I have mastered many of the English accents from all over Great Britain and, indeed, from all over the world. At that time, I had a good base in most of the European languages and some international languages learned from the many nannies that I had over the years. This natural aptitude was discovered, not surprisingly, by my Oxford language professors early in my first week there. They tested me, of course, and I found that this was great fun. Then they picked a language for me to learn: Greek. It was a language that I had not been introduced to and it had a structure that I had not encountered. They also had six professors who spoke Greek as a first or second language and these people had several dialects. So, I learnt Greek in about five weeks."

"Five weeks!" said Dorthea.

When Bedard had started to speak about languages, Dorthea looked amazed and put her hand to her mouth.

"Do you speak any languages other than English?" he asked Dorthea.

Dorthea babbled out a few sentences in six different languages, and it was Bedard's turn to be amazed.

Dorthea opened the lunch of sandwiches, juice and sweets that she had brought, and they started eating.

"I am now beginning to understand a number of things that happened to me," she said. "First of all, I was what they called an advanced student. Although I went to grammar school and so on, I skipped three levels because I learned faster than my classmates, and I had my mother coaching me all the time. I applied to several universities for entrance at a relatively young age: fourteen. This was very difficult to do for a woman, especially for a young girl. Few of them would even consider me, and none would allow me full membership. Women who gained entrance could attend lectures, take examinations, and do very well in those examinations, but they were, however, unable to receive the degree to which, had they been men, their examinations would have entitled them. I had visited many of these universities, and I had fancied going to Cambridge. It is beautiful there, as you undoubtedly remember."

Bedard nodded.

"But Mother fancied Oxford," she said. "And that is where I went."

Bedard shook his head and stared at the ground.

"Initially," said Dorthea, "I was not happy, and I don't think that the university was particularly happy either. Few of the professors liked young students, let alone young *female* students. At that time, there were only two other women at Oxford, and they were much older than me. I think that Mother endowed a chair in languages to get me in."

Both Bedard and Dorthea smiled while Bedard continued to shake his head.

"I also started in September, but the fuss continued for several months as I crammed to catch up in several courses. I wanted to focus on languages because I already spoke a number of them fluently and had been introduced to many more on what mother called our summer adventure tours. Mother had done something that I did not understand at that time. The last name that I had used all my life was Wotheringspoon, her maiden name. I knew that your surname was Bedard, but she said that you and she were separated and that my surname would be Wotheringspoon. But when she registered me at Oxford, all of a sudden, I was a Bedard.

"We had all started classes on a Wednesday, and I had a hectic weekend setting up some cramming schedules. On Monday morning, about twenty minutes before my first class, which happened to be a course in the Greek language, one of the students whom I had met briefly the previous week and who was five years older than me came up to me and said, 'My father thinks that he went to Oxford with your father. He would like to meet you. Would you follow me now, please?'

"So, I followed him, and I met Sir Ralph Hamilton."

Bedard was beaming from ear to ear.

"I remember him," Bedard said. "He was also a young student a few years older than me, at the time perhaps your age, and one of my few close friends at Oxford."

"Anyway," Dorthea continued, "his son Abel, who was also a language student and whom I got to know quite well later on, led me to the office of Dr. Everest, the Dean of Languages, a man I had met the previous week. In the office, there was the Dean who was, as I recall, grinning like a Cheshire cat, and six very old men, two in wheelchairs!"

Bedard started to laugh.

"Well," Dorthea said, "I did not know what to make of this! Very slowly they were introduced to me, and they all said that they had known you as an amazing scholar and linguist and were very pleased that I had chosen Oxford. That made me feel very good. They all told me stories about you, and I missed my first class completely! One of them asked me if I spoke Greek, and when I flippantly said not yet, they all laughed.

"Of course," Dorthea said, "then I understood where my aptitude for languages came from. Now I understand the Greek language reference. They did not mention the five-week learning period. Incredible!"

Bedard was very impressed with Dorthea's story. He gazed at her with something akin to wonder for a moment then continued with his own tale.

Eleven
January 16, 1858
(Afternoon at Fort Victoria)

"The professors were all very good teachers," he said. "And of course, I appreciated what they were trying to do. The subsequent Greek language testing was a pleasure not only to me, but to all of the professors who participated. When that session, which took most of one afternoon, ended, the language department head, a very old, wizened gentleman named Sir Thomas—who is long dead now, of course—told me that my skills were incredible and that if at any time I wished to study a specific language at Oxford, he was prepared to move Heaven and Earth to facilitate that. I recall that his words were received by a round of applause.

"I am not sure how many languages I now know, about forty I think," Bedard said. "But it still remains a lot of fun to learn another."

Dorthea then spoke in very passable Musqueam, and Bedard laughed and replied using both the island and mainland dialects. It was Dorthea's turn to laugh, and she replied using the mainland dialect. After this they were both quiet, and Bedard turned and hugged his daughter. They were both crying and did not know why. Liz appeared briefly, and Bedard called in both of his dogs for ear scratches.

While still holding Dorthea, Bedard continued. "Oxford was incredibly interesting for me as I can now imagine that it also was for you. Over the next two years, I dabbled in ancient Greek, Latin and philosophy, of course, along with ancient history, advanced mathematics and physics, and several languages that I liked.

"Later in the second year, I discovered that a whole world existed outside of the classical education that universities like Oxford focused on.

"I had been back in Spain to visit my aunt and others in my family. As I recall, the visit was not much fun for me, but as I passed through Paris on the way back to London I overheard three people speaking about developing a school of business and commerce in France outside of the formal educational system. I spoke with them for some time and missed my ferry back to Dover that night.

"When I returned to Oxford the next day, I talked to my advisors, and they introduced me to a part-time professor who was a well-known businessman in London. He then wrote letters of introduction to a number of business leaders of the time who were all based in London.

"Looking back, I was very fortunate as a fifteen-year-old to get audiences with some of these men. Many of them were well educated—Oxford, Cambridge, etcetera—and had heard of me as a very young scholar and were curious as to why my educational mentors would be asking them to meet with me. Before each meeting, I was usually able to spend time researching the scope of their commercial operations. As a result, I was able to gain and hold their attention early in the session and learn a great deal more about them and their businesses than perhaps I should have.

"I remember the pleasure of finally meeting Sir Bentley who was, at that time, rumored to be one of the wealthiest men in the world. Unbeknownst to me, he had already heard a great deal about me through some of his club and business friends that I had already met. And he had done a bit of research on me! We met in his office on Oxford Square, which had rather large windows overlooking London and the Thames. He sat in his chair with a huge desk between us and asked me why I was there. This was a normal response and I had a fairly good answer. I recall it was about his wharfage operation on the Thames.

"This was a very small part of his worldwide operation, but I had discovered that it was definitely very profitable, and as such he would probably have more than the usual general operational knowledge. I asked him if that was correct. He did not answer the question but sat there looking intensely at me. After a few minutes, I became quite uncomfortable and started to rise with the intent to try to escape.

"He then came out of his trance and smiled and started to ask me a lot of questions about his wharfage business. He then quizzed me about what I called at that time the other end: What ship lines was he using? Where did they come from? Did he own any of these ships? What goods were being transported, the people involved, and so on. I did not have the answers to some of these questions and said so. Then he stopped and looked intensely at me again.

"I then apologized, saying that I had spent most of the previous day reading about his businesses down at the *Times* office, a favourite haunt of mine, and smiled. 'A day!' he said, and I nodded. He shook his head, reached down and opened a drawer, took out a file and passed it over to me. He said, 'Take a look at that.' I opened the file and found a report on the wharfage operation addressed to him dated the previous day—obviously highly confidential. I immediately looked up at him, and he said, 'Read it.'

"So, I did. It was about ten pages long, handwritten in beautiful small and tight but very elegant English script. I read quickly, and it was very interesting. After a minute or so I placed the file on the desk, looked up at him and decided to keep my face blank waiting for him to set the tone of the next interchange. He reached into his top desk drawer and withdrew a pair of half glasses and another file. He put on the glasses and looked over them at me, and we both smiled.

"He then opened the file and said, 'Reginald Edward Bedard the Third, born in Antipy, Spain, on September 22, 1798.' He stopped briefly and looked up at me over his glasses, and I gave a small shrug because I did not know when I was born.

"He went on, 'Not confirmed because of an unfortunate church fire.' He looked up again, and I gave a brief nod. He continued reading from the file. 'Educated at home, few friends, some travel with his father. Both parents died three years ago.' He stopped and grimaced at me, saying, 'Mine died when I was young too.'

"'Came to England where he is staying with his mother's brother, Mr. Homer Castelancaisa.' He then looked up at me. 'Do you know anything about this man?' I squinted at him and decided to be noncommittal and shrugged. He said, 'You should.'

"'Went to St Vickers for two weeks,' he said, 'and then sent to Oxford. He had just turned thirteen years old at the time, the fifth youngest student in Oxford's seven hundred years. Master Edward, or Bedard, as he likes to be known, has almost perfect visual and audial memory and an incredible aptitude and ear for languages.' He then switched from English to Greek. 'Learned Greek from scratch in five weeks!' He then looked up at me smiling and said, 'You did not know that I spoke Greek, did you?' I was indeed surprised and shook my head. Then I decided to have some fun and said in Greek, 'On which of the Aegean Islands where you born, Sir?'

"Sir Bentley dropped the file on the desk, put back his head and laughed uproariously. His glasses slipped off and he grabbed them. Then a door to his right opened and a woman looked in anxiously. 'It is all right, Rose,' he said, withdrawing a handkerchief from his pocket and wiping his face, still chuckling.

"That was very good indeed, Bedard. I now have a better understanding of you. Your visits to some of my business friends brought me glowing reports of you. You are indeed very interesting. I was born and brought up on Mikonos of French parents who were also linguists, but not of your class, of course. So, I speak a smattering of European and other languages. This amuses me and occasionally helps me in some business dealings. My parents both died before I was twenty.' He looked down at the desk, nodding his head a bit, obviously reminiscing.

"He then looked up at me and said, 'Do you wish to hear the rest of my notes?'

"I thought briefly about that, thinking that Sir Bentley must have some Spanish information and that that would be very interesting to me at this time, so I nodded. 'The Antipy Castle,' he started, briefly looking up at me, 'is located in the Pyrenees surrounded by the thriving town of Antipy. Both the castle and the town are directly managed by Mr. Bedard's aunt on his father's side, Madame Catherine Bedard, who is about forty years old and is an astute business woman. The value of these remarkable assets is unknown and perhaps incalculable. The cash flow from these operations after expenses is thought to be several million British pounds per year.'

"Sir Bentley looked up at me and raised his eyebrows. I kept my face a mask. He continued, 'The family agricultural land holding is not known due to the complexity of land holdings in Spain, but it is thought to be in the order of a thousand square kilometres. The value of these land holdings is unknown, but this could be in the order of fifty million British pounds with a probable cash flow from agricultural and associated operations after expenses in excess of five million British Pounds per year. According to documents of registry, Mr. Bedard will be the sole owner of all of these assets: the Antipy Castle, the town of Antipy, and the agricultural land holding, when he reaches twenty-one years of age.'

"Sir Bentley then closed the file and pushed it across the desk toward me saying, 'I don't need this anymore.' My mind was going furiously. This was indeed an incredible package of information. I looked across at Sir Bentley with raised eyebrows.

"Sir Bentley said, with a small laugh, 'As far as I know, the information is reasonably accurate. My team had four days to assemble it. Now, what do you think of our wharfage operations?'

"With great difficulty, I brought my mind back to the question and said that I had concluded the previous day that the operation was very profitable, and I thought, since he sits with a view of the Thames, that he would be knowledgeable of it in spite of the fact that it is a very small part, much less than one percent, of all of his total worldwide operations. Then I said, 'Today I think that I should try to purchase it from you!'

"Sir Bentley again threw back his head and laughed uproariously. His glasses slipped off again, and Rose looked in anxiously. 'It is all right, Rose.' He again withdrew his handkerchief from his pocket and, still chuckling, wiped his face. 'I think that a better deal for both of us would be for you to come and work for me!' he said.

"So I did!" Bedard said to his daughter.

"You went to work for Sir Bentley? Amazing!"

"Well, at fifteen years old, it was an unusual working contract. Of course, my guardian had to sign some documents on my behalf. I had read the first draft and modified it to fit my new objectives. Sir Bentley read the modified contract and immediately signed it with a flourish! Homer did not read it, and probably got a payment under the table. I was not overly concerned about that. I worked for Sir Bentley three days a week and went to school three days a week. At Oxford, I continued taking a wide variety of courses and undertook some self-study so that I could graduate from Oxford after three years of study with both a bachelor's and a master's degree. At World Corp., Sir Bentley's holding company, I spent two weeks or so in each department in order to understand what each group did and how the whole organization worked as a single unit. At first it was a little tricky. A fifteen-year-old who was obviously very clever but was also a bit of a nuisance—perhaps even a potential threat. Sir Bentley supported me fully and said so.

"After a few weeks, I was welcomed into new departments because it was discovered that I was a significant problem-solving resource. After ten weeks, I had made the rounds of the holding company and was now interested in moving on and visiting some of the independently run businesses that were located in Great Britain. Sometimes I was asked to return to World Corp. for a special assignment, usually a financial study or analysis.

"The next year was quite incredible," Bedard continued, "I developed a staggering amount of business acumen and became very valuable to Sir Bentley. I met Walter Dinsbrook, who became my closest friend. Walter was about forty at that time and was a semi-retired, very sophisticated criminal who taught me many things that I still value enormously, including the art of disguise.

"Walter said that life was often a balance of truths, and frequently the good winneth out, so to speak. With his help I became a professional criminal at a very early age. I also became a saint, as your mother has probably mentioned."

Bedard smiled.

"Yes, she said that you are both a criminal and a saint, which is something she always had difficulty with. What does she mean?" Dorthea said. "I am still confused."

"Much to my surprise, and to my family's surprise, my uncle, Homer Castelancaisa, was also a professional criminal. Walter and I managed to deal with Homer very effectively by forging an association of interested parties. This included an improbable group of people including Homer's wife, an incredible Cockney family and Sir Bentley and his very clever assistant, Rose. We called this a conspiracy.

"When we had dealt with Homer, we also managed to take over his very profitable criminal interests. This project was very interesting and introduced me to the criminal world. I was then able to use these profits—and the profits were substantial—to finance other projects that I was involved with that were very different, very good projects, such as bringing good health and schooling to small areas of London that had been poverty-stricken for hundreds of years.

Dorthea said, "I still don't understand how the good things came about. How does a criminal become a saint?"

"That is a good question," Bedard said, smiling. "The answer is a bit complicated. Sir Bentley had been living in England for thirty years or so. He was very much impressed with the potential future of the country and felt that land ownership was the best long-term conservative investment that a person could make. He invested in both industrial and agricultural land, as well as in properties in London City and in the areas around London that he said would be part of the city someday.

"I became interested in London City property when I found that some of them were incredibly cheap because no one wanted to own properties that were full of poor people who had difficulty in paying their rent, or who were squatters and did not pay any rent. It was very difficult to get rid of the squatters at that time. One would clear out an apartment one day and it would be full of more squatters the next day. These properties also had many young abandoned children sleeping in the doorways and hallways. It was very sad!

"So I formed a company with Walter and Sir Bentley to purchase a whole block of tenement buildings near the centre of London. In the central area of this were several businesses and piles and piles of junk. I then spent most of a month with a small team trying to find out exactly what we had purchased. It was impossible to determine the exact population, but we guessed about ten thousand people.

"The first thing we did was to start carting away the junk from the central area. We initially had difficulty stopping the existing businesses there from simply moving in on these cleared areas. The plan was to rent these areas for profit to other small businesses. We also wanted to create a small park and plant some trees and grow some vegetables and plants. Most people thought that this was crazy.

"We also had other projects. At one corner of this huge area we started cleaning the hallways and the rooms—filling holes in the walls and painting everything. Now most people knew that we were crazy.

"Mrs. Arentha Castelancaisa, Homer's wife, was one of the project's closest advisers. She was also a well-known London aristocrat and benefactress. She and I visited a facility that I think was called Northampton Institute one day. It was located about two blocks from our property. We told them what we were doing and said that we wanted to start a private school and we needed a teacher and some help with the curriculum. They were initially a bit stunned but introduced us to their weird-looking english department head, Dr. Palmer, who became very supportive.

"He introduced us to a woman who was looking for work that would make a difference. She thought that our school project would be perfect for her. She wanted to work for nothing, but I wouldn't have that, so the first meeting with your mother did not start altogether well!"

"My mother! But she said that she was eighteen when she started teaching school," said Dorthea.

"We were both eighteen," said Bedard, "and we both had families who were very wealthy. The school project started in a small apartment in one of the buildings that we were fixing up. It was a bit challenging for Donna in that she had four students, girls, on the first day and had to ask for two tubs of water and soap to wash them. She also had to ask for clothing to replace the rags that they were wearing. We eventually adopted a uniform and provided breakfast and lunch to all the students every day, and a morning wash if necessary.

"Donna was then, and is now, not only a very clever teacher but also a very intelligent and resourceful person, but of course you know that."

Dorthea smiled.

"Over the next ten years she helped us develop our medical services and many other projects, including making the lives of the many prostitutes who lived in our buildings a bit better. She also improved the lives of the hundreds of children who were sleeping in our doorways every night. We now own eight blocks of tenement buildings, and we are definitely not considered crazy anymore. All of these projects make money. But not all the problems of our area have been solved, London City has a long way to go yet. I think that we should return back to the fort for supper."

Dorthea looked startled and glanced up at the sun. "Yes. It must be about four o'clock already. Mother will be wondering what has become of me! That was a very interesting story. But you have also travelled extensively, have you not?"

"Well, yes," he said, "I wanted to travel and to see for myself what Walter and Sir Bentley had seen before me. So, I travelled for two or three years and then returned to London for a year or two. I have not been in every corner of the Earth, but I have enjoyed much of it."

Twelve
January 17, 1858 (Fort Victoria Visit)

Bedard was out for a run at his usual very early time, going to the southwest again. This time he had both Liz and Hy with him. They started out fairly close together, Liz in front and Hy trailing. As he passed Cowen and Aroga's longhouse, Cowen unfolded himself from the doorstep and ran down to meet him. Aroga waved from the doorway. Two young children then poked their heads out the doorway and also waved. Bedard waved back.

Bedard slowed down to a fast walk and called the two dogs in to meet Cowen.

"Good morning," he said. "This is Liz, and he is Hy. They are part of my security team."

"Good morning. You have four dogs, don't you?"

"Yes, the other two are fairly large dogs, mastiffs. All four dogs have been part of my family for more than nine years."

"Chief Cobalt was very interested in the village children security plan that was first developed in Tsusnahm. He sent one of his older sons over there to see how it was set up. We now have a very simple version of the plan covering some of the trails leading east from our village. We are close to Fort Victoria, so we find that village security is a bit more complicated to set up. We all have said many times that some of our dogs are very intelligent, almost human. I told the chief yesterday afternoon that you were at the fort, and he would like very much to meet you. Perhaps we could set that up sometime today if you have time. We can talk more about this at the morning meal." He smiled. "Aroga insists."

"I told you I would be back. That is my favourite eating house here." They both laughed.

Bedard sent Liz out in front again with Hy following still fairly close. As soon as they turned east and entered the brushland, he positioned both the dogs farther out.

Cowen said, "Not likely that we will meet anyone this early in the day."

They followed the trail alongside the ocean for about an hour at a fairly good pace. The trail had turned south briefly and then east, and then north. When they reached a large sandy beach, they stopped for a quick rest and turned around.

"We must be fairly close to the landing that I used two days ago," said Bedard. "If I had less gear, I would certainly prefer to use this trail to get to Fort Victoria rather than the road I used."

They continued on and met only one person walking on the path close to the village. After a cool-down walk, they entered Cowen's longhouse where Aroga gave Bedard a hug. Bedard met Aroga's two young daughters. Like their mother, they were very pretty, but they were shy, just like Adrona's twins. They tended to stay in the background most of the time. The meal was a small fish that was very tasty.

"Would you like to visit Chief Cobalt now?" asked Cowen. "I know where he is this morning, and I am certain that he will have time to meet with you."

"Yes," said Bedard, "that would be fine. I have a meeting set up with James Douglas for later this morning, and I will be leaving the fort this afternoon to return home."

Bedard said goodbye to the children, received another hug from Aroga and followed Cowen out the door into the morning sunlight. They walked through the village toward the fort and entered an elaborately decorated longhouse. Bedard had his two dogs stay outside by the open doorway and wait for him.

Cowen turned to Bedard. "This is Chief Cobalt's office," he said, using the English word and smiling. "He and his large family actually live next door."

"The artwork is exceptional," said Bedard. "Has it been done by local artists?"

"I do not know. It was done before my time."

Inside the longhouse were a number of rooms and areas in which many different activities were in progress.

"Much of our weaving and small artwork is done here in the winter where it is always warm and dry." Cowen said. "Behind this longhouse is where the boat builders and the plank makers work all year round. We also store firewood there for the whole village to use. This area is still very active at this time of the year because, although it is unusually warm in the daytime, it is still cold at night."

A large man came out of one of the rooms and came toward them. "You must be Copco. I am pleased to meet you. I am Chief Cobalt. Good morning, Cowen."

They all shook hands and followed Chief Cobalt back into the room.

The room had a large table set close to the ground, and ten men and three women unfolded themselves from a sitting position. Cowen took Bedard around the room to meet all of them. Bedard and Cowen were then directed to sit down on two seat mats near the middle of one of the long sides opposite to where Chief Cobalt was sitting.

"This low table is a good idea," said Bedard. "I am going to try that when I get back to England."

The group smiled.

"Yes," said the chief, "this table, as you can probably see, is an English table that was purchased many years ago. We like this height, but many chiefs have used it at different heights. I like the table because it separates those with differing opinions very well, and we often have that here in our village."

The group liked that and smiled and nodded.

"We have heard that you are a student of languages. Although a few of us speak some English, I wish to ask your permission to use our native dialect. Perhaps Cowen can translate for you when you need assistance."

Bedard said, "Of course."

Chief Cobalt collected his thoughts for a moment. "As Cowen has probably told you, we adopted the village children security plan first developed in Tsusnahm. This works well although the waterfront area remains a problem, but we continue to work on that. We now understand that, under your guidance, Tsusnahm has started a security dog training program and that you use personal dogs for protection. Today we have briefly talked about this and have concluded that it is a great idea.

"All of us have family dogs that have been trained to protect our young children from the dangers of the ocean and the forest. These dogs are often considered and treated as family members. Some of us have hunting dogs that are surprisingly useful. Many of us have said that the intelligence of our dogs is remarkable. Could you please tell us something about yourself and your dogs and the new security dogs program?"

"I am a businessman based in England who likes to travel," said Bedard. "Unfortunately, I have some enemies, and I currently have four dogs that I use to protect myself. My family"—he paused, and the group smiled at that—"have been with me for more than nine years, and there were others before them. They are very well trained and serve me well in almost all the situations that I have found myself, but they work most effectively in forests like you have here.

"In Tsusnahm, they have only just started training some dogs that will eventually be able to provide some measure of detail security in the forest that surrounds the village, especially at night. You are no doubt aware that they have a lookout tree that is manned in the daytime, and this gives very good security over the river channels.

"A security dog program will be difficult to set up here because your village is so close to Fort Victoria and to the village that has already started to grow around the fort. This village will no doubt grow very rapidly this year, which will not be good for you in many ways. You will try to protect your village land from the encroachment of the expanding village and their use of your waterfront. This will lead to many confrontations that you will probably lose."

Chief Cobalt nodded. "A topic that comes before this council almost every week is our close association with Fort Victoria and James Douglas. Many of the issues that we talk about are minor irritants involving one villager or one white person or one dog. Some of the topics are much more serious, including, unfortunately, someone's death.

"One thing that James Douglas does very well is listen. He is our friend and has strongly supported our village over the years. But there is a change coming, and he sees this. He has told us what he sees every time we meet with him. He told us last month that there is a gold rush coming to the Fraser River much like the gold rush that came to California several years ago. He said that there will be many white men arriving, and that the village around the fort will become very large. Last week he showed us his plan for the new streets and new homes and businesses. We were astounded, and some of us were afraid. Now you come saying the same thing."

Bedard spoke further with the group and told them about his assignment from the Queen to find the killers on his list and his success to date, including identifying the white men in the corral to the west of the Musqueam villages. The chief and his council members had good relevant questions and Bedard tried to answer them.

When Bedard got up to leave, Chief Cobalt thanked him for coming and said that he hoped that he would drop by the village the next time he visited.

One of the women on council addressed Bedard. "Do you know a woman teacher here named Dorthea? I ask this question because she is also English, and she knows many languages like you do. She also looks a bit like you."

Bedard stopped and smiled. "Yes, she is my daughter."

Everyone was astounded, including Cowen.

As they were exiting the longhouse, Cowen turned to him.

"I was initially surprised, but now I am not. Dorthea is exactly the sort of daughter that you should have. Our two daughters go to the school, and it has improved considerably in the year since Dorthea became involved. She now comes twice a week to teach English and to meet with our teachers in an idea and teaching session. Everyone in the village is very pleased."

"Thank you for those words," said Bedard. "I knew that she was teaching, but I did not know that she was involved here in your village. That is wonderful!"

Bedard arrived back at the fort and went up to the room that James was using as an office and study. He entered just as a light lunch was being served to quite a large group of people, including his wife and Dorthea. He immediately went over to Dorthea.

"I have just returned from a meeting with Chief Cobalt and his council where I learned that you are involved with their school system."

"Yes," said Donna, "she has been involved for more than a year and it continues to be both interesting and challenging. I told you that she is a good teacher!"

Dorthea just smiled.

Amelia came over. "Just in time for a bite to eat before your meeting with James. Bring the two clever teachers with you and sit down over here with us."

The meal could have been created in Tsusnahm except for the silverware and the tea. Bedard was pleased to see some cooked shrimp and what tasted like the river fish that he really liked. He was introduced to many of the village leaders that had been meeting with James for most of the morning. After lunch the crowd thinned out, and a large conference table was moved to the centre of the room with ten chairs arranged around it.

James Douglas wasted no time with formalities and started talking before everyone had seated themselves.

"Today I wish to again focus on the gold rush that will be upon us soon. Copco," he said, pausing to looking at Bedard, "these people are the smartest men and women that we have in the communities around Fort Victoria. Some of them are not employees of the company but are working hard in our community or have farms and are working harder."

The group all smiled and some of them laughed.

"Yesterday we sent a large sample of the gold that we have been collecting for several years to the San Francisco Mint for evaluation. We have had two meetings this past week to talk about the coming gold rush and the large influx of miners and settlers that we expect this year and the following years. Some of us continue to be confused and remain unconvinced of its widespread impact on this part of the world. I think that you see this change in our lives from a slightly different perspective. We would benefit from hearing what you have to say."

"Well," said Bedard. "First of all, I am a businessman from London, England, and I have had the pleasure of travelling extensively throughout the world. I have visited several gold mining areas in the past, including Australia and California. The news of your gold sample's arrival will soon be known widely in San Francisco. I believe that some miners will arrive in small groups over the next three months. Larger groups of miners will probably start to arrive in April. Most will probably pass through Fort Victoria because the sailing ships cannot go up the Fraser River. Some of the miners will travel directly north overland to Fort Langley from the United States, and some will travel north overland much farther to the east.

"The number of miners that will come here this year is difficult to estimate. The gold mining in the San Francisco area is petering out, and only the large companies with large mining equipment are continuing to have success. I would guess more than five thousand miners will arrive before July and more than fifteen thousand over the rest of the year. The actual number of people arriving this year might be double those numbers."

The group gasped.

"The first large ship to arrive at Fort Victoria might have five hundred men on board. You must be ready for this."

Many just shook their heads in disbelief.

The discussion raged on for two more hours, with James trying to allow people to have a turn speaking without being interrupted, which was very difficult. Eventually, James, Wilber Abercrombie and Bedard left the table and met in another room to discuss other matters of concern to James and Bedard.

Bedard started by saying, "For the past four years, the Haida Nation has been active up and down this coast attacking many villages, killing adults and abducting young children for slaves. The Musqueam village of Tsusnahm lost thirty of its children and many adults to a marauding group of Haida four years ago. This could happen now to any of the native villages on the coast. Are you prepared for that?"

James and Wilber were shocked by Bedard's aggressive words and tone of voice.

Bedard continued looking directly at James. "For many years, including this year, there have been large numbers of Haida camping near Fort Victoria. If you continue to allow this Haida presence, the Musqueam Nation and other nations living on the Lower Fraser River and on this coast, including the native village beside you, will not be pleased. This would not be good, especially this year, with the anticipated huge numbers of miners coming."

There was a silence before Wilber spoke.

"James and I have been talking about the aggressiveness shown not only by the Haida Nation on this coast over the past four years but also the terror that the Tongass, the Yakamas, the Cowichan and other nations have spread over the past many hundreds of years. With the coming of the white man trading for furs, these terrible activities have lessened perhaps, but they have not stopped. As each year passes, new atrocities are reported."

"The Haida that come in the summer to trade and work in this area are from the village of Skidegate and are no longer warlike," said James. "It is the Haida from farther north and the Tongass that continue to be dangerous."

"With all due respect," said Bedard, "you cannot tell the difference between northern and southern Haida. If you ask them where they come from, they will lie because they profit greatly from the association with your community here. I believe this to be a high risk for you. If you ask them to return home, they will just move farther up the island and continue to be a dangerous presence. You have created what I believe to be an impossible situation. I hope that you do not have to pay for it.

"The Musqueam are planning to travel north to find the children who were taken from Tsusnahm four years ago. A small group will go up to find where the children are now. A second much larger group of warriors will follow in order to actually take back these children. I will be involved in a planning and leadership role. What we need is the use of a large ship, like the *Beaver*, to transport and hide us on both trips north."

"I will look into that," James said. "This sounds very dangerous."

Bedard shook his head. "I do not think that it will be as dangerous as it sounds. Most people, probably including the Haida, do not like confrontation. For this reason I feel that something can be negotiated. We are now just starting the planning stage."

James said, "I am concerned with the native camp at our fort. We will try to create a plan that will eliminate the Haida from this camp. Thank you for your concerns. We value them."

Wilber was somber and nodded in agreement.

James continued. "I had a message yesterday from Fort Langley. They believe that there are two or three white men living in a camp upstream on the north bank of the Fraser near the Harrison River. So far they have kept to themselves. They have been there about two weeks."

"Thank you. I will definitely investigate the camp. I also would like to thank you for introducing me today as Copco. I appreciate that."

The three men got up and shook hands.

The Fort Victoria trip had been successful, and the late afternoon trip from there back to the coast went very smoothly. Douglas had insisted on providing Bedard with carriage transportation east to the boat landing which Bedard greatly appreciated.

It had started to rain lightly again, and he had not been looking forward to slogging over the muddy trail on foot. As it was, the carriage driver, his assistant and Bedard had to help the two horses through two quagmires, and this had ruined his last set of travel clothes. The two dogs had easily followed the carriage by keeping to the light forest on either side of the road. The carriage turned around in a clearing about half a mile from the boat landing which worked well for everyone. The carriage driver had decided to return to Fort Victoria by another road to the south that was much longer than the road that they had just used, but was, he hoped, in better condition.

Bedard arrived at the coast in the late afternoon. It was now raining quite heavily, and it was cold with a light breeze off the water. After retrieving his hidden packs, he used his two ground tarps and some small trees to create a lean-to to get out of the rain. He then changed his sodden pants and wet jacket and built a fire to warm up and dry his clothing.

He then tried to plan the remainder of his day. He had brought some food from the fort for the late and early morning meals, and he would build a cooking fire near the lean-to. The cliff rubble would allow him to create a fancy fireplace, which he was looking forward to doing.

He also needed to build two beacon fires in case the boat arrived after dark. When he had arrived three days ago, he had decided that one of the beacons would be placed near the bottom of the path that wound its way up the one-hundred-foot cliff, and the second one would be built on the beach near the high-tide line. He now located a good place on the path for the cliff beacon fire and then, sighting out on the water to where the boat had travelled past an island, picked a location for the beach beacon fire and marked it with a stick. When he was satisfied with these locations, he went up the cliff path with two simple dragging harnesses and called in his two dogs. He proceeded to find some very dry wood for the two beacons and his fireplace.

Fortunately the rain stopped, but the wind picked up and it was really cold. Dry firewood was easy to find, and he created a huge ten-foot-tall tangle of wood at each beacon fire location, plus a huge supply of wood for the fireplace near his lean-to in case it remained cold all night. After all this work, he sent the dogs back up the cliff to their security positions while he warmed up again at the fire. With a great deal of pleasure, he created a cooking fireplace. It was a masterpiece, and he was very satisfied.

Tomara's boat showed up just after nightfall as he had predicted, and Bedard was able to fire up the two beacons soon after he heard the horn over the water. The beacon fires were enormous, and when the boat arrived at the beach Bedard got quite a ribbing from Roanyon and Tomara for trying to burn down all the trees in the area.

Roanyon had a surprise passenger, Mothana, who was introduced as an old friend. She was very pretty and had a great smile for Bedard. Bedard introduced his two dogs and started cooking the meal. Roanyon built a second lean-to with Tomara's help. Tomara said that he would sleep on his boat.

Mothana said that she had grown up in Tsusnahm and was very pleased to be going home. Given the way Roanyon and Mothana exchanged glances, Bedard assumed that Roanyon's trip had also been successful.

Thirteen
January 18, 1858

The next morning the four campers rose in the darkness, and Bedard cooked a morning meal on his fancy fireplace.

"Roanyon," said Mothana, "this is good food. Do you think that we can eat at his place in Tsusnahm all the time?"

"Adrona is an even better cook than he is," said Roanyon. "So that would be a great plan."

They all laughed, and Bedard said, "The fort kitchen was very kind to provide me with some food."

With a following wind, the trip over to the mainland was smooth. Tomara took advantage of having the two expert sailors with him again and piled on the sail. They arrived at the sailboat's landing place well before noon, a record time according to Tomara. A fog bank had followed them up the river and this made it quite gloomy.

Mothana had quite a bit of baggage. Bedard suggested that rather than making three or more baggage trips he would call in his two other dogs and rig them up with dragging gear.

The welcoming ceremony for the four dogs was a sight to behold, with all their jumping and bumping. The four adults enjoyed it almost as much as the dogs obviously did.

Bedard went west with Haus and JoJo and fitted them up with the harnesses that were hidden with his canoes. Roanyon had cut some small trees, and the three men rigged the platforms for the baggage.

Tomara was most impressed with the result. "This is very professional," he said.

The trip back to Tsusnahm was easy. One of the small boys popped out of the brush and raced down the path to the village so that Mother and Adrona were on hand to welcome everyone home again.

Mother gave Mothana a very long hug, and both were crying as they turned to walk toward the longhouse where Roanyon lived.

Bedard and Adrona touched hands, and Bedard said, "I met your sister Aroga and Cowen. She is almost as beautiful as you are."

That earned him a big hug. Adrona had not seen her sister for three months, so she asked him to tell her what she had said. He reported the two meetings, word for word and minute by minute, much to her amazement and entertainment.

After the midday meal, Bedard eventually met up with both Modan and Towaba, who reported that they had great success working with Haus and JoJo over the past three days. The dogs seemed to know what the two men were trying to do, and they had made a significant contribution.

"They are so intelligent and responsive," said Modan. "Absolutely amazing."

Bedard decided to take an afternoon run with his family so as to get them back into the personal security pattern again. The weather continued to be foggy and gloomy but still quite warm. Hy met him on the river trail at the east edge of the village. Bedard wanted to follow the trail to the east past his landing place and the spot where they had found Noua. He called the rest of the dogs in from their stations and dispatched them in their usual tight security net around him.

This again left the village a bit unprotected, but he had talked to Mot's two brothers about taking the dogs away and they continued to be aware of Bedard's priorities.

The family group moved onward. Bedard could only occasionally see Liz running ahead of him in the gloom. Hy was acting in the rear this morning, and he soon gave a very soft bark and came up closer, wagging his tail before moving off into the heavy brush to the north of the river trail. Bedard slowed down and soon heard a figure running on the trail behind him. A person soon materialized from the mist, and Bedard recognized Roanyon.

"I hope that you do not mind if I join you again," Roanyon said.

Picking up the pace a bit to match Roanyon's, Bedard said, "Of course not. You have been doing this longer than I have."

"I really doubt that," Roanyon said, and they both laughed.

"I chose this route today because I have not travelled very far on this side of the Fraser, and I am curious to see where it leads."

"Not very interesting until Fort Langley can be seen on the far shore," said Roanyon. "Although there are some small villages scattered here and there on both sides of the river."

"We will try to skirt any villages that we see. I do not want to expose myself any more than I have already." They both laughed again.

Sometime later the mist lifted, and occasionally they could see across the water to the south shore. They had run for the better part of an hour and a half at a medium pace and had skirted only one small Kwantlen village consisting of two longhouses.

On the return trip, they stopped at the spot where Bedard had found Noua and searched the area with the hope of finding some evidence of why the baby was left in that specific spot. About one week had passed with only two periods of light rain. They found two pairs of interesting footprints. One looked to be made by a large white man's boots, and one set of small smooth imprints, suggesting a woman or older child, perhaps a local resident. There was also evidence that a canoe had beached there recently. Bedard wondered if the baby had been accidently, or even purposefully, left behind by someone. *Why was a local resident involved in this?*

They soon moved off to the west.

Roanyon was intrigued by Bedard's story of his initial arrival in the village as he had not been at the tree meeting when Bedard had come with Noua.

"We had been told briefly about the loss of the baby," Roanyon said, "and I participated in the organized search of a large area around the village on the first day. The next day several groups made searches of other areas. I went with a group of six men and women who travelled north to the Squamish communities along the arm of the ocean there. We returned that night after two days of travel, and we were very pleased to find that the baby had been found."

At his landing area, Bedard uncovered one of his stashed canoes and the packs that he had left there. He removed a large pack of clothing and rummaged through two others for small weapons and other tools that he had decided to add to his arsenal.

Roanyon was not surprised to see the cache again and noted that Bedard had selected his set of Hawaiian throwing knives.

"I like those knives too," he said.

"I think that the group at the corral must be dealt with sooner rather than later, and I feel that some of the encounters might be at close range," Bedard said. "These knives are very effective, as you know."

Roanyon nodded. "I still like the bow, and I make my arrow tips similar to the way you showed some of us many years ago."

"I, too, still have them made in the same way, but there have been some improvements in the materials," Bedard said. He rummaged in the canoe and brought out an arrow and gave it to Roanyon.

Roanyon first measured its length against his arm. "You still have an incredible reach. This arrow must be at least four inches longer than mine and much straighter."

He looked along the shaft of the arrow and shook his head in admiration.

He then examined the metal tip and found that it was almost the same diameter as the shaft of the arrow.

"I need my spectacles," he said smiling, "what is the metal?"

"Steel. It starts off as iron with other metals added. A rod of this metal mix is heated, cut and milled with the tip pointed and smoothed as usual. Then they heat up the tips again to quite a high temperature and the properties of the metal mix change and the metal becomes extremely hard. The tips no longer break, bend or dent. I do not have many of them left, so I try to retrieve them after I have used them. A bit tricky sometimes."

Roanyon nodded.

"With my standard longbow," said Bedard, "I think that these new arrows travel about thirty percent farther."

Roanyon examined the feathered end and shook his head. "Fantastic," he said. "May I borrow this? There are two craftsmen in the village who will be very interested in seeing this arrow. At both Fort Langley and Fort Victoria there are forges, but I do not know anything about forges," Roanyon said. "The blacksmiths seem to concentrate on horses, small tools and household utensils."

Bedard nodded. "Might be worthwhile looking into."

"Have you heard about Chief Big Bon on the island?" asked Roanyon.

Bedard smiled and told him about the arrow and the three fires on his first morning in the area.

"You must meet him. He and his family are very nice people. And Chief Big Bon has a longer reach than you do. He is the best archer in this area. He has won almost all of the archery competitions here for twenty years."

"Ah, but I have two special bows that he will enjoy. Then we will see who can really shoot an arrow at great distance with accuracy!"

It was now late afternoon, and despite the heavy packs of Bedard's gear that they now carried, they moved off at a fast pace to finish the afternoon run. At the entrance to the village, Bedard stopped, dispersed his family to their perimeter roaming security assignments and followed Roanyon into the village.

Entering his new home from the front of the longhouse, Bedard found Adrona with Noua talking to Mother at the central cooking area. Adrona was stirring a pot of something good that he could smell as he came closer. He went into his sleeping area to drop off the two big packs with the weapons, tools and clothes and returned to sit in the cooking area next to Mother.

Mother said, "Have you met Chief Enthica yet?"

"No."

"He will definitely be joining the selection camp this week. He is about your age, and he is very fit like you are. He is also one of the cleverest men I have ever met. He is well known on the river and up and down the coast.

"When he was a young man he was elected chief of the small Musqueam village of Massuxkumiy, which you will recall is on the south bank at the mouth of our river. He married the daughter of a Nooksack Nation chief and they had a son. Every year they paddled south to visit her family during the summer high-water period.

"Then one summer, as they were returning, he tried to beat out a storm. Instead of keeping to a safe shoreline route he decided to cut across the water from headland to headland. The storm arrived sooner than he anticipated and was ferocious. His canoe overturned when he was still half a mile from the shore, and his wife and son drowned. Neither of them could swim and he could not save them. He barely survived himself. He made it ashore and managed to return to his home with the help of some men from a nearby village.

"Shortly after this, he disappeared from his village for five full years. When he reappeared again, he said that he had spent most of his time up on the large mountain that we can see to the southeast of us here."

Bedard nodded. This was the mountain that he thought was an old volcano.

"He said that he had a vision and was going to try to follow the directions that had been given to him. He began teaching swimming. He said that those who lived by the water and fished the water for food had to know how to swim in the water. At that time there were few of us, including himself, who really knew how to swim. There was an Englishman living in Khwaykhway who swam every day of the year in the ocean. Chief Enthica searched him out and swam with him for four months. The man—I can't remember his name now—was a very experienced swimmer and taught Chief Enthica a number of different swimming strokes. They also practiced water survival: how to right a tipped canoe, how to get in and out of the canoe when you are in the water and how to help others save themselves. The most important thing that this man taught Chief Enthica was how to teach other people how to swim.

"Chief Enthica has spent the last thirty-five years going from village to village teaching children and adults how to swim. I would think that every village for many miles from here has two or three villagers who teach swimming as part of the program that he started. Suan is our senior swimming instructor here, and she and others swim every day of the year. This program has the complete support of every chief that I have ever met, and the results are quite incredible. There are very few people in our villages now who cannot swim. Even those who have difficulty walking at a young age can swim. I have seen babies less than one year old swimming, much to the complete amazement and pleasure of their parents.

"Chief Enthica is also called upon in his travels to help villages with problems that they have been unable to solve. He is very clever and has developed an enormous reputation in this manner. He travels now with an assistant most of the time who helps with the swimming and water survival projects and paddles his canoe with him. He did have a woman assistant for a number of years, but that apparently did not work out for some unknown reason."

Roanyon then entered the room with Mot and two other villagers and came over to where Bedard and Mother were sitting. Bedard got up, and Roanyon introduced the two men as Ortho and Melleran. Roanyon switched to Musqueam.

"The four of us have been examining your arrow and comparing it to mine." He placed an arrow on the table.

Bedard picked up the arrow and examined it with interest. "It looks like one of my best arrows two years ago," he said smiling.

Then Ortho placed an arrow on the table. "This is my best arrow as of yesterday." He laughed, a bit embarrassed.

Bedard picked up this arrow and examined it. "The feathers are very good, perhaps even better than mine, but the tip is a bit larger than both Roanyon's and mine, so it will not travel as far in the air. Too much wind resistance." Wind resistance took a while to translate with both Mot and Roanyon participating. Melleran and Ortho were thoughtful and spoke to each other for a while with Mot translating for Bedard.

Mot then turned to Bedard and said that Melleran was the feather master and Ortho created the bows, but there was no one in the village who could create an acceptable straight arrow and build arrow tips, so the two of them were most interested in Bedard's arrow.

Roanyon said, "Chief Big Bon makes very good arrows, and he would be interested in yours."

The four of them looked at each other.

"Tomorrow?" Roanyon asked.

The others nodded.

Ortho said, "After lunch would be perfect."

Mot turned to Adrona who was listening to the conversation with some interest and said to her, "When is Suan doing her swim today?"

"About now, I would think," Adrona said.

Mot rushed out the front door and ran toward the water. Suan was sitting on a log waiting for her friend to come by in a canoe to accompany her on her daily swim in the freezing cold seawater.

Mot said to her, "We need a message to be given to Chief Big Bon. Is that possible?" She nodded.

"Tell him that Ortho, Melleran and Roanyon will be visiting him tomorrow afternoon, along with his new friend who he met about two weeks ago. Just add the words 'three fires, one arrow.' He will understand," said Mot.

Suan repeated the message and nodded. Mot returned to the longhouse just as the three were leaving. "Message sent," he said, and they smiled.

"We have arranged for Roanyon to go over with Bedard and for us to go over directly from the village," said Ortho. "Are you going to join us?"

"Yes," said Mot, "if I may."

"Of course," said Ortho. "We are thinking to meet here after the midday meal tomorrow to make final plans."

With that, Mot entered the longhouse with Bedard and Roanyon. Mothana had joined Adrona to prepare the late meal with Mother still sitting smiling with her arms crossed. Mot was introduced to Mothana and was invited to join them.

The conversation turned to Bedard's obvious skill in languages. Mothana had noted, of course, that Bedard's knowledge of Musqueam was fairly good, but she did not realize that he had only been speaking it for six days.

Mot and Roanyon had the advantage over the others by having had the opportunity to actually observe Bedard's incredible language abilities.

Mothana asked, "Just how many languages do you now know?"

"About ten fluently and about thirty proficiently. But languages are complex and there are many dialects." Then he smiled. "My current favourite is Musqueam, and I thank you all for your contributions."

"But you learn a new language so fast," said Mothana. "How is that?"

"Mot and others have been translating Musqueam into English for me, and so I have built up a fairly large memory of words, but I am still learning how the words and the sentences go together. Along with a large memory of many language vocabularies, I also have a good idea of many language structures and how thoughts and communications can be expressed. I have a unique mind. I remember everything that I hear. Languages are complex, and I enjoy learning them."

Both Adrona and Mothana shook their heads. "Amazing," they said.

The group managed to finish eating the meal, which was another delicious fish stew that Adrona enjoyed making. Bedard was smiling and the group burst into laughter, remembering a similar occasion a week ago. Roanyon explained the occasion to Mothana.

Bedard said, "Well, the shrimp and fish dishes were so fantastic."

And at that all six of them burst into laughter. Adrona had tears in her eyes again.

Mot, Roanyon, Mothana and Mother left.

Noua had been awakened by the laughter, and Adrona moved over to feed him. Bedard watched closely but no show evolved, so he went into his room and examined the weapons and tools that he had selected.

The six throwing knives had a special shoulder harness with holsters. The knives needed to be sharpened. He had brought a stone for that. He had also brought a small pair of binoculars that he felt would be useful when he wanted to view the corral from a distance. He had left his bow and arrows at the cache because they were ungainly and difficult to conceal. He would need them tomorrow. He had also brought a large assortment of other knives and short bars and clubs. He wanted to look them over and choose a selection that he thought would be useful in the battle that he envisioned to rid the area of this group of dangerous thugs.

At the end of the day, as he snuggled closely to Adrona in bed, he was very pleased to be back in Tsusnahm.

Fourteen
January 19, 1858 (Morning)

Bedard and Adrona had an exciting early morning time, with Noua participating by giggling and wriggling, much to their amusement. Bedard left them both to sleep for another hour and went out for his early morning run. Roanyon did not join him this time, and Bedard decided to take the river path again. He called in the dogs, sent Liz out ahead and had Hy follow him with both JoJo and Haus not far inland in the thick forest.

Running strongly and smoothly, he ate up the miles rapidly. In just over two hours, he passed around two small villages and came upon a large Kwantlen village at the waterside, with Fort Langley clearly visible in the morning mist on the opposite bank. He did not enter the village but went down to the water's edge for a quick rest.

Using his telescope, he inspected the fort and a small Kwantlen village of lean-tos and fires at the waterside on the west side of the fort. It had only six canoes pulled up on its beach, and he saw that a longhouse was under construction. He thought that it must take a long time to build these homes in the small villages because of a manpower shortage. It took a lot of people to hunt, fish, gather food and look after the children, leaving not much time to build the homes.

On the east side of the fort near the water there was an area that Bedard thought could hold up to about ten small camps of miners. Four of the campsites were currently occupied by ten or twelve men in all. These were miners on the way to Fort Hope. They had no doubt come overland from the south and needed to rest for a few days, stock up on provisions and perhaps rent or buy a canoe. Bedard needed to visit this area soon although he did not think that anyone on his list would travel this overland route. Perhaps he could come this way and borrow or rent a canoe in the village in order to inspect the men at the camps. He would discuss this with Roanyon as he would certainly need help. He could not do this by himself.

The run back was uneventful. When he arrived in Tsusnahm he sent his dogs to their security runs. He then went in search for Mot, who was in the dog sleeping area with Modan and Towaba, working on some hunting harnesses and leads.

"Mot," he said, "I need some more language training. Do you have some time now?"

"With pleasure, but I do not know how much more that I can help you. You already speak better than I do." The others thought that this was pretty funny.

The two of them wandered off up the northerly path. Bedard spoke and had Mot correct his speech. This was a manner of language training that Bedard had used all his life and it worked very well for him. They returned to the village just in time to eat a midday meal prepared by Adrona and Noua, assisted by Aurora and Basso. Ortho, Melleran, Roanyon and Mothana had also been invited. The children continued to squeal and giggle throughout the meal, much to the amusement of the group.

After the meal, the five men got up to move on to their afternoon's adventure. They thanked Adrona for the food and said goodbye to everyone.

"Adrona," said Bedard, "it is probable that Chief Big Bon will insist that we stay for the late meal tonight."

They looked at each other carefully, touched hands and parted.

Bedard picked up a small pack and the binoculars from his room and joined the others out near the big tree in front of the chief's building. All the other men were carrying bows and quivers.

"I am hoping to have some fun with our bows, and then I would like to go to the west end of the island and look at the corral. We must do something about those people," said Bedard.

The others nodded.

Roanyon said, "I will go and get my telescope."

"That's a good idea," said Bedard. "I also have a telescope as well as these binoculars. The more of us looking at the corral, the more we can see and understand, and this will help in the planning of that adventure."

Bedard, Roanyon and one of the dogs would take Bedard's canoe and travel out of sight of the tree lookout near the corral, to the east end of the island.

Mot, Ortho and Melleran would travel directly over to the island. Skwisahthun, or Skwis, the village on the island, was actually near the east end. Chief Big Bon, having some advance warning of the pending visitors, would send someone to meet Bedard and Roanyon and bring them to Skwis. Visitors between Tsusnahm and the island were commonplace, so this trip would not raise the suspicions of the men at the corral who were monitoring the waterways.

Roanyon arrived with his telescope, and he and Bedard started off down the river trail again. Bedard had decided to take only Liz with them, leaving the others in their normal security screen around the village. Mot's two brothers had dealt with some minor native traffic on the upper trail over the past two days, and Bedard was impressed with the way they interfaced with the dogs. The dogs, on their part, seemed to enjoy working with these two men. This was a very unusual situation for Bedard, and he was very pleased with how many of his initial issues and concerns about living in this village had disappeared, allowing him to concentrate his thoughts on his main task of identifying and dispensing with the people on his list.

The light run down to the landing was uneventful. Bedard had Liz ranging out in front for the run and had her circle forward and back behind them when they reached the landing.

Bedard and Roanyon moved the canoe out of hiding and transferred it to the riverbank. He also found his telescope and his package of bows and quivers. He moved a large package to the canoe.

"What is that?" asked Roanyon.

"It's a very old type of bow that you are familiar with from our Hawaiian adventures called a crossbow."

"Yes, I remember those. I also used one when I was with the Spanish Navy. It was very useful."

They prepared to push off, and Bedard whistled for Liz who materialized at the last moment and jumped onto the boat, tail wagging furiously. She loved adventures!

The trip over was short, and they were met by two men who introduced themselves as Dorono and Fenciao. They handled the canoe onto the shore and helped Bedard hide it from view.

Bedard sent Liz out to circle the area. Fenciao carried the large bow package and Bedard brought his other bow pack with him, plus the binoculars and his telescope. The group climbed the bank and moved in the direction of Skwis, the small village consisting of one building, just back from the north shore of the island. At Skwis they met with the other three members of their party, and Bedard finally met Chief Big Bon.

Bedard had not met many very tall people in his life, and he was impressed to see that Chief Big Bon was not only a giant of a man but that he was also in very good shape. They stopped in front of each other and sized the other up.

"I thought you would be taller," Bedard said.

The whole group laughed.

"I thought you would speak better Musqueam," said Chief Big Bon. "After all, it has been seven days."

This brought more laughter.

The two men moved forward to shake hands and then patted each other on the back.

Chief Big Bon stepped back. "I understand that you have a great ability for learning our language, and that is good. Language is where the land and the people and the sky become one."

"You are very wise," said Bedard. "You already have a good start in becoming a great legend of your nation, and I am very pleased to finally meet you. Thank you for your arrow and the three fires. That very clever action saved my life."

Chief Big Bon smiled. "Yes," he said in English.

Bedard was surprised. Chief Big Bon switched back to Musqueam. "I know six English words and learning them has been very difficult for me."

Bedard laughed lightly.

"I understand that you have brought some toys with you," said Chief Big Bon. "Some bows, I am told. I am also told that you will show me how to shoot accurately at distance. I hope that this is so. I have always wanted to shoot accurately at distance."

The group exchanged wry glances.

"Yes, I have brought some bows, most will be too short for you but perhaps several will be interesting. Maybe you will have Dorono here make some for you to try. That would please me."

"Let the fun begin," Chief Big Bon said, turning and starting off down a trail. He picked up two bows from a large woman who had been carrying them for him.

Chief Big Bon said, "This is my wife, Dotena, or Dot as she likes to be called. She's a strong leader of our small village and is greatly appreciated."

Dot had obviously heard those words before, but she appeared a bit shy. She smiled and nodded at Bedard.

A group of men, women and children followed Chief Big Bon and his guests. *This is apparently going to be a village entertainment afternoon,* thought Bedard.

Liz came by, wagging her tail. She had been gone for some time, so the area did not seem to offer anything that worried her. Bedard was pleased, but he sent her off again to continue circling the area.

They passed over a ridge that seemed to travel down the centre of the island in an east–west direction. Soon they came to a meadow which reached some distance westerly along the island.

Immediately in front of them were four large straw bundles built on small wood pole structures. Bedard smiled. *Very professional.*

Chief Big Bon turned with a huge smile. "I'm told that these are the same as the targets that you have in England. I met an Englishman from one of the English boats many years ago who showed me how to make these."

Bedard went forward and took some time to examine the targets. There was a small cloth fixed to the front face of each of the straw bundles with two circles drawn on the cloth, one about six inches in diameter and the other about eighteen inches.

He spoke in English. "You've imported them from England."

Mot translated, having some difficulty with the word "imported," then the whole group laughed and Bedard could see that Chief Big Bon was very pleased.

Bedard took his bundles of bows and quivers from Dorono who was carrying them for him and began to pace westward down the meadow. Chief Big Bon and some of the others followed. Bedard stopped at a marker at what he believed to be close to seven hundred feet and turned around to look at Chief Big Bon, who shrugged. Bedard then went farther to the nine-hundred-foot marker and stopped to unwrap one of his packages.

Two of his bows could handle more than thirteen hundred feet, but he wanted to provide a bit of a show because this is what was apparently expected today.

The first bow that he chose was a simple longbow, similar in nature to the local bows. He offered it to Chief Big Bon to look at, and Chief Big Bon gave Bedard one of his bows to examine. Chief Big Bon's bow was a finely crafted solid wood bow. Bedard could not tell what the wood was but suspected that it was yew. Dorono was the local bow master, so Bedard assumed that he had made it.

"Is this yew?" Dorono's eyebrows went up and he nodded.

Dorono and Chief Big Bon were examining Bedard's bow.

"This is also made of yew," said Dorono, "but the sapwood section is almost perfect. It has about the same stiffness as Big Bon's bow. I have a very difficult time getting good long sections of yew wood now. I will have to examine this more carefully when we return to the village. The dimensions are slightly different from those that I am currently using. Very interesting."

He continued examining Bedard's bow and talking to Chief Big Bon about what he was seeing.

"All of the modern bows and arrows that I have with me are made by the same craftsman who used to live in England but now lives in New York. He is very famous, by the name of Robert Doyen," said Bedard.

Dorono nodded. "I saw two of his bows about ten years ago. They, like this one, were very finely crafted."

Chief Big Bon moved away from Dorono and exchanged bows with Bedard. Bedard placed the end of his bow on the ground and compared its length with Chief Big Bon's very long bow. They both smiled.

Continuing to smile, Bedard drew a line in the earth and looked up at Chief Big Bon.

Both Bedard and Chief Big Bon did some simple arm and chest stretches and stepped up to the line. Chief Big Bon gestured that his guest should shoot first so Bedard fitted an arrow to his bow and looked down the range. There was a very light wind off the ocean to the southwest and Bedard tested it with a bit of straw. He drew back and released the arrow. Bedard was a very good archer, and he expected his arrow to place well. It did, arriving just within the small circle. Bedard was pleased when the report carried by a young girl came.

The chief also tested the wind and stepped up to the line, and drew back and released. The young girl came again to report that it was a tie. Chief Big Bon was relieved, and Bedard was pleased that a conflict had not developed on the first pull.

Six other archers, including Roanyon, Ortho and Melleran, then moved up to the line and released arrows. It was reported that all six were within the small circle. *This is an expert group,* thought Bedard. Chief Big Bon's pleasure was evident in his smile.

Then Bedard turned and marched off another hundred feet. He turned and looked at Chief Big Bon, who again shrugged, and Bedard went on another hundred feet. Chief Big Bon and the others followed.

Bedard took the remaining three bows from his first bag. They were individually wrapped in special waterproof bags. Two were considerably shorter than the previous bow. He handed these shorter bows to Chief Big Bon and Dorono.

"These bows are very special. They are *recurve* bows, and the curves at the ends are designed to store energy. I obtained these two shorter bows while I was in Hawaii. They are very old and were probably made somewhere in China. They are both very easy to use and their pull distance is the same as the longbow," Bedard said. "I use them for shooting at relatively short distances, say, less than four hundred feet. This one is a recurve compound bow. It is very old and is my favourite."

The group passed the bows around. Dorono was particularly interested in the compound bow.

"What is this made of?" he asked.

"The core is obviously wood," said Bedard. "I do not know what the wood is. The belly is horn and there is sinew on the back." With both Mot and Roanyon translating, the word sinew took a bit of time to understand. The three materials had to be fixed together, and that was a new idea for those present.

"When the bow is drawn," Bedard said, "the sinew stretches and the horn is under compression, and this stores more energy than a longbow of the same length. The construction takes at least a week, and the drying and curing time is very long, several months in fact, and the bow is very sensitive to moisture. In this climate, I keep all three of these bows in special bags to protect them."

It was some time before the translation of all of this was understood by the group.

"I do not like these bows," Ortho said. "They are killing bows!"

The others were surprised at this outburst and murmured amongst themselves.

Chief Big Bon looked at all three bows again and spoke with Dorono about the compound bow.

Chief Big Bon said to Bedard, "Is this bow a very good bow?"

"It is the most useful all-purpose bow that I own."

Chief Big Bon turned to Dorono. "Can you make such a bow?"

"I can make any bow," Dorono said. "I will make a bow like this for you."

Chief Big Bon nodded and grunted.

Chief Big Bon then chose the second bow he had been carrying. It was slightly longer than the first one that he had used. Bedard examined this bow, which was also slightly heavier and extremely well crafted from yew.

"This is the best bow that I have ever seen," he said.

Both Dorono and Chief Big Bon were delighted with Bedard's approval.

Bedard stepped up to the line and used a special body movement to pull the string back and sight the arrow. He exhibited an enormous amount of physical effort. He was very pleased when the arrow was reported to have landed again inside the six-inch circle.

Chief Big Bon was very impressed. "At this distance, everyone should stand well back from the target area." The group laughed with him.

Chief Big Bon moved back from the line to talk to himself. Bedard understood later that Chief Big Bon often did this, especially in a competition. Chief Big Bon stepped up to the line and released an arrow. The report was that it had also landed just inside the six-inch circle. He was very pleased. "That is a long shot," he said.

Bedard just shook his head and looked at Roanyon, who smiled. No others attempted to shoot, not wanting to be embarrassed.

Bedard turned and marched off another two hundred feet to thirteen hundred feet. He looked back to see that Chief Big Bon had not followed him.

Roanyon, of course, knew what was going to transpire next and he placed his arm around Chief Big Bon and explained that Bedard had a new toy to show him. Chief Big Bon slowly moved forward to where Bedard was standing.

As he came up, he said to Bedard, "So, show me this toy!"

Bedard then took back all the bows and with Roanyon's assistance slipped two into their watertight bags, and then into the long carry bag. He left the compound bow out.

He took the other bag and placed it on the ground.

Bedard lifted up the device from the bag.

"That is a *crossbow*," Dorono said, using the English word for crossbow. "I have had it described to me many times."

Mot and Roanyon tried to translate and then decided to use the English word instead.

"Yes, it is a crossbow, a large modern bow made last year. The crossbow has been in use for more than eight thousand years," said Bedard. The time was very difficult for the group to believe.

Bedard turned to Roanyon. "You said that you used one of these when you were with the Spanish fleet."

Roanyon nodded. He reached for the bow and looked it over carefully, trying the cocking mechanism and then releasing it.

"This is much larger than the crossbows I have used. It has a much longer bow and I am wondering about the ribs in the centre portion. I believe that this design will support more than the usual compression. It certainly takes a fair bit of effort to cock."

"Yes," said Bedard, "it stores a lot of energy. Try it."

Roanyon took a special arrow from Bedard and walked over to the line. He put the front of the crossbow on the ground and drew back on the lever to cock the unit again. He then called Mot over to help him. Mot was a bit apprehensive.

"Just stand there and I will rest the bar on your hand at the end of your shoulder. That's it!"

Then Roanyon knelt down on the grass with one leg and aimed the device. The arrow's release scared Mot quite a bit but nothing hit him.

The small girl again ran up to them and reported that the arrow had struck just outside the six-inch circle.

"That was a good shot!" said Bedard, and the others agreed.

Chief Big Bon and Dorono were surrounded by the others as they examined the crossbow.

"This is very interesting," said Chief Big Bon. He turned to Roanyon. "Is it easy to use?"

"There are many different designs," Roanyon said. The crossbow is slower to use than a longbow of the same energy but quite accurate, especially at very long distances, as we have just seen. For someone who could not use a longbow because they are not strong enough, the crossbow could be the answer. It is also heavy and clumsy, but it does hold the tension in the string for a long time, which is very useful in some situations. I used one from the heaving deck of a ship. It allowed me to wait for the perfect time to shoot, something I could not have done with a longbow of the same strength. I could also shoot many arrows with no problems."

Bedard, taking both the crossbow and the compound bow, turned and marched off another one hundred feet to fourteen hundred feet. He looked back to see that Chief Big Bon had again not followed him.

This time the group's reaction to these incredible distances was laughter.

Roanyon walked slowly alongside Big Bon up to where Bedard was standing smiling. The others followed.

Chief Big Bon was shaking his head. "I do not believe this! Dorono, what is the longest distance that you have shot an arrow in practice?"

"I have just started practicing from nine hundred and fifty feet with our new bows made from the yew we obtained from the south last year.

Looking at Bedard, Roanyon said, "Which bow are you going to try first from this distance?"

Chief Big Bon groaned.

"I have never tried the crossbow from this distance before and it would be a remarkable test."

Chief Big Bon, Dorono and the others moved back a bit.

Chief Big Bon was still shaking his head. "I do not believe this," he said again.

Looking at Mot and smiling, Bedard said, "I will volunteer to hold the bow."

There was still a slight breeze coming in from the south, and Bedard and Roanyon tested the wind several times with small pieces of grass and discussed the results.

Roanyon cocked the bow and inserted the arrow. Then Bedard crouched down and held the bow stock and Roanyon took his position behind him.

"What elevation should I use?" Roanyon asked.

Bedard turned his head toward Chief Big Bon. "Do we get more than one try?"

Chief Big Bon said, "Of course, we will allow two tries." The group laughed and clapped at this generous offer.

One of the small girls that was manning the target had arrived, wondering if the session was over yet. Dorono explained to her that there would be several more tries and they should report the result of each try as usual. They would signal to her when the session was over. He added that the girls should stay well back from the target. Everyone laughed at this.

Bedard said, "I think that the elevation should be at least six feet."

Roanyon and Bedard discussed this for some time. For the first try, they decided on about eight feet. Roanyon tested the wind one last time and then settled in for the shot.

The report was that the arrow had passed just above the centre of the target structure. Everyone was amazed.

Roanyon cocked the bow again and inserted another arrow. He tested the wind again. They decided to reduce the elevation by about two feet.

The report was that the arrow had landed just outside the eighteen-inch circle in the middle to the side.

"Dammed wind," Bedard muttered.

The whole group laughed and clapped in appreciation of this shot.

"That was a marvellous shot!" Chief Big Bon said. "An incredible bow!"

Bedard picked up the compound bow and inspected it carefully. Roanyon tested the wind several times for him.

Bedard stepped up to the line. He used the same special body movement to pull the string back and sight the arrow. He once more exhibited an enormous amount of physical effort. He did not have very much hope for the placement of the arrow and was surprised when it was reported to have again landed inside the six-inch circle.

Chief Big Bon shook his head. "That was hard to believe. I am glad that I was here to see it." And then he moved forward and shook both Bedard's and Roanyon's hands.

Chief Big Bon said to Dorono, "I must have a bow like that!"

Dorono nodded, smiling.

Roanyon looked up at the sun and turned to Bedard. "If you want to look at the corral today, we should start to move."

Dorono signalled to the target team that the session was over.

"Copco," said Mot. "I will take your bows and arrows back to the village."

Fifteen
January 19, 1858 (Late Afternoon)

Most of the group did not wish to travel to the far end of the island at this time.

Bedard, Roanyon, Chief Big Bon and Dorono moved off to the west at a light run with Dorono leading the way.

The trip took more than an hour, and Bedard realized that they might have only an hour of sunlight left for this project.

The ridge continued almost to the western tip of the island and the grassland and light bush gave way to sand dunes. The sand along the island's south shore was compact near the water with rocky sand and scrub bush above the high-water line. It was very easy going.

Dorono stopped and turned to the others. "Anywhere here on the ridge would be a good place to see the corral. I suggest that only one person at a time take a look. The lookout tree is still manned at this time of day, and the observers will have a good view of this area of the island."

Bedard took the first view. He used his binoculars to sweep the whole area and better understand the coastline.

Bedard soon came down, and Roanyon took his place with his own telescope. While Big Bon and Dorono took their turns, both using Bedard's high-powered telescope, Bedard and Roanyon discussed what they had seen.

"It is a classic small fort," said Roanyon. "Like many I have seen in my travels."

"Yes," said Bedard. "It has three buildings, each built into one of the walls except for the entrance gate wall. There are gun slots everywhere. The ground has been cleared for more than five hundred feet in all directions to minimize surprise attacks."

Chief Big Bon came down to join the conversation. "That is going to be very difficult to overcome. They finished the rear building last fall and reconstructed the large gate on the water side. I have no idea why they have built this. They must have very ferocious enemies. Do white men in other parts of the world do this?"

Bedard just grimaced. "We all have had some very bad experiences and tend to be protective and conservative."

"I think that they have started an internal watch system," said Dorono. "There seems to be men circulating around the inside of the walls and buildings, looking out the gun slots as they pass them."

Bedard went up to the berm again, this time carrying his high-powered telescope.

Roanyon followed him and used the same telescope.

Bedard started to draw a map of the corral in the sand. The four men gathered around it.

"The three buildings seem to be similar but have some differences. It would be helpful to find out why they are different. All have wide front doors, meaning that they have thick barriers with two small gun slots just inside. They might also have platforms at the corners of the walls."

Roanyon talked about this, explaining that the barriers prevent anyone from entering the building and creating havoc. This also allows two defenders to shoot through the barrier at attackers coming at the doors. The corner platforms allow men to shoot down on any attacking force along all the walls.

"I, too, saw the internal watch system," said Bedard, and he looked at Roanyon. "Do you remember the watch system that we used in our south coast fort in Hawaii?"

Roanyon nodded. "Yes, we had the men go past the front door of the building and look out the next wall slot before entering the building itself."

"Right," Bedard said. "That is what I see here!"

Again, Roanyon talked about this, and Bedard drew another small plan in the sand to support the explanation.

Chief Big Bon and Dorono just shook their heads.

"Each building must have one or two emergency exits," said Roanyon. "I wonder if we can find them."

This caused further discussion.

Chief Big Bon said, "I did not realize how serious these people are. I wonder if it would be possible to set up a spy tree or spy bunker here on the island."

"That would be a very dangerous venture," said Roanyon.

Chief Big Bon and Dorono discussed this possibility for some time.

"We might be able to build a one-person fort with a very small opening to the north," said Dorono, "but we would also have to set up some sort of security. The security alone would require many people. We do not think that this project is feasible."

"I agree," said Bedard. "We would not be able to get the type of information that we now need from a lookout on this island."

As they prepared to leave, Dorono said, "It is going to rain tonight, and the rain will wipe out most traces of our visit here."

Nevertheless, they all spent some time smoothing over the sand where they had made their maps and the marks in the sand that they had made when they crawled up the bank to look over to the corral. The tide was coming in and would cover their footprints on the sand along the water.

Bedard was very concerned about what he had seen. The Wolverine had built a sophisticated fort with only three apparent weaknesses. One was the short five-hundred-foot cleared distance to the forest. They must have something in place, perhaps in the forest, to further protect them in this regard. The second was the security exits. These should be easy to find but were probably protected in some way. The third weakness made Bedard smile as he thought about it: *Everything is made of wood, and wood is very flammable.*

On the return trip east to the island village, Bedard admitted to Roanyon his surprise that the Wolverine has allowed Skwis to exist. He felt that there might be a spy in their village somewhere. In any case, he said that they should try to move everyone to Tsusnahm where the security was much better with the dogs and the children.

Roanyon was a bit startled. Bedard thought about these concerns for some time. Chief Big Bon was jogging in front of him and he moved up and allowed Roanyon to pass them. Jogging beside Chief Big Bon, Bedard said that he had a terrible question for him.

They both slowed down to a fast walk.

"You may have heard," said Bedard, "that we found a person in our village who was on the way to meet someone from the corral to tell him that I had arrived in the village. If that information had been passed on to the Wolverine, it would have made life very difficult for everyone in Tsusnahm. The Wolverine and I know each other very well. He is already concerned because he lost two people on January second. One of those people was named Martin. I knew him too. Martin was probably the one who instigated the search for the unknown person who arrived by a small boat on January first. He was very clever and sensitive to situations like that. I am certain the Wolverine misses his contribution very much. The second man, Woolsome Taylor, was a well-known professional killer. It is probable that the Wolverine moved forward and built a more sophisticated fort because he does not understand what happened on January second. He doesn't really want to antagonize you but he must protect himself."

Chief Big Bon said, "You are thinking that our village should have been wiped out some time ago!"

Bedard said nothing. Chief Big Bon moved ahead until he was running beside Dorono. They talked briefly. Dorono moved forward at great speed. The remaining three sped up a bit but Dorono was soon out of sight.

They arrived at the village to find that another party was in the making. Bedard immediately saw Mother, who gave him a dreadful glare.

Oh-oh, I am in the doghouse again.

Much to Bedard's surprise, Modan was also here and he came over to him.

"There was a canoe that travelled by Tsusnahm this afternoon with two white men paddling it with some expertise," Modan said. "The canoe was of a type that is made in a village near Colville over on the island. The canoe went in to the north shore where you found Noua and then returned. It did not stop at the small landing where your second canoe and supplies are hidden. They were not travelling very fast and they were looking at our village intently. We followed them carefully, staying well back from the water. I don't think they saw us. Your dogs were also tracking them, but of course they would not have been seen either. The canoes travelled past Mahli and Stsulawh just as the sun set. I assume they returned to the corral."

Bedard said, "Thank you for this information."

Then Bedard reported what the group had seen: A sophisticated well-designed fortress with formal security systems in place. He drew a small plan on the ground for Modan. Modan just shook his head in amazement.

"It is probable," said Bedard, "that this village will move over to Tsusnahm for the time being. There might be some risk for them to remain here."

Modan nodded. "We have lots of space, but it will need some work before it will be comfortable. I can return now and start that activity today."

Bedard said with a smile, "How is the new dog team doing?"

Modan and Towaba had been so impressed with Bedard's dogs that they had chosen six dogs from the hunting pack to see whether they would respond to security training.

"They have had five days of training, and we think that they will all be able to make a contribution in a month or so. We were amazed how smart the dogs are. It is very enjoyable, especially after you showed us what to do."

Bedard continued to smile and said, "Let us go and talk to Chief Big Bon and Dorono and find out what they have decided."

It was very close to dinnertime, and Mother was, of course, in the middle of the preparation effort.

Bedard was surprised to see Adrona and Aurora at the cooking fireplace. Both of them had their babies slung in packs on their backs. Adrona saw Bedard and waved, much too busy to come over for a visit.

Not so Mother. Seeing Bedard, she marched over and steamed him for not telling her that there would be a special dinner here that night, and turned away without waiting for Bedard's reaction. Both Adrona and Aurora were laughing as Bedard gestured with both hands in the air.

Modan and Bedard found Chief Big Bon with Dorono, Fenciao and two young women talking together.

Chief Big Bon said, "These are my granddaughters, Inchesca and Bella. They already think that they are smarter than me, so I always ask them for their advice." He smiled greatly, and the two women nodded at Bedard and looked down a bit embarrassed.

Dorono gave a proud smile. "They are my daughters. Their mother passed away two years ago, and we have found that they both have her great wisdom and the ability to understand their visions. They talk well together, and their ideas and recommendations have always been well received."

"We have been concerned about the corral," said Inchesca, "and have been watching its construction for almost a year. We understand that you think that it is finished now, and that it is a danger to our village."

"We have been discussing two problems," Dorono said. "The first is why Skwis has not been wiped out by the white men, and the second is when should we move across the water."

"Our father mentioned that there might be a spy in our village," said Bella. "And Mot told us the story about a similar case in your village. We do not know what to say. Nothing is impossible. We need to think and talk about this more. There are not many people here."

"We have almost agreed to move tonight," said Inchesca. "We can then come back over next week in the daylight to move most of the personal property and temporarily close down our home."

Modan said, "I will return to Tsusnahm and start work on your home there." He moved off toward the water where his canoe was located.

The two women talked together while the men moved over toward the benches set out for the feast.

Mother came over to Bedard, all smiles now. "I was impolite to you, and you must forgive me. It is difficult for me to understand that everyone is not my child. I have heard the results of the archery competition. Your special toys appear to be very unusual. I have also heard of the plan to protect the villagers. That will be very good for Tsusnahm because there are some unique people who live in Skwis. If they move, they will make

Tsusnahm a better place to live, even if they only stay a short time. They have much to share with us. I will try to be kinder to everyone all the time."

She gave Bedard a big hug and ran off to the cooking area again before he could respond. Bedard saw Adrona near the fireplace laughing and holding up her arms as Bedard had done a few moments before.

Sixteen
January 20, 1858 (Morning)

The next morning was crisp and the air was, as usual, heavy with mist. Bedard had noted on his early morning run that the snowline was still visible on the mountains to the north. Mother, of course, had all the guests for the early meal in Tsusnahm.

"Copco," Chief Big Bon said, "do you think that we will be able to do anything on our own here?"

Dorono, Roanyon and Modan, who were seated nearby, laughed with them.

"How was the building? Were you comfortable?" asked Bedard.

"It was perfect," said Chief Big Bon. "Dorono had two hours. We expected nothing less. I even got to sleep with my wife!"

Dom looked at him sternly and then the two of them laughed.

"You are very kind to say that," Modan said. "My team will continue to work there today and perhaps tomorrow. It will be perfect then!"

Chief Big Bon smiled widely.

"We will have more guests this morning," Roanyon said. "Perhaps within the hour. We were told this morning by their runner, Young Joie, that the chiefs from both villages downriver are going to arrive mid-morning. I think that they are coming to find out what caused you to move over to our village last night. They also might have some concern about the canoe that came by yesterday."

He turned to Bedard. "What should we report to them at this time?"

"Well," said Bedard, "we can start by telling them the truth. I will tell them why I am here in this beautiful land." He smiled.

"Dorono, perhaps you can report on our trip up your island yesterday, and Roanyon and I will tell them what we saw and what we think of the corral. Chief Big Bon, you can talk about Skwis and the possible risks of staying there. They will understand you, and they will probably have some similar thoughts to share with us. After all, they are much closer to the corral than we are."

"I have continued to think about Skwis," said Chief Big Bon. "And I am very pleased with the idea of coming over here to Tsusnahm. I feel like a very heavy weight has been lifted from my shoulders."

When he finished speaking, the group looked very sombre.

"We then need to talk about a plan of action to get rid of the Wolverine and his corral," Bedard said, to the agreement of everyone. "We may need several meetings after everyone has thought about the information to be exchanged today and after all the chiefs have shared their wisdom with us."

"The villages, no doubt, have been monitoring the corral closely and will have important information to share with us today," said Towaba, who had joined the group.

Chief Big Bon nodded. "There is still some unfinished business from yesterday; we need to inspect your arrows."

The group was amused by that, and Mot said, "I have all of them right here!" He put six arrows on the table.

Bedard picked up each one in turn and described them. Both Ortho and Melleran joined the group. There was much discussion, especially about the new steel-tipped arrow.

Bedard said, "They definitely fly farther than the previous metal-tipped arrows I used."

Bedard took Dorono aside. "Did Inchesca and Bella come to any conclusion regarding a person of interest in your village?"

Dorono looked very sad. "There are only fourteen adults in our village, and they are all family. If Inchesca and Bella have some thoughts, they have kept them to themselves. I am not even certain that I want to know anything!"

Bedard nodded. "Thank you. I know that it was a very difficult question for you to answer."

"I hear the canoes coming now," said Mot.

Within ten minutes, four small canoes with twelve men and two women arrived at the beach and were welcomed by Chief Sparrow and Mother.

As the group came up the beach toward the big tree, Chief Big Bon moved over to Bedard and offered introductions.

"The man in front is Chief Wanso. He is the chief of the Mahli village. He is the same age as Chief Sparrow, and he is very fit and very wise and well respected. Some say that he was, in his youth, a ferocious and feared warrior, and a legend is developing around him. He is considered the senior chief in our area. His wife, Amoroa, who is following him, does not say much, but when she does everyone listens. They both have travelled and speak several languages. This is a very powerful family. Two of his many sons, Dobera and Wantano, are next. I do not know what their current responsibilities are, but we will surely find out today.

"Then comes Chief Tamburo and his wife Tomala. He is chief of the larger Stsulawh village, which is a little closer to the corral. He is much younger and has been chief for only about five years. He has also travelled south and speaks both Spanish and English quite well. I think that his wife does also. Roanyon and he are very close long-time friends, although they are not directly related. His oldest son, Tosby, is next. I do not recognize the four men following them, but one looks like he may be from one of the Squamish villages. That is interesting."

Chief Tamburo yelled and started to run up the slope, and he and Roanyon met in a fierce embrace with much pounding of backs. Tomala and Mothana hugged each other like old friends. Everyone was smiling. A great start to the gathering.

Bedard was still standing back from the trail with Chief Big Bon, trying not to be in the first rush of old friends meeting again.

Mother immediately brought Chief Wanso and Amoroa over to meet Bedard.

Chief Wanso said, "We have been looking forward to meeting you. The reports of your unique language skills amaze us. Your *worldly*"—using the English word followed by a huge smile—"experience can only benefit us."

Chief Big Bon moved forward to catch the last part of the conversation. Chief Wanso turned to him and the two embraced and held each other for a moment. Then Chief Big Bon said to Bedard, "Chief Wanso knows ten more English words than I do." The small group around them laughed at that.

Amoroa then said to Mother in English, "You did not tell me he was so handsome."

Amoroa gave Bedard a hug and they both smiled greatly. Bedard realised that he had not tested Mother's English yet. He just shook his head and addressed Chief Wanso in Spanish.

"Are there more beautiful women in your village?"

Chief Wanso smiled, and Amoroa flushed a little, laughed and walked off arm-in-arm with Mother. She obviously told Mother what he had said because Mother turned, laughed and waved.

Roanyon brought Chief Tamburo and Tomala over to meet Bedard. Chief Tamburo was a tall, lean man, although not a tall as Big Bon. It was obvious that he was indeed very fit. They shook hands but Tamburo did not release Bedard's hand for a moment. He was looking into Bedard's face.

He then nodded and said in English, "You have already become one of us."

"That is a great compliment," said Bedard, and bobbed his head slightly.

Roanyon said, "I wish to suggest that we continue to speak Musqueam unless we have something private to share, then we can use Spanish." He paused for a moment and said, with his eyebrows lifted, "Or French, or Italian." The four of them laughed heartily at that.

Chief Tamburo said, "You have me mixed up with my wife." And again they laughed.

Tomala introduced herself to Bedard and, having heard his wordplay with Amoroa and her husband, Chief Wanso, said, "We will talk later about what language *we* will use when we are together."

At which the men were very amused.

The gathering around the big tree was developing in a different fashion than what Bedard had seen before. Roanyon stayed with Bedard, introducing him to the other men in the visiting party, including the man who called himself John-John from the Squamish village of Khwaykhway to the north. He was an archer and a bow-master.

Roanyon then guided Bedard to the area where Chief Sparrow and Mother were about to sit down. Chief Sparrow and Chief Big Bon sat on one side with their wives and the village elders.

Across from them were the two other chiefs and their wives. Their three sons and the men who accompanied the two chiefs sat with them.

Others at this meeting were few. Bedard, Roanyon, Dorono, Modan, Towaba, Ortho and Melleran sat behind Chief Sparrow and Chief Big Bon while Mot sat close to Bedard.

The senior elder, Kom, who Bedard had met with Mot in the beaver dam meadow, stood up holding an ornately carved rod and moved to the space at the side between the two groups, and officially welcomed the visitors to Tsusnahm. Chief Sparrow stood up and smiled at the two chiefs and the visitors. Bedard later learned that the beautifully carved rod was known as the talking stick.

Roanyon stood up, moved to the same area as Bob had used and graciously received the talking stick from Bob. "You have all met our special visitor, Copco. We have asked him to share with you some thoughts and ideas that we think will be interesting to you."

Bedard stood up and moved forward, and was offered the talking stick by Roanyon. Mot followed and stood close, ready to translate if necessary.

"I am from England. Some of you have met others from my country, most probably sailors from quite large ships. I have been sent here by our queen, our supreme leader, to deal with what her advisors consider a very difficult and perhaps unusual problem."

Bedard looked directly at the two visiting chiefs. "How many people live in your villages?"

Chief Wanso said, "About a thousand people."

"About fifteen hundred people," said Chief Tamburo.

"This year," said Bedard, "we believe that a large unorganized group of white people from the United States will pass by your villages and continue up the river. These people will be looking for the gold that has been reportedly found farther up the river. Perhaps twenty thousand people, eight times your combined population will come."

The group was obviously confused.

"They will travel in ones and twos and perhaps in very small groups. Over the next few years, there will be more and more people. Some of these people will go south again during the summer river-flooding period. Some will stay and wait for the water levels to go down. Others will go south in the late fall and return again in the spring."

Tomala made a little squeaking sound, removed a necklace from around her neck and gave it to her husband.

Chief Tamburo took it from her gravely. "This is what we believe to be a very old gold coin that I acquired for Tomala last month from the captain of a Spanish ship."

The coin was passed around the group. Some had seen similar coins.

When the coin came to Roanyon he said, "Yes this is a coin from Europe, perhaps Italy."

He passed it to Bedard who examined it. "Definitely an old Roman coin. It is probably very valuable because it is gold, but also because it is very old, perhaps more than two thousand years old."

Tomala said to her husband, "Tell them how much you paid for it."

Chief Tamburo frowned at her. "No."

She continued to stare at him. "It will help us to better understand why all these people are coming here."

She turned back to the group. "When we were in the new state of California ten years ago, we heard that a gold rush was about to happen there." She looked at Bedard, who nodded.

"And when we left there about six years ago," she said, "we heard tales of a gold rush in a faraway place called Australia."

"Yes," said Roanyon, "I have been there. That gold rush is still going on."

She again looked at her husband. "Tell them or I will."

Chief Tamburo scrunched up his face. "I am either very stupid or very much in love." He and his wife exchanged large smiles and the tension that was developing in the group dissipated.

This time Chief Tamburo looked beseechingly at his wife. "You really want me to tell them?"

She nodded.

He again grimaced. "Thirty Hudson's Bay blankets."

The group gasped.

Tomala said, "Continue!"

"Four muskets and a small amount of shot but no powder."

Tomala said, "And?"

Chief Tamburo turned his face down. "Five of my best bows." Then he looked up smiling. "But no arrows."

The group was obviously shocked. Mot whispered to Bedard, "Wow! That is more than five years of my income."

Chief Wanso was holding the necklace at the time and looked down at it with great respect, shaking his head. He passed it over very carefully to his wife Amoroa who, of course, had seen it before, but now looked down at it with her mouth open. She got up, went over to Tomala and carefully placed the necklace around her friend's neck and embraced her.

"Ah, love," she said—or something like that, Bedard did not hear the exact words.

"For a very skilled gold miner," said Bedard, "that amount of gold can be found in only one day." The group was now very stunned. "For someone who is not very skilled, perhaps three days. Some of these people will come across the water from Fort Victoria. Some will come overland through the forest from the south to Fort Langley. Some will come overland from the south beyond the eastern mountains and then west to the northern portion of your river. Many of these people have travelled in woodlands and forests before and can look after themselves quite well. They will need food, so they will fish, hunt for animals, pick the berries, and some of the more experienced people will find the good edible roots and grasses. Over time, you may have to go farther for food for yourselves. Others will die accidently in the water because they cannot swim or travel on land because they cannot find or buy enough food. Some will hurt themselves and die because they have no one to care for them. A small number of these people will be very bad people who will not look for gold but will steal gold from others, perhaps killing them in the process."

Bedard held up a piece of paper. "My queen has given me this list of twenty-eight men and two women who are very bad. Some of them were told to leave California because they had created too much trouble. I have also been to California and I know many of the people on this list. I killed two of these people on my second day in this beautiful part of the world. Quite incredibly, I had the help of Chief Big Bon, who I just met yesterday."

Bedard and Chief Big Bon exchanged big smiles.

"Tommy Hunter, known as the Wolverine, controls the corral. I have met him several times in my travels. I have seen him kill someone because he did not like the way he was looking at him. He is very clever and very evil. His name is at the top of my list. You may also be aware that there is another small group near Harrison Lake and another group forming at Fort Langley. Others are already mining for gold north of Fort Hope, and there are perhaps more miners on the Fraser and Thompson Rivers to the north.

"I plan to take action against these bad people when I find them. The corral is a unique and difficult problem."

Dorono came up to address the group, taking the talking stick from Bedard who returned to his place.

"Yesterday was a very interesting day for all of us at Skwis." He and Chief Big Bon exchanged smiles. "Copco visited us with what can only be called an incredible collection of bows and arrows. Mot, Roanyon, Ortho, Melleran and Modan accompanied him. We went out to our shooting range and Bedard demonstrated the bows that he has with him. The final range was fourteen hundred feet."

Two of the men behind the two visitors scrunched up their faces and shook their heads in apparent disbelief.

"And," said Dorono, "at fourteen hundred feet one of his bows placed an arrow within the six-inch target."

The visitors all shook their heads.

"The last bow was a *crossbow*."

At that, most of the male visitors nodded their heads.

"Roanyon, who has experience with this bow, and with the assistance of Bedard, placed an arrow within the six-inch target from thirteen hundred feet and within the eighteen-inch target from fourteen hundred feet.

"You all must see Bedard's bows. The arrows are also very modern. After this incredible demonstration, four of us travelled well down the island and looked over the sand dune ridge at the corral with high-powered telescopes."

At that, one of the visitors brought forward a large package and unwrapped it to show a large-scale model of the corral. It was about three feet by two feet showing all the ramps and platforms and gun slots. The roofs of the three buildings were removable, showing some detail of the building interiors.

Bedard and Roanyon moved forward and knelt to inspect the model.

"Now, this is very professional," said Bedard.

Chief Tamburo nodded. "We have some clever artists in our villages. This was put together over the past two weeks when we were starting to conclude that the corral was not good."

"When we returned to Skwis," said Dorono, "Chief Big Bon decided to move our small family over to Tsusnahm."

Chief Big Bon then got up, took the talking stick and addressed the group. "We had not been monitoring activity at the corral for some time. It was too far away, and we were too busy living." He smiled at the group.

"This was a good opportunity to look at the corral from some distance away, but with high-powered telescopes and in the company of Bedard and Roanyon, who both have had experience with similar forts in other parts of the world. They explained what we saw and what it perhaps means to all the villages here. I was not happy. On the run back to Skwis, we continued to talk. One of the terrible questions that came up was why the corral had not just wiped Skwis out. Of all the Musqueam villages, we were in the best position to monitor their activities, although we were not doing that. Four of their men could come in the middle of the night and that would be that.

"Another question: Do we have a spy in our village? Perhaps it was the spy who was protecting us! We had a short village meeting. You all know Inchesca and Bella. Mother was there and graciously invited all of us to live in Tsusnahm, so we moved here last night. I feel that a great weight has been lifted from my shoulders. We may move back eventually, but we have been so welcomed here. I have not done anything. Everything is being done for me."

The whole group laughed.

Roanyon got up to take the talking stick and Chief Big Bon returned to his place.

"We saw that the corral was almost complete and that a sophisticated daytime security system was in operation within the corral. There are probably six escape tunnels in place."

This was obviously an unfamiliar concept to the visitors.

"There are probably more security systems in the forest fringe."

Again, this was an idea that was perhaps new to the visitors, who were now talking very quietly and animatedly.

"We thought that there were platforms inside at the corners of the walls, and I notice that your wonderful model shows that. The two main weaknesses that we saw were, firstly, the distance from the corral to the forest is not great, and secondly, the corral is made entirely of wood which is, of course, flammable."

The visitors all nodded.

"We also wonder what the real purpose of the corral is, given its obvious weaknesses," Roanyon said. "The report of two men passing by in a canoe yesterday may indicate that they are going to take some sort of action soon, which is why Bedard and I feel strongly that Skwis is in danger. We are very pleased that the villagers decided to move here on such short notice."

Amoroa then spoke up. "Roanyon, please tell us more about the escape tunnels and the security systems in the forest fringe."

"I will ask Bedard to answer that question," said Roanyon. "He and I met in Hawaii five years ago, where he directed the construction of three forts similar to the corral."

Bedard got up, taking the talking stick.

"Any fortification like the corral is somewhat confining. There are usually only one or two entrances to the fort, and activities can usually be monitored fairly easily by the enemies; therefore, the builders usually incorporate … *secret*"—he paused to use the English word—"person passageways that are usually tunnels and sometimes very long ones. They can be walkways but are, more usually, crawlways. Depending on the soil, they may need a ceiling and side supports so that they do not collapse under the weight of the soil above. There are many different designs. Roanyon and I believe that there are probably three escape tunnels from the corral most likely leading to old deadfalls or exposed root systems of a large tree, perhaps even to a very large rock or an outcrop of bedrock." That word proved difficult to translate. "There may also be a cleverly designed door at the tunnel end intended to hide the tunnel exit. It is possible that one of the tunnels is only known by one or two of the corral's inhabitants. This one may not even be finished and is used only as a last minute, desperate attempt to escape. It may even have a stock of food and water, allowing someone to survive hidden for several weeks."

There was obviously much to think about in and around this concept.

Bedard continued. "Security systems in the forest can easily be put in place so that the occupants of the corral are forewarned of a pending attack or of someone who is inspecting the corral from the assumed safety of the forest. You get too close, and a tree falls on your head."

The men pursed their lips and shook their heads.

"The Wolverine probably has someone at the fort that is expert at security systems. The internal daytime security system that we saw is certainly a very good one. Roanyon actually remembered it from one of the forts we used in Hawaii."

"In other words," said Bedard, "closing down the corral is not going to be easy in spite of its apparent weaknesses."

Adrona had come to up to where Mother was sitting and quietly said something to her. Mother then rose.

"We have some light midday refreshments coming in a moment. If you would like to stand up and stretch or wander off, now would be a good time."

Everyone smiled and stood up. Modan and Towaba moved over to talk to some of the visitors.

Bedard and Roanyon were now standing together.

"I think that went fairly well," said Bedard. "But it has perhaps caused more problems than solutions."

Dobera, one of the two sons of Wanso in attendance, came up to Bedard. "We have been talking to Modan from time to time over the past week, and he has reported good progress with training the dogs to help with village security. We hope that you might have time to visit us and help us start a similar program. It is a very good idea. As you know, we use the dogs as friends and hunters but also as guardians for our children to safeguard them from the water, the forest animals and from straying too far from home. We think that some of the dogs are very smart, and we have talked about that before. I have brought one dog with me today, Bobo— Well, yes, my son named him."

Bedard smiled. "It is a good name for yelling, I think."

Dobera turned and slapped his leg. A beautiful yellow dog came rushing out of the light brush by the river and arrived in a massive skid in sitting position with his head turned up to Dobera, and received a good scratch for his work.

"I was hoping that he could meet one of your dogs and perhaps even join in a short security run. I think that Bobo could do that, and this would be interesting for me to see. I am planning to stay here overnight so we could fit this *experiment*"—he used the English word with a smile—"at your convenience."

Dobera indicated with his hand that Bobo should meet the others. He bumped Roanyon briefly as an old friend and Roanyon greeted him in English.

"Hi Bobo."

Then Bobo went over to Bedard and gave him a thorough sniffing.

"Bobo obviously smells my dogs," Bedard said.

"Yes," said Dobera. "That is unusual. I have never seen him give … anyone such a thorough greeting." Just then Bobo jumped up with his paws on Bedard's chest and Bedard gave him a thorough scratching.

Dobera laughed. "I have never seen him do that before to a new friend. He obviously approves of you."

"I have never tried this before," said Bedard, "and I do not know if it will work. But over the many years that I have had a family with me, I have become convinced that they can communicate with each other. I usually try to feed the dogs near the end of the day, so that would be a good time to try the experiment."

Seventeen
January 20, 1858 (Afternoon)

The midday meal was indeed quite light, consisting of both cold vegetables and small pieces of hot meat and fish. After a short time, the group again sat down under the big tree.

Mother got up and asked Roanyon, Bedard and Chief Big Bon in turn if there was anything that they wished to add. They all shook their heads, so she sat down and, after a brief moment, Chief Wanso got up and moved to the speaker's space with the talking stick.

"This has been a very interesting morning for us. We are pleased that Chief Big Bon has moved here, and we are all looking forward to much better arrows in the future."

All the group clapped lightly, and Chief Big Bon dropped his head slightly with a great smile on his face.

Chief Wanso turned his head toward Bedard. "We must see your bows. The shots from thirteen hundred and fourteen hundred feet are quite remarkable. Chief Big Bon, who has been our champion archer for more than twenty years, told me that he has ordered some bows like yours."

The whole group clapped loudly.

"Surprisingly, we actually have two crossbows stored somewhere in our village. We never knew how to use them, and they probably need repairs. We are now very excited to drag them out and test them and perhaps even build more of them. Hopefully, we will have time for a short archery demonstration today. Some of us need to return to our responsibilities right away, but some will stay overnight. We are pleased that our model of the corral has been useful. We actually found one of the tunnel exits in the forest but did not think that there would be more. We have a *report* on that." He smiled and looked at his wife. The group laughed at his use of the English word.

"The existence of dangerous security systems installed in the forest was our greatest surprise this morning. This is terrible information. We have been moving around in that area for many months and are fortunate not to have had any injuries. We have sent a runner back to our villages this morning to stop any trips to the forest area around the corral until we have more knowledge and better planning. And finally, we look forward to implementing a plan to destroy the corral. It will be done. We are very fortunate to have Copco and Roanyon with us to help us do this. Our villages are now on first-level war-command status. Chief Tamburo and others will speak of that."

Mother, Chief Sparrow and the villagers behind them shook their heads in dismay.

Roanyon turned to Bedard. "Just like the Hawaiian fort and community war status systems."

Bedard pursed his lips and nodded. "This is very bad news."

Chief Wanso then sat down and the group clapped lightly.

Chief Tamburo got up and moved over to the speaker's space with the talking stick.

"This has indeed been a very interesting morning for us. We are also pleased that Chief Big Bon has moved here. We are all looking forward to not only much better arrows in the future but also to more of his famous archery lessons so that we can become better hunters and warriors."

All the group smiled and clapped, and Chief Big Bon again dropped his head slightly with a great smile on his face.

"We are also very pleased that Inchesca and Bella are closer to us. We have met with them, and their mother before them, many, many times for their ideas and counsel."

He stopped for a moment in thought. He then turned toward Bedard.

"We have been very interested in your family, Copco, and in the work that Modan, Towaba and Mot have been doing with some of the village dogs under your guidance over the past week. Modan has participated in our strategy to use some of our young children in responsible positions as path security and our version of this has served us quite well. The idea of having a security network completely around our villages is a great idea. We must also do this. You spoke this morning of the arrival this year of a great group of people attracted by the promise of finding gold and in so doing becoming very rich. We would benefit from more discussions with you to better understand the impact that this will have on our community, both good and bad."

Bedard nodded his head.

"And now what I believe is very bad news," said Chief Tamburo. "Yesterday, with no notice, the ten youths that stayed at the lookout tree near the west point were told to go home by the men at the corral. They arrived at our village in the early morning, confused and disappointed but none the worse for wear."

Bedard and Roanyon shook their heads. Mother, Chief Sparrow and the villagers behind them gasped.

"This was the event that caused us to decide to travel east to the beautiful village of Tsusnahm on short notice. We are very concerned about this development. We would benefit from your help and counsel. This morning Roanyon mentioned that the report of two men in a canoe inspecting the villages and the shoreline yesterday caused Bedard and him some concern, for they felt that some sort of other action may soon follow. We also saw them and found that to be troublesome. It has never happened before. This activity, along with the return of the youths from the lookout tree, caused us to call a two-village war council meeting yesterday evening which lasted more than four hours. As Chief Wanso has said, our villages are now on first-level war-command status. We have sent some of the younger children and older people north to our Squamish friends in Khwaykhway and Wh'mullutsthun. We have assigned lightly armed men in positions all around our villages. They are instructed not to engage anyone but report what they see immediately. We have special warrior groups guarding the pathways in and around our community. They have been directed to stop and talk with anyone they meet. We had sent a warrior party out to watch the corral from the forest, but today they have been told to fall back until we can assess the forest for security systems.

"This morning we have also sent a warrior party of four men plus two runners on a long trail up and across the mountains to an area we call West Cove. This is where the white men who have travelled here from Fort Victoria have been storing their boats. There are twelve small boats hidden there near a beach at the bottom of a seldom used trail. We also have a small party on the island near where you were yesterday. They actually saw you leave." He smiled. "They also have long-range telescopes and three runners who report every four hours. They reported once early this morning that there is no change to the daytime security system in the corral that you saw yesterday, and that they felt that they had not been spotted yet. We are anticipating another report soon "One of the conclusions that we came to yesterday at the war council was that the people in the corral were not entirely stupid and that, even after initial quizzing of the young men from the lookout tree, we had absolutely no information as to what they were going to do next, if anything. My *support staff*"—and he smiled—"have more to say about our situation."

Chief Tamburo moved over to his seat and sat down. His son Wantano got up and went over to the speaker's space with the talking stick.

Wantano said softly in English, "I used to be his son, and now I am *support staff*."

The group laughed loudly. Several people were translating.

"I was volunteered, a year ago, to try to get to know the group of white men who had come to our area and camped in a small clearing. My English was reasonably good because my mother had set up a school that included English teaching. I am certain that the men appreciated dealing with someone in English. At that time, there were four of them led by Tommy Hunter." He looked over at Bedard. "I only recently heard that his nickname is the Wolverine. Last week there were twelve men. They are good hunters, and the only thing that we initially sold them was fish. And that was acceptable. They offered only American currency in payment, but we prefer British currency. I went to Fort Langley and found out what a reasonable exchange rate would be, and Hunter immediately accepted that. We were pleased that we had very little to do with them because they were really different from us in many ways."

Wantano again looked at Bedard and put his hands in the air a little bit. Bedard nodded and smiled.

"Soon after I had met him, Hunter came to me and said that they wanted to build a home and asked me to help them choose a good place. Our village family leaders and elders had already talked about this eventuality, so I showed them the small meadow with a small stream running by that used to be an ancient village called Kullukhun, and he said that that would be perfect. Initially, we helped him find and cut suitable trees for the building. They knew how to build, and we thought that some of their tools and building ideas were very good. They also chose not to take down many trees around the meadow. They said that the area was very beautiful, and that they did not want to change that. All in all, they were very good neighbours. Then one of the men took one of our young girls away into the forest. I had to go and speak to Hunter about that, and he just told me to go away. So that really ended our good relationship. We did not help them or sell them anything for more than six months."

Wantano looked at his father for a moment.

"My father's father and his father before that, forever—all were chiefs and ran their villages as chiefs. In their travels, my father and my mother had seen some systems of what we now call *democracy*"—using the English word—"and felt that it offered some advantages to our society. So, when my father became chief, he tried very hard to listen to everyone who had an opinion and wished to talk. He has never liked the corral." Wantano again stopped and looked at his father for a moment. "But others saw benefits and wished to re-establish relationships with the white men. Because of their wishes he agreed, but he maintained a close watch on these relationships. I was asked to meet with Tommy Hunter to try to encourage them to buy some fish from us again. Hunter agreed immediately but had a problem with my insistence that he control his men. Our village women were off limits. After several short meetings, he agreed to this. Again, they were good neighbours, and they organized the lookout tree and we participated. Most of the youth involved knew English, but we still think that the white men never knew that, so we had a very good understanding of what they were doing.

"Then a man named Don arrived at the corral. It was soon apparent that he was a very experienced womanizer. For this reason, our relationship with them started to fail. Don never approached any of our villagers, but he was very active elsewhere. We determined that all of his relationships that we could identify, until recently, were mutual, and because of this we did not take any firm action. I did, however, bring his name up at several meetings with Hunter, but again he just shrugged and said that he was controlling his men as per our agreement."

At that point, one of the small children involved in the village security came running to Modan and pointed at the river. They all looked over and saw a canoe flying through the water from the island.

"This is unexpected," said Chief Wanso. "They are part of the island group."

He and several others rushed down to the water to wait for their arrival.

At the same time, Young Joie was sighted running down the trail toward the village, yelling something. Chief Tamburo got up and rushed up the trail to meet him. Bedard and others followed them. Young Joie was on the verge of collapsing, and they had to wait a few minutes for him to collect himself.

"The corral now has only two men, and both of them have been captured. They are Spanish and speak a little English, but they are refusing to say anything. The corral has not been entered in case there are traps.

"Five small boats are missing from the west cove. It is probable that the other ten white men sailed off early this morning before daylight. The war committee has sent twenty warriors to secure the west cove and another twenty warriors to secure the beach at the corral. The committee has also taken all the men off the mountainside and assigned them to the water side. There are many small beaches, all of which will be monitored. Twenty warriors are on their way here and will arrive momentarily."

Chief Tamburo looked at Bedard with great concern.

"They are gone," said Bedard. "But the corral will not be abandoned. Other men will come who must be stopped. The war committee's plan of action is a good one."

Then Chief Tamburo and Bedard turned and made their way back to the tree area where the report from the island group was being received by Chief Wanso, Dobera, Wantano, Roanyon and others.

Dobera turned to his father. "They saw the warriors capture the two white men and assumed that the other white men had gone. A runner from our villages came over by canoe and gave them a full report. Our other two men have gone to the south side of the island to see if they can see anyone. The wind and tides do not favour paddling up the river today, if that is their objective. So, the white men have probably landed and are travelling by foot on the south side river trail toward Fort Langley."

Roanyon said, "It is possible that they had a lookout hidden on the island watching Tsusnahm and perhaps discovered who you were, Copco. Or they decided that you were the person that was a real danger to them, the one that killed two of their men. They could not find you initially, even if they did not look very hard, because it was too dangerous to search for you in this wild forest. The two men in the canoe also caused some concern. Perhaps Don also reported no-show meetings with some of his women spies. Perhaps they even saw us yesterday on the dunes looking at them. They could have been manning the lookout tree after our young men had been dismissed. That would give them a better sight line."

"This is not a good development," Bedard said. "Once they reach Fort Langley, they will mix with the larger population there and be much harder to cull. It will be very difficult to stop them on the trail because they all have guns. It is unlikely that they are travelling with any more than small to medium packs because they know that even with a four-hour head start, we might be able to catch up with them if they have heavier packs. But they are probably still carrying their rifles, and they are heavy. They will not reach Fort Langley until sometime tomorrow."

"They might break up into two groups," said Roanyon. "Say one group of three men travelling very light and fast and the second slowly, even walking. It might be possible to stop the second group if we take action now, but this is very dangerous."

Bedard and Roanyon looked at each other for a long time. The other men waited patiently.

Bedard said, "You are very wise, Roanyon."

"Definitely two groups," Roanyon said. "The second group will be well spread out for better defence and will have one guard in front and two guards following."

A call from the water drew their attention to a flotilla of canoes coming up the north arm of the river.

"These are our warriors coming now," said Chief Tamburo. "They will continue east to the middle arm and then go south and across the shallows to the south side river trail."

Bedard said, "I will go to my canoe storage area and get my bow and perhaps my rifle or a revolver. A canoe can pick me up. I will take all four dogs. I will need one man to come with me."

Six people immediately volunteered, including Chief Big Bon and Roanyon.

Bedard smiled as Mother objected. "No! You are all too important to our villages and your families."

"I will go with Copco," Wantano said. "He will need *support staff.*"

The group laughed lightly.

Chief Wanso looked at his wife. Amoroa nodded slightly.

He then turned to Bedard. "That would be good as he needs more training."

The group laughed again.

The two lead canoes came to shore and Chief Tamburo, Chief Wanso and Roanyon went down to talk to the warriors about the plan.

Bedard went to his quarters and took the throwing knives and harness. He decided not to take anything else. Roanyon came back up to talk to Bedard.

"We will send another small group to follow you. You may need some help after you capture the slow group."

Eighteen
January 20, 1858
(Late Afternoon & Evening)

Bedard and Wantano went off up the hill at a light run. They stopped to stretch and the four dogs were called down. Then they all continued rapidly to the east with Hy out front and Liz behind them.

Bedard was thinking about what he should take from his storage area. Certainly a small pack, with a few clothes and a bow and quiver. He also decided to take one of his rifles and a rifle support pack but no revolvers.

They soon arrived at Bedard's storage area and uncovered the canoe that held his bow and guns and some clothes. Wantano was impressed with the camouflage and was very surprised when Bedard showed him where the second canoe was hidden.

"I never would have found them," he said.

Bedard worked the area to protect the canoe and gear, and they joined the canoe that had come to the shore to pick them up and set off to catch up to the flotilla that was just in front of them. The trip to the main landing of the south side river trail was quite long.

Upon landing, Bedard dispatched the dogs immediately on perimeter surveillance, much to the amazement of the twenty warriors as well as Oban and Wantano. Bedard and two of the warriors inspected the trail and agreed that the white men had passed by many hours ago. They also agreed that some were dragging what were probably baggage carriers, and this seemed to support the idea that these men had split into two groups.

Liz came back with a positive report within ten minutes. Bedard then sent her and JoJo off on a distance run east toward Fort Langley on the south side river trail. He planned to use Haus in the forest to the south and have Hy bring up the rear. Bedard sent Hy down the south side river trail to the south and he soon returned wagging his tail, having found the two men from the island.

These two arrived just as the group had hidden their canoes in the forest, and the men did a sweep of the landing area. It had started to rain lightly which would help mask the group's footprints at the landing.

A strategy meeting was held and several of the party had very good ideas to offer, not only regarding the task of finding the white men but also various plans on how to capture them. Bedard described how the dogs would respond when the trailing white men were encountered and what the dogs could do within some of the plans that had been described. The warriors were very impressed, and all of them looked forward to this adventure. The final plan would be decided when the white men were found and the local terrain known.

The group also decided to break up into two parties with two warriors in front accompanying Bedard and the remaining warriors following at a slower pace.

Bedard assigned Hy to follow the second group just off the trail and Haus to remain in the forest to the south of the second group.

All of the front warrior group had bows. Bedard had left his rifle and bag with the second group. There were fifteen guns altogether, including Bedard's and Oban's. All of the warriors had been chosen for this particular adventure because they knew how to use a gun. Bedard was impressed.

About half an hour into the run, the front group saw Liz who turned around immediately without approaching Bedard. She did not have anything to report yet. This happened three times. Then Liz came within a hundred feet and went into the bush to the south. Bedard said to the others that someone was coming toward them, so he stayed on the trail and the other two hid in the forest.

Very soon a local native and his wife passed him. One of the warriors stepped out of the forest. This at first startled the couple, but they and the warrior knew each other. The warrior found out that the large party of white men that they were looking for was more than an hour ahead. Bedard and his two companions continued their run.

About an hour later, Liz arrived and stood on the trail waiting for instructions.

It was early evening, and the white men ahead of them would soon have to stop to camp overnight. It had been a long day for them.

Bedard thought that one of the best and simplest plans that had been discussed earlier was to quietly capture or kill the men guarding the camp and then capture or kill the replacements, assuming that the guards were doing two- or three-hour shifts. This would leave one or two to deal with in the camp.

Bedard sent Liz up the path again while the three men followed rapidly but more cautiously. Liz came back frequently and refused to go forward. Bedard gave her a hold-and-report-later assignment and she went off into the forest to the south.

"I think that the group that we are following is just up ahead," he said. "Perhaps they have stopped for the night."

Bedard sent one of the warriors back down the trail to intercept the second group of warriors and stop them. He and the other warrior went south into the forest and found some good game trails that allowed them to move farther east toward the camp but off the main trail.

The party of white men had indeed set up camp. It took Bedard almost half an hour to find the location of the sentry in the forest to the south of the camp area. The guard's position was very cleverly concealed in the lifted root system of a deadfall. The other two sentries were easily spotted just south of the trail some distance east and west of the camp.

Bedard returned to the trail, leaving his partner near the hidden white man, and met up with the rest of their party. He called in each of the dogs for a scratch and redeployed them around the area.

Bedard described the plan that he liked for this location and the group easily agreed.

He insisted that everyone wear masks to keep them from being recognized. He said that these men were clever, strong and evil. If they were to escape, these criminals might return for revenge.

Immediately, six volunteers moved out to capture the three existing sentries. The three white men were brought west to a small clearing near the warriors' temporary base. The same group of six went out again to intercept the replacements. Two warriors volunteered to capture the remaining white man in the small camp—he was apparently the cook and would be very busy, and therefore reasonably easy to take.

As they were captured, the first three white men had been immediately knocked unconscious, gagged and tied. At the small clearing, they were tied to trees and inspected by Bedard, Wantano and the two leaders of the group of warriors.

The four agreed that one man was Don and that the other two men were involved mostly with the walk-around security. Don was on Bedard's list and he remembered that his real name was Donatello Markashino, an Italian who had worked for the Wolverine in California. He had never met Don, but he knew the name well.

The first prisoner to awaken was very frightened. Bedard had him taken some distance away and his gag removed. The man stated that, because it was partially in sunlight, the first sentry shift was a long one that would end in about one hour. He had nothing else to say, so Bedard replaced his gag and brought him back to his tree where he was once more securely tied up. The warriors were obviously impressed with the concept that no one was going to escape and return for revenge.

The second group of sentries was easily captured, brought to the clearing and tied to trees. Shortly after, the cook arrived. He was conscious and his eyes bulged with terror. Don and several others had awakened.

Bedard left two warriors to watch over their captives and took the rest of the warrior group out of earshot for another discussion. He was pleased with the result and said so. The group appreciated that.

The campsite had to be dealt with. It was decided to take all the guns, bullet bags, belts and packs and leave the campsite as if it had been abandoned in a hurry with no indication of what had happened and no indication of where these men had gone. This included a visit to each of the sentry locations to make certain that all traces of the warrior attacks were masked. The group liked this. This was good fun. Copco was a clever person and a good leader.

Bedard did not like the next step. He brought each of the captives to the questioning area one at a time, and sometimes a second time, when he found that the answers to his questions were incorrect. Four of the masked warriors spoke reasonable English and some Spanish. All of the warriors except the two guards listened to the questioning with a constant buzz of translating going on. This was something new to this group, and they were very much into it. They wanted to learn, and they had already acknowledged that Copco was clever. This was good stuff.

Bedard first searched the captives' clothing for small weapons and then their bodies for tattoos, especially prison numbers. He asked them what their names were. Some of the warriors had been in contact with some of the white men before, and from time to time suggested questions for Bedard to ask, which was very useful in getting at some of the truth.

Don was the last person to be questioned.

Bedard spoke to him in Italian. "So, Donatello Markashino, what are you doing in this part of the world?"

Don was stunned.

Bedard translated this into Musqueam, saying that Don was Italian from far-away Europe. The warriors liked this. They had all heard that Bedard spoke many languages and had only been speaking Musqueam for eight days. Because it was so similar to

Spanish, Wantano actually spoke some Italian. He clapped his hands and laughed at Don's reaction.

After receiving no response from the prisoner, Bedard pressed on.

"What part of Italy are you from?"

This time Wantano translated.

No reply.

Bedard adopted a Sicilian accent. "I think that you come from Sicily."

Again, Wantano translated and guessed correctly that Copco had adopted a Sicilian accent. The group was amused.

Don was again stunned.

"Did you know Monsignor Dobera?" Bedard asked.

Don's jaw dropped.

The warriors were being well entertained. Wantano could hardly contain himself and said that Copco knew the small village that Don came from on the small island of Sicily and knew the name of the Roman Catholic priest there. Wantano went on the say that Bedard must have visited this place at some time.

Bedard looked over at Wantano and nodded.

Bedard said, "Now that you have agreed that you name is Donatello Markashino and that you come from Sicily, answer the first question: What are you doing in this part of the world?"

No answer.

Bedard got up, took a rifle from one of the warriors, turned and shot the man in the head.

The warriors all jumped back, shocked.

"This was a very terrible, evil man," said Bedard, "and the world is better off with him dead. Drag him to the prisoner area and prop him up against his tree so that they all can see what has happened to him."

Bedard and the warriors processed the group of prisoners again, and Bedard was pleased with the results. He felt that he had the truth from all of the men except one.

It was now dark, and the warriors had eaten a small hot meal and were now gathered around a smoldering fire, discussing what to do with the six prisoners.

Liz arrived with her tail wagging and disappeared into the darkness. In a few moments, Roanyon arrived with a group of ten men including Towaba and Oban. Oban had come with Chief Tamburo's group and was reported to be a gun expert.

Bedard briefly described all the action and said that he was very pleased with the *professionalism* of the group of warriors. Wantano beamed and the warriors were very pleased to again hear these words of praise.

Bedard once more had the one man brought to the meeting at the fireplace to see if any of the newcomers knew him.

Oban immediately identified him as the gun master.

Bedard went to the pile of confiscated guns and picked up a new slick side-loading rifle that was much like the one he had. Bedard knew that it had only recently been available in the eastern part of the continent, northeast of New York in the Boston area. He laid the rifle on the ground in front of the prisoner and went back to his place in the circle.

The man looked at the gun for some time and then closed his eyes.

After some time, Bedard got up again and picked up the gun. The man watched him. Bedard levered a bullet into the chamber with obvious experience and pointed the gun at the man.

The man's eyes bulged. "No, no, no!"

Bedard lowered the gun, crouched on the ground in front of the man and started speaking to him in American English with a pronounced Boston accent. The man looked up and nodded his head and said that his name was Art Rossland. He then began a long story of how he had travelled from Boston to California and up to Fort Victoria and across to the Wolverine's fort, arriving three months ago. His stock of six new guns had been confiscated by the Wolverine and he was made to examine all the rifles they had and repair them if necessary. This was difficult work, he said, because they did not have any parts and only a very crude forge. Two days ago he was told that they were leaving soon, and he was given back one of his rifles and six bullets.

Rossland identified the three that went on ahead as the Wolverine, Bill Lomax and Bill Thompson. Lomax and Thompson were both hunters, bushmen and killers.

"I tell you I've seen both of them kill men. I'm a gun master, not a killer."

To Roanyon and Wantano, Bedard said, "All three are on my list. We must leave here tonight, in case they change their minds and come back. I believe this man, but he has more information to share that will be valuable to us. He is, no doubt, also an experienced hunter and bushman, so we must be doubly careful that he does not escape."

Bedard asked Towaba to bring in a small deer so that they could feed the prisoners. Towaba just looked at him in surprise. Bedard whistled and Liz came in for instructions.

Bedard smiled. "Liz will help."

Towaba shrugged, asked a warrior friend to join him and they both jogged off after Liz into the darkness. In fifteen minutes, the two men jogged back into camp with a small deer between them.

Towaba grinned at Bedard and shook his head.

The warrior, Tomkins, was very excited and reported to the other warriors still seated around the fire, which was now a larger cooking fire.

"We just went into the forest not three hundred feet along a faint trail, and Towaba moved me to the side and suggested that I put an arrow in my bow. I had just done that when this deer dashed past us and we both put arrows in her shoulder from four feet!"

"We really must train our dogs properly," said Wantano, and the whole group laughed.

A group of three warriors and three newcomers was immediately sent back to the canoe storage areas to prepare for the return to Tsusnahm, taking with them some of the confiscated guns and gear.

Two prisoners at a time were brought into the fire area and fed and then sent south with escorts. Within an hour, the fire was doused and buried and the area had been swept, with the remaining group also travelling south with the rest of the guns and gear.

The canoe trip was again long and uneventful. It was an incoming tide, and this helped balance the river current.

Chiefs Tamburo and Wanso, their wives and most of their party had been invited by Mother to stay on in Tsusnahm, and they were given a full briefing. It was now well past midnight and a mid-morning meeting was planned.

When she saw him, Mother approached Bedard.

"My husband and I have been talking all evening about the gold rush. This is difficult for us to completely understand, and we have some questions for you. We know that this is very late in the day, but Chief Sparrow needs to understand what is going to happen to us, or he will not be able to sleep."

Bedard followed Mother to her home where Chief Sparrow greeted him with great pleasure, with Mother translating his guttural speech.

"Thank you for coming to visit us at this late hour. We understand that the effort today was successful, which is good. My father was the chief of this village before Chief Komchowa, Roanyon's father. They both died young. When I became chief thirty years ago, all of a sudden I became interested in living to be an old man." The three of them smiled. "I spent much time with the elders and determined when I was born. When were you born, Copco?"

Bedard said, "I was born in a country called Spain, but the records of my birth were destroyed in a fire. I believe that I am sixty years old."

"I have a similar problem," said the chief, "in that there are no written records of those times, of course. However, each year is different and unique. With the help of the elders I determined my age, and I believe that I am now sixty-two years old. I am very relieved that I am older than you." The three of them laughed. "Mother, of course, is much younger." Mother blushed but joined them in laughter.

"My wife and I have been talking about the good life we have lived. We enjoy doing that." He looked at her smiling. "We have also been discussing the gold rush that you have predicted, as she has no doubt told you. I think that she understands what is going to happen to us better than I do. We remembered hearing years ago that there was a gold rush near the place you call San Francisco and also in a distant land called Australia."

"Yes," said Bedard. "The gold rush in Australia started seven years ago and is still going on in various parts of that very large country. The gold rush in California started ten years ago and ended about three years ago. The miners could not find enough gold to cover their cost of living, so most of them went home, although many of them are still in the San Francisco area."

Mother said, "We also remember hearing about six years ago that there was gold to be found to the north on the islands that the Haida control."

Bedard smiled. "Yes. Not much gold was found in that area, but it did attract a number of gold seekers, many of whom disappeared and are presumed dead. As I said earlier today, not everyone can survive living in the woodlands and forests. In addition, the Haida were not pleased with the arrival of the miners, and the Haida have a violent reputation, as you know."

"Several years ago," said Chief Sparrow, "some of our friends who live near where our river is joined by another large river north of our very narrow river canyons visited us. They said that they found gold and sold some of it to the Hudson's Bay Company."

Bedard was quiet for a moment. "You are very well informed. Yes, the Hudson's Bay Company has some gold found in that area and has sent some of it down to San Francisco for evaluation. I believe that soon the rush of people from that area of the world will start in earnest. I understand that there are now gold miners working on the river beyond Fort Hope."

Mother looked concerned. "When will the large number of these gold seekers come to our lands?"

"There is no doubt," said Bedard, "that most of the gold miners will travel here from San Francisco on large boats. I think that the first boatload of miners and other people will arrive at Fort Victoria in three or four months, but many more will follow. I estimate twenty thousand or more people will pass by your home this year, and more will come next year. Your ability to feed yourself will require some initial planning because all of these people will need to eat. I think that it would be reasonable to try to protect the land that you are using by not allowing people to stop there. In about five to ten years, the settlers will come and that will develop into a major problem for your nation. They will take the land, and you will not be able to do much about that. If you fight them, you will be killed."

Chief Sparrow looked at Mother for a long time, and then he shook his head. He turned to Bedard.

"Thank you for joining us. We appreciate the information and your wisdom."

Bedard got up and shook the chief's hand, gave Mother a big hug and left their home.

He has a real problem, Bedard thought. *Under normal circumstances he would be chief until he died or found himself at death's door. I think that he is now going to resign and let a younger man take them into this very difficult future.*

Nineteen
January 21, 1858
(Morning & Early Afternoon)

The morning meal was strung out a bit as those who had difficulty sleeping managed to extract themselves from their quarters.

Mother had announced to everyone that her husband had requested a special council meeting of the assembled chiefs that morning on a very important matter.

In due course, Chief Tamburo, Chief Wanso and Chief Big Bon arrived at the meeting place under the big tree where the elders, Chief Sparrow and Mother received them. Bedard, Roanyon, the visiting chiefs' wives and families and almost all of the village adults and visitors sat in a large circle around this powerful group of Musqueam leaders.

Bedard found Roanyon very quiet and introspective but sensed this was caused, for the most part, by the previous day's excitement, so he did not quiz his friend.

With the assistance of his two granddaughters, Chief Sparrow, who was not known to mince words, began to address the visitors, his long-term friends and the villagers.

"For more than a year, I have been seeking advice from the elders of our village, my very close friends, and of course, Inchesca and Bella who, as all of you know, are blessed with the wisdom and insight of their mother. Their counsel has guided all of us through this world for many, many years." He paused, looking intently at both Inchesca and Bella.

"I have decided to step down as chief of Tsusnahm today, now, at this meeting!"

The three chiefs facing him were stunned but silent. A soft murmur of discussion could be heard around the circle.

"As is our custom, our elders have put forward the name of a new chief to follow me, and I was extremely pleased with their choice." He sat down and the Senior Elder, Kom, rose to address the three chiefs.

"We have in our village a man who has only recently returned to the village where he was born. He is the son of one of our village's most famous chiefs, Chief Norman Komchowa."

Again a soft murmur could be heard around the circle. The three chiefs were smiling. Bedard looked at Roanyon who was still looking at the ground in front of him.

"He has spent many years travelling the world and has gained an understanding of many cultures, including the English. These assets are going to be very important for our communities in both the near and distant future. He has shown himself to be wise, with a wide range of practical skills and, most importantly, he is very considerate and thoughtful of others. He has found himself a very beautiful and strong woman from Tsusnahm to be his wife. We believe this to be very important."

Bedard noted that Roanyon was now looking at the speaker with a small smile on his face.

"The only negative thing that we have discovered..." Kom paused and carefully looked at Roanyon with a smile. "Is that he has no children yet!"

The group enjoyed this and laughed softly.

"There is no doubt that he will be as famous a leader of Tsusnahm as his father was before him. I am pleased to introduce to you Roanyon Komchowa."

And with that, Kom moved back.

The whole group stood up and started to sing softly. Everyone was smiling. The three chiefs had turned around to face Roanyon. Roanyon was slow to get up because he was looking for Mothana. When he found her, he went over to her and took her hands. She stood up and they embraced. The singing intensified.

Roanyon and Mothana, holding hands, moved slowly toward Mother and Chief Sparrow and embraced them. They went to the three chiefs and embraced them, each chief saying something to both of them.

They then returned to the front of the group and Chief Sparrow stepped forward with an elaborate ornate blanket and his conical looking hat, and with the assistance of his grandchildren, put these on Roanyon.

Kom then moved up again. "I am pleased to introduce you to Chief Roanyon Komchowa."

The whole group now began singing a song that Bedard had heard several times before. It was a combination of chanting and singing; he had not learned it yet but obviously everyone in the village knew it.

Bedard was surprised and pleased with the effectiveness of this simple ceremony.

Mot came up to him and said, "This is very clever of Old Chief Sparrow, because he only needed one visiting chief for this event, and he has three. The three chiefs are now endowed with the obligation of helping Chief Roanyon in the future. Being a chief is not an easy job."

Chief Roanyon and Mothana started moving around the circle, talking to and embracing everyone. Mothana, who was leading, embraced Bedard and smiled up at him through her tears.

"Roanyon will benefit enormously from your energy and support," Bedard said. "I only hope that I will be able to provide some assistance to both of you from time to time."

She smiled and hugged him again.

Roanyon and Bedard first made a one-arm clasp, hand to elbow on the forearm, and stared intently at each other from close range for a moment. Then they embraced.

"And so, the world turns," said Chief Roanyon.

This was a favourite expression of Bedard's in recognition of an unusual occasion or event.

Bedard laughed. "Your humble servant."

This was one of Chief Roanyon's favourite expressions after doing some very difficult and exacting tasks for Bedard.

Chief Roanyon and Mothana returned to the centre of the circle and addressed the old chief and Mother for some time. Bedard heard the words but could not understand much of what was being said.

Mot moved to Bedard's side again. "Chief Roanyon is speaking in an old language that is not used much anymore. Most of the elders and those older than about sixty years, including, of course, Old Chief Sparrow and Mother, can still understand this language which is called Hunguminum. I am very surprised that Chief Roanyon still speaks this language. He obviously learned it as a child from his parents. I think that the three visiting chiefs also understand most of what he is saying. By speaking this language, Chief Roanyon is bestowing a great honour on Old Chief Sparrow and Mother."

Tears were running down the faces of Mother and her husband.

Mot translated the old tongue for Bedard. "He is saying that he is greatly honoured to follow in the footsteps of Old Chief Sparrow and that he hopes that Old Chief Sparrow will honour him by becoming his chief advisor for many years into the future. I do not know this language very well because there are few who have the skills to teach it. It is on my list." Mot smiled.

Chief Roanyon then turned to the visiting chiefs. "I am greatly honoured to be chosen to be the chief of Tsusnahm. I am blessed a hundredfold to have you witness this incredible event, and I am feeling very humble in your presence."

He bowed down before them. The three chiefs stood up and gathered around him in a very tight group. The villagers and guests continued singing quietly. Everyone was smiling.

Bedard was very impressed by all of this. Chief Roanyon would certainly continue Old Chief Sparrow's practice of speaking clearly and succinctly.

Adrona materialised at Mothana's side and the two embraced. Adrona said something, Mothana put her hand to her mouth, and the two of them laughed so hard that tears ran down their faces.

They were too far away for Bedard to hear, but Mot arrived at Bedard's side again and could hardly contain his mirth. He had been close enough to Mothana to hear some of the exchange.

"Adrona has decided that Mothana should announce that lunch is available, and this was very funny, apparently. I did not hear all of what Adrona said."

Mothana composed herself and, with Adrona still clinging to her side, spoke in a loud voice that Bedard thought was very similar to Mothers' distinct accent.

"We have some light midday refreshments coming in a moment. If you would like to stand up and stretch or wander off, now would be a good time."

The whole group instantly exploded into laughter.

Mother was immediately on her feet, laughing loudly and clapping her hands over her head. She ran toward Mothana and Adrona to envelope them in her arms. The three had a hard time staying upright because they were laughing so hard. Everyone continued to laugh and stood up, clapping loudly. The four chiefs did not know what to make of all this. Chief Roanyon came over to Mothana, Adrona and Mother. He was all smiles and gave them each a hug.

Old Chief Sparrow, accompanied by his two granddaughters, moved over to where the three visiting chiefs were now standing. They exchanged handshakes and embraces and began talking amongst themselves.

The meal was similar to yesterday's except that there was even more food, enough to feed everyone. It was quite light, consisting of cold vegetables and small pieces of hot meat and fish. Bedard thought that Adrona and her team were magicians and that he would have to remember to say something to her later.

After a short time the villagers dispersed, and the chiefs, now five in number, including Old Chief Sparrow, sat down facing each other under the tree with their wives and some of their families and support staff behind them. Bedard tried to keep unobtrusively in the background, but that was not to be.

Chief Roanyon stood up with the talking stick, smiled and addressed the small group.

"The meeting that I had envisioned last night for this morning did not turn out to be quite what I expected."

The group smiled and clapped lightly as was their fashion.

"We were, as I recall, listening to Wantano report on his dealings with the corral. Although this topic is somewhat modified now." The group laughed softly. "I wonder, Wantano, if you have anything more to share with us."

Wantano took the talking stick and again moved into the space at the side between the two groups.

"You will all recall that I accompanied Copco and our warriors on yesterday's amazing adventure. I am very happy that I can report to my father that not only was I pleased to have had the opportunity to play some small part in those activities but also to have seen Copco in action as a group leader. He is formidable. In particular, and I do not wish to embarrass him, his ability to draw out good ideas from our men and incorporate these ideas into the final action plan. And then, after the action is completed, to reward the group of warriors with praise for a job well done. I only hope that I can emulate these skills and utilize them some time in the future."

Bedard stood up, moved in beside Wantano and put his arm around his shoulders.

"Thank you for those kind words, Wantano. I am also pleased to report to Chief Wanso and Amoroa that Wantano will continue to have a successful career within this nation. He already has many skills."

Everyone was smiling and clapping lightly. Chief Wanso and Amoroa were very pleased.

"It was also interesting," said Wantano, "to watch the smooth interaction between Copco and Chief Roanyon yesterday. They have obviously operated together before and have developed a great deal of respect for each other. At the ceremony today, when they met in the circle, the exchange of emotion between them was very powerful. I was very pleased to see that."

Wantano and Bedard moved to their seats as Chief Roanyon rose and took the talking stick.

"Yes, Copco and I have been part of groups that have greatly benefited from Copco's inspired leadership. We now find ourselves greatly in need of his inspiration, and hopefully his understanding of some of the challenges that are about to descend upon us in this coming year by the gold seekers."

"We do have a number of unfinished tasks. The first has to do with the six prisoners who we took yesterday and the two prisoners from the corral."

Chief Roanyon moved to his seat, and Komchowa, one of the two warrior leaders, moved forward with the talking stick to address the group.

"As we decided last night, the prisoners have been hidden in one of the village buildings and are in close custody. Chief Roanyon's cousin, Tomara, was contacted early this morning, and he agreed to sail to Fort Victoria right away to deliver the message that Copco wrote to Mr. James Douglas who is there now. Two of Tsusnahm's warriors travelled with Tomara to help him and perhaps learn how to sail a boat. They will visit

Cowen and return next week with him and others. Hopefully, we will receive a reply late this evening. You will recall that we are hoping to arrange to send these prisoners south.

"We also decided to bring the two Spaniards here later today after they have been used to clear the corral and the surrounding forest of dangerous traps. I am certain that our warriors there will like that idea. We hope to be able to question them and find out more about other men who may soon come to the corral.

"This morning we again had a meeting of some of our *support staff*."

This brought on a tangle of comments from Wantano and his brother and other visitors behind the three chiefs as well as guffaws from some of the Tsusnahm men behind Chief Roanyon and Old Chief Sparrow.

"We interviewed the cook again. We find that this skill is a very difficult one. We thought that there might be an opportunity to hire this man, but it turns out that he does not have enough cooking skills to be of use to us. We were disappointed.

"Then we interviewed Art Rossland, who is the gun master from the corral. Oban, who is our gun master, participated."

Oban then joined Komchowa. "I immediately recognised Art Rossland. I had met him in San Francisco a few years ago when he was using the name Ansel Pancrest. He was very surprised to see me and gave me a long-involved story of why he was using a different name. He was very frightened. He said that he had been accused of killing someone, but actually he had been framed by the Wolverine. I have no idea if this is the truth or whether it is just another story. There is no doubt that Art is a very experienced gun master. I had brought a number of guns that had been confiscated from the prisoners to this meeting with him. Some of these guns were very modern and he told me about them and where he got them. I believe that this was truthful. There is no doubt that we could use his skills, but I do not know if he is reliable. He is also a very experienced bushman and trapper, and if he decides to escape he may turn out to be very dangerous to us."

Oban then went back to his seat.

Komchowa nodded his thanks. "When Copco was questioning Art," he said, "our group felt that he was not telling the whole story of how and why he came to the corral. Copco in his assessment of his last interview with this man suggested to us that the Wolverine must have had some other sort of hold over him, because the killing story did not sound strong enough to hold him. Art, or Ansel, gave us the impression that he did not like the people at the corral. He could have easily escaped but he did not, so we talked to him for a long time about what his name really was and why he stayed at the corral. In due course, he admitted that he had a niece in Colville Town on Vancouver Island and the Wolverine said that if he did not stay at the corral and do what he was directed to do that they would go over and seriously hurt her.

"We remembered that Mothana had lived in Colville Town for some time, and she remembered the woman who Mothana said was an English *medical practitioner* named Elizabeth Rossford. She said that Elizabeth helped with births and deaths and treated cuts, burns, broken bones and so on. Mothana also said that Elizabeth was very knowledgeable about and skilled in treating and coping with some of the white man diseases that have killed many of our ancestors and friends.

"We could certainly use another experienced gun master. We talked to Inchesca and Bella about what Mothana had said this medical practitioner was doing, and they gave us some more general information and were very supportive. They suggested that we talk to Tomala and Amoroa who may have met up with similar people in their travels. We did this over lunch. We became very excited because a *medical practitioner* was more than an English nurse—and we understand what that means—but not quite an English doctor. We could really use someone like that, but it might be very difficult to convince her to leave the small, comfortable and familiar English and Scottish community of Colville Town and join the relatively large and unfamiliar Musqueam community here. It was also noted that other villages here might want to consult her as well, and that might become too much for her to handle.

"Our group realizes that we are perhaps getting too far ahead of ourselves, so we moved Art to more comfortable quarters and set up a special security system for him using three of Tsusnahm's new security dogs. As Oban said, he is a very experienced bushman and trapper, and we do not want him to escape. We also want to show him a bit more respect in the hope that we can arrive at some sort of contract with him. We are planning to confer with Copco, and perhaps have Copco interview Art again. We now think that his real name is Art or Ansel Rossford and that Elizabeth Rossford is his daughter." Komchowa sat down.

The chiefs were obviously very pleased with this report.

Chief Roanyon again came to the speakers' area with the talking stick.

"As you know, we are planning to create a special group of warriors to travel into Haida territory this year to find our children that were taken from us by the Haida four years ago. The warrior selection camp will start next week. The selection process will be very difficult. A focused training period supervised by Copco will follow, leading to the exploratory trip northward. The plan is to then make a trip north with a large group of warriors to recover our children. This is a very dangerous enterprise requiring fearless warriors with great skills. We anticipate that a number of our warriors will not return, but we feel that we must try to find our children and also try to convince the Haida to never do this to us again."

Chief Roanyon stopped and looked at the chiefs sitting before him. They were obviously very concerned. The Haida were very powerful and fearless warriors and had been so for many hundreds of years. All of the nations in the area had had many opportunities to discuss the Haida nation and to exchange ideas on how to minimize the Haida's violence and their influence on their lives.

"Last week Adrona told us that there were six Haida families living near Fort Victoria. The English cannot differentiate between the Haida and the Musqueam. We feel that they do not yet understand the potential danger to everyone, including themselves, from these warlike people. The Hudson's Bay Company, with James Douglas as its leader, has a clear policy of supporting us and protecting us as much as they can from the negative influence and actions of the white men, but rarely gets involved in actions between nations. The Haida had some experience with gold rushes in their lands about six years ago. A Hudson's Bay Company prospecting party was attacked by the Haida and lost half of its gold. Several other prospecting parties of white men were never heard of again. We think that these Haida families have been sent to Fort Victoria to specifically monitor the anticipated influx of gold seekers. They will want to benefit from this gold rush as much as they can, and they have many skills to offer. We also think that there are other small Haida families in other communities along the Fraser River. We need a plan to identify and perhaps remove these people from our territory. We certainly do not want them learning of our plans to attack the northern Haida to recover our children."

Chief Roanyon noticed Bedard indicating that he wished to speak, so he gave him the talking stick and moved to his seat so that Bedard could come forward.

"The Haida have been amongst the villages and nations here for many, many years. The intermarriage between villages and nations has been going on for centuries. Some of these men and women still have ties, some with very strong ties, to their families up north."

Bedard stopped speaking as the three visiting chiefs moved over to confer with Old Chief Sparrow and Chief Roanyon. In a moment they returned to their seats, and Chief Tamburo remained standing to speak to Bedard.

He said, "You know that we are aware of this group of people in our midst. When the children were kidnapped four years ago we carefully spoke to most of them, those who we knew. Most were aghast and helped us to identify a few who were undesirables for one reason or other."

"We did identify two Haida men who we felt had in fact participated in the planning of this specific kidnapping. Our elders decided not to kill any of these Haida men and women because we did not have any proof, only suspicions, of their involvement. We asked ten men and four women to return to their northern Haida villages. Unfortunately, they did not complete the trip. They were all killed by an unknown group of people."

Chief Tamburo stopped for a moment, and the group was very quiet and reflective.

"Over the past four years," Chief Tamburo said, "our villages and others in this valley, including those of the Squamish Nation to the north of us, have refused to have Haida men or women join our villages, and we have tried to convince them to return home. We have firm evidence that some Haida are living up the river to the east, but we have not established a system to track them. Perhaps we should."

The other chiefs pursed their lips and nodded. This would obviously be a very difficult task, especially since manpower was at a premium.

"We also know that the Haida came back two years ago. Raiding parties of Haida attacked a Coast Salish village at Port Gamble some distance south of us and kidnapped a number of children and women for slaves. There was a fierce battle between the Haida and some white men with quite a few casualties on both sides. We monitored the straits for some time after we found out about this attack but did not see the returning Haida warriors. We assumed that they travelled past this area in the dark. They apparently returned the next year, last year, and killed a white settler in retaliation for the death of one of their chiefs."

Chief Tamburo sat down. Bedard waited a moment, collecting his thoughts, then spoke again.

"We can explain the warrior training as a simple protective measure from the anticipated onslaught of the gold seekers. When the larger group goes through the training period, it will be relatively short as we will be able to use part of the northward travel time for further training."

The chiefs nodded their heads in appreciation of this tactic.

"Perhaps," Bedard said, "we should continue the training program beyond what we need initially and invite other villages and the Squamish Nation, for example, to participate in this exercise. We could expand the program to include security issues and the use of young children and dogs in village security activities. My information suggests that there are several gold seekers already working on the river above Fort Hope. The first mass of gold seekers will probably arrive in three- or four-months' time. I would be pleased to speak more about this later today before you leave for home."

Chief Big Bon got up. "These are very interesting and difficult ideas. We need some time to think about them and to confer with our advisors."

"Of course," said Bedard. "Well, perhaps we can take a break now and inspect the bows and arrows that I have previously shown to Chief Big Bon."

Chief Big Bon seemed pleased with the suggestion.

"That is a good idea. My *support staff*"—and the group gave an appreciative laugh at his use of the English term—"has set up an archery range in the wet low-lying marshes to the west of the village. Two of Copco's *support staff* have brought his selection of bows and arrows here earlier this morning. We can go there immediately."

Twenty
January 21, 1858 (Mid-Afternoon)

The large group that made their way to the west down the river trail included Chief Roanyon, Chief Big Bon, Chief Tamburo, Tomala and Tosby, Chief Wanso, Amoroa, Dobera & Wantano and Bedard. Then came Ortho, Melleran, Dorono, Komchowa, a bow master named Johno and Mot, who was carrying some of Bedard's equipment. All of the men and both wives were carrying bows and arrows.

They came out of the dense forest by the river onto a small ridge of light grass leading toward the marshlands. In the distance, two of Chief Big Bon's targets could be seen.

Chief Big Bon was very pleased as the group squinted down the range at the targets. He led them to the very edge of the swamp where a white pole marker was buried in the silty-sandy soil.

"This marker," he said with an enormous smile, "is exactly nine hundred feet from the targets."

The two women immediately berated him, saying that seven hundred feet was a politer starting point. The group exchanged amused glances.

Chief Big Bon then shook his finger at Tomala. "You came first last year, and I know that you have been practicing with Chief Wanso and his sons. The chief beat me two years ago when I was at death's door."

Most of the group had attended that memorable battle and smiled at the memory.

"He is a very good archer and an exceptional teacher. I should know because I taught him myself!"

There was approval for this comment as all assembled thought it an appropriate start to this special event.

"We also have Chief Roanyon with us today," said Chief Big Bon. "His father, Chief Norman Komchowa, was a master archer and I was his student. I have seen Chief Roanyon shoot, and I fear that this year's competitions will be very difficult for me indeed, so much so that already I have begun to feel ill again."

Someone gave a brief laugh.

"And then there is Copco, of course, who has some very interesting bows to show us today and who is also an incredible archer himself."

Bedard showed them his longbow, similar in nature to the local bows. They all inspected it. Dorono said that it was made by Copco's friend, Robert Doyen, an outstanding craftsman in New York.

"Johno," Dorono said, "you will remember that you and I saw two of Doyen's bows about ten years ago."

Johno nodded. "Yes, that is when we started making our bows from yew and experimenting with other woods."

Chief Big Bon said, "Copco, will you please start off first because then we will be able to try to better your shot."

The group murmured its assent.

Bedard stepped up to the line, fitted an arrow to his bow and looked down the range. There was again a very light wind from the southwest, and Bedard tested the wind with a bit of straw. He drew back and released the arrow. It was a good shot, arriving within the small circle. Bedard was pleased when the report carried by a young girl came.

Chief Big Bon, the other two visiting chiefs and their wives and fourteen other archers, including Chief Roanyon, moved up to the line two at a time and released arrows. It was reported that everyone was within the small circle.

Big Bon was not smiling when he once more shook his finger at Tomala, who was beaming. Chief Tamburo had his hand over his mouth and was laughing with great pleasure.

Chief Roanyon was also smiling and shaking his head as he followed Bedard with the others. Bedard passed by the one-thousand-foot marker and went directly to the eleven-hundred-foot marker.

Bedard took three bows from the bag that Mot was carrying. They were individually wrapped in special waterproof bags.

"These three bows are very special. They are recurve bows, and the curves are designed to store energy," said Bedard.

He described them carefully and then, choosing his favourite recurve composite bow, stepped up to the line to shoot. He was very pleased when his arrow was reported to have landed inside the six-inch circle.

"I am in the process of making two of these bows," said Dorono. "It is very difficult, but Copco has been most helpful."

Chief Big Bon stepped up to the line and released an arrow. The report was that it had also landed in the small circle. He was very pleased. "That is a long shot," he said.

Then both Chief Tamburo and Tomala stepped up to the line.

Tomala turned to her husband. "When was the last time you shot from this distance?"

He smiled at her. "I don't remember."

Chief Tamburo shot first. Then Tomala, emulating Chief Big Bon, stepped back from the line and dropped to one knee for a moment before approaching the line and releasing her arrow. A young girl was seen running toward them with the results.

"Oh my goodness," Tomala said in English. "I must have killed someone!"

Just then the report was delivered that both had been just inside the six-inch circle.

Chief Big Bon said, "I knew it, I knew it, I knew it!"

The whole group rejoiced, with Chief Tamburo and Amoroa hugging Tomala.

The other fourteen archers then moved up to the line and released arrows. It was reported that Chief Roanyon, Dorono, Johno and Komchowa were all within the small circle and the others just outside of it.

This is indeed an expert group, thought Bedard.

Bedard surveyed the dense forest immediately behind them. "Chief Big Bon, do we have more markers?"

"Of course!" The chief then addressed the group. "You will now all see some magic."

Chief Big Bon led the way into the forest along a new path that eventually arrived at a small meadow surrounded by tall trees and light brush.

When all the group had arrived, Chief Big Bon, standing by yet another marker in the ground, said that it was exactly thirteen hundred feet from the target and there had been a sight line cut through the trees.

Tomala asked her husband, "Are you going to shoot from here?"

"No, I would definitely kill someone!"

The group burst into laughter.

Bedard picked out the compound bow again and inspected it carefully. Roanyon tested the wind several times for him.

Bedard stepped up to the line and used a special body movement to pull the string back and sight the arrow. He exhibited an enormous amount of physical effort. He was surprised when the arrow was reported to have again landed inside the six-inch circle.

Some of the group had seen this demonstration before and continued to be very impressed with Bedard's skills and bows. The rest of the group was stunned. Chief Big Bon was shaking his head and looking at Bedard.

Chief Tamburo looked over at Chief Wanso, and they also shook their heads. Johno and Komchowa looked at each other, speechless.

"That is the longest shot I have ever witnessed," Komchowa said.

"I have yet another toy," said Bedard, reaching for the third bag.

Chief Big Bon laughed. "This is the best one."

Bedard lifted up a device with a small bow and Johno and Komchowa both immediately said, "That is a *crossbow*."

Johno was very interested in this new bow. "Chief Wanso said yesterday that we have two of them in storage somewhere."

Chief Roanyon took the special arrow from Bedard and walked over to the line. He put the front of the crossbow on the ground and drew back on the lever to cock the unit. He then called Mot over to help him. Mot was a bit apprehensive again.

"Just like we did it the first time. That's it!"

Chief Roanyon knelt down on the grass with one leg and aimed the device. The arrow release again frightened Mot quite a bit but nothing hit him.

The small girl again ran up to them and reported that the arrow had struck within the eighteen-inch circle.

Bedard and Chief Roanyon were surrounded by the others, who examined the crossbow.

"There are many different designs," explained Chief Roanyon. "The crossbow is slower to use, but for someone who cannot use a longbow because they are not strong enough, the crossbow might be the answer.

After a few moments, Chief Roanyon said, "Perhaps we should return to Tsusnahm now and find a table so that we can examine Copco's arrows. You will all find them interesting."

The group followed Chief Big Bon back to Tsusnahm.

A table was found and placed in the shade of the big tree. Mot placed six arrows on the table. They discussed all of the arrows, including one of Ortho's bone-tipped arrows, for some time.

Bedard held one of the arrows up. "This is the type of arrow that I have been using for some years now. The tip is made from a modern gun bullet such as this one." He pulled a cartridge-type bullet out of his vest pocket. It was relatively soft and would get damaged easily.

"But *this* arrow tip"—here he held up a second arrow—"is relatively new for me. An iron rod with other metals added is heated, cut and milled and then the tip is pointed and smoothed on a forge. Then they heat the tips again to a high temperature, and the properties of the metal mix changes and the metal becomes tempered steel. It is extremely hard, and these tips never break. I do not have many of them left so I try to retrieve them after I use them. A bit tricky sometimes."

They all laughed.

"With my standard longbow, I think that these new arrows travel about thirty percent farther because they are much smoother than the bullet tips. I have worked on feather sets with Robert Doyen, but I still have much to learn."

Melleran grunted. "All of Copco's feather sets are very good. When we last talked, he introduced me to many other feather ideas that I will be experimenting with soon. This is all very interesting. Thank you, Copco."

Johno spoke up. "At both Fort Langley and Fort Victoria there are forges. They seem to concentrate on horse gear, small tools and household utensils. Hopefully, Big John, who is now at Fort Langley learning this trade, will be able to support some of the ideas that we now have thanks to Copco."

"This has been very interesting to all of us," said Tomala. "We also need you to meet with us and discuss guns. In many situations, guns and pistols have a distinct advantage over bows and arrows. We need to understand more about guns and those who use guns exclusively. We have recently seen some examples of modern rifles and pistols, and we would be pleased to hear you talk about the future of these terrible devices."

"Yes," said Chief Tamburo, "this has been very interesting. We also would like you to meet with us, perhaps after dinner tonight, and talk more about the gold rush."

"Of course," said Bedard. "I would be pleased to join you to talk about these ideas."

Chief Roanyon turned and addressed all assembled.

"I am very pleased that you all could take the time to see Copco's equipment. I am certain that Copco will accommodate those of you who wish to examine some of the bows again."

At this, Bedard nodded.

Twenty-One
January 21, 1858 (Late Afternoon)

Wantano walked over to Bedard. "I wonder if you could spare some time now to talk to Art and perhaps the two Spanish prisoners."

"Yes, I was thinking about that," Bedard said. "I wonder if you should ask Oban to join us when we talk with Art."

Wantano nodded. "Of course, that is a good idea. Perhaps we can also include Komchowa. His quietness hides the fact that he is very wise. His size is imposing, and he is well respected in our communities. He speaks almost fluent English."

"We need more Spanish speakers in order to interrogate the Spanish prisoners," said Bedard. "I will speak to Chief Tamburo and ask his advice."

"Very good. I will meet you under the big tree in a few minutes."

Bedard approached Chief Tamburo, who smiled broadly when he saw him.

"That was a fantastic demonstration, Copco. Thank you."

"I think that the most fantastic part of the demonstration," said Bedard, "was Tomala's incredible shot!"

Tomala, who was standing beside her husband, blushed and smiled sweetly.

Bedard then switched to Spanish. "Wantano and I are going to talk to the two Spanish prisoners in about an hour or so. We will be wearing masks to keep us from being recognized. If they were to escape, these criminals might return for revenge. I feel that we need more skilled Spanish speakers for this task. I am going to approach Chief Roanyon. He and I have done this sort of thing together before. I was wondering if any of your party would be useful. It is probably going to be very nasty."

"Tosby speaks Spanish," Tomala said. "He speaks it very well, but he is still a young man."

Chief Tamburo said, "If we are wearing masks, I will go."

Tomala objected. "Masks or not, they will recognize you because of your size and composure."

Bedard had to agree. "I also find myself a bit uncomfortable with your idea. But you could sit in the background, perhaps even behind a curtain, and we could confer with you from time to time if necessary."

"With respect," said Chief Tamburo, "I am not interested in sitting in the background."

Tomala said, "Both Oban and Komchowa are very clever, speak fairly good Spanish and are the same size as you are. Perhaps the three of you should attend this session."

Chief Tamburo looked at Bedard, who considered it for a moment.

"That would definitely work well."

Chief Tamburo said to Tomala, "You know more about our villages than I do!"

"That is why you pay me these huge salaries in gold coins!" said Tomala.

They both laughed and hugged each other.

Bedard smiled and moved over to Mot and Dorono, who were carrying his equipment bags.

"Almost all our experts," said Dorono with a smile, "want to examine your bows and arrows again, so we are going to your building and will examine them there."

Mot said, "We will take very good care of all of the bows, especially those that are in moisture-tight bags."

"Thank you," said Bedard.

As he passed by Chief Roanyon, Bedard said, "Are you interested in taking part in the questioning of the two prisoners? We will be wearing masks and I think that it is going to be interesting. Chief Tamburo, Oban and Komchowa are joining Wantano and me in about an hour from now."

"The chief is going to participate?"

Bedard smiled. "Yes, the three of them are all big men and Oban and Komchowa both apparently speak reasonable Spanish, so it will be a formidable group."

"I will try to attend," Chief Roanyon said, "but I must check with my *secretary* to see that I do not have a *conflict*."

They both laughed. Bedard thought that Mothana was already playing several important roles in the life of the new chief.

Wantano, Oban and Komchowa were waiting for Bedard under the big tree. The four of them moved east up the river side trail until they came to the last building where a warrior with a rifle was standing guard outside with a huge dog on a leash.

Wantano smiled. "We decided that Komchowa would be a quiet but imposing figure and wear a masking hood."

Komchowa smiled as he started to put on the hood. Footsteps were heard behind them, and the group turned around to find Mothana approaching them at a run.

She arrived a bit out of breath. "I wish to attend this meeting, please. I have met Elizabeth Rossford, so I think that I may be of some help in this discussion."

Bedard looked at Wantano, who shrugged. "There is no doubt that she could help us if we have a problem confirming the identity of Art's daughter."

"Thank you for coming, Mothana," said Bedard. "I do not want to insult you, but I must ask you if Chief Roanyon is aware that you are here to help us?"

"Yes," she said smiling. "It was actually he who suggested that I could be useful at the meeting."

Bedard turned to Wantano. "Should she start off wearing a hood?"

Mothana said, "Roanyon suggested that I do that and perhaps take it off later in the discussions if we feel that it might be useful. He also advised me not to speak unless I thought that I had something important to say. Perhaps we can use Musqueam to talk amongst ourselves. I do not think that Art knows our language."

Wantano looked at Bedard and nodded. At that, Komchowa and Mothana put on hoods and the group of four approached the building. The smiling warrior talked to Komchowa briefly and let the dog smell the visitors before they entered.

Art was at a table behind the central fireplace and cooking area in the middle of the big room. Two more warriors and a smaller dog were stationed inside near the door. The dog was also allowed to smell each of the visitors. Komchowa lifted his hood briefly so that the guards could identify him. Bedard suppressed a smile. *Very professional.*

Art was writing, and the only restraint was a metal leg clamp and a short chain to a metal pin in a big six-foot-long log on the floor.

He was startled by the entrance of the group. He had not been told about the meeting in advance. A bench was dragged over in front of the table and Komchowa, Oban and Mothana sat down, with Bedard and Wantano remaining standing to the side.

"Good afternoon Art," said Oban. "How are you?"

Art looked frightened. "What is this about?"

Oban spoke softly.

"Art, you are a prisoner. You need to reflect on that. You should just focus on answering the questions accurately."

He then brought his rifle up, smoothly levered a bullet into the firing chamber and placed it across his lap with both hands in the firing position.

Art contemplated these words for a moment while looking at the hooded Mothana and Komchowa, and noted that all of the men had rifles.

"I am fine, thank you," he said.

"What is your name?" Bedard said. "Your *real* name."

Art looked at Bedard. "I told you before, it is Art Rossland."

Komchowa stood up. He was a big man. He smoothly took his rifle from a side bag attached to a shoulder and chest strap, cocked it and pointed it at Art—all this in an obviously practiced professional movement.

Art stood up. "No, no, no!"

Wantano repeated Bedard's question. "What is your name?"

Art looked down at the table; he was shaking a little. "My name is Art Rossford."

Komchowa sat down again but still held his gun at the ready.

"You have a middle name," said Bedard. "What is it?"

Art stood up again and looked a bit startled. He thought for a moment and sat down. "Ansel. Arthur Ansel Rossford."

Then Wantano spoke. "Your daughter lives in Colville Town. What is her name?"

"No, no," said Art, "she is my niece, the daughter of my brother."

Komchowa stood up and pointed the gun at Art again.

Bedard said, "We have talked to her. Her name is Elizabeth Rossford. She is a very well-respected medical practitioner in Colville Town. She told us that you were her father. You must be very proud of her. She is a very nice person and a real professional, like you are."

Art's head was on the table and he was crying.

Mothana spoke in Musqueam. "I take that for a yes?"

Both Bedard and Wantano sat down and waited for Art to compose himself.

Wantano too spoke Musqueam. "This man is not stupid. He is very skilled and very smart. He survived the corral."

"He is about fifty years old," said Bedard in Musqueam, "and he has been through many trials and tribulations. I think that we should leave now."

"Yes," said Wantano, "we should not rush this. We can have another meeting tomorrow."

Bedard resumed in English. "Oban, please come back to visit Art after dinner and ask him about his life, his family, where he was born. Why his daughter is in Colville Town and where in the world he has visited over the past fifty years, anything like that."

Bedard smiled and said in Musqueam, "Do not talk about why we want this information. We are not ready to negotiate a contract. I think that the only way we will be able to get him to join us is to also have some sort of contract with his daughter."

Oban nodded.

Art was sitting up now looking very sad. The group left. Once outside, Komchowa and Mothana removed their hoods.

As the group was walking back to Tsusnahm, Mothana said, "I wonder if Elizabeth Rossford has a husband or a gentleman friend. I cannot remember. I was not really directly involved with the English community, although I have met with Elizabeth many times. She is very good and always very kind to us, especially to our women and children."

"Well," said Bedard, "if we are successful in creating a contract that we feel would work for Art, we will probably need to visit Elizabeth in Colville Town. We will probably take Art with us."

The group continued down to the big tree where Chief Roanyon and Chief Tamburo were waiting for them. Mothana talked briefly to Chief Roanyon.

Chief Tamburo addressed Wantano. "So how did that go?"

Wantano smiled. "We are now at the beginning. Art confirmed what we had guessed, and Mothana's presence was significant. Art knew that there was a woman present."

Bedard, Chief Roanyon, Chief Tamburo, Oban and Komchowa followed Wantano west through the village to the last building, which had a warrior with a rifle standing guard outside with another huge dog on a leash.

As the group stopped outside to put on their hoods, Chief Tamburo said, "The presence of the dogs in security situations continues to be very useful."

Wantano nodded. "The only downside is that everyone has to be very careful and not move in an abrupt or rapid fashion so as to minimize unfriendly contact."

The warrior talked to Komchowa briefly and let the dog smell the visitors before they entered.

Two more warriors and a smaller dog were again stationed inside near the door. Komchowa was leading the group through the door, and he turned and lifted his hood so that the warriors could briefly see his face. The dog was allowed to smell each of the visitors. Komchowa stayed to talk briefly with the warriors. Bedard smiled. *Again very professional.*

The two Spanish prisoners were tied spread-eagle, face-down on a floor pad. Four warriors moved out of the darkness and untied them. They led them in turn to chairs behind the central fireplace and cooking area in the middle of the big room where their arms and legs were tied to the chairs.

One large bench was moved to a position in front of the two prisoners.

Bedard and Chief Roanyon sat on either side of Wantano on the bench. They lifted their rifles, cocked them and held them on their laps ready to use. The others, all big men, stood behind them with their arms folded. Their rifles were obvious, hanging in side bags or on straps over their shoulders.

There was no doubt that this was all noted by the two Spanish prisoners.

"Do you speak English?" Wantano said.

They looked at each other and one said, "Yes, a little bit, but my friend does not know much English."

"What are your names?"

"My name is Pirano, Joseph Pirano. My friend is Alfonzo Gorrani."

Wantano switched to Spanish. "What is your full name, Pirano?"

They were surprised by the switch to Spanish.

"Joseph Sabastian Torano Ecrano Pirano."

Bedard stood up abruptly and aimed his rifle at Pirano. He too spoke Spanish. "That is not your real name! What is your real name?"

Pirano was very surprised that this other person could speak Spanish.

Gorrani said to Pirano in very rapid Spanish, "You fool, they can all speak Spanish. You must be careful or you will get us both killed."

This was enough for Bedard to pick up Gorrani's accent and Spanish dialect. He swung his rifle toward Alfonzo and spoke to Alfonzo in his Spanish dialect, which was unique.

"Do you know Cristóbal Quintero in Seville?"

Both of the prisoners' jaws dropped.

Chief Roanyon jumped to his feet and pointed his rifle at Pirano.

"Answer the question!" Bedard said.

Both the prisoners were now sweating profusely. It was Gorrani who answered. "Yes, of course, he was the mayor of Seville."

"Yes," said Bedard, "and you live on the southern edge of Seville near Señor Quintero? Be careful that you answer correctly. We obviously have a lot of information about you."

Gorrani slumped forward. "Yes, but not for a number of years."

"How many children do you have?"

"I have four daughters and two sons."

"And your wife and children are all happy and safe?"

"Yes."

"Do you think that we are a threat to your wife and children?"

After a long pause, Gorrani said, "I don't know. Possibly. I hope not"

"You are right to hope," Bedard said. "When you were working for the Wolverine, were you a threat to our wives and children?"

This stunned both men. Gorrani tried to stand up but his bonds prevented him. "No, never!"

"What is your real name, please?"

Alfonso looked at Pirano and then back to Bedard. "My name is Alfonzo Afraid Torano Bellini Gorrani." He looked back to Pirano. "We are first cousins on our mothers' side."

Pirano spoke up. "My real name is Joseph Sillibon Torano Ariana Pirano." He looked at Bedard. "I am sorry."

Wantano spoke softly but with a tone of menace. "You are a prisoner. You need to reflect on that. You should just focus on answering the questions accurately."

The two prisoners nodded their heads.

Both Bedard and Chief Roanyon sat down again.

"And so," said Bedard, "you arrived in this area with the Wolverine, and you participated in the construction of his fort."

They both nodded.

"How did you meet the Wolverine?"

Pirano looked at his cousin. "We helped him build a fortification to the west of San Francisco and followed him after he had to leave that place. When he decided to come up here, he invited us to come along. He paid well, in gold coins. We have sent most of the coins back to our families."

He slumped forward onto his bonds.

"So," said Bedard, "you are hired killers and troublemakers."

Gorrani again tried to stand up. "No, no! We were construction carpenters and workers. We never carried guns. We just did what we were told—anything and everything that they said we should do."

Komchowa growled at them in Spanish. "You were carrying guns when you were captured in the fort."

Pirano said, "There were no bullets in the guns, and we dropped them as soon your warriors entered the fort."

Wantano got up and turned around to the group and spoke in Musqueam. "We must know more about the Wolverine and his instructions to these two people as they left the fort. It is getting late, and I propose that we do that tomorrow."

Everyone nodded and got up to leave.

Wantano and Komchowa spoke to the leader of this small group of warriors.

"We will be back tomorrow with more questions," said Komchowa. "You can reduce the arm and leg binding a bit so that they can be more comfortable, but they are still at risk to escape, and that must not happen." The warrior leader nodded.

"Also," said Wantano, "we do not want them to talk to each other tonight, so perhaps you can now move one to the next building temporarily."

Komchowa nodded. "That will be easy to do."

The group assembled outside and removed the hoods.

Chief Tamburo was thoughtful. "We knew that they were the carpenters in the construction of the corral. I wonder if they also made some of the boats that that group had."

"It would be very helpful if they could share their skills with us," Chief Roanyon said. "The boats that we currently build take a long time to construct and last a long time. It might be useful to learn how to build boats faster using a different design."

"That might also be profitable," said Bedard. "The boats could be sold and *rented* to the gold seekers." Chief Roanyon translated "rented" for Komchowa.

"Perhaps we need two types of boats," said Komchowa. "One for ocean travel and one for river travel."

Bedard thought that Komchowa was a warrior leader and a village elder because he was very smart and wise.

Wantano saw Bedard looking at Komchowa. "No, you cannot recruit him, as he is too valuable to us." All but Komchowa laughed at that. "Copco thought that was a very good idea. He is only now realizing how wise you are."

Incredibly, Komchowa blushed. Komchowa thumped his chest and took a warlike stance. "Me Warrior! Me Kill!"

The group including Komchowa all laughed at this. Komchowa was indeed a big man.

"Copco," said Chief Tamburo, "Komchowa is the great grandson of one of our chiefs. He is one of a number from our two villages that are meeting with Amoroa and Tomala to learn or improve their English and Spanish and to listen to tales of adventure."

Komchowa nodded. "There are about twenty of us including my son." He was obviously very proud of that. "Some of us are pretty old." He looked at Chief Tamburo and they both laughed.

Chief Tamburo rolled his eyes. "Komchowa is the youngest elder that we have ever had."

Bedard and Komchowa looked at each other for a moment. "We will talk," said Bedard.

Then the whole group broke out in laughter. Komchowa was obviously very pleased with the compliment.

"Very good," said Chief Tamburo. "We must leave early tomorrow morning, but any or all of our *support staff* and warriors can stay to clean up loose ends."

"With luck," said Bedard, "Tomara will arrive back from Victoria today and we will be able to plan how to get rid of our other prisoners."

"You have been thinking," said Chief Roanyon, "about the three men from the corral that have escaped to Fort Langley and perhaps beyond."

"Yes, I think that I would like to find out where they are."

They arrived at the big tree to find Mothana and Tomala waiting for them.

"Good, just in time," said Tomala, grabbing her husband and Bedard's arms and leading them away toward the ornate chief's building. Mothana and her husband followed hand in hand, smiling at each other.

"So Mothana," said Chief Roanyon, "Tomara has not arrived back yet?"

She shook her head. "But the lookout tree is active again, and Young Joie arrived about an hour ago. He reported that a small British vessel is just off the coast and will be entering the middle branch of the Fraser River sometime before dusk, so they will anchor somewhere for the night. We have made plans to meet this vessel in case they have information for us."

Tomala was obviously also reporting this information to Bedard and Chief Tamburo, and as Bedard turned around he exchanged thumbs-up signals with Chief Roanyon.

Twenty-Two
January 21, 1858 (Evening)

The late meal had been prepared by Aurora with several others helping, including the usual gaggle of teenaged girls and several men tending the fire. The small group of twelve at the tables included the three chiefs and their wives: Chief Roanyon and Mothana, Old Chief Sparrow and Mother and Bedard and Adrona.

Adrona later reported to Bedard that Mother had a difficult time not being involved in the meal preparation for such an august group. She had first hovered around and then, even though it was still her home, had left the building and disappeared until dinner was announced.

After they were all seated, Old Chief Sparrow rose and, assisted by Mother, addressed the group.

"I have to admit that I am selfish. I could not resist having you all for dinner today because, in talking to Copco for many hours, I now believe that our world is going to change dramatically. We may never again have this chance to meet all together in a peaceful time."

He sat down and Mother stood up.

"I was not happy to find that I was not involved in leading the food preparation today, so I went to one of my favourite thinking places. I now feel that a great weight has been lifted from my shoulders."

Chief Big Bon jumped to his feet and clapped loudly, and the whole group laughed until tears ran down their faces remembering the quotation from Chief Big Bon. All the women, including Aurora from the food preparation area, came for a group hug. Mother was smiling greatly at her success in dealing with what was for her a significant change.

The meal started with a huge fresh salmon followed by Bedard's favourite, prawns, then more fresh salmon. It was excellent.

At the end of the meal, Chief Roanyon got up and invited Aurora to the table where she received enthusiastic clapping. She immediately noted that Tomara and Mothana had also made significant contributions.

Then Chief Roanyon said that he had arranged a meeting down by the big tree for this group and their *support staff*. This continued to attract a small laugh.

"We would all benefit from further discussion of the impact that the gold seekers will have on our nation."

The group was pleased with this and all rose, exited the building and made their way down to the big tree where about thirty people were already gathered.

In due course, they were settled into the now familiar grouping of the three visiting chiefs opposite Chief Roanyon and Old Chief Sparrow, with staff and family seated behind.

Everyone was smiling. Fresh salmon had been served throughout the village.

Chief Roanyon stood with the talking stick and addressed the group.

"We strongly believe that in two or three months a large unorganized group of people will start to pass by our villages and travel up the river. They will be looking for gold. Gold seekers. There will be an incredible number of these people; perhaps they will number as many as twenty thousand people this year, eight times our combined population."

Most of the group had heard this before, but there was still a murmur of discussion.

"I would like to ask Copco to further lead our discussion so that we can better understand the impact that this will have on our nation, both good and bad. It will be useful to gain an understanding of what we must do to protect ourselves and perhaps also to take advantage of some opportunities to profit from these people's needs."

Bedard stood up, took the talking stick and moved over to the speaker's position.

He started by speaking Musqueam.

"I would prefer that if you have a question that you ask it rather than not ask it. I now have a good understanding of this village, some understanding of other villages and of your nation and the nations that surround you. But there is much that I do not know yet."

Bedard smiled. He then decided to switch to English because he thought that his Musqueam was not strong enough to express the thoughts and ideas that he wanted to share with this group.

"What I do know is that England and the United States do not like each other. Both of these very large and complex nations do not have a good record in dealing with native populations. The settlers will come, the governments will come, and they will take all the land that you currently use for hunting, fishing and gathering, and you will be left with almost nothing."

The background noise of ongoing discussion and translation continued.

"You have heard about, and some of you have personally seen, these problems in the United States. Some of the wars between the settlers and some other nations have been just five days' journey to the southeast of us.

"The very large English company, Hudson's Bay Company, has English government control of the large island to the west. They are calling it Vancouver Island. This company also has English government control over what they call the fur industry in these lands that they call New Caledonia. You all know that they have many forts throughout New Caledonia, including, of course, Fort Langley.

"The head man in this area is James Douglas. He lives in Fort Victoria on Vancouver Island. He has always tried to be fair to all of the native peoples his company has encountered. Settlers on Vancouver Island as far north as Colville Town have had problems with the natives, and these problems have mostly been resolved, but not always in favour of the natives. The men that he has running the many forts in this land, including Fort Langley, have been specifically told how to deal with the natives, and they have generally accepted that. It is my understanding that England will soon take stronger control of these lands. I believe that this will be better than if the United States controlled the land.

"Once England takes control of these lands, the settlers will follow rapidly. They will take and occupy almost all of the land. You might object, but you will lose because you do not have enough people to resist them, and you do not understand their government and their laws."

This concept took a long time to translate, and Bedard was not certain that everyone understood it.

Adrona stood up.

"Why are you telling us this? What has this to do with the gold seekers?"

"That is a good question. The simple answer is that more than half of the people who will arrive and travel up the river this year will be United States citizens. This may give the United States a claim to these lands. The English government works very slowly and may not react fast enough to control the land, and there may be a very serious war between these two very powerful nations on this river.

"The complicated answer starts with the fact that although most of the people who arrive here will actually go and mine for gold, many others will be selling services and products to these miners. The mining community will be a complex community. It has already been decided by the Hudson's Bay Company that miners will require a permit from England in order to start mining. These permits are now only issued in Fort Victoria. Since there are many routes that lead up the river, including a well-known route from the southwest to Fort Langley, I think that mining permits will also be issued there in due course.

"The miners will need boats to take them from Fort Vancouver to the Fraser River. Some of these travellers will die because their boats will capsize and they cannot swim, or because they have never been in the wilderness, or because they do not have the skills to hunt for food. Others will die because that do not have enough money to buy food and will starve to death. Still others may meet the wrong people who will take their money and their gold and kill them. Many will die just because they are stupid and do the wrong thing or say the wrong thing to the wrong people.

"The Wolverine, the man who controlled the corral, has killed many people for just looking at him. He is incredibly bad, and I will kill him when I next meet up with him."

The group continued to contemplate this. The translations continued.

"Some of these early travellers will be settlers looking for land to clear and farm similar to the farmlands that Fort Langley has developed in the grassy plains to the south of the fort. A large number will be merchants and business men. Others will be gamblers and generally just bad people who plan to live off the weaknesses and real needs of the miners, settlers, merchants and all the rest of the people here. Not many will stop in your area because the forests are too difficult to clear, but some of the shorelines and the river delta islands may attract some of the more experienced settlers. I think that you should try to stop these early settlers if you can. Once the settlers come in number protected by governments and English guns, you should just go away and let them be. Otherwise, the English will send for more guns and you will die.

"Initially the miners will travel in ones and twos and perhaps in very small groups. There are already about twenty miners panning gold in the river above Fort Hope. Later this year, the miners will be travelling in larger groups in larger boats. Over the next few years there will be more and more people. Not all of these people will speak English. Some will go south again during the summer river-flooding period. Some will stay and wait for the water levels to go down again. Many of the natives will also try to seek gold, and this will soon result in hostility between the natives and the white miners. There will also be conflict between the native fishermen and the miners. Learning how to effectively use the bow and arrow is difficult and time-consuming. Everyone, including natives, will be using rifles and pistols because guns are more effective in killing people."

The group was obviously now upset at all this news, and the chiefs were talking amongst themselves.

Chief Tamburo stood up. "Do you think that we should focus on rifle and pistol shooting skills and abandon the bow and arrow training?"

Bedard and Chief Roanyon looked at each other for a long time.

Bedard looked over at Oban. "You and I know that this is a very difficult question for this nation as represented by these five chiefs. I also know that you must have seen this coming. When was that? When did you decide to specialize and become a gun master?"

"More than twenty years ago," said Oban.

Bedard asked, "How far can a gun shoot a bullet and kill a person?"

The group became very noisy as this idea was not completely supported by several of the group, including Ortho, of course.

Oban smiled. "You know as well as I do, the answer is changing. It seems that this is changing every month. Three years ago, I would have said one hundred and fifty feet. Late last year, I obtained my first breach-loading percussion rifle. They have been on the market for some time now. I found that six hundred feet was fairly easy for a warrior learning this skill. I am a good shot and am very patient. I can now easily shoot very accurately at nine hundred feet."

He smiled and said, "Both you and Chief Roanyon are better than I am, but I practice every day and I am catching up! Then we captured Art Rossford." Oban looked at Bedard who nodded. "He had three rifles that were very new, and I have examined them. In fact, I have taken one apart. They are made by a United States company named Winchester. I have decided that they are still handmade but are being mass-produced. I found small but insignificant errors in the construction of the rifle that I took apart. I was able to easily correct these errors when I reassembled the rifle. This is a huge move forward because the rifles will now be relatively inexpensive to purchase. I hope that I will be able to speak more to Art about these rifles."

Oban looked at the chiefs. "Yesterday morning I took all three guns out to my new shooting range with one of my students." He smiled at Chief Big Bon. "My student, who is a fairly good rifleman now, was hitting the centre one-inch target more than half the time at nine hundred feet." The group gasped. "To my surprise, the rifle that I had reassembled performed the best. I do not have a fourteen-hundred-foot firing range here yet." The group laughed lightly.

Though Bedard knew the answer he asked anyway. "Who is the fairly good rifleman?"

Oban smiled. "Dobera, of course!"

Everyone looked at Dobera, who was studying the ground. Chief Wanso and Amoroa were very pleased with that.

After Oban finished speaking, Bedard continued. "Some of these people will be looking for the gold that has reportedly been found farther up the river above the rapids. The direct route is along the vertical rock cliffs of the canyon past the rapids and, as you all know, this is very difficult and dangerous. The alternate route to the north will take a much longer time. A shorter, easier route may be found. I do not know if or when this will happen. Somehow you must protect yourselves, protect your villages, protect some land so that your sources of water, fish, berries and roots remain available. Initially, these miners will need small boats to cross the water from Fort Victoria to the river.

Some will walk up river trails perhaps needing natives to carry their packs of food, clothing, and tools. Others will use boats to travel up the river and will perhaps need natives to paddle or row their boats. All of these people will need food: fish, meat, berries and so on.

"Other villages and nations will compete with you to service these people. The early merchants that come here will need help in carrying their goods up the river. Some will use mules and horses to carry their goods. Then they will use the larger boats. Very soon all the deer and other animals will be gone from this area. You may have difficulty feeding yourselves."

Bedard was interrupted by Mot, who had gone down to the water's edge a minute ago.

"Boats coming," Mot said. "More than five, probably from the large ship."

Bedard turned to the group. "This is a good place for me to stop tonight. Mot reports boats coming soon, probably from the large ship."

The first of the boats could be seen coming around the river delta island.

Bedard saw something in the first two boats that caused him to turn and run to his home building. He soon emerged holding his short telescope against the door frame. He could now see seven boats in the water. The first two were large canoes from the village and the last five were rowboats from the small vessel *Cobalt,* with three huge boxes in each of them.

He trotted down to the water's edge to join the large group that had moved there.

He touched Chief Roanyon on the arm.

"That is my daughter, Dorthea, at the front of the first canoe. I am guessing that the woman at the front of the second canoe is Art's daughter, Elizabeth Rossford."

Modan arrived at Chief Roanyon's side.

"Modan," said Chief Roanyon, "thank you for being so observant."

Modan nodded. "I assume that one of these English women is Art's daughter. Oban is still with Art. I have sent a warrior over to ask Oban to come here and report to you. We can easily set up temporary accommodation for her in the same building as Art. He is still chained to that log. I do not know who the other English woman is."

Bedard smiled. "She is my daughter. You are very clever. I will leave the setup of her accommodation to you."

Bedard had never seen Modan speechless before. The young man turned and raced off.

Mothana, Mother, Tomala and Amoroa had been talking together and now, as the boats were approaching the shore, they came over to where Bedard and Chief Roanyon were standing.

"The first boat has Copco's daughter at the prow," said Chief Roanyon.

The four women gasped and looked at Bedard, who was smiling greatly.

"Surprise, surprise!" he said.

Chief Roanyon said, "The second boat probably has Elizabeth Rossford at the prow. She is Art Rossford's daughter who Mothana knows from Coleville Town. She is an English medical practitioner, and her father, Art, is a gun master and is currently a prisoner who we are talking with."

They all nodded, very surprised.

Bedard moved down to the water's edge as the first boat arrived. He waded into the water, swept his daughter up in his arms and carried her to the shoreline. She was beaming.

"Please do not be angry with me. Mother and I had a terrible argument two days ago, so I decided to leave and join you. I know that this is going to be very tricky. You are Copco, and who should I be?"

"You are my daughter, Dorthea. You do not need a last name for now. You are more than welcome. You will like all the people here just as they will like you. Your teaching skills are in high demand, so everything is perfect!"

She gave him another big hug and turned to face the very curious crowd. Mothana immediately recognized her, ran to her, gave her a big hug and took her up the beach to the small group of women and introduced her. Bedard followed along.

The first thing that happened was that Dorthea started speaking Musqueam with a local accent and all the women squealed with laughter. Dorthea was a bit startled by this. Tomala said something to her in Spanish, and of course Dorthea replied in Spanish. Amoroa spoke to her in Italian, and Dorthea got it and said in English, "Yes, I have the same disease that my father has."

The group was very happy with this and Bedard gave his daughter a squeeze.

When Dorthea was introduced to Mother, Dorthea stopped and looked at Bedard. Bedard explained that Mother's Musqueam name was very long and for at least five years she had been addressed as Mother.

Mother squeaked and the group laughed.

"More like forty-five years," she said in English, put her hand to her mouth and looked at Bedard, who waggled his finger at her.

Bedard went on to say that she had been, and still is, the mother of this beautiful village of Tsusnahm. Mother was obviously pleased with that.

Modan arrived back. "Copco, Adrona is making the room next to yours suitable for Dorthea."

The second boat had arrived, and the woman was carried to the shore by Dobera who had a good eye for beautiful women, and she was indeed beautiful. Mothana also recognised her and ran down to give her a big hug.

Mothana and Dobera brought her up to the small group of women where she was introduced as Elizabeth Rossford. The group was all smiles and obviously pleased that she had come for a visit. They all spoke English to her, and she was understandably very relieved by that.

Dobera said that he would escort Elizabeth to see her father, and Modan said that he would follow with her baggage. The three moved down to the waterside where all the bags and boxes were being unloaded. Elizabeth identified the three that were hers.

Bedard and Dorthea went down to the water followed by Mothana, Mother, Tomala and Amoroa. There were fifteen huge boxes and steamer trunks and numerous boxes, bags and suitcases.

Dorthea turned to her father. "I had difficulty deciding what to take, so I decided to take everything. Perhaps I can open up a dress shop."

Bedard laughed. The ladies were shaking their heads in amazement.

"I know," Amoroa said in English. "You can give us a fashion show!"

The group laughed. Tomala translated for Mother who was not familiar with the word "fashion." She looked at Dorthea with interest.

Towaba had supervised the unloading, and Bedard asked him if they could have all of Dorthea's things brought up to his building for the time being.

Towaba agreed, and he and his team of six men conferred as to just how the bigger boxes would be moved, as they were very heavy.

Then Bedard and Dorthea walked slowly across the grassy area toward his building.

"I'm sorry this is so sudden," Dorthea said. "Mother was very unpleasant to me, incredibly unpleasant! As far as I was concerned it was a choice of coming to you or returning to England. Of course, if this does not work out, I can always go to England."

"You are here," said Bedard. "Everyone is pleased. I am very pleased. We will see how this plays out. I think that it will be perfect. Your mother and I have had many angry discussions over the years, and that is why we chose, some many years ago, not to associate with each other anymore. I do not think that we will get together again."

Dorthea nodded her head.

"You are about to meet Adrona, who is my very close friend here." He smiled. "I hope that you will like her."

They entered the building. Dorthea had been in similar buildings before.

Coming to meet them were two very pretty women, obviously sisters. One had two babies in her arms. Bedard, speaking Musqueam, introduced the women. Dorthea, also speaking the local dialect, asked what the babies' names were.

Both women were quite startled and Dorthea immediately apologized and continued in Musqueam.

"I am sorry, I have the same appreciation for language as my father. I particularly like your language and have been studying and practicing the various dialects for more than two years near Fort Victoria on Vancouver Island." Looking at Bedard, she laughed and said, "I probably speak it better than him now."

Both women laughed and shook their heads.

Adrona took Bedard's hand. "When you told me about your daughter you forgot to say that she was so beautiful." Then she frowned. "And you certainly did not tell me that she spoke many languages like you do!"

The four of them laughed.

Then Aurora introduced Noua and Basso. "I have the privilege of looking after Noua when Adrona is busy."

Dorthea looked at Adrona. "My father has told me the story of how Noua was named. That is a very good story, and I think that Noua will become a very famous person in this nation."

Adrona gave Dorthea another hug. She was very pleased and happy with these words.

Aurora said, "Noua is already a very famous person in our nation."

The four of them laughed again.

Dorthea said, "I have also met your sister, Aroga, in Victoria, and Cowen too, of course."

Adrona and Aurora were not surprised.

Adrona said, "We have prepared a room for you. There is more work to be done on it tomorrow and perhaps the next day, but I think that it will do for tonight. Please come with me."

She led Dorthea away to the room next to Bedard's. Bedard and Aurora followed. In the meantime, the first of the huge shipment of boxes came.

"Where do you want these?" Towaba asked.

"Just put them over here for now," said Bedard, "and we will arrange them later."

Bedard turned to Adrona and Aurora. "Dorthea will fill this building with her boxes."

Towaba laughed as he went out the door. Over the next hour or so, the fifteen big boxes and twenty-two smaller boxes and suitcases were delivered.

Adrona and Aurora, of course, had never seen anything like this in their lives. Dorothea was not embarrassed as she had gone through this many times before. She searched though the smaller containers, and Bedard moved three of them to her room.

Dorthea spoke with Adrona and Aurora. "I love clothes, and since my father gives me a big allowance, I spend almost all of it on clothes. Amoroa has suggested that I give you all a *fashion show,* which means that I will show you many of my dresses and other clothing. Just for fun."

"What a wonderful idea," said Adrona and Amoroa agreed.

Bedard thought to himself that they really did not know what that meant, but they would like it.

Dorthea was tired from her trip and decided to go directly to bed, which was a large bunch of small fir branches enclosed in a light cloth bag. It looked very comfortable, and she was pleased to find that it was.

Bedard also decided to retire although there were other things that he wanted to do and to know. Tomorrow was another day.

Adrona came in with Noua. "Your daughter is very beautiful. Is it true that she also knows many languages?"

Bedard shrugged. "She has not travelled as much as I have so she does not have as many languages as I do, but those that she knows, and those that she finds interesting, like the mainland and island dialects, are very strong and complete. She obviously finds learning languages very interesting and rewarding like I do."

"This is really none of my business," Adrona said, "but she said that her father gives her a big allowance. What does this mean?"

"I have a lot of money, a lot of gold coins. She is my only daughter, and so whatever she wants she gets. I think that it is fantastic that she has developed strong skills. She is known as a very good teacher. If she wants to stay here for a while, she can make a big contribution to this community."

Adrona nodded and smiled as she removed her top robe and exposed her beautiful breasts.

Bedard always appreciated the show. Noua appreciated it, too. After a few moments, Adrona, still smiling at Bedard's reaction, pulled the top robe over her head to cover herself and Noua.

When Noua finally went to sleep, Adrona moved over with her sleeping blanket and nestled her bare breasts into Bedard's bare body. *This continues to be good.*

Twenty-Three
January 22, 1858
(Morning & Early Afternoon)

The next morning, Adrona escaped before Bedard could capture her to make love, something that he had tried to make part of a pleasurable morning ritual.

Bedard picked up the bags of bows and the arrows that Mot had left for him and went out the front door with the large load. He then picked up some meat for the dogs, put it in a backpack and moved up the path to the ridge trail. Dobera and Bobo were waiting for him there.

Bedard said, "This is a good time to introduce Bobo to my family."

The four dogs were brought in individually to feed. Liz and Bobo hit it off well almost immediately, so they were sent off together.

"I have been working with dogs for about forty years," said Bedard, "and with these four dogs for nine years. I have come to the conclusion that they can talk to each other, but I do not know exactly how they do it. It must be a complicated combination of voice and body language." Dobera just shook his head in wonderment.

"May I join you on your run this morning?" Dobera asked.

"Of course."

Bedard called in all five dogs and sent them out in the usual security net, with Liz and Bobo leading.

Dobera was watching Bobo carefully. "Bobo did not even give me the time of day!" They both laughed.

"Please let me carry some of those bows."

They did some easy body stretches and started off in a medium run.

As they ran, Dobera said, "The small vessel *Cobalt* that arrived last night is going on to Fort Langley this morning. It has quite a large shipment of goods for them plus twelve miners who will disembark there. These men do not include any of the ones that you told us that you were looking for. Tomara was initially very concerned and boarded the ship late last night, and with the captain and some of his crew personally checked out all of the miners.

"The *Cobalt* will return here in two days and will pick up the prisoners. It will stop at Colville Town for coal and then move on to Fort Victoria for an hour or so to pick up some goods. The ship will then make its way south down the coast, stopping at several ports and eventually get to San Francisco. The captain is going to keep the prisoners in chains and turn them over to the authorities there. I assume that if they are not on anyone's list, they will be released, but maybe not." He shrugged.

"Tomara has some information for you. He spoke with Wantano last night. From his reaction, I assumed that it was not critical. He gave Wantano a sealed letter from James Douglas and another from his wife, Amelia. I assume that Wantano will give those to you this morning. Also, I listened in on Oban's report to Chief Roanyon about his discussion with Art which was very positive. Chief Roanyon and Oban agreed to speak with you this morning. I am just full of information this morning. Am I not the perfect *support staff*?"

Bedard nodded with mock gravity. "Absolutely."

"After the morning meal," Dobera said, "you will be busy down at the big tree. Firstly, a short discussion with Wantano and Chief Roanyon on how to handle the two Spanish prisoners, Alfonzo and Joseph, and about who should go to the planned morning meeting with them. Secondly, a further meeting with Oban and Chief Roanyon on how to handle Art and his daughter. And don't forget to pick up the two letters from Fort Victoria that Wantano has for you.

"And finally, my father and Chief Tamburo left last night with their *security warriors*, but their wives, their three sons, and a few of our warriors are still here. Tosby, who you will recall is Tamburo's young son, has been involved with Modan and Towaba and their group who are training the security dogs here. He, like Mot, enjoys being with dogs, and he has trained many hunting and family dogs in our villages. He is the only one who can work with Bobo other than me. He is very excited and will probably return home today so he can start a dog security training program for our villages."

Bedard's run was a short one that allowed him to place the bows and arrows under his hidden boats. When they returned to the path leading back to Tsusnahm, he stopped and called the dogs in for a scratch. Bobo was still quite frisky with Liz, but Dobera managed to get him to follow him back to the village. Bedard was quite impressed with Bobo and said so. Dobera was pleased with that.

When Bedard returned home, he found that Dorthea was up and seated at a table near the central cooking area. She got up and gave him a big hug. She had on a dark dress and a Cowichan sweater that was obviously custom-made for her figure.

"I had a great sleep last night on that beautiful bed that Adrona and Aurora made for me. I am going to try to get used to the daily routine here. Do you always go out for a run in the morning?"

"I try to run in the morning, although sometimes I run at night. I try to feed my family every morning. You must meet my other two dogs, Haus and JoJo."

She nodded.

"I think that you will find that Tsusnahm in general, and this home in particular, does not have much of a daily routine. There are not many people who live in this village, and they are all busy doing something all day long. Although they do have some artists and some specialty crafts persons, including clothing makers, even these people might also be fishermen and gatherers. For example, my friend, Chief Roanyon, is an expert with knives. He is often found cleaning and filleting fish, which he does very rapidly, three times faster than anyone else here. Therefore, that is a reasonable job for him in spite of the fact that he is the chief of this village."

Dorthea thought for a moment and then put on an obviously phoney pout.

"They," she said, pointing to Adrona and Aurora, "would not let me help with the morning meal!"

Adrona laughed. "Guests get one free day from work! We are expecting Tomala and Amoroa to join us for the morning meal in a moment. Mothana said that she would be a bit late because of her *secretarial duties*. And Mother said that she was having difficulty getting up now that the old chief did not have as much to do in the morning."

That amused Bedard.

Dorthea obviously didn't get it and looked at Bedard, who switched to French.

"The old coot is still pretty active in bed."

Dorthea put her hand to her mouth to stifle a laugh. The other two women laughed again and shrugged their shoulders, appreciating what Bedard had discreetly told Dorthea.

Then Tomala and Amoroa arrived, and there were hugs and smiles all around. Dorthea again praised the sleep she had in the bed the sisters had prepared for her.

"Yes," Tomala said, "these two have many skills."

Food was offered, and the group sat down at the long table, and Bedard and Dorthea were asked to sit at the ends. Mothana and, incredibly, Mother, who was looking very fresh, joined the group before the meal was ended, and both hugged Dorthea and had a small morning snack.

"This is a very powerful group," Mother said, "and there was no way I was going be absent from this *meeting*. I woke him up early!"

She looked at Bedard with her eyebrows raised—there was a great deal of smirking among the group.

Soon the discussion came around to the schools that had been established in the three villages. Tomala and Amoroa described the three schools for their young children that now had been running for about four years.

"We both have visited other English schools in our travels," said Amoroa, "but there is no person in any of the villages that has any experience as a teacher. We know that our *curriculum* and our *teaching methods* are very basic."

Tomala nodded. "We have recently started classes in English and Spanish, and we were very surprised at the men and women who turned out, including Komchowa and his older son."

Bedard turned to Dorthea. "Komchowa is a very large man, a warrior leader, a wise man and a village elder. He has done some travel and has a good basic start in both of those languages."

"Yes," said Tomala, "we try to include stories of some of our travels into this program, and that is well appreciated by the group that now numbers about twenty." She looked at Amoroa who nodded.

Amoroa said, "We are very pleased that you have come to visit your father. We were astounded at your language skills but now, having a bit of time to think about it, we understand how this comes to be. Your father is very handsome, so it is not surprising to us that you are very beautiful."

Dorthea blushed at that.

"You are a teacher," Amoroa said, "and that, of course, was of great interest to us."

"Well," said Dorthea, "my father thinks that I have several pieces of furniture in my boxes." She swung her hand around at the many boxes behind her. "So he thinks that I may stay for a while."

The group was amused by this.

"I received my education in England, and because I have a mind similar to my father's, I became a teacher at the fairly young age of fifteen. I then went to work at a private English school developed by my father in London, England, that specializes in teaching people who have never been to school before. Some of my students were in their twenties."

Bedard nodded.

"I own buildings in an area of London that is very poor," he said. "Most of the people who live in these buildings have never been to school. I started a school because I believe that this is the only way to become not poor. The concept of going to school was very difficult to sell to many of these poor families."

Tomala and Amoroa agreed. Some discussion evolved because the idea of being poor was not familiar to all of the group.

Dorthea said, "I have subsequently taught for about seven years in four other places in the world: one short term in Spain and then three other English places, including a school near Fort Victoria. I have been at that school for two and a half years. During that time, Cowen and Aroga introduced me to Chief Cobalt. About one year ago the chief asked me to start a school in their village because my understanding of his dialect was quite good by that time."

She looked at her father and shrugged her shoulders. He smiled.

Mothana, Mother, Tomala and Amoroa looked at each other and were astounded.

"And so," said Dorthea, "I would be pleased and honoured to participate in this project. Children everywhere are very eager to learn, and above all I enjoy sharing knowledge with them."

Just then, Towaba burst in through the door and said that Bedard was urgently requested to go down to the big tree to see Chief Roanyon.

Bedard rushed off.

The seven women continued to talk. Tomala and Amoroa decided that they would go home just after the midday meal. Mother beamed and said that that would be at her place.

"Politics, politics!" said Mothana.

Mother blushed, but it was obvious to Dorthea that she enjoyed the banter.

"I will visit Mahli and Stsulawh," said Dorthea, "just as soon as I have settled in and unpacked my furniture."

Bedard followed Towaba down to the big tree where Chief Roanyon was talking to a group of twenty warriors armed with rifles and bows.

Seeing Bedard, Chief Roanyon turned to him. "The man in our local lookout tree has sighted a canoe coming slowly downstream from the east on the north side of the river with three white men paddling it. They are keeping very close to the shore and the overhanging brush. I think that they know that we have a lookout tree here. They have rifles. They may be our friends from the corral."

Bedard looked around at the group. "We should go upstream and see if we can intercept them, but we cannot leave the village unprotected. They may want to capture our prisoners. They may have other men coming here from another direction. Can you contact the other lookout tree?"

"Yes," said Chief Roanyon. "Our Morse code system is not perfect, but we have had several tests and it has been operational for two days now. They already know about the canoe."

"Good," said Bedard. "I will take three warriors with me and try to deal with this canoe. If we had a Morse signal bowl with us, we could be in contact with our lookout tree. Wantano, will you come with me?"

"Yes, of course!"

Bedard turned to him. "You pick two others."

Chief Roanyon said, "We will close up the buildings and set up three warrior teams to protect the village. I think that I will also try to contact Mahli and Stsulawh directly and see if they have any ideas. I suspect that they have already taken some action because of the remaining visitors that we have here."

Bedard nodded, and the four men moved off rapidly to the east. Bedard called in Liz and Hy to help and sent both of them forward in a long and short defensive pattern. He stopped to pick up one of his bows, a quiver, a rifle and a few bullets from his hiding place. Wantano contacted the lookout tree during this brief stop, and it was reported that the canoe was still about a mile upstream, still moving slowly and keeping to the north shore of the river and to the north side of the large island there.

"We will go farther east to the small landing where we found Noua. It is not very far from here. I think that that is where they may be heading. You must be very careful. These are very experienced killers. We have two options: kill them just as they are landing or kill them just after they pass by us."

The men nodded and moved off at a fast run.

The group soon arrived at the small landing; Bedard left Hy on the trail to the east and placed Liz near the water just east of the landing. He chose three hiding places for his team, gave them further instructions and moved upstream near the water to join Liz.

He heard the boat. Bedard could see that it was indeed his three enemies: Tommy Hunter, also known as the Wolverine, and his two partners, Bill Lomax and Bill Thompson.

Lomax was paddling in the stern with Thompson in the bow. The Wolverine was in the middle of the small canoe with his rifle aimed at the shoreline. They were definitely going to come in at the small landing.

Just as the canoe touched the sand, two rifle shots hit the heads of Thompson and the Wolverine. The stern paddler, Lomax, must have seen movement in the brush because he slipped rapidly over the side of the canoe near the stern and into the water.

No one on the team moved. Bedard heard a third rifle shot from Wantano, who had been positioned downstream from the landing.

"Got him," yelled Wantano.

Bedard advanced toward the canoe with Liz, checked the two men in the boat and, joining the other two warriors, ran west along the path for a short distance. The three of them then went through the light bush toward the water and helped Wantano pull the dead Lomax from the water.

"That was a very good shot, Wantano!" said Bedard.

Wantano was smiling. "I think that the bullet skipped once on the water."

The other two warriors laughed.

"Let's contact the others," said Bedard, "and see if there is any news."

After a long communication with the lookout tree, Bedard looked pleased.

"The lookout tree has observed the short battle and has already reported this to Tsusnahm. No further enemies have been sighted yet. Mahli and Stsulawh have sent more than two hundred warriors down to help, and the village is overrun with people. Everyone in Tsusnahm heard the gunfire and is now preparing for a victory lunch supported by four boatloads of food that came down with the warriors!"

"We can bring the dead enemies down to Tsusnahm in their canoe," said Wantano, "rather than leaving them for the animals to eat. There are two paddles still in the canoe."

Bedard agreed and sent two warriors back for the canoe.

Bedard and Wantano talked about this new adventure and agreed that they were very fortunate to have such quick success against such formidable adversaries.

"Lomax's escape over the back of the canoe is a good indication of his experience and the high level of his skills," said Bedard.

Wantano nodded. "I am not certain that I could have moved that fast," he said, still in deep thought.

The canoe arrived and they loaded Lomax's body into it.

Wantano and Bedard followed the trail back at a medium run, stopping only to hide Bedard's bow, quiver and rifle again

At the village they were welcomed like returning heroes. The boat and its cargo had arrived before them, and the experts had noted the locations of the single shot that killed each of them. The village was overrun with people.

Chief Tamburo and Chief Wanso were amongst the first to congratulate Bedard and Wantano as they arrived under the big tree.

Chief Roanyon also arrived smiling, and Bedard said, "I am still uncomfortable with the idea that there are only three men. Surely they did not think that they could recover the men we captured without help."

"We have three teams of four warriors, each under the supervision of Komchowa over on the south side of the river," said Chief Roanyon, "and they will stay there for at least two days, monitoring that area and the trail leading to Fort Langley. They will search the south side of the big island. We also have two teams of hunter-trackers with dogs led by Fenciao searching the island beyond Skwis and one team of hunter-trackers, also with a dog, searching this side of the big island."

The group moved off toward Mother's for the midday meal as Chief Roanyon continued to brief Bedard.

"We have had several meetings today, and one of the ideas was to create a third and perhaps even a fourth lookout tree on the south side of the river. It is thought that this will be useful to monitor the gold seekers later this year."

The group seated around Bedard and the three chiefs had expanded to include other notables, including Chief Big Bon, other warrior leaders and *support staff*.

"The three bodies have been moved to the east edge of the village," said Wantano. "We need to show the bodies to our prisoners so that they know that these terrible men will not be part of their lives again. We think that Art, both the Spaniards and most of our other prisoners are very worried that the Wolverine will find them and kill them."

"That is a good idea," Bedard said. "I am still concerned that there are several groups of the Wolverine's men on the islands opposite us watching for an opportunity to recapture the prisoners."

"If there are men there," said Chief Roanyon, "we will find them and deal with them today."

Wantano said, "I have two letters from Fort Victoria for you, Copco, and Tomara is here somewhere and wishes to talk to you."

Bedard took the letters and, having finished his meal, thanked Mother and left the building.

The letter from James Douglas was short. He was going to try to deal with the Haida camped near the fort, but he thought that they would only move up the coast and not return home. He was sorry to lose Dorthea, who he said was a very good teacher. The letter also included a new list from England, and Bedard noted the addition of two more names, both of which he recognized.

This did not put him in a good mood.

The letter from Amelia was also short, bemoaning the loss of Dorthea and reporting that Donna, in hindsight, had finally realzed that she had again made a terrible family mistake. This pleased Bedard and he resolved not to make a similar mistake, so that he could get to know his incredible daughter before they possibly parted ways at the end of the year.

He returned to the group gathering again under the tree to find that Dorono was assembling a small team to pick up the three bodies to show them to the prisoners.

"Dorono," said Bedard, "what is the name of the cook?"

"I think it is David."

"I am going to see Art and Elizabeth now. Bring David over to their place, please. Leave him with the guard outside the building. I want to talk to him before I go in."

Dorono nodded. "That will be easy to do as we are leaving now."

Wantano arrived with Tomara who said, "I talked to Cowen briefly, and he said that he would be coming over later this week with Aroga and that about five or six other warriors would follow early next week. The two warriors who went over with me were novice sailors but learned very rapidly, and we almost beat our previous trip time back here. It was again great fun for me and for them. They told me that they had walked through the small Haida camp of about six families near Fort Victoria and did not see any rifles or pistols, so they assumed that they were hidden. They did not like that. Just as we were leaving, this Haida group was in the process of breaking camp and the warriors found out from one of the children that they were moving somewhere farther north."

"Thank you, Tomara," said Bedard. "We must do that trip to Fort Victoria again sometime." They both smiled.

Chief Roanyon came up to Bedard just as Tomara left.

"We need to see the two Spanish prisoners again. Wantano has talked with them this morning and found that they were left behind because they were not needed anymore. The Wolverine said that he was not going to build anything. They think that they can adapt what they are calling a "British boat" for use in these waters. They made a few of these lightweight boats in Corsica when they were younger."

Wantano said, "I went for a walk with them on the path along the river to give them some exercise after being tied up for so long and decided that they did not have any wilderness skills whatsoever. They were always searching the forest for danger. When we returned to their building I posted more guards and cut all of their bonds. I then found them some paper, pen and ink so that they could try to draw the boat from memory. Apparently, they were used to creating things from drawings. I also arranged for two of our senior boat builders, who both speak some English, to visit with them and talk about the lightweight boat project. They were both very excited about that."

"That is a good plan," said Bedard. "We should visit them again today and see how the drawings are coming along. It is good to understand why they were left behind. With no wilderness skills, the Wolverine would have no use for them. We also need to talk about what kind of contract we should try to negotiate with them."

"Yes," said Wantano. "Chief Roanyon and I have been discussing that, and we have some ideas."

The chief nodded.

"Now," said Wantano, "Oban here has a report for you on his meeting with Art last night."

"Yes," said Oban. "It was very enjoyable. Art was relaxed and talked readily about his life. He is from a town on the east coast of England north of Lancaster called Halton. His father had a horse tack business: saddles, stirrups, bridles, halters, reins, bits and so on. It was fairly successful, and he and his brother became involved in the business at an early age.

"Art liked the mechanical part of the business and eventually apprenticed to become a blacksmith and iron forger. With the very large forest to the east, Bowland Forest, the family business supporting the horsemen prospered. Art soon became interested in shotguns and rifles and started to specialize in those. Then his father died and his mother soon after. His brother was not strong enough to run the tack business, so the family business was sold and Art was on his own.

"The disaster continued, and Art's wife died. His son was newly married and doing well and his daughter, Elizabeth, moved to Lancaster to live with relatives. He had always wanted to see the United States and so he immigrated there. He was forty-two years old. He readily found jobs in the small gun industry and enjoyed that. In ten years, he found himself in San Francisco and did a bit of gold panning.

He met up with Tommy Hunter and was hired to buy and service the best pistols and rifles available to Hunter's team. He could do that and still do some hunting and fishing on his own, something that he really liked to do, especially in the wilderness to the east of this large town. Hunter invited him north. The pay was very good, so he travelled up here to join him, but when he found out what they were planning to do he attempted to escape and failed. As far as he knew, his daughter did not know that he was here. He was very surprised when she arrived, needless to say!"

"Thank you, Oban," said Bedard. "That was a good report. I would now like you and Wantano to join me in a visit to Art and Elizabeth."

"Yes," said Chief Roanyon, "Mothana and I would like to join you."

"Of course," said Bedard. "That would be very good. We might be able to work out contracts with both Art and Elizabeth."

Twenty-Four
January 22, 1858 (Afternoon)

The group started to walk east toward the building that currently housed Art and Elizabeth. This area was a very popular area of the village. Previous generations had planted shrubs and flowers and arranged sitting logs to take advantage of the long water view of the junction of the north and middle arms of the river. The flowers weren't in bloom, of course—not in January. The weather continued to be cool but the sky was clear and sunny.

As they walked, Bedard asked Chief Roanyon, "Do you have any ideas about what type of a contract would work in this very unusual situation?"

"Mothana has been working on that problem."

"First of all," said Mothana, "we need to offer accommodation and food and any other simple utilities that he needs: blankets, clothing, cooking utensils and so on. He is a hunter, and he may want to augment the food from time to time, especially since he apparently enjoys hunting and fishing in the wilderness, and we have quite a bit of that here. Oban and he will work together initially and will probably become friends." She looked over at Oban who smiled and nodded. "They will, no doubt, develop a base of professional and technical respect. Oban will introduce Art to other gun masters in this area. There are several in the Squamish villages to the north of us. I sense that this will be pleasing to everyone.

"We need modern rifles, and we should be able to increase his personal collection of rifles and pistols on a regular basis. We need to ask him what a reasonable compensation over and above his accommodation and food would be. For Elizabeth, I do not have any great ideas; perhaps we can offer her a monthly stipend of some sort, something simple."

They had arrived at the building where David was waiting with one of the warriors from his building. Bedard stopped and said that he was going to talk to David before they entered. There was a pair of sitting logs not far from the building near the water and the group moved over to those.

Bedard went up to David. "We have met briefly before. My name is Copco, and my home is in London, England. What is your name?"

David looked very sad and weary. His clothes were torn and his face was dirty. He looked at Bedard and said nothing. Bedard took the small lead rope from the warrior and untied David's hands. He took David's arm and led him over to the logs where the others were sitting. When David sat down, Bedard undid the ropes that hobbled David's legs, moved back a few feet and sat on his knees facing him.

"Your name is David and you come from a town on the east coast of England north of Lancaster, called Halton."

David looked sadder. "You have talked to Art."

"No," said Bedard. "I have not talked to Art about you. I am a linguist of sorts and I determined that you have the same accent as Art, and therefore you come from the same town as he does."

"I do not believe you," David said.

Bedard shrugged. "I also assume that you know Elizabeth."

At this David jumped to his feet, startled. "Where is she? What have you done with her?"

"These people are from this village of Tsusnahm," Bedard said, "and they all speak English. We have met Elizabeth and have great respect for her courage and her skills."

"Yes," said Chief Roanyon, "I am the Chief of Tsusnahm. Elizabeth is an honoured visitor to our village and is now staying with her father here."

David sat down.

"I have undone your cords," Bedard said, "but you are still a prisoner here. You need to reflect on that and answer our questions, please. What is your name?"

David thought for a moment.

"David, David Anderson," he said. "And yes, I come from Halton. And yes, I know Elizabeth very well. I was, and I still am in love with her, but alas…"

He dropped his head and tears came to his eyes.

Bedard switched to Musqueam and addressed Wantano. "Can you have your people clean him up a bit? Perhaps some clothing would help. And then bring him back here and come get me out of the building."

Wantano called over both guards and the big dog and gave the men instructions. They went off with David.

Bedard led the group into the building. It was similar in nature to the other longhouses in the village, with rooms along the sides of the building enclosed with curtains and a central heating and cooking area. There were no warriors standing inside the door, but Bedard knew that there were two with a dog somewhere in the building.

Art and Elizabeth were sitting at the table behind the cooking area. There were no bonds on Art.

Elizabeth stood up. "I wondered when you would visit."

Bedard introduced himself and the others to Art. They all shook hands. Elizabeth had met all of the visitors yesterday upon her arrival, but it was good for her to hear their names again.

"I live in London," Bedard said, "and I am visiting this beautiful area for a year or so."

He turned to Elizabeth. "You have met my daughter, Dorthea, who came on the boat with you yesterday."

Elizabeth nodded.

"And your father," Bedard said, "has no doubt told you the story of his recent adventure." He looked at Art. "The *true* version, I hope?"

Art dropped his head.

"Yes, the true version. I have nothing to hide from her. I want desperately to be with her, and she knows that. We think that this beautiful village is a good place to start to get to know each other again."

Elizabeth went to her father, sat down and took his hand.

"Elizabeth," Bedard said, "as you know, Oban spoke with your father for two hours just before you arrived yesterday. So, we have an outline of his life after the disasters that befell your family back in Halton. How did you end up in Colville Town?"

"I was living in Lancaster with relatives. They were very good to me, and when I showed an interest in medicine they encouraged me to become a nurse. It was not a great occupation, but I could not become a doctor so I became a nurse. I worked very hard and enjoyed it best when I actually helped a doctor do his work. I then became friends with an older nurse who had just returned from the Crimean War and was pioneering modern nursing along with a number of other nurses with Crimean experience. We both worked directly for Doctor Ryan, who soon married my friend.

"Soon after, I met and married a coal mine manager. Just after we were married, he was recruited to work as the manager of a coal mine incredibly far away in Colville Town. I thought that it would be a great adventure. We were both well received by the small community of Colville Town, and I found work with the Hudson's Bay Company doctor who was living there. My husband unfortunately died in the first year, and I was miserable for some time. But I decided to stay for a while. Then, to my amazement, I heard that my father was close by and in some sort of trouble. I decided to come over to see him and help if I could."

"Elizabeth," Chief Roanyon said, "the community here would like you both to stay in beautiful Tsusnahm. Our nation and other nations nearby all have gun masters. We believe that guns will soon be replacing bows, and we must continue to protect ourselves. We would benefit by having Art in our community helping and teaching. We also need more modern medical help, and so we would also benefit by having you, Elizabeth, in our community helping and teaching."

"We have many specialists in our community," said Mothana, "and we would like to make some sort of agreement or contract with the two of you. Art is a special consideration in that he was our enemy last week and he is still our prisoner. But we appreciate his skills, and we know that he was kept at Tommy Hunter's fort by intimidation. We do not think that he is a threat to us now."

"Furthermore," Bedard said, "today we killed Tommy Hunter, Bill Lomax and Bill Thompson."

Art jumped up. "I must see them."

"Come with me," said Wantano, and the two men left the building.

At the same time, a warrior came in and approached Bedard, saying that the man was now outside.

Bedard excused himself and went out to meet David, who looked like a different person.

The man smiled. "Thank you. I feel much better now."

Bedard brought David in to meet Elizabeth. They both stared at each other, and David collapsed onto the floor sobbing. Elizabeth went to his side and helped him up onto a bench. It was some time before David calmed down.

"Oh David," Elizabeth said, "Dad told me that you were here somewhere, so I am not surprised to see you."

"I am sorry," David said. "I also knew that you were here, but I just could not help myself."

Art returned with a small smile and joined Elizabeth on the bench. He nodded at David.

"David," Bedard said, "we need to know who you are and why you are here."

David looked at Bedard for a moment and then at Elizabeth and Art. He lowered his head.

"My father is a veterinarian in Halton and has a good practice that includes boarding hunting horses and occasionally racing horses. My three younger brothers and I were involved in the business from a young age. Dad wanted me to become a horse vet so I did, but I didn't like it much. I liked the small animals: cats, dogs, sheep, even rabbits."

He stopped for a moment and smiled at Elizabeth.

"Then when I was about nineteen, we were constructing a new barn and my mother took over the project and added large windows to one corner of the building. When it was finished, she said that this was my space to provide vet services to my small animals. I built some outside cages and dog-run cages and moved all my inside cages over to the new space. It was fantastic! Then I met Elizabeth and my world turned upside down."

He looked at Elizabeth again and smiled. "I think that I can talk about it now."

Elizabeth said, "You don't need to talk about it if you don't want to."

"I fell in love with her, but she did not feel the same way toward me. In any case, I left home suddenly and moved to Lancaster to be closer to her. My parents were not happy. I started up a vet service for small animals there, and many of my Halton clients followed me. Halton was not far away from Lancaster. Then I managed to get a part time job in the small clinic where Elizabeth worked. At first I did all the gopher work: cleaning, taking out the garbage, making the beds, emptying the bed pans—just like a nurse in the large hospitals."

"He was, and is," said Elizabeth, "a very nice person, and our friendship continued, but it was not going to develop further. I made certain that he knew that. Doctor Ryan knew that he was a vet and found out that he had very strong and sensitive hands and a great deal of knowledge and skill that was easily transferrable to working with human problems. Dr. Ryan soon added David to his medical support staff, and David showed how clever and skilful he was." She smiled at him again.

"Then she got married," David said. "It almost killed me! I returned home and suffered the verbal abuse from my father. My mother, who understood what I had been going through, said that I should start up my small animal vet service again. Then I heard that Elizabeth had left the country to go to a place I had never heard of before. She was gone, and I did not even have a chance to say goodbye."

It was Elizabeth's turn to look at the floor. "I'm so sorry, David."

"I travelled to Liverpool," said David, "and went to the library and found some maps and studied them. It was obvious that travelling through Upper and Lower Canada would not work. The United States had an immigrant recruitment service in Liverpool, so I went there and signed up.

"I then went to a pub near the recruitment centre and talked to some people who had been to the United States and found that I could go directly to San Francisco and then up the coast by boat to a place they called Fort Victoria, which I knew was near Colville Town. I also determined that they were shipping work horses from Liverpool to San Francisco, so I scoured the wharfs until I found some horse pens and a boat that looked like it was about to load some horses.

"I found a huge sailor on the boat who looked like he was in charge. When I said I was a vet, he hired me on the spot at a very good salary and told me to go down to the pen and look over the horses. As it happens, on the last trip, half of the horses died and the rest were sold at auction in San Francisco for a pittance. He and the crew were paid by a share of the profit from the sale of the horses, so they did not want that to happen again.

"I briefly inspected the horses in the pen. It was easy to see that many of them were malnourished and some had nasty gashes on their legs and backs. I went back to the boat and the huge sailor took me to see the captain, and I reported what I saw to him.

"The captain was furious and took some of his sailors down onto the dock and went in search of the horse salesman. To make a long story short, the salesman avoided a significant beating, perhaps even death, by promising to provide eighty perfect horses within two hours. Which he did. I examined them all one by one as they were being loaded by slings onto the boat, and only rejected six. In the course of the three-month voyage around Cape Horn to San Francisco, we lost only two more. The horses were judged to be in premium shape when we arrived in San Francisco and earned very good prices at the auction. I received a bonus, and afterwards, at the bar to celebrate our success, the crew collected another two hundred dollars for me. I was quite rich and pleased with myself.

"The gold rush was on, of course, and I tried some panning, but it was hard work. I then ran into Tommy Hunter who had some horses running grinding mills and needed some help. His cook disappeared one day so I started to do that, too. He paid well, and when he decided to go north he invited me along, saying that he planned to have a number of horses or donkeys hauling goods up the river to the goldfields, and I could start off by being the cook. I thought that I could somehow make my way over to Colville Town to visit Elizabeth, but that was not to be. I did not have any experience living in the wilderness so I just kept quiet, did what I was told to do and cooked as best as I could. You know the rest."

Elizabeth turned and met Bedard's gaze. "David would be very useful working with me. He is skilled in some areas of medicine that I am not." She smiled. "Also, you have a great number of dogs and he could monitor their health as well."

Art was sombre. "Are you certain that this is what you want?"

"Dad, David has a problem. If he does not find a way to fit into this community, he will be sent back to San Francisco, and that might be a disaster for him."

Chief Roanyon said, "We would be pleased to have all three of you join our community. But as we said before, we need some sort of contract to protect us and to protect you. We are willing to provide sleeping space, shared living space and meals plus some reasonable additional compensation for your services. Perhaps you can talk about that before we meet again. David, if you will come with me, I will show you a room in the adjoining building that you can call home."

"David," Elizabeth said, "please come for breakfast tomorrow morning, and we will talk together."

David gave her a big smile. "Thank you, Elizabeth." He turned and followed the villagers out the door.

Mothana stayed behind briefly. "You may need some more cooking utensils and other useful items. I will return shortly with some. Meanwhile, you can make a list of other items that you could use. We are not a very sophisticated society here, but we will try to provide whatever you need."

Elizabeth smiled and came over and gave her a big hug.

David was shown to a room in the next building with a new fir-bough mattress bag that he tried immediately and liked. He examined the big bearskin blanket.

"I hope that I do not have to kill any animals. This blanket is going to be very difficult for me to use."

"We will assume that this is your room for now," Chief Roanyon said. "If there is a change it will happen tomorrow. We will gradually assemble some clothing and other useful things, like a bowl for water. I think that we have some Hudson's Bay blankets that we can lend you instead of this bearskin blanket. Perhaps you can buy some blankets next month. In about two hours, someone will come here and bring you to another building for dinner. As the first week progresses, you will understand how to live in this village. I hope that you will enjoy yourself."

They shook hands and Chief Roanyon left to join the other four waiting outside the door.

"I think that went very well," Mothana said. "Copco, it was quite remarkable that you identified David from his accent. I now realise that there are many aspects to the language skills that you and your daughter have that you can use to your benefit and ours. You used these same skills when you were talking with the two Spaniards. Amazing!"

"Yes," Bedard said, "it can be a lot of fun sometimes."

Oban said, "Do you plan to visit with the two Spaniards now or after the late meal?"

"I think now," Bedard said. "It should not take very much time. We can all go there directly and then go to eat."

They all agreed and moved off through the village to the building where Alfonzo and Joseph were currently being held. Bedard liked this end of the village. There was a wide variety of vegetation growing in the mucky inter-tidal land, and this attracted a great number of birds and small animals.

The front door of this longhouse was not guarded from the outside, but there were four warriors and two dogs on the inside of the building. Wantano had a few words with the warrior inside the front door, who had his dog sniff all the visitors.

Alfonzo and Joseph were sitting at a table covered with paper behind the cooking area. They stood up to meet their visitors. They had no bonds.

Wantano said to them, "You met some of our boat builders today. How did that go?"

"It was very interesting," Alfonzo said. "We had, of course, seen some of their boats and had previously decided that they were made by expert craftsmen. So that is where we started. Surprisingly, one of the builders actually spoke a bit of French and Spanish, so we were able to communicate in a mish-mash of languages and enjoyed our time with them immensely."

Both Alfonzo and Joseph were smiling and nodding their heads.

"The builders reported that they had experimented with what they called plank boats several times, and then proceeded to allow us to draw out their designs. We had been working on our design from memory and not having much success, so this was exciting for us. The designs were very good, and after about two hours we had a drawing that we really liked." He pointed to the table. "Joseph and I have been playing with the plan all day, and we are very pleased with the result. We are looking forward to meeting with the boat builders tomorrow morning. They said that they would take us, with your permission, of course, to the place where the construction occurs. Then we can start immediately to build the first"—he switched to Spanish—"*new plank boat.*"

Chief Roanyon talked to them about joining the community and the need for some sort of work agreement. He went on to identify the services that would be provided to them, including meals, and suggested that he would be willing to provide some additional compensation.

"Perhaps you can talk about that before we meet again. In the meantime, we would like you to move to another building now."

The two Spaniards followed the local group out the door, and in due course entered the same building where they had relocated David. David stood up immediately and the three men greeted each other in Spanish and shook hands.

Bedard, who was the first in the door, was surprised at that.

"Tell me David, how many languages do you know?"

It was Alfonzo who answered.

"He has French, Spanish and a bit of Italian and a bit of English."

David looked embarrassed.

"My family have a summer home in Southern France near Nice that we went to for years and years. So, I learned French and, in addition, took French in school. Italy was only forty miles away so I picked up a bit of Italian, too. In my last year of school, we studied both Italian and Spanish because, as you know, they are so similar to French. I really enjoyed learning them. At the fort the three of us often talked about..." He paused, looking at Alfonzo and Joseph. "Well, the *world.*"

The two Spaniards looked at him and nodded.

Bedard shook his head.

Alfonzo and Joseph were shown to rooms in the building. They both tried the mattress bags and were very pleased. They examined the big bearskin blankets, and both liked them very much.

"Dinner will be in less than one hour. Someone will come here and accompany you. I hope that you will enjoy yourself here."

They shook hands and Chief Roanyon left to join the other four waiting outside the door.

"That was a plus!" Bedard said. "Imagine David speaking Spanish!"

Twenty-Five
January 22, 1858 (Evening)

Bedard, Chief Roanyon, Mothana, and Wantano made their way back to the big tree. Mothana excused herself and went in search of some cooking utensils for Art and Elizabeth.

"Well, Wantano," said Bedard, "is there anything else we need to do?"

"We are now down to four prisoners for the boat tomorrow," Wantano said. "That is not a problem, but it might be useful if you and Chief Roanyon talked to them briefly tonight so that they know exactly the predicament they have got themselves into. I have also arranged to have them recover their packs and bags if we have them in our collection. Also, Komchowa arrived back with two more prisoners that you should see."

Bedard was pleased and sought out Komchowa amongst the teeming masses of warriors that filled the village.

Komchowa was beaming. "We found the two men hidden in a cave on the north side of the middle arm of the river. Actually, it was the dogs who found them. This security dog training is absolutely incredible."

"We have a bit of time now," Bedard said. "Can we visit them?"

Komchowa turned and led the way. "I left the other island teams to complete their inspections. That will be finished by midday tomorrow, and I left three teams on the south side monitoring the well-used trail there. Later this week, we will decide when we will bring some or all of them back to our village."

The building that held the two prisoners had the usual warrior and big dog outside at the front door and another team inside. Komchowa talked to each man briefly. It was obvious that this was the team that had found the two men now tied to the floor and gagged with their arms and legs spread.

Bedard approached the two prisoners and sat down on a nearby bench. They looked at him. He did not say anything.

Komchowa came over and joined him. "They look like men from California. We gagged them as soon as we captured them. They both had two modern rifles, two pistols and a pack full of ammunition. The two dogs pinned them before they could react to our attack. Our team was very efficient." He looked over at the three warriors, who were listening and smiling.

Bedard decided that the new prisoners were not on his list but that they were probably recruited by the Wolverine at Fort Langley.

"Right," said Bedard, "let's take this one, tie him to a chair and remove his gag."

Bedard guessed that the man spoke English. "You are in a serious situation, and you may die shortly."

The man was obviously very frightened but did not say anything. To Bedard this meant that he was a professional.

"What is your name?"

The man again said nothing. Bedard inspected the prisoner's head and arms and found a number printed on his inside wrist. He had been in jail somewhere. The number was a very common marking for prisoners in many countries of Europe, the United States and even the Far East.

Komchowa came over with the four rifles. Bedard took one, levered a bullet into the chamber, pointed the rifle at the man in the chair and shot him.

Everyone was stunned, including Komchowa.

Bedard said, "Let's take the other one, tie him to a chair and remove his gag."

"What is your name?"

"John Timothy."

"Do you have a middle name?"

"David. John David Timothy."

"Do you know Tommy Hunter, the Wolverine?"

"Yes."

"Tell me how you know him."

"I worked for him briefly in the California goldfields. He is very erratic and likes killing people, sometimes for no reason. I do not like him."

"And yet you worked for him here."

John David said nothing.

"Who was your friend?"

"He was not my friend. The Wolverine hired both of us for this project at Fort Langley. We did not know each other before. His name was Bill. He did not talk much."

"What was the project?"

"The Wolverine said that these natives had captured several of his men, and he wanted to get them back again. He and his two buddies planned to find out where they were being held and then take them back to Fort Langley. He said that this would not be much of a problem because the natives did not have many guns, just bows and arrows. We were to provide covering fire from across the water there." He smiled, showing two teeth missing at the front of his mouth. "We arrived on that island just this morning, and we soon saw that everyone had guns. We also saw that you killed the Wolverine and his two buddies. We were running across the island to where our canoe was hidden to return to Fort Langley when the trackers came with their dogs. We knew that we were sunk. The cave was a good hiding place but not from the dogs."

"The guns and the ammunition are yours?" Bedard asked.

"No, no. The Wolverine bought all that from a guy in the tent camp outside of Fort Langley. Very expensive!"

"I have not visited the area north of New York," Bedard said. "What part of that area are you from?"

John David looked surprised and he hesitated before answering. "On the coast of Maine. How did you know that?"

"Why did you leave there?"

John David looked down. "My wife left me last year and took the two boys. I was unhappy and my parents were not particularly supportive, so I went to California. This was not the best decision I have ever made."

He looked over at Bill, still slumped in his chair.

Bedard said. "You should remember that this nation and other native nations on this river and up and down this coast are very sophisticated and understand the white man quite well. They are very different from the natives in California. We are going to send you back to San Francisco if you agree not to come back here again."

John David nodded emphatically. "I agree, no problem."

Bedard turned to Komchowa. "Would it be more convenient to hold this man with the other prisoners?"

Komchowa nodded, and Bedard left the building.

The warriors were now seated in various groups near the big tree eating the late meal. Bedard entered his home building and was told by a villager making the evening heating fire that he was to go to Mother's for the late meal, so he did.

Mother got up, gave him a hug and pointed him to the table where Dorthea was sitting talking to the two Spaniards. Art, Elizabeth and David, who were also at the table, got up and everybody shook Bedard's hand, and he joined them. Immediately, a plate of shrimp was placed in front of him by Adrona who gave him a quick kiss on his ear and escaped.

"Oh, a special meal for you!" said Dorthea in Spanish.

Bedard smiled and dug into his favourite food, saying nothing.

Amused, Alfonzo said, "I have met more people in this village who speak Spanish than I had expected to!"

Bedard said, "Have you met Chief Wanso and Amoroa yet?"

"Yes," said Joseph, turning to his cousin. "What was the name of that huge, jolly man? Oh, I remember now: Komchowa. He said that he had not spoken Spanish in many years, yet I thought he did very well."

Bedard merely smiled.

"His story is similar to mine," said David. "Those romance languages are very similar and easy to absorb once you have one down, more or less."

"So that is eight and counting," said Alfonzo.

The group enjoyed that.

Dorthea said, "We have all been busy this afternoon making lists of supplies that we think we will need in our special areas of work over the next year. These have been given to Mothana."

Bedard nodded; that was a good idea.

Just then Chief Roanyon came by. "Copco, there is a meeting at your place in about ten minutes."

"Parties, meetings, parties and more meetings," Bedard said. "This is just like my home life in England!"

David smiled. "If you don't mind me asking, just what do you do back in England?"

"Well," Bedard said, "over the past thirty years I have been travelling throughout the world about half of the time. When I am in England I find myself focused on running the commercial business that I have established there over the years. I still enjoy that very much, but I also enjoy travel and, of course, the opportunity to learn new languages and dialects."

"How many languages do you know?"

"I do not know exactly. Let's say about forty, some more proficiently than others."

"Languages are complex," said Dorthea, "and we both enjoy learning them. Musqueam is our favourite and my father has some very good teachers."

Bedard wandered around, saying hello to many of the people who were just finishing their meal. He went up to the cooking area where Adrona was brandishing a pot, but Bedard still managed to get a hug and a kiss before he left for the meeting.

At his home building, the five chiefs and their wives were seated at a table where Mothana was arranging some paper. Others were lounging around in the gloom behind them. The fire was burning bright, and it was quite warm.

Mothana looked up at Bedard. "We have five lists of materials: the new school program, mostly books; the plank boat project, mostly small barrels of screws and nails and some tools; a small number of vet products and a rather large list of medical products, supplies and equipment. Then we have a large complicated list of guns and ammunition with no quantities attached and a few speciality tools. We have no way of estimating the cost of all this, but the chiefs have just voted a few minutes ago, and they don't care what the cost is. They just want to proceed with it all."

Bedard sat down and Mothana passed him the school sheets.

"Dorthea, Tomala and Amoroa spent most of the day creating that. Dorthea found these in her small school box."

Bedard read it rapidly and turned to Dorthea. "Four hundred students, sixteen books, average book about one dollar?" Dorthea scrunched her face. Bedard said, "Let's say seven thousand dollars."

There was a bit of a gasp from someone in the back who understood the American dollar.

"Do you think that San Francisco would have that many in stock?"

"No," said Dorthea, "but Fort Victoria has about half of the order in stock and the balance may be in stock in San Francisco or back ordered from England or New York, arriving here in about three months, which would be acceptable."

Bedard said, "I would have guessed about a thousand students."

"Yes, but the students will be concentrating on learning English first because the books are in English, so we really have four hundred sets of sixteen books shared by a thousand students as a start, so that is about six books per student. Then we will need different books as this large group progresses and as the school curriculum evolves."

Bedard smiled. "Very good. What's next?"

Mothana passed over the plank-boat list and Bedard studied it. "This looks very simple." He looked at Old Chief Sparrow. "Have you bought hardware in San Francisco lately?"

Old Chief Sparrow talked to Mother for a few moments, and she said, "There are a number of very large hardware businesses there. We have never had any problems, although this order is quite large."

"I have no idea what this will cost," Bedard said. "Anyone like to make a guess?" There were no answers, so he said, "We will say two thousand dollars. Next!"

Mothana passed over the vet products list and turned to look for David, who said, "Two hundred pounds. I do not know the current currency exchange rate."

"Five hundred dollars," said Bedard.

Mothana passed over the four-page list of medical products, supplies and equipment which Bedard studied. Most of the quantities had British Pound prices. Bedard took a pen and ink pot from the table and made some calculations.

"Fort Victoria will have small quantities of most of the medications," said Elizabeth, "but probably will not want to share any with us. It is difficult to estimate how much of everything we need. Some of this may stay in our inventory for some time and then be used up in one week. We just don't know. I was quite pleased with the inventory in stock now. Inchesca and Bella and the others are all very modern practitioners."

Bedard said, "Looks like about ten thousand dollars." There were some gasps from around the table and in the background.

Then Mothana passed Bedard the gun list without comment.

Bedard looked at the two pages and grimaced.

"We pulled in a number of people who have purchased guns lately," said Mothana. "They all said that the price of guns was going down and the designs were changing. They also said that the quality of workmanship was going up, so they did not have any clue as to current wholesale costs."

Art came to the table and Oban followed him.

Art said, "I think that you should probably assign a budget amount and buy as many guns as it will allow."

Bedard nodded. "That is a very practical solution. Perhaps the nation as represented by the chiefs here today cannot afford to go from minimum guns to top-of-the-line guns for everyone in one day."

There was a clank on the table. It was Amoroa's gold coin necklace. It did not need any accompanying statement.

The chiefs all looked at Bedard with steely eyes. No one said anything.

"On the other hand, the world is turning rapidly." Bedard looked at Chief Roanyon, who laughed. This broke the tension, and everyone stood up and clapped.

"So this is the way I think you should proceed. You need a representative in San Francisco to act on your behalf. I have a fifty-man office there run by Phillip Goren. He is a very competent man whom I have known for thirty years. We should submit the lists to him, and he will get the best deal that he can for you." He looked at Dorthea. "I don't think that we should get any of the books from Fort Victoria. Donna would not be pleased."

Dorthea nodded her head and smiled.

"I also propose that I fund the purchases and that you reimburse me when we have received the statement of accounts from Phillip."

"We thought that you might offer to do that," Chief Tamburo said, "and we are uncomfortable with that idea. But we realize that this is a very unusual situation for us, and we easily agreed that if we are going to be more modern we must also adopt some of white man's methods. We need to discuss and plan the actual split between the villages and the families, depending on the services and product distribution. This is not new to us, but we decided today that we need to review everything again, including the fishing, hunting and gathering activities so that every individual living here is fairly treated." Again, everyone in the room stood up and clapped.

"That sounds very modern," Bedard said, and everyone looked very pleased. "We now need quantities on the gun list."

Art moved up to the table. "The discussions on this gun list took a long time today, and I made some notes as the chiefs discussed various distribution plans. I have made several copies of the summary sheet that I made. You all might want to look at this before you move toward a final decision."

Art placed three sheets of paper on the table, which the chiefs studied with the assistance of Art and David. They then reviewed the various options that they had previously discussed.

Bedard was impressed with Art's initiative and looked over Chief Roanyon's shoulder at the notes. He judged that it was going to be about a hundred and fifty thousand for everything. Quite the sum.

He took some blank paper and the pen and inkwell and composed a letter to Phillip Goren. He folded up the letter and waited patiently for the chiefs' decision on the quantity of guns. He had Phillip's address in his room in a small case with some envelopes and a wax-sealing kit. He would get the letter ready immediately and give the envelope to Wantano so that he could give it to the captain of the *Cobalt* when it came for the five prisoners tomorrow.

Everything was finally decided and the large group left the building. Bedard addressed his envelope, sealed it and went out to search for Wantano. He found him down at the big tree talking with Komchowa and Chief Roanyon.

"Here is a letter to give to the captain of the *Cobalt* for delivery in San Francisco. You said that we need to visit the prisoners. Can we do that now?"

"Yes, of course."

"I think that I will pass," said Chief Roanyon. "It has been a long day."

"I will come," said Komchowa.

The three men moved off in the darkness to the building where the prisoners were held. They put on masks. The usual guards and dogs let them in, and they saw that the prisoners had washed up and were wearing cleaner clothes. They were now on thin mattresses and securely tied to boards on the floor.

Bedard sat down at a fireplace bench where they could all see him in the firelight.

"Tomorrow you will board a ship bound for San Francisco. It will not be an enjoyable trip for you because you will remain tied up as prisoners. If you survive the trip and are allowed to walk away from the boat, do not try to return to these lands again. If you come back here, you will be recognized and killed. We know who you are."

Bedard got up and walked over to one man and repeated what he had just said in Spanish. The man nodded his head and Bedard returned to the bench.

After a long period of quiet, the three men left the building and took off their masks.

Adrona was almost asleep when Bedard finally turned in. With all the guests, she had a very long day. They were both asleep in a few moments, pleasantly entwined.

Twenty-Six
January 23, 1858 (Early Morning)

Bedard left his bed early without waking Adrona because she had Noua curled up against her, sound asleep. On his morning run, he passed by several warriors in guard positions on the paths above Tsusnahm. Taking only two dogs with him this time, he directed Liz to be the front guard and JoJo to follow.

Bedard decided to take the northern path for a change and, after JoJo gave a warning woof, slowed down and found to his amusement that not only Chief Roanyon but also Chief Big Bon were approaching. Dobera and Wantano were steaming up the trail behind them with a group of six heavily armed warriors stripped to the waist and sweating profusely.

Chief Big Bon was leading this impressive group as he pulled up beside Bedard. "Please do not say anything or I might laugh, and if I do that I will not be able to keep up with you."

Chief Roanyon was running just behind Chief Big Bon. "The two chiefs and their wives left for home early this morning, but then we received an early runner from the Squamish village of Khwaykhway. The Squamish chiefs from both Khwaykhway and Wh'mullutsthun are coming to visit Tsusnahm in the late morning. The messenger said that they wanted to be among the first to congratulate me on becoming chief, but I suspect that the real reason is related to the warrior action yesterday. These people have many information sources, and all of the Squamish villages in that area are probably very concerned and need to know what is happening here. We were not surprised to hear that they are coming to visit today."

"Only some of the warriors were sent home," said Dobera, "so we still have very heavy security for the village."

Wantano nodded. "My father and mother will never miss a party and they, along with Chief Wanso and his wife, will come back to Tsusnahm this morning."

Bedard slowed down to a walk and spoke with Dobera and Wantano. "Well, what is the plan here?"

"We will need a vote to determine further action."

"As I recall," said Wantano, "the path branches off in about another mile. I think that we can make it that far." The warriors groaned. "Then you and Chief Roanyon can proceed further if you wish. We will get a volunteer warrior to follow you."

The warriors immediately all turned and pointed to Fenciao, who was Chief Big Bon's only warrior.

"Oh no, not me!" he said in English, and the whole group laughed.

Bedard knew that Fenciao was not only exceptionally strong and skilled but also very popular amongst the warriors. Chief Big Bon was obviously pleased with this.

Bedard and Chief Roanyon started off again with Chief Big Bon and the group following. At the spot where the path branched off, Dobera and Fenciao followed behind Bedard and Chief Roanyon who took the northeast path, while Chief Big Bon and the rest of the group turned around and proceeded back toward Tsusnahm. Bedard noted that both Dobera and Fenciao carried rifles and Chief Roanyon now had a bow and a small quiver.

Bedard looked at Chief Roanyon with raised eyebrows, but Chief Roanyon just shrugged.

"The committee chaired by the women said that we were still on high alert and that we had to continue to be careful."

After another three miles, they reached Bedard's favourite marshland meadow where they stopped for a rest. Bedard called in the dogs for a scratch and introduced them to Fenciao.

"So these are the famous dogs," the warrior said in English. "They are very good-looking animals. They certainly look big enough to look after themselves in any action. I know that they are very well trained and have a long history of working with you. I also understand that you have four dogs. How long have you had them?"

"More than nine years."

"All the villages will have trained security dogs this year," said Dobera.

"You will remember that I have a dog," Fenciao said. "I should get him assessed to see whether he has the potential to participate in the security training."

The small group turned around and started running home, led by Liz some distance ahead. When they reached the ridge above Tsusnahm, Bedard directed the two dogs to their current security areas and the group moved down into the village, which was quiet at this time of day. There was still quite a number of sleeping lean-tos but not many people.

They entered Old Chief Sparrow's building and found Mother at the door welcoming everyone for the early meal. The place was full, and Adrona and Aurora were supervising the cooking area, of course, and they gave the new arrivals a wave.

Mother gave everyone a hug.

"I am starting to understand how my new world works now. When Chief Big Bon awoke the first day that he was here, he said to us, 'Do you think that we will be able to do anything on our own here?' I now understand exactly what he meant."

Chief Big Bon and his wife were seated nearby, and he got up and gave Mother a big hug.

Bedard waved to Dorthea, who was eating with a group of women. Wantano came over to Bedard, bringing his plate, and sat down on the bench.

"Everything is under control, more or less. The two Spaniards were invited over to Art and Elizabeth's building with David for the early meal, and I managed to find them and take them there. David and Elizabeth seemed to be doing the cooking. I don't know where the food came from, probably Mothana's team. She seems to be everywhere this morning. What a mob of people!"

"I really enjoy these parties," Bedard said, to the approval of all assembled.

Wantano said, "We have two boats set up to take the five prisoners away. And we are waiting for the lookout tree to signal that the *Cobalt* is in sight."

As Bedard was making ready to leave the building, he addressed Old Chief Sparrow. "I need a drum, a small drum like the ones that the girls use."

Old Chief Sparrow said something to his wife, who immediately got up from the bench, went back into one of the sidewall rooms and came out with two drums, one fairly small and the other a bit larger. She smiled and gave them to Bedard.

Bedard tried each of them with his finger and found, not to his surprise, that the larger drum had a deeper resonance. He smiled at Mother and Old Chief Sparrow.

"Perfect," he said in English.

Mother laughed, and Old Chief Sparrow said something to her. She put her hand to her mouth and laughed some more. Old Chief Sparrow beckoned over one of his grandchildren and said something to her. The girl then relayed it to Bedard.

"He told her to be careful or you will find out that she speaks English."

Bedard went outside and walked down to the big tree. He squatted down and tried the two drums. He decided that the girls probably used the smaller drum, so he started playing it in their usual manner of a constant drum roll with no pauses or variants. He watched the buildings to the east and immediately noticed small faces poking out the doorways, followed by their mothers' faces.

At Adrona's building, the two six-year-olds who Bedard knew were drummers came flying out with their drums. Adrona followed them with both babies in her arms. These two children were the first to arrive and sat down facing Bedard on a blanket that they had brought with them. They immediately played their drums in the same manner that Bedard was playing his. Everyone was beaming.

In short order there were six drummers. The sound was deafening, and an audience was building behind them.

Bedard hit his drum with two big swats and the whole group stopped drumming. All of them were smiling broadly.

Bedard played a sequence of hits and pointed to one of the girls, who caught on immediately and mimicked his drum pattern. Bedard pointed to each one in turn until all six had repeated the pattern. He then played the same pattern again, lifted his arms and rapidly dropped them. Nothing. Then he did the same again and some of the drummers responded. Several tries later every drummer responded. They were all smiling.

Bedard then played another sequence of hits, lifted his hands and dropped them again. They all responded immediately. He played it again but this time he did not lift his hands. The girls all giggled.

Bedard then used his hands in the air to represent the pattern and played it again, this time both lifting his hands in the air and showing the pattern. Several tries later they got it, and it sounded great. He joined in with them, and they all played the pattern. The girls really liked that. The large audience behind them, composed mostly of warriors, clapped. The girls giggled again.

He talked to the drummers and said that he was going to play the patterns together, and that they should join him and not worry if they made the odd mistake. They played non-stop for about five minutes until Bedard again hit his drum with two big swats. The whole group stopped drumming at the same time. All of them were falling over laughing, and the audience was clapping behind them.

Then, to everyone's complete surprise, a drum roll was heard from the top of the ridge to the north. Everyone turned around to look. Bedard could see in the distance a number of people walking on the path down to the village, and he assumed that they were the group expected from the two Squamish villages. It was obvious to him from the sound that there were a number of drummers there. *This is fun.*

Bedard clapped his hands to get the attention of his young drummers and started a drum roll to match the one that they all heard from the ridge. They all joined in. The drums on the ridge stopped. He hit his drum with two big swats again, and his group stopped.

Bedard lifted his hands like an orchestra leader and rapidly mimicked the beats of the two patterns that the girls had learned. He held his hands over his head and brought them down on his drum, and the whole group started the drum patterns in unison. Bedard smiled. *Wow!* Some of the girls were laughing so hard that they missed a few notes, but the overall result was magnificent.

Bedard was not surprised to hear the drummers from the hill joining in with the same patterns. The Tsusnahm villagers and assembled warriors were all clapping.

Coming down from the ridge was a procession led by two chiefs in full ceremonial robes, followed by their wives also clothed in beautiful robes. Then came four drummers. Bedard thought they were teenage girls, but they could have been a bit older. Following them was a group of some twenty men and women, all smiling and clapping.

The villagers rushed up the hill following Chief Roanyon with Mothana and Old Chief Sparrow and Mother. The four chiefs and their wives exchanged hugs and the following group surged by them to greet their friends from Tsusnahm.

Bedard noticed one person in the group coming down the hill who kept to himself.

My God! he thought. *I think that might be Roger. I haven't seen him since I was in China more than ten years ago.*

Bedard got up and left the group of drummers hammering away. Roger saw Bedard and started to run toward him. The two met in a huge clash of bodies and they fell over laughing.

Bedard said something in Chinese and the two of them exploded into laughter again.

Now sitting on the grass facing each other, they quieted down and looked at each other.

Bedard shook his head. "You are the last person in the world that I expected to see here!"

Roger just smiled.

"So, talk to me," said Bedard.

"I left China about ten years ago, shortly before you did, and went to Australia to see my family and do a little gold mining. Then I went to San Francisco and did a little more gold mining." He smiled. "It really is contagious, you know! Then in early 1854, I travelled to a group of islands to the north of here called the Queen Charlottes. I was following a rumour that there was some gold to be found, but there was very little. Actually, I was three years too late!

"I decided to try to stay there for a while, and I was fortunate to find a Haida chief who liked me. About two years ago I came south again and did some trapping and pretty well kept to myself. The first winter I hooked up with a small Squamish village on the coast that was not doing very well, and I managed to help them through the winter. The next winter I came back to the same village. They liked me, and we got along fairly well. I do not have your strength in languages, but I do all right. This winter I came down to the area just north of here with two Squamish friends of mine. Earlier this month I heard of you, but I did not know who you were until this week. Well, I did not really know it was you, but there was too much action happening! It could not have been anyone else!"

Bedard looked up and saw that Chief Roanyon and Mothana were walking toward them with one of the Squamish chiefs and his wife.

"We have visitors," Bedard said, and they got up.

"You will like these two people from Khwaykhway," Roger said. "They are very nice and both of them speak English and a smattering of other languages, including Musqueam, of course."

Bedard put on his reception smile and Roger moved back half a step. The chief was a big man and the robe made him look even larger. His wife was another very good-looking woman.

Chief Roanyon spoke in Musqueam. "Copco, I would like you to meet Chief Whernacowa and his wife from Khwaykhway. She likes to be called Joan."

They shook hands.

Joan spoke English. "I heard some of the story of Joan of Arc's life, and I thought that Joan would be a good name for me."

Her husband laughed, having obviously heard her say that many times, and said in Musqueam, "A good name for her. She is a good leader."

Joan was pleased with that.

Chief Whernacowa looked intently at Bedard. "We have heard stories of your strength in languages and your fighting and leadership skills. You do indeed look like you have lived here all your life."

Bedard spoke in halting Squamish. "I have not had the pleasure of visiting you yet."

The group laughed, with both Chief Roanyon and Roger both shaking their heads.

Joan switched to Musqueam. "You must come for a few days. Your Squamish is terrible!"

The group again burst into laughter.

Bedard turned to Chief Roanyon. "Do you remember me talking about Roger when we were in Hawaii?"

"Yes, I do," said Chief Roanyon, looking at Roger. "You are very skilled in hand-to-hand combat, as I recall. I forget the names of those systems. We had run into some Japanese fighters and Copco was wishing that Roger was with us at that time."

The two men shook hands.

"Roger has been helping one of our small villages with winter planning." Joan said. "Over the past three weeks he has been explaining these activities and ideas to us. It has been very informative and useful. We are a large village and do not have the same challenges that small villages have. With this information, we think that we can now help our small villages, which is a good thing for us to do."

Chief Whernacowa nodded. Roger was very pleased with the compliments.

Mother and Old Chief Sparrow were approaching the group with the other chief and his wife. Bedard thought that both the chief and his wife looked very young.

Mother spoke in Musqueam. "Copco, I would like you to meet Chief Andoronowey and his wife, Orelotta, from Wh'mullutsthun."

They both shook hands and Chief Andoronowey said, "Chief Big Bon has just confirmed that you have held several archery demonstrations to show some bows that perform well from very long distances. Because we knew that Chief Big Bon and Dorono and their families had moved to Tsusnahm, some of our senior archers and craftsmen came with us today to visit with them. They hope that you will have time to show these bows to them."

"That would be a pleasure," said Bedard.

Orelotta spoke in English. "We understand that you have information regarding a gold rush. We hope that you will be able to help us understand what this means. I understand that you are a skilled linguist and have rapidly learned Musqueam."

"His Squamish is not very good yet," Joan said with a smile. "So I have invited him to visit our villages for a few days so he can learn it properly."

Roger said, "This is an amazing skill that Copco has. I have witnessed him learn several languages and dialects very rapidly."

Chief Roanyon nodded. "I spent five years with Copco in Hawaii. He has many skills. It was he who was leading our young drummers as you descended from the ridge today."

"Our drummers were not expecting that," Joan said, "and enjoyed playing with them. I see that the two groups have met. The drummers here are very young."

They could see the two groups of drummers talking together.

"I have heard them several times at our meetings," Bedard said. "But today was the first time I have played the drums with them. It was very enjoyable. I really get pleasure from young children. This is something that I do not have enough of in my current life."

Orelotta smiled. "We have three young children, and we enjoy them very much."

Mothana said, "We have time for a short meeting underneath the big tree before our midday meal. We should all go there now."

Mother smiled. "Oh, I am so glad that you are here now!"

The two women laughed and moved off with their arms around each other.

Twenty-Seven
January 23, 1858
(Late Morning and Early Afternoon)

As the group followed Mother and Mothana toward the big tree, Mot arrived.

"Canoes will arrive soon from Mahli and Stsulawh."

In the distance to the west, they could see two huge canoes being paddled furiously, with several more canoes in the far distance.

"This is part of an enormous rivalry that the two villages have," said Mot to Bedard. "Their war canoes race each other at every opportunity, and the race to and from Tsusnahm is by far their favourite because it is so short—about three miles in fifteen minutes. This will have special significance because both chiefs and their wives are aboard. The paddlers will be absolutely exhausted when they arrive."

"My God, look at the bow waves," said Bedard. "They are really travelling."

Everyone could now see the two figures standing in the bow of each of the enormous canoes. Old Chief Sparrow, dressed in the splendour of his chieftain robes, was standing at the edge of a sandy portion of the beach.

Chief Roanyon said, "I remember when my father was chief, he also went down to that portion of the beach and would indicate the winner of the race with his arms. The two boats will arrive on either side of him. The boats will hit the sand at full speed and will travel up onto the land almost half their length, coming to a stop very suddenly."

Most of the villagers and all the visitors had assembled to watch the spectacular finish to the race.

"I have never seen this before," said Chief Andoronowey

Chief Whernacowa smiled. "I think that Joan and I have witnessed this perhaps three times."

Joan nodded. "My only concern is that no one gets hurt. It really is a ferocious finish."

The two boats were almost upon them. They could see the two chiefs standing in the bows with their arms wrapped around their wives and a special support stanchion. The paddlers were all yelling at the top of their lungs in order to gain the last scrap of energy to finish the race.

The two boats hit the beach with a thunderous sound and Old Chief Sparrow swung both arms out, signifying a tie. The paddlers drooped sideways and backwards in exhaustion. A small team of villagers emptied pails of water on them, and others made drinking water available.

The two chiefs and their wives stepped out of their boats, laughing, hardly able to stand.

Chief Tamburo said, "We won again, right? We were at least two feet in front of you!"

"No," said Chief Wanso, "it was judged a tie! But that was a political result because we were at least four feet in front of you!"

And the four of them collapsed in the sand laughing. The villagers were all clapping and laughing, too.

The two chiefs and their wives got up, brushed themselves off and moved up the grass toward the big tree and the other group of dignitaries.

"We heard the drums just before we left home," said Tomala, "so we knew that we were going to be late. We are sorry."

"That is fine," said Chief Roanyon. "We appreciate the entertainment."

The whole group laughed. Chief Roanyon introduced Roger to the four newcomers.

"Roger is a close friend of Copco from his China visit more than ten years ago. I did not have the pleasure of meeting Roger then, but when Copco and I went to Hawaii Copco often said that he wished that Roger was with us. So, it was very interesting for me to finally meet him today."

Joan said, "Roger has been visiting us for the past month. He was trapping on our far northern coast and living in a small Squamish village. He has now been helping us to understand how we can support our small villages up there. We, of course, are a large village and do not have many of the challenges that our small villages have. Nor do we have knowledge of their problems. Roger is very clever. We are going to start what he calls an *outreach program* to support these small villages, especially during the cold season."

"Yes," said Chief Whernacowa, "this is something that we want to do, and we appreciate Roger sharing his experiences with us."

"Roger also spent three years living in a Haida village," said Bedard, "so he will have an important contribution to make to our planned project up there."

Roger was a bit embarrassed. "My personal philosophy is to have fun, and this looks like a great party in the making!"

The group laughed and moved off toward the big tree. Bedard took Roger in tow, and they settled on the grass behind Chief Roanyon. Bedard pointed out to Roger the various support staff from Tsusnahm and the two large Musqueam villages to the west. Dorthea came over and sat beside Bedard, who introduced her.

"Your daughter? You never told me that you had a gorgeous daughter!"

Dorthea gave them both a bright smile. "I sense that Roger was brought up just south of Sydney, Australia, don't you agree father?"

"Oh my God," said Roger, "not another one!" The three of them laughed as Roger just shook his head.

"Dorthea is also a very accomplished teacher who actually worked as a teacher for a while at one of my schools in London. She has been teaching just outside of Fort Victoria for more than two years, and her mastery of these dialects is better than mine! She decided to move here three days ago. I am very pleased with that."

He gave her a hug. Roger continued to shake his head.

Roger said, "You must let me introduce you to the group that came down with the two chiefs. They are all clever experts. I especially like the two warriors over there, both named Tom." He laughed. "We have been practicing some of the Shaolin style of kung fu fighting techniques, which they really like."

The ceremonies started, with Old Chief Sparrow assisted by his granddaughters welcoming the two Squamish chiefs and introducing the new chief of Tsusnahm.

Chief Roanyon moved over and the visitors all rose and clapped for a long time. Mothana joined Chief Roanyon, and the clapping intensified.

Chief Roanyon thanked the two Squamish chiefs for coming to visit.

"You have missed ten days of non-stop parties."

The assembled villagers and guests all laughed.

"I knew we should have come earlier!" said Joan.

Just then Mot came up and spoke softly to Bedard. "There are a number of canoes approaching, and Modan thinks that they are Squamish canoes."

Bedard moved quietly up behind Mother. "I think that there is a shipment of Squamish food and party favours coming in about ten minutes." Mother eased herself up a bit and looked over the water to the west at the oncoming canoes, and managed to locate and wave at Adrona who had also seen them. Adrona came over and talked briefly with Mother and rushed off, trailed by Aurora.

Joan also saw the canoes coming and interrupted Chief Roanyon.

"That is good to know, Chief Roanyon, because we felt that a party tonight and tomorrow would be most appropriate for this occasion. I see that our supplies are almost here."

She pointed at the canoes, now clearly visible. Everyone thought that was very funny and burst into laughter and clapping.

Just then the drum corps arrived, composed of both the youngsters and the older Squamish drummers who marched through the crowd toward the water in celebration of the arrival of the canoes.

Chief Roanyon came over to Bedard. "I think that there will be a large group of people joining you on your run tomorrow morning!"

Bedard smiled. "I think you're right."

Chief Andoronowey and Chief Whernacowa joined them, and Chief Andoronowey said, "So tell us the story of why there are a hundred extra warriors in camp."

"Well," said Chief Roanyon, "the short version starts with the fort that the white men made west of Mahli and Stsulawh, the one that we call the corral."

The two chiefs nodded.

"They suddenly abandoned the corral one evening, and we did not know about it until the next day. Bedard and Wantano rushed over to the south river trail with a team of warriors and managed to capture seven of the ten men, one of whom was killed. Two more that had been left at the corral were also captured. The three that escaped to Fort Langley came back yesterday, creeping up on us slowly along the north shore in a canoe. Their objective was to recapture the nine prisoners. They were seen by our lookout tree. We had about two hundred warriors here yesterday from Mahli and Stsulawh within a half hour, because we have recently adopted a communication system called Morse code. You probably know of it.

"We had already sent out a small warrior team lead by Bedard and the three men were killed. Two other men were also captured yesterday on the island over there." He pointed across the water. "We still have a number of warriors and trackers on the island and on the south river trail, but we do not think that we will find anyone else."

"The good news," said Bedard, "is that Elizabeth, the daughter of one of our prisoners, came here two days ago. She is a medical practitioner and her father, Art, is a gun master. Fortunately, we have managed to put them both on contract. Another prisoner who, incredibly, is from the same small town in England as Art and Elizabeth, David, also agreed to a contract. He is a horse and small animal vet and will help us with the multitude of dogs that the three villages have. He has also worked with Elizabeth at a medical clinic in England and will be able to assist her from time to time. This is a very good addition to the communities here. Two more prisoners are actually carpenters, and they are now also under contract and will start by assisting in the construction of what they are calling plank boats. These are small four- and six-man boats that are easy and fast to build and repair. This is a very interesting project.

"And then, finally, my daughter arrived here two days ago. She is a teacher and has been working at a school on Vancouver Island near Fort Victoria. She is also a linguist and will make a big contribution to this community over the next year."

The two chiefs just shook their heads.

Chief Roanyon said, "But the first party that you missed ten days ago was when Copco first arrived. You will recall hearing that one of our babies had been stolen, and Copco found him. Absolutely incredible."

"That was when I decided that I liked shrimp," said Bedard, and the group laughed.

Chief Whernacowa screwed up his face. "I don't know if we brought any shrimp. I will ask Joan."

Mothana was circulating amongst the distinguished guests, inviting them to the midday meal at Mother's home. Down at the boats, several tables had been set up and, as if by magic, food from the boats covered the tables, and the large crowd of villagers, warriors and other visitors moved down in orderly lines to sample the offerings.

Roger led Bedard and Chief Roanyon around the area, finding and introducing them to the group that had accompanied the two Squamish chiefs and their wives. Bedard said that he would be pleased to show them his archery equipment in the afternoon sometime. The archery experts were pleased and said that they were looking forward to that.

Some of the visitors were also interested in any new rifles and pistols that were in the village. Chief Roanyon said that they did not have many, about fifteen rifles and a selection of pistols, he thought. He said that these would also be available for inspection. He added that there was a six-hundred-foot rifle shooting range in the meadow to the west of the village with a nine-hundred-foot range being constructed. The gun experts wiggled their noses at nine hundred feet.

Roanyon smiled. "Talk to Oban and our new gun master, Art. They have been working on the new range this morning when we knew that you were coming."

As they were moving toward Mother's home, Inchesca and Bella intercepted Bedard.

"We have met Elizabeth and David this morning," said Inchesca, "and we had a very nice visit. Two Squamish shaman friends came down today, so we are all going to meet again this afternoon to discuss modern medicine, amongst other things. David has a very interesting background, and he said that his personal philosophy based on his veterinarian experience was not too dissimilar from ours. We talked about that for some time. We found that this was very remarkable indeed."

"I am pleased that you like them," said Bedard. "Their background is very different from yours, and you all have an opportunity to learn something new. I think that is good."

"We completely agree," Bella said.

After a delicious midday meal of cold fish and meat, Bedard and Roger found Chief Big Bon. Bedard introduced Roger to him and gave him a bit of the background that they shared.

Chief Big Bon gave a theatrical scowl. "I hope that he is not an archer. Is he?"

"Only when I have to be!" Roger said.

"I may have to lend him one or two of my bows, as he did not bring any today."

"I tell you," said Chief Big Bon, "we have a group of Squamish archers who would really like to see your magic bows this afternoon. I was thinking in about three hours because there will be a rifle demonstration soon and their nine-hundred-foot range uses the same marker as we do." He shook his head.

Bedard had the same opinion. Nine hundred feet was a questionable distance for any rifle that he was familiar with, but he had heard Oban talk about it as if it was possible with the new rifles he had acquired.

Roger just shook his head. "I do not think I have ever shot an arrow that far."

Chief Big Bon said, "I have seen this man shoot an arrow fourteen hundred feet into a six-inch target!"

Roger looked up at Bedard.

Bedard and Roger went west to the shooting range and joined a small group of people sitting on the grass watching the shooting demonstration from the six-hundred-foot marker. Very few of the shooters were hitting the one-inch circle. Twenty of the warriors and assembled experts shot twice, and only two men, Oban and Wantano, were successful twice. Six others hit one bull's eye.

The group then spent almost an hour examining and talking about the various rifles and pistols that were on display. Art and Oban were in the middle of the group pointing out the technical changes that they were seeing in the manufacture of rifles. Mot and others were translating into Musqueam, Squamish and English.

Bedard and Roger did not participate in the shooting, but both examined a number of the rifles, especially those used by Oban and Wantano.

At the nine-hundred-foot range, the same twenty men shot. Only two, Oban and Wantano, came within the six-inch circle, with Oban winning by doing this twice. Art did not shoot at either distance, saying that his eyesight was not what it used to be.

Oban came back to Bedard and asked him to try the shot using his rifle. Bedard was encouraged by Roger so he got up, and the group, all of whom knew Bedard either personally or by reputation, became quiet.

"Mot," Bedard said, "do you have my bows for later?"

The group murmured good naturedly.

Bedard hefted the rifle, feeling its weight, then took a straw to test the wind and turned to Oban.

"Do I get four shots?" The group laughed and clapped.

Bedard's first shot was a bull's eye, and many of the group nodded their heads in appreciation of this man's skills.

Oban grinned. "Not fair, you were practicing at noon today."

A second straw by Bedard got the same reaction.

Bedard's second shot was within the six-inch circle.

"Damn wind," said Bedard.

The group laughed and clapped.

Bedard said, "I will purchase this rifle from you, Oban."

"I will sell it to you in three months," Oban said.

"Ah, but then you will have better guns."

Oban smiled, and the group talked excitedly amongst themselves.

Bedard brought the rifle back to Roger and took it partially apart under the watchful eye of Oban.

"The sights are unusual and very adjustable," he said. "I like that. I am surprised that I shot so well without the opportunity to set up the sights for my own eyes. I also like the feel of this gun, but I do not know why."

Oban nodded. "Oh yes, I agree. It is one of the new rifles that we confiscated from those two men found on the island yesterday. It is a little bit lighter than my favourite rifle that I have been using until today, the Winchester. As you say, the sights are more flexible for adjustment, but it is the balance of the rifle that makes it feel good. I really like it. The other three rifles are exactly the same, but this one, for me at least, is the best one."

"I am surprised," said Roger, "that no one is interested in the pistols. Do they all have them?"

"Most of these people have not seen pistols in action," said Bedard. "Pistols are not much use for hunting. They are used to kill people. They will learn about this in due course."

Several other warriors and experts stepped up to try Oban's rifle from the nine-hundred-foot marker. Everyone liked it, but no one else hit the six-inch target.

Twenty-Eight
January 23, 1858 (Late Afternoon)

Most of the small group watching the rifle demonstration were also interested in archery. They were supplemented by a much larger group of warriors and archers, and all seven chiefs and their wives.

Mot and Modan brought Bedard's bags of bows and placed them near the nine-hundred-foot shooting mark.

Chief Big Bon addressed the dignitaries.

"I have decided that I feel ill today and will not be competing."

This was received with light laughter from the group and some sly comments from his more serious competitors.

"There are so many archers here today," said the chief, "that we have chosen only ten of you to participate in today's competition. We are going to focus on Bedard's bows. You will all enjoy them. One of these bows is so interesting that we have started to try to replicate it and have managed to bring the work in progress along today for you to see. Unfortunately, we cannot use it yet because it needs more curing time. Some of the arrows are also quite remarkable."

Bedard got up and joined Chief Big Bon. "I hope that Amoroa will not be shooting today."

"Of course not," said the chief. "We do not want to embarrass our visitors on their first day here."

Amoroa's success at the last competition was well known by all the archers, and they all cheered.

The archers came up near the nine-hundred-foot shooting mark and began doing some simple arm and chest stretches. Bedard was asked to shoot first with his longbow. He and all of the ten archers placed their arrows within the small six-inch-circle.

Chief Big Bon smiled at Bedard, who just shook his head and followed him another two hundred feet farther back.

Roger, who was walking beside Bedard, said, "I think that this is going to be a bit different than the last competition that you told me about."

Bedard looked at him and smiled.

Bedard took the remaining bows from the bag that Mot was holding. "These three bows are very special. They are *recurve* bows, and the curves are designed to store energy."

He described them carefully and, choosing his favourite recurve composite bow, stepped up to the line and released the arrow. The report was that it had landed just inside the six-inch circle again.

All ten of the archers then shot. Four arrows were within the six-inch circle and six were just outside of it.

Chief Big Bon and Bedard looked at each other with amazement.

"I think that I am going to retire this year," said the chief. Those close by him laughed. The group then moved farther back still.

They were now thirteen hundred feet from the targets.

Chief Big Bon held up his arms and addressed the crowd. "Now you are going to see some magic."

Bedard inspected the compound bow carefully. He stepped up to the line and used a special body movement to pull the string back and sight the arrow. He released.

In the distance, they could hear the small group yelling. She ran toward them at all speed and arrived completely out of breath. After catching her breath, she said that the arrow had landed within the six-inch target.

Some of the group had seen this demonstration before and continued to be very impressed with Bedard's skill and his magic bows. The rest of the group were stunned. Big Bon was again shaking his head and looking at Bedard.

Chief Andoronowey and Chief Whernacowa just looked at each other.

Chief Andoronowey called over a warrior who had successfully shot from the previous mark.

"Have you ever tried to shoot from this distance?"

The warrior shook his head. "That was amazing!"

"I have seen this bow in action twice," said Johno. "It is easily the longest shot that I have ever seen."

"I have yet another toy," said Bedard, reaching for the third bag.

Chief Big Bon laughed. "This is the best one."

Bedard lifted up another device with a small bow. Several of the Squamish archers who had moved to the front of the group immediately identified it as a crossbow.

"Chief Wanso said that we have several of them in storage somewhere," said Johno, "but we have not yet found them."

Chief Roanyon reached for the bow. "This bow is larger than any *crossbow* that I have used, and it has a very heavy draw weight and a simple method of cocking."

He took a special arrow from Bedard and walked over to the line. He put the front of the crossbow on the ground and drew back on the lever to cock the unit. He then called Mot over to help him. Mot was again a bit apprehensive and flinched at the release.

The small girl again ran up to them and reported that the arrow had struck within the eighteen-inch circle. The group continued to be impressed with these incredible bows.

"Perhaps we should return to Tsusnahm now and find a table on which we can examine all of Copco's bows and his arrows. You will find the modern arrows interesting. We can also see the compound bow that is being fabricated by our experts."

The group now followed Chief Big Bon back to Tsusnahm. Four tables were found and placed in the shade of the big tree. Mot and Bedard placed all of the bows and six arrows on the table.

Bedard picked up an arrow.

"I have been making this type of arrow for some years now. The tip is made from a modern cartridge bullet such as this one," he said, pulling a bullet out of his pocket.

"Most of the arrows that I have examined here are very well made. The feathers are very good, perhaps even better than mine, but the tip is a bit larger than mine so it will not travel as far in the air. Too much *wind resistance*." This took a while to translate with Mot and Roanyon and others participating.

The arrow was passed around the group. The experts—Dorono, Melleran, Ortho and Johno—spoke with some of the visitors from Squamish for a while.

Johno went over to his carry bag, brought out about twenty arrows and put them on the table. Bedard picked one up.

"Now, this is good," he said and looked at Johno, who was beaming.

"These are the result of a *joint venture*," Johno said. "Chief Big Bon provided some of his excellent arrows, Melleran added the feathers and Ortho and I have been working on the bullet tips. These arrows definitely perform much better at a distance and are very accurate for hunting at short distances, especially in the forest. We are very pleased."

Bedard passed another arrow to Johno, who examined the metal tip and found that it was exactly the same diameter as the shaft of the arrow. He said with a smile, "Yes, this is what you are calling steel. We have not set up our forge yet."

"These tips never break any more," said Bedard. "I do not have many of these tips left, so I try to retrieve them after I have used them. A bit tricky sometimes." They all laughed. "I have also worked on the feather sets, but I still have much to learn."

Melleran grunted. "All of his feather sets are good. When we last talked, he introduced me to many feather ideas that I have been experimenting with."

Joan said, "We also need to understand more about guns and those who use guns exclusively. Today we have seen some of examples of the modern rifle and pistol, and we would be pleased to hear you talk about the future of these terrible devices."

"This has been very informative," said Chief Whernacowa. "We would like you to meet with us, perhaps after dinner tonight, and talk more about the gold rush. Since the corral and the people there have been dealt with it is now the people that you have said will come to seek gold that we must better understand."

"Of course," said Bedard. "I would be pleased to join you to talk about the future."

"I am very pleased," said Chief Roanyon, "that you all could take the time to see Copco's equipment. If some of you wish to examine the bows and arrows further, I am certain that Copco will facilitate that."

Bedard nodded.

The evening meal at Mother's was supplemented by the food shipment from the Squamish nation and was very well received by all. Bedard had shrimp again. He thought he must have eaten shrimp for four out of the last six days. He was pleased.

After the meal, the visitors gathered to hear what Bedard had to say about the gold seekers and the settlers who would follow. This was not well received. The Squamish Nation would escape from most of the friction this year, but in subsequent years Bedard feared that they would be very poorly treated by the anticipated wave of settlers and the so-called law and order of the British government.

Art and Oban then joined Bedard to talk about rifles and pistols. The two Squamish villages had some guns but not many modern rifles and pistols. Their two visiting gun masters agreed with Bedard, Art and Oban that guns had a shorter learning period than bows, were better for hunting and, in most cases, were better for killing. Everyone also agreed that the new modern rifles demonstrated were remarkable in their accuracy at a distance.

Chief Roanyon, who was also at the meeting, reported that the three Musqueam villages had just placed a huge order for rifles from San Francisco with the assistance of Copco, who had a large business office there that would process the order.

Chief Roanyon also stated that, with the assistance of Copco's daughter, who was an accomplished teacher, the villages were going to upgrade their school system. Joan was very interested in this and eventually met with Dorthea.

The meeting ended with a very long discussion in Squamish where the two chiefs, their wives and *support staff*—they easily adopted this phrase—discussed what they should do in light of all this new information.

Roger expressed his view that, with an increase in the English-speaking population over the next few years, hunting would be more difficult and guns would help to solve that. He also said that the villagers needed to continue discussing how to protect themselves and how to conserve the land that they now occupied. He felt that this was important. The white men would bring guns so they needed to have guns of their own. The meeting ended with everyone frowning and unhappy.

Bedard had managed to get Roger a room in the same building that he was staying in, so the two of them continued the discussion there for some time. They decided that there were no good solutions to the problems identified.

Adrona was asleep when Bedard completed his day, and he quietly snuggled up to her in a satisfactory manner and went to sleep.

Twenty-Nine
January 27, 1858 (Morning)

A powerful group assembled by the water under the big tree in Tsusnahm just after the early meal. Bedard had called the meeting because he wanted help creating a master plan of action for the first trip north. He could then plan the warrior training sessions.

Chief Roanyon, Old Chief Sparrow, Chief Big Bon, Mot, Dorono, Fenciao and Chief Enthica had arrived at the tree first and were deep in conversation with Cowen, who had arrived from Victoria late the previous day. Wantano, Dobera and Komchowa, who had travelled up the river that morning from their villages, were listening intently. Roger, who had been sitting by himself deep in thought, was now listening.

There were also four very grim-looking men who had arrived several days before from the Squamish villages to the north. Immediately behind all these men were assembled most of the villagers and numerous visitors. Many of the women had their arms crossed and looked particularly hostile.

When Bedard arrived, purposely a bit late, the large group fell silent and the men moved into a half circle facing him. He picked up the talking stick and surveyed the group; specifically noting the angry appearance of the women in the background.

Bedard spoke without preamble.

"It has been proposed that the time has come to take action and respond to the terrible event that occurred four years ago. As you will remember, a small group of Haida warriors came and kidnaped thirty young children from the village of Tsusnahm for their use as slaves. They also killed twenty-five villagers. The Haida and other nations have been doing this for many hundreds of years. This assault was a surprise to everyone because they had not attacked any village on this river for many years. Two years ago, the Haida came again to a village farther down the coast and kidnapped more children and some women. We have, at this time, a very basic plan of action that we need to expand It has been proposed that we assemble a small group of volunteers to travel north into Haida lands in search of information as to where these children are currently located. I will lead a short training program, and I will personally lead this first group north.

"A second much larger group of warriors will then follow later in the year and try to rescue as many of these children as can be found and bring them home. Some sort of physical retaliation to the Haida has also been suggested. We have very little information about anything. But what information we do have is very good, thanks to Old Chief Sparrow and Mother." Bedard stopped a moment and looked at them. "We have sketches and descriptions of some of the Haida. We also have some good maps of the area given to me by James Douglas at Fort Victoria. We have several people here today who have recently travelled in Haida lands, and we would like them to come forward now and talk to you."

Bedard looked directly at Roger.

Bedard had discussed this project with Roger, and Roger knew that he was going to be called upon to participate in the initial discussions. He arose from his position on the grass, came forward and sat immediately in front of Bedard. Roger was joined by Mot, Cowen, one of the four Squamish men named Robert who was well known in Tsusnahm, and a surprise visitor, a woman who had come down from a small Staulo village some distance upstream of Fort Langley.

This woman and Mother had hugged and cried when she and her husband had arrived by canoe the previous day.

Bedard looked at the woman and smiled. She arose and took the talking stick. She spoke in Musqueam.

"My name is Arentha. I am a Skidegate Haida. I was up there last year for a short visit to my family." The group became quite noisy as they reacted to this.

She turned around to address the group and continued. "Some of you might know my husband, Pisano, who is the brother of Tosca, both of whom have lived here in Tsusnahm. Tosca died here two years ago." She stopped for a moment. "Tosca lost one child in the Haida attack."

Again, the group became noisy while absorbing this information.

"Pisano and I married last year." She looked at him and smiled.

She turned again to face Bedard.

"We heard of this planned action only last week, and we decided to come and help if we can."

She sat down.

Roger stood up. "I lived in a small village south of Skidegate called Cumshewa for two years. I left there two years ago." He sat down.

Cowen stood up. "I visited Skidegate last year to arrange to purchase some carvings from the carvers there. As a trader, I have visited many Haida villages in the last ten years."

Mot stood up. "I have not visited the Haida lands, but I speak their language." He smiled at Bedard, who was surprised at this news.

Bedard thought, *Mot is bound and determined to go on this first trip north.*

Robert stood up. "My three brothers and I are Haida from an old village on the west coast near Skidegate called Cha'atl. It is abandoned now, and most of our remaining family have moved to the small new village of Haina, which is located on an island near Skidegate. My brothers and I have lived in the Salish village of Khwaykhway for thirty years. Many of you know me. My wife Doris was born in Tsusnahm. She is ill and could not join me, but she sends her greetings. My brothers and I left our homeland because we did not like the fighting and the slavery. We have never been back. We hope that we can help here."

Bedard looked across at the five people in front of him. "Yesterday this group met for most of the day and examined the sketches and descriptions of the Haida who came to this village. I was surprised and very pleased with the results of that meeting."

He looked at Arentha and nodded his head.

"Quite incredibly," Arentha said, "we identified and named all of the people sketched and most of the people described. Each of the four warriors and two women sketched were identified by at least two of us. One of the warriors was confirmed as dead. Each of the remaining five people is believed to be living in or near Skidegate. We were not surprised to find that all of these warriors and one of the two women were remembered as evil people. People that we did not like. People that we all remembered as liking to hurt other people. People who were perhaps natural killers."

Tears were running down her face and she buried her head in her lap.

Cowen spoke up. "I recognized only one of the men sketched. He was the leader of a group of men at Skidegate involved in what our trading party decided was waterfront security. I met with him once when we first arrived at the Skidegate beach last year. He has a speech impediment that makes him very difficult to understand. The two Haida translators that were travelling with us convinced him that I was indeed a trader. Otherwise, I would not have survived. He was extremely aggressive and had pushed me to the ground with a wicked-looking long spear that had a sharp metal tip."

Roger said, "I recognized all four of the men and both of the women sketched. And I participated in the further discussion that helped identify the two men with limps. We agreed that there are many men in Skidegate with facial scars, but two of the four described were probably identified because their scars are illustrated very well."

Robert said, "One of the men sketched is from my family. He married one of my sisters. She is dead. I have been told that he killed her. I have also been told that he is now dead. He was a terrible person."

Roger stood up and moved to where Bedard was standing. "Last night this small group spoke of the inherent danger in any contact with the Haida. We are very concerned that the Skidegate Haida, although not as fierce and warlike as the northern Haida and the Tlingit, have security systems in place to protect their villagers from their many enemies. We concluded that having a small group of our warriors visit this area to gather information will be very difficult and dangerous. The second idea that we talked about is that child slaves are often traded or gifted to other Haida chiefs. After four years we may find that almost none of our children and young people are now in the Skidegate area."

This caused a great rumble of conversation in the larger group. Two people stood up and Bedard beckoned them to come forward.

Chief Roanyon came over behind Bedard.

"The first person is Aunt Betty, followed by one of her granddaughters who is married to one of my father's family."

Bedard turned to look at him. He shrugged his shoulders. "I am only now getting to know them all again, and I am not good at names."

"You have not met Aunt Betty because she stays at home in bed almost all the time. I am very surprised that she is here and amazed that she is coming forward to speak. She, like Old Chief Sparrow, does not speak clearly now, so the granddaughter will translate. Aunt Betty is seventy or even eighty years old, and in her lifetime has travelled extensively up and down the coast. She speaks all of the local languages and dialects and knows everyone for hundreds of miles around. She now says that she will die soon. But Inchesca and Bella disagree, telling us that she has several more years to go.

"Aunt Betty has visitors constantly, and as a result she knows everything that is going on in this area. Some of her visitors have travelled three days just to visit with her for a few hours."

Aunt Betty had now reached Bedard and the people sitting at the front. The group had all stood up and were clapping lightly.

The woman with her came to Bedard. "I am Rosa, and I will help Aunt Betty talk." Aunt Betty faced Bedard.

"I am pleased to meet you. You are even better looking than what Mother told me."

There was a squeak close by that Bedard thought was Mother. The clapping intensified briefly and most of the group were now smiling.

The large group settled down again, and it seemed to Bedard that this highly respected woman's presence had removed all the frowns. She took the talking stick and turned to look at her friends and family.

"I think that the plan to try to identify and then retrieve our lost children is a good one," she said, and the group started to rumble again. "But many of the younger children will be difficult to identify because they will have lost the ability to speak our dialect and probably have been adopted into Haida families where they are now living good, comfortable, ordinary lives. Possibly they should not be taken from their new homes and families. Also, some of the older children are now adults and may be happily married with children of their own."

The group continued to rumble as many of them talked to their friends and family.

"Older Musqueam children may be able to identify some of the younger Musqueam children, but these older children may not now be living in the same villages because some slaves are traded, as you all know. I do not know how the first group of warriors from Tsusnahm will accomplish its mission."

Bedard looked at Roger who continued to frown. They had talked at length about this same difficult problem.

She turned to look at Bedard. "One of the first ideas that I had was for you to capture all the children and young people that you can find and bring them all back here. That would in theory be very simple. But of course, this would bring problems that the Musqueam Nation, even when supported by both our Squamish and all of our Salish brothers, may not be able to deal with.

"You mentioned the large raiding party that attacked and enslaved some of our Salish sisters and children at Port Gamble two summers ago. That group of warriors was composed of northern Haida from the Northern Masset area and from the islands to the north of them, and a large group of Tongass people, actually from the Tlingit Sea Lion tribe. I know this to be true. The United States sent a large warship to battle these invaders, and the Haida and the Tlingit lost many warriors, including a Tlingit Chief. A small group of Tlingit warriors returned last summer and, in retaliation for the chief that they had lost, killed a United States war chief named Ebey who had settled on Whidbey Island. I know this to be true. Mr. Douglas knew of this massacre and did nothing. I was very sad when the confirmation of this battle and the news of Mr. Ebey's death finally reached me last September.

"I was also advised of another Haida attack that also took place two years ago. A village of the Qualicum people at the mouth of the Qualicum River was completely destroyed, and almost all of the people living there were killed. This attack was probably carried out by some of the same large warrior group. The village was left in ashes and there was only one survivor, an elder hiding inside a tree stump."

The group was now very quiet.

Aunt Betty was silent for a long time, and the group continued to be quiet, thinking about what she had said.

"I have thought about this matter for some time. I have not talked to any of my visitors about it for fear that they might unintentionally pass on information that could reach the Haida. I continue to be very disappointed that Mr. Douglas allows a group of Skidegate Haida to remain camped near Fort Victoria. They are there year-round and increase to a very large number in the summer. They are *undesirables*."

She turned to face Bedard. "The next time you visit your friend, Mr. Douglas, I would like you to ask him to review his records—and he does have good clear records—of the death and devastation that the Haida, along with the Yakamas and others, have brought to the people living peacefully along our river and the coastal lands."

Bedard nodded his head. He'd heard of the battle with the USS *Massachusetts* in February of 1856, and the killing of Colonel Isaac Ebey the following summer. These were fierce warriors.

Aunt Betty and Rosa returned to their seats in the grass amongst their family and friends, and the group again rose to their feet and clapped lightly in appreciation of her words.

A group of three women stood up and Bedard beckoned them forward. Bedard soon realized that they were Lois and her two sisters whom he had met on his second day in Tsusnahm. They were not smiling.

When they reached the front, they introduced themselves. It was Lois who spoke.

"We represent the largest family in Tsusnahm, and we lost the most children to the Haida. The Haida killed ten of the older men and women of our family when they attacked us four years ago."

The group was very quiet.

"We agree that the plan to try to identify and then retrieve our lost children is a good one."

The group started to rumble in conversation again.

"But we think that this effort will cost too many lives due to the inevitable violence that will occur during our actions and for many years afterwards. Hundreds of our men will be lost. We cannot afford this."

The group was really rumbling now.

The three women then yelled in Musqueam at the top of their voices.

"STAY HOME, NO WAR, STAY HOME, NO WAR!"

They repeated this over and over again. Many people, mostly women, stood up and shouted the same words. It was quite deafening.

Bedard and Roger exchanged glances again. Both were nodding their heads and grimacing. Reaction to any action was definitely possible. The three women continued their chant as they returned to their places and moved off toward their homes followed by most of the village women.

When they left, Bedard looked around.

"Aunt Betty and the other women of this village have given us much to think about. We will have another general meeting today after the late meal. Thank you all for coming."

Bedard and Roger went directly to their home. They were followed by a number of people who wanted to better understand how Bedard would respond to what they had just heard. Bedard paused a moment at the door and asked Dorono if he would find Lois and her two sisters and Aunt Betty and Rosa and invite them all to this smaller meeting.

The group crowded into the room. It was quite warm and they arranged benches and floor blankets near the fireplace.

Bedard started speaking right away.

"Aunt Betty provided us with more detailed information on the Haida attacks two years ago, and that was good. She asked me to talk to Mr. Douglas, and I will."

Dorono appeared at the door and shook his head.

Bedard continued, "Lois and her two sisters made it clear that if we go north to visit the Haida we must have a perfect plan, or we may subject this area to a horrible Haida reaction that may go on for years with great loss of life. As you saw, most of the women in the village agree with her and probably most of the men too. Last night, Chief Roanyon, Roger and I also spoke of this and we agree with Lois. We talked well into the night and came to several conclusions that I would now like to put forward for your consideration.

"Firstly, we concluded that if we decide to go north, the Haida will know that we are coming and will confront us. Moreover, our plan to select and train warriors for this first exploratory visit will not go unnoticed."

There was quite a rumble of voices as the listeners reacted to this. Bedard waited to see if anyone wished to speak up, but no one did.

"Secondly, if they believe that our first visit is not an aggressive one, they will not confront us in an aggressive manner. The Skidegate chief, Chief Taan, his elders, his family leaders, his warrior leaders and his advisors are very intelligent and competent people. We believe that they will somehow try to meet with us and negotiate."

Bedard stopped and looked around the room as several small groups of people were talking amongst themselves. Again no one wished to speak up.

"Thirdly, Chief Taan does not have the full support of all of the people who live in and around his village. Some of the warriors may not agree to negotiate and may decide to attack us while we are there or at some time in the future, perhaps even here in the village of Tsusnahm. It is possible that these warriors will be the same warriors who came here four years ago."

Once more there was a rumble of voices as the group reacted to this.

"As some of you know, we plan to travel north for the first visit in a large British ship. If we were to have this vessel travel in and anchor close to Skidegate, we might be able to meet and negotiate with Chief Taan and his group in the relative safety of this large boat. We also talked about negotiating with them at a distance, perhaps sending messengers back and forth. We then tried to think of what exactly we would say—what we would be prepared to negotiate. We did not, however, have any reasonable ideas on how to deal with any rebellious warriors. It was getting late and we ran out of ideas."

Mothana stood up and said that there would be a midday meal under the big tree for those that did not have any other arrangements.

Thirty
January 27, 1858 (Afternoon & Evening)

The group gradually moved out of the building. Bedard had a chance to talk with several people.

After the meal, Bedard wandered east down the waterfront trail to the end of the village where there were a number of sitting logs by the water. He sat on the grass with his back to a log and a good view of the river flowing past. He plucked a blade of grass that was just starting to grow. It tasted very good and he smiled.

Chief Roanyon, Roger and Mot had been sitting together eating, and when they were finished they saw Bedard walking down the path to the east and decided to follow him. Not saying anything, the three sat down on Bedard's log and also watched the river. Roger eventually got up and went to the water's edge to throw flat stones out onto the water to see how many times he could get them to skip.

Another hidden skill, thought Bedard, and he smiled.

Roger looked over at him and smiled. Then Chief Roanyon got up abruptly and walked rapidly back toward the centre of the village.

In due course, a number of others wandered down the trail and found Bedard, Roger and Mot. Chief Big Bon, Dorono, Chief Enthica and Fenciao with Cowen arrived first and sat on a log. Then the heavyweights came—Wantano, Dobera and Komchowa, who also sat on logs. Then the remainder of the group that had met last night arrived: Robert and his three brothers and Arentha and her husband Pisano.

Chief Roanyon came back with a number of maps of the area around Skidegate that Bedard had obtained from Fort Victoria and had given to him. He spread these on the ground, held in place with small rocks.

To everyone's amazement, along came Aunt Betty with Rosa and Mother carrying one of the few chairs in the village. Old Chief Sparrow and a few villagers followed. Of course, everyone stood up when Aunt Betty arrived. She directed Mother to place the chair near Bedard's log facing the river.

She did not say anything. Roger, down at the water's edge, decided to continue skipping rocks.

Aunt Betty called out to him with Rosa translating. "I had a son by my second husband who was good at doing that. He is dead now. I think that you do it better!"

Roger turned and gave the group a small bow.

Aunt Betty turned slightly toward Bedard who was now sitting on the log.

"I received a report of your short meeting just before *lunch*. Thank you for considering my thoughts and ideas."

Bedard nodded and smiled.

"I think that you are right," she said. "The Haida will know that you are coming to Skidegate before you arrive, although I have not received confirmation of this yet. If I do, I will let you know immediately."

Bedard nodded. He was not smiling now.

"I also think that it is a very clever idea to plan the travel north in a large ship. I agree with you that the Skidegate chief and his advisors are probably very intelligent and competent people. I do not know these people. They are too far away from here, and they have a terrible reputation. I find it interesting that you sense that if the chief and his advisors believe that this first visit is not an aggressive one, they will not confront your party in an aggressive manner and might be willing to meet with you and negotiate. This is something that I had not considered, and the more I think about it, the more I find it quite plausible.

"I also had the thought today that it is possible the raid on our village was accomplished by a small group of warriors without the approval of the chief and his advisors. The chief would then be very angry and embarrassed by this action, but he would not admit to others that these men had done something that did not have his approval. But he might eventually evict them from his village as a punishment in spite of the slaves that they had brought back. All of our villages expel undesirable members from time to time. These people live in buildings that they construct well away from their previous homes. If some or all of these rebellious warriors have also been expelled from Skidegate, I think that they would move west, away from the coast, to live. I doubt if they would move north, up the coastline. The weather is not good there.

"It is also possible that only the leaders of the raiding warrior group were expelled. And as you have said, if some of the warriors who were on the raid are still living in Skidegate, they may not agree to negotiate and become dangerous. It might also be possible that warriors who have been expelled may come back at the time you are there. A very dangerous situation!

"I have come to you again today because my memory is not as good as it used to be. I understand that you have a strong mind. That is good. We in the village of Tsusnahm have already benefited from your thinking. I now find that things that I used to know and thoughts that I had yesterday sometimes disappear. Perhaps you will find that also when you become more mature."

The group found that amusing, and that pleased Aunt Betty as she rose to leave.

"And I still think that we should make this trip," she said. "I think that the plan to try to identify and then retrieve our lost children is a good one."

Bedard said, "Thank you, Aunt Betty and Rosa, for coming and sharing these thoughts with us."

A polite cheer came from the group as Aunt Betty left, leaning on the arms of Rosa and Mother. Some of the villagers left with her.

Bedard thought, *Aunt Betty is an incredible person who has made considerable contributions to this group today.*

He faced the twenty people who remained and addressed them.

"We have all been thinking about how best to negotiate with Chief Taan. The first important idea that Aunt Betty left with us is to question whether the warriors who came here did so on their own rather than with the support of their chief and his advisors. It would indeed be useful to know if some or all of the warriors who came here four years ago have actually been expelled from Skidegate. Aunt Betty suggests that if they have been expelled they may have moved west, away from the ocean, to start their own community. If some have been expelled, then the question becomes who remains and are they likely to become a problem? If we had answers to these questions it would help us understand what we should put on our negotiation list."

Bedard moved to the maps that Chief Roanyon had placed on the ground. Everyone followed him and moved in closer as he knelt down to examine the map of the Skidegate area.

Chief Roanyon said, "This place with the stream would be a good place to build one or two longhouses. It is some distance from Skidegate, about six miles. Another good site is just beyond the large island. Another location may be inland near one of those small lakes."

"These are people who have lived their entire lives near water," said Bedard. "I would also choose the place with the stream. They could also have a lookout in the grass on the hill at this point, not far away. The location beyond the island would be difficult to protect and these people will have lots of enemies. Unfortunately, we do not have any information about the warriors, and we are unlikely to learn anything about them before we leave here. So, the plan is to travel in a large boat and anchor near Skidegate. We should be able to see the longhouses, if they exist, with our high-power telescopes."

"During my visit last year," said Arentha, "no one mentioned to me that some warriors had been evicted, but perhaps they would not say anything because these people were so terrible that they were not to be referred to again. I do remember that there were two old longhouses facing the beach near that large stream, but they were abandoned many years ago."

"I visited Skidegate several times," said Roger. "But I did not travel to the west of the village. I did travel across the water from the south, but I do not remember seeing anything to the west. I was not carrying a telescope. If we were to stop at Cumshewa to trade before we go to Skidegate, I may be able to get some information from the chief there. I know him quite well, Chief Tsang. Skedans is located right here, not too far away from Cumshewa, at the mouth of the Cumshewa inlet on the south side. Tanu is located here farther to the south of Skedans on this island."

Bedard nodded. "Stopping to trade at Cumshewa is a good idea, Roger. Perhaps we should also stop and trade at Skedans and Tanu. When we reach Skidegate, Chief Taan will send a few canoes out to meet us. He will assume that we have something to trade, which will be true. We will then send an invitation to Chief Taan to visit us on the boat. I think that he will come. When he comes, we will have to decide how many of his advisors to allow on board with him. We will need to decide what to say to him when he comes on board. Does anyone have something to add at this time?" He waited a moment and when no one answered said, "Right, well, we will meet again under the big tree after the main meal tonight."

Most of the group left the area until only Bedard, Roger, Mot, Cowen and Chief Roanyon remained. They moved on to Bedard's building and sat thinking for a long time. Then Robert cautiously opened the door. Bedard got up and motioned for him to come in. Robert was followed by his three brothers.

The eight men shook hands, and Robert smiled. "We have been thinking and talking amongst ourselves about the ideas that have been put forward today. We are most impressed with Aunt Betty. We had heard a little bit about her, of course, but we had never met her. Her reputation, as you are no doubt aware, is that she knows everyone on this coast and everything that is happening. But we did not appreciate how intelligent she is, nor did we realize how old she is. We just did not think about her in that way. We thought that *we* were old, now we think that there is yet hope!"

The group laughed.

"Her theory that the marauding warrior group who came here four years ago did so without the support of Chief Taan and his advisors sounds reasonable to us. At that time, the people of Skidegate were being constantly attacked by several of their enemies, and the chief would not have wanted any of his warriors to be absent for any length of time. It was a very difficult time there for many years. The population was still dropping due to sickness, and they had lost some of the battles. Their enemies had taken some of their children as slaves. We also agree that, if Aunt Betty's theory is correct, some or all of these warriors may have been banished from Skidegate. We know Chief Taan, and he has a vicious temper. Over the years he has not mellowed as some of his contemporaries have."

Roger and Cowen nodded.

"We suspect that children brought back in such a raid would not have been appreciated by the chief even though he needed more children and slaves at that time. If that is true, he would have sold, traded or gifted many of these children to other Haida villages and other nations. Perhaps a few older children may still be in Skidegate, but we doubt if there would be more than one or two remaining. In such a case, the villages of Cumshewa, Skedans and Tanu will have no doubt received some of these children, perhaps even the small village of Haina where some of our family now live. However, it is likely when the chiefs of these villages heard the story of the children's capture and the expulsion of the warriors from Skidegate that they chose not to keep the children out of respect for the Skidegate chief who is very influential.

"As you know, Skedans is the largest village in this area. Traditionally, the chiefs of Skedans and the Tsimshian village of Kitkatla have had a special relationship. Kitkatla is located on an island near the mainland and the relationship between the two villages goes back many hundreds of years. Their trading ties are very strong although they occasionally find themselves at war with each other." The brothers shook their heads and looked down in disgust. "We think it possible that many of these children and some of the young people will have gone over to Kitkatla in trade or as gifts. We agree it is likely some or all of this warrior group have been expelled from Skidegate, and they might have quite a few of the children and young people that you will be looking for in their new community."

"Thank you," said Bedard. "Thank you all for sharing this information and your ideas with us. I think that we will now be able to plan our first trip north with a minimum of risk."

Robert and his brothers then left the building, followed by Mot, Cowen and Chief Roanyon.

"It would certainly be useful to have some confirmation of these ideas," Bedard said to Roger, "but if we continue to be conservative about our plans for the trip, it is probable that we will be successful and find the location of many of the children and young adults."

"Agreed," said Roger. "But we still need to plan what to say if we have the chance to negotiate something with Chief Taan. If the children are now generally centralized in the warrior village west of Skidegate and in the Tsimshian village of Kitkatla, this would simplify our second trip considerably."

Bedard nodded. "I wonder if we could get an agreement from the local Haida villages not to interfere with a large Musqueam war party intent on destroying the warrior village."

Roger looked uneasy. "I have never been involved in an attack on a family village. I wonder if it is possible to have a plan to minimize children and women casualties. If the attack was planned for a time when many of the men were away fishing or hunting, then the village could be easily captured and we could wait for the return of the men."

"Perhaps," said Bedard. "Except that the fishermen often take their families with them and fish for several months."

"If the weather was expected to be rainy and cold," said Roger, "perhaps many of the families would stay home."

Roger and Bedard sat for a while thinking. Adrona came in to announce that the late meal would be served at Mother's very soon, and the two men followed her through the doorway and down the path to Mother's building.

After eating and talking to many of those in attendance, Bedard and Roger went down to the big tree and joined the early arrivals to talk about the day's interesting discussions. Soon the group was quite large as the villagers and their visitors arrived. Bedard took the talking stick and started to address them.

"I am very pleased with the progress that we have made today in developing a plan for the two trips north this year. Many people have come forward to share their ideas and thoughts, and we thank them for that.

"It is possible that most of the warriors who were involved in the attack here at Tsusnahm have been expelled from Skidegate and have many of our children and young people with them as slaves."

The large group was quiet, listening intently.

"It is also probable that most of the remaining children and young people have ended up at the Tsimshian village of Kitkatla. The first group to travel north will be travelling in a large British sailing ship that will be trading with various Haida villages just to the south of Skidegate. We will hopefully obtain very good information from these people as to the whereabouts of the children and young people. We still have a number of problems mentioned by Aunt Betty. When we first visit Skidegate, it is probable that Chief Taan will be expecting us and will also understand that this initial visit is not an aggressive one. We hope that they will meet with us to talk and negotiate.

"Now," said Bedard, "Does anyone wish to take this opportunity to come up and speak to us?"

He waited a few moments but no one came forward.

"Thank you all for coming again tonight. We will have other information meetings as our plans become firmer."

Thirty-One
February 10–12, 1858

Bedard was leading a group of ten warriors who were running at a fast pace eastward along the familiar well-worn trail on the north side of the river. This was Team Red's first training trip and the group, headed by Chief Enthica, was nervous. Mot was in the middle of the group following two of the warriors carefully. He was attached to them with stiff six-foot cords, and he was very excited. He was running for the first time in his life. Liz was in front and the new crossbreed, Bobo, was trailing the group. Bobo, a mature seven-year-old hunter, was showing great promise. A second group of local security dogs was being trained and evaluated, and the warriors appreciated their potential contribution.

Although it was a training trip, the objective was very serious. Two white men had been reported encamped near the Harrison River and they needed to be identified and perhaps dealt with. Everyone was in full gear and carrying the regulation eighty pounds of supplies, including fighting equipment. This group's head feathers were red and their faces were all painted the same black and red. Fearsome indeed! This was a very unusual transformation for these men. Their ancestors had rarely if ever used war feathers or war paint, but everyone liked the effect.

Bedard had created several fighting forces before, but none of the previous groups had been so focused and eager to get into action. He had decided to make the training sessions serious from the very first day so as to take advantage of the natural energy that the men had relative to the main objective: to recover family members from the Haida. Thus, face paint, feathers, war chants, custom fighting equipment and latent anger.

The selection camp had been most interesting in that two hundred and six men showed up, including six men from Vancouver Island led by Cowen. Almost all of the men were very fit and very serious. They were all members of family groups who had lost children to the Haida attack four years ago.

The actual selection process focused initially on fitness and body mass. This created a group of eighty-eight large men, many of them tall.

These men were interviewed by the three Musqueam village chiefs who were supervising the selection process, and those who were married with young families were asked to go home. This reduced the group to sixty-one warriors. This also caused a huge ruckus that took all of Bedard's negotiating skills and physical strength to calm down. Several very fierce men with families were shocked and indignant that they would not be included in the first group. The three teenagers from Tsusnahm were watching with obvious interest.

One man, Oricon, actually took on Bedard man-to-man in a fierce fight that ended only when Bedard had him in a full nelson with his face in the ocean. His friends took over and talked with him for half an hour before he approached Bedard a bit sheepishly to apologize. No one had seen Bedard fight before, and they were most impressed with the obvious controlled skill with which he contained and then subdued the massive Oricon, who was easily twice his size.

Bedard's early morning meeting with Mot was one of the most difficult sessions Bedard had ever experienced. Mot was adamant that he wanted to be included in the warrior training group. He was small, not in good shape and almost blind. He was, however, a linguist—not at Cowen's level, but close. He felt that he could get in shape very rapidly and that his personality was such that he could augment Cowen's skills in the contact with the communities to the north. The Haida would be more comfortable with Cowen and him together.

Bedard then had a session with Cowen, who knew Mot very well. Cowen agreed that contact with the communities to the north, especially those under the influence of the Haida, would benefit from Mot's presence and contribution. Bedard finally agreed to recommend that Mot be included in the warrior training group but did not want his inclusion in any of the planned warrior actions. Mot was not completely happy.

Cowen was married with children, and Bedard wanted to include him in the warrior training group but could not. Cowen's valuable linguistic capabilities and current direct experience with many of the northern communities presented Bedard with a serious problem. Cowen recognised the conflict and suggested that he and Mot would be specialists who would be involved in the warrior training group but would not participate in any future combat. Bedard agreed to recommend this.

In the early afternoon of that same day, the chiefs requested a meeting with all the adults of the village of Skwis at the big tree. They had decided that the decision not to include married men with families included Chief Big Bon. Bedard was very sad because Chief Big Bon had become one of his close friends in the village, due in part to the fact that the chief had saved his life and also because he was a very nice person. Chief Big Bon and Mot were similar in that they both started out the training session needing concentrated and focused effort to become fit. Now both of them were well on the way to accomplishing that objective.

Chief Big Bon and his wife had lost four small children to the Haida. This was probably not going to be an easy meeting.

Dorono and his wife sat to Chief Big Bon's right. Inchesca and Bella sat on either side of Chief Big Bon's wife. The rest of the family formed a circle. This group was at the big tree about half an hour before the time that the chiefs had requested, and they were talking adamantly. Fenciao refused to sit down and roamed around behind the group in some distress.

Bedard, Adrona and Noua sat on the front step of their building watching and saying nothing. Chief Roanyon and Mothana joined them and also said nothing.

The large group of warriors in Tsusnahm disappeared. They knew the issue that needed to be resolved. All the warriors liked Chief Big Bon and appreciated his leadership and warrior skills.

As the time for the meeting neared, a group of villagers arrived at the big tree and, supported by the drummers, began a chant accompanied by soft clapping. Chief Big Bon was obviously greatly admired by everyone.

Bedard and the three chiefs approached the group and sat down on the grass.

Chief Big Bon rose to his feet and faced them.

"I cannot be included in the warrior fighting force being selected. Neither can my son, Dorono. Our family, our village of Skwisahthun, will be represented by our best warrior, Fenciao. We are very pleased with this decision. Fenciao has the full support of our entire family."

Chief Big Bon's family and the villagers started to clap. Quite incredibly, the other warriors materialized clapping. Fenciao was quite surprised. A number of his close friends approached him and gave him big hugs and slammed him on the shoulder.

Bedard thought that this was the perfect solution and he was not surprised that this incredible family had pulled together to support Chief Big Bon in what must have been a very difficult decision.

Two weeks had passed since the first training session and all of the warriors were progressing extremely well. A number of the married warriors, including Chief Big Bon, Dorono and Oricon, continued to participate as active trainers and support personnel.

As a result of the success of this selection camp, Bedard changed his mind and decided to recommend the creation of two teams of nine men plus two team leaders for the ongoing training period. He further proposed that Roger and Chief Enthica be the team leaders. These decisions were well received by the whole warrior group.

Roger did not have the same body mass as some of the others, but he was easily the most fit. He also had two years of Haida coastal experience that was thought to be crucial to the success of the initial venture. He was highly respected not only for his leadership skills but also his fighting prowess. He had a thin build but had incredible hand–eye coordination and punishing physical kung fu fighting dexterity, as several of the warriors found when they survived scrimmages with him. Roger's incredible flying body fighting style was impossible to escape, and they ended up on their backs with large chest bruises. Roger was only a passable archer but one of the best riflemen of the group.

Chief Enthica was very pleased to be chosen as a team leader. He spoke English quite well and understood many of the local dialects, although not to the same extent as Mot and Cowen. He was not discouraged by Roger's presence and obvious skills because he felt that they both were very fit and intelligent and would be members of the first group.

On the first morning after the selection process, Bedard was very impressed by the final group of twenty men.

Addressing the larger group, he stressed that all warriors would participate in the fighting force that would be assembled later in the year. But he was adamant that the initial force would be a smaller group that would explore the islands of the Haida and bring back essential information in order to focus the main force's efforts.

Team Red moved at a steady pace for ten hours with two half-hour rest periods. They did not anticipate meeting anyone. Most travellers used the south shore because Fort Langley was located there. The north shore trail, although well used by native fishermen just before and after the summer flood period, was ignored the rest of the year. Bedard had heard that some white men had recently been seen using the trail off-season. He felt that the ferociousness of his group would create a situation where it would be easy to deal with any white men that they might encounter. In any case, the training trip was exactly what this group of warriors needed at this time.

At the end of the first day, they had dealt with one encounter with a small family of local natives. Mot successfully provided the social interface. They had arrived at the target campsite on schedule, and although weary were pleased with themselves. All of the group had a reasonable rest overnight with campsite guard duty shared by everyone. The two dogs were stationed some distance up and down the main trail.

The second day was similar. They had one encounter with two native hunters, again smoothed over by Mot, who was quite pleased with his contribution to the group. Mot was now very fit, and although he did not carry a full pack had no problem catching up to the group after the encounters.

The warriors' second camp was relatively close to the Harrison River where the white men were said to be encamped. The number of men in this camp and its exact location was not known. Again, the warriors' campsite guard duty was shared by everyone, with the two dogs positioned strategically to the east.

The next morning the group split up into five teams of two. Using maps created by those familiar with the area, four of the teams moved forward to investigate and search for the target camp. One team stayed in the vicinity of the campsite to protect the rear end of the operation. This was all part of the training sessions that Bedard had led the warriors through over the past two weeks. Bedard and Mot stayed in the camp area as well and allowed the warriors to do the work.

The target camp was not easy to locate even by the very experienced hunters and trappers who were part of this team. Just after noon, the warrior group reassembled at the base campsite, and the target camp was marked on the map based on three long-distance sightings.

This camp was well hidden, and the group was impressed with the skill of the white men. It was on the east side of the Harrison River well back from the water in the forest and thought to be in a sand cliff cave. All four teams had spent more than six hours moving toward the river from different directions searching for the camp. The three teams that had identified the target camp had spent about three hours in the tall grass near the river before they sighted activity on the far side of the river. A small boat was found hidden near the shoreline, and one man moving in the forest near the sand cliffs had been seen by two teams.

The fourth team, which was assigned to a more northerly path, reported an occupied lean-to and two local natives fishing in the lower Harrison River.

A plan was devised by the group, wherein the fishermen's boat would be borrowed to transport all the warriors to the east side of the small river. Then a new base camp would be set up and further investigations would fix the target camp and allow contact with the white men.

Bedard was pleased with the progress so far. The campsite security was carefully planned for the evening and the early morning. One team of two plus Mot went to the area of the lean-to so that they could contact the fishermen in the morning and obtain the required transport for the rest of the group.

They crossed the river early in the morning without incident. The fishermen were quite cooperative although bemused by this ferocious group in paint and feathers.

A new campsite was located for the group and the three teams again set out to find the exact location of the target camp and, if possible, determine how many people were there.

Before noon, one of the teams reported back to the campsite confirming the location. The other two teams had set up a perimeter watch of that camp. The consensus was that there were more than two men at the target camp at this time, and that the men did not seem to have any security system. Two trails were identified: one continuing east along the river and another going in a northerly direction toward the Harrison Lake Village. Best reports indicated that the village population was currently about fifty. Several of the warriors had friends living there.

Bedard was reluctant to approach the target camp directly because this could be dangerous. It was suggested that one of the white men could probably be captured and used as a hostage in order to start communication with the other men. Bedard agreed to this approach, so the perimeter around the camp was expanded and the group waited patiently for the opportunity to entrap one of the men. Bedard also thought that there would be at least one emergency exit from the cave, so two of the warriors searched and found one potential exit in a nearby wind-fall and another between two very large rocks. A watch was also set up at these positions.

Just after midday, one man left the cave and moved down a trail toward the boat. He was carrying a rifle over his shoulder. When he was at the boat and about one thousand feet from the cave, he was approached by Bedard and Chief Enthica. With two warriors close in the forest as backup, he was subdued without incident. Bedard did not recognize the man, who said that his name was Bill Bennet. He readily volunteered that there was only one other person in the cave and that his name was Julius Voight. This name Bedard *did* recognize. It was the second name on the list, and Bedard knew him well. Bennet said that he was on the way over to Fort Langley for supplies and that he had planned to stay there overnight and return the next day in the early afternoon.

Although the capture had gone well, Bedard was not completely comfortable with Bennet's claim that there was only one man in the cave. He felt that the upcoming negotiations would not be as simple as the group had anticipated.

Bennet was tied up and lightly gagged with one warrior left to guard him. A second warrior was positioned close in the forest as a security action, and Bobo was stationed up the Fraser River trail as further security.

Liz and one warrior were positioned to the north on the trail to the village.

Bedard went around to all of the perimeter positions and talked with each of the warriors, sharing his concerns about the danger associated with the next step in their proposed action.

In the early afternoon, one of the warriors reported to Bedard that he had heard a woman's voice coming from the cave. Bedard took a warrior who knew most of the Harrison Lake village families and they cautiously positioned themselves closer to the front of the cave. Soon a woman came out, took some wet clothes out of a basket and placed them on some nearby bushes to dry and returned to the cave. The warrior nodded, signaling that he knew the woman, so they moved carefully back so they could talk.

Her name was Tonka, and she was a newcomer to the village from a large native nation much farther to the south and east. She had arrived alone on foot about a year ago. She'd said that she was a hunter and she spoke a similar language to the dialect spoken by those in the Harrison Lake village. She was very tough, aggressive and impolite and not well liked by the villagers, but had nonetheless managed to attract a man named Thorn to live with her. The couple did not live in the village but farther east up a small creek, but the warrior did not know much more about her.

Bedard did not like this development because he thought that Voight could easily use her as a hostage.

Shortly after the discussion about Tonka, she burst from the cave laughing and giggling and ran down the trail toward the boat, with Voight running closely behind her. As per the basic plan, a warrior stepped out of the bushes and brought down Voight with an arrow in his leg. Tonka stopped and turned around and was grabbed from the rear by another warrior. She fought both warriors fiercely and was eventually subdued. Bedard directed that both Voight and Tonka be securely tied and gagged.

Bedard cautiously entered the cave and found a third man on the ground tied to a stake. He was identified as Tonka's companion, Thorn. He was carried out and lightly tied and gagged. Bedard directed the warriors to make a stretcher for the man and tie him to it.

This was starting to become very complicated.

A warrior reported to Bedard that Liz had arrived and that Bedard was needed up the village trail. Leaving Chief Enthica to complete the action near the cave, Bedard sped off up the trail with Liz and came upon another man with an arrow in his leg. He had apparently gone to the Harrison village to obtain some food supplies.

"Lorne Thompson," said Bedard. "How wonderful to meet you again!"

Another name on his list! He directed the two warriors to drag Lorne to the cave and then come back for the supplies. One of the warriors would then guard the trail to the village with Liz.

Returning to the cave, Bedard found Voight, Bennet and Tonka tied to trees near the cave and not looking very happy. Tonka's companion, Thorn, was tied face down to a stretcher. Bedard inspected the cave and found nothing of interest. Mot had taken some papers out of the cave. Bedard read them and learned that Voight was soon to be joined by others from San Francisco.

The two warriors arrived dragging Lorne Thompson. He was already gagged so he could not communicate with anyone. He was also tied to a tree.

Bedard went over to where Bill Bennet was tied up and, without speaking, shot an arrow into his leg. Bennet fainted.

Thirty-Two
February 12–14, 1858

Bedard called the warriors to follow him from the cave area to a small clearing about two hundred feet away. Here the remaining group of five warriors, plus Chief Enthica and Mot, sat in a circle with Bedard. The four other warriors were on guard duty with the dogs on the two trails.

Bedard congratulated them for their work in clearing the cave. "You have done very well. We were lucky to avoid a serious confrontation with Voight and Thompson who are powerful enemies to all of us."

With a small smile, Bedard said, "You now can see the advantages and disadvantages of having a woman companion that you cannot control."

The group was not amused. Two of them had serious bruises and cuts from apprehending and subduing Tonka.

"It is very important," Bedard continued, "to have security set up around our camps and positions even when we are in friendly lands. We have much to learn about how to do this." The warriors nodded their heads in agreement. "The dogs that we are training will be very useful to us."

Again, they all nodded their heads.

"I plan to talk to the three men and then kill them. Voight has killed hundreds of people in his lifetime. I do not know Thompson as well, but I have personally seen him kill three men because they disagreed with what he said. I do not know the third man, Bennet. We will talk to him. Tonka and her companion, Thorn, present another problem for us. We need to know exactly what their relationship is to the three white men and to each other. I suspect that Voight wanted her to himself but that she serviced the other two men from time to time."

The group did not know what to make of this.

"I suspect that Tonka is quite volatile and would possibly say to Voight that she was going to leave if she did not get her way. It was perhaps easy for him to stop her or at least manage her. He captured Thorn and tied him to a stake on the floor of the cave as a hostage in an attempt to control her. I suspect that this was only partially successful." The group now started to get angry. "This is not too different," Bedard continued, "from what has probably happened to some of your family members up north with the Haida. Now you see why it is important to find the truth about this group of people and then eventually find the truth about the Haida and how they have treated your families."

Bedard then asked two of the warriors to bring Bennet to the meeting area.

Bennet was favouring his leg with the arrow still sticking in it. Bedard asked Mot, who was one of the group's medical experts, to remove the arrow and bind the leg.

Bennet was obviously afraid of what was going to happen to him next.

"You lied to me," Bedard said. "You may die of your wound. If you continue to lie to me, you will receive another arrow that kills you."

Mot translated for the warriors although some of them had reasonable English.

"I will not lie to you. Ask me anything," said Bennet.

"You were going out in the boat. Why?" said Bedard.

"Voight told me to go to Fort Langley and pick up two men named Conner and Craig and bring them to the cave. I don't know their last names," said Bennet.

"How did he know that they would be there?" said Bedard.

"The last two men who came through two weeks ago told him when these two would arrive at the fort," said Bennet.

"How many men have passed through here?"

"Only two men came here that I know of. Lorne and I arrived at Fort Langley by boat just before Christmas, about seven weeks ago. Voight picked us up in the canoe. We had previously arranged this with him when we met him in San Francisco in September. Then two weeks ago I picked up two men at Fort Langley, Thomas and Bill. They stayed only one day. I don't know their last names. They weren't very friendly and apparently had a terrible trip so far. Voight gave them some food and supplies and they went on toward Hope on the south trail, walking with big packs."

"How long have you known Voight?" asked Bedard.

"I met him twice before in California," said Bennet. "He pays well, but he is sometimes very difficult to work for and with."

"Difficult. How difficult?" asked Bedard.

Bennet was very quiet for some time before he replied. "Voight likes to kill people," he said. "I just try to keep to myself, do what I am told, and survive."

"And Lorne?" asked Bedard.

Bennet thought for a moment.

"I know both Voight and Lorne quite well," said Bedard.

Bennet was surprised. "Lorne is usually quiet, almost mousey. He knows Voight very well, and I think that there is some sort of mutual respect between them. Lorne is a very heavy drinker and he is violent, disruptive and vicious when he is drunk. He is also a killer. There is no alcohol in the cave and amazingly, to me at least, Lorne does not seem to crave any."

"How does Voight pay you?" Bedard asked.

"With gold," Bennet said, "after the job is done. He has always paid. Never a problem." He thought for a while and added, "Until now."

"Go on," said Bedard.

"Voight has a contact at Fort Langley," said Bennet. "I have not met him yet, but it should not be difficult to determine who this is."

Bedard thought that this was another lie, but he did not react, even when Mot and two others looked at him questioningly. *These men were definitely not stupid.*

"Gag him and take him back to the cave area and tie him to his tree," said Bedard.

"I have been very helpful to you. What is going to happen to me?" asked Bennet, becoming very frightened again.

"You are going to die for lying to us again," Bedard said and turned away.

Before Bennet could say anything more, he was gagged. Two warriors dragged him away as he struggled frantically and mumbled.

When the group assembled again, Bedard asked, "Well, what is your reaction to that information?"

"He is lying," Mot said. "He must know Voight's contact at Fort Langley, or at least have a good idea who it is."

The others nodded in agreement.

"I have a plan for all of you to consider," said Bedard. "We should tell Bennet that he is free to go back to California because he was so helpful to us. If we let Bennet go to Fort Langley in the boat, he will meet with Conner and Craig. Bennet can tell them that Julius Voight and Lorne Thompson have been killed by a wild band of natives and that they should return to California because this group knows that both of them are at the fort. He should be encouraged to tell them that he luckily escaped with the boat and he is going back to California, too. We can send two warriors to tail him and find out what he does and who he speaks to, and if Conner and Craig continue on toward Hope we will know that. With any luck, Bennet will not make any mistakes. It would not be good to have to find him again."

Chief Enthica spoke up. "The two men, Thomas and Bill, who passed through two weeks ago going to Hope, need to be identified and stopped."

Bedard nodded thoughtfully. "They have been gone for two weeks, so it now might be difficult to find them."

"We need to take Thorn into the Harrison Lake village in order to get him some care and see if he has any information that we can use."

He directed Mot and two of the warriors who were familiar with some of the villagers to take Thorn.

"I will catch up to you before you reach the village," said Bedard. "But first, before you go, let's talk briefly with Tonka."

Bedard asked two of the warriors to bring Tonka to the meeting area.

She was definitely not pleased with her current situation. When the gag was removed she started protesting loudly and pulling at her bonds.

Bedard ignored her and spoke to the group.

"You will note that her bonds are loose. She has been tied up before, perhaps many times. When we tied her up, she tensed her muscles and arched her body in such a way as to provide her with relatively loose bonds. This in theory is a strategy that would help her escape. She is reported to be a warrior, just like you, and I sense that she has many skills. Some of these skills we may never know until she decides to use them on us. She is now by far the most dangerous of the four prisoners, and we must be very careful."

The group was shocked at this information, and they all looked at Tonka carefully and with new respect. Tonka did not know the language, and she became silent when she realized that no one was paying attention to what she was trying to say.

"I know that you speak English," Bedard said to her. "I have some questions for you." Mot started translating for the warriors.

Tonka showed surprise at this because she had thought that Bedard, who was obviously the leader of this wild group, was himself a native. She squinted her eyes and looked carefully at him.

"Yes," said Bedard. "I am English from England, as one of your family was, probably your mother's grandfather. It is a very useful language to know in this part of the world."

Tonka continued to stare at Bedard, saying nothing.

"I would be surprised if you have any more use for your friend, Thorn. It is unfortunate that Voight brought him here. We will take him to his family in the Harrison Lake village and he will probably survive his ordeal. In order to help Thorn as much as we can, we need to know how long he has been in the cave and what condition he was in when he arrived here."

Bedard stopped talking and waited for Tonka to respond. She did not. Bedard got up.

"Take her back to the tree and tighten her bonds so that she cannot move. I think that we should soak the rope and stretch it before we tie her up so that the bonds are really tight."

Tonka spoke in English. "No, no! He has been here for a week but he has refused to eat, so he is not in good condition now."

"Take her away," said Bedard.

Bedard supervised the transport of Thorn to the village and checked the condition of the four remaining detainees. He went off in the direction of the village and passed the two warriors carrying Thorn on the stretcher. Bedard doubted that Thorn was in any condition to provide them with any information of value at this time.

Arriving in the village, Bedard found Thorn's family with the assistance of Rugard, one of the two warriors who had subdued Tonka. Bedard told them that Thorn was coming home in poor condition because he had not eaten much in the past week. They were pleased that he was returning home and agreed to look after him.

Bedard arranged to borrow a canoe for a week.

Bedard and the four warriors returned to the cave area with the canoe. It was hidden temporarily from the captives to be used the next day to follow Bennet to Fort Langley.

The next day they brought Bennet to his canoe and told him to go to Fort Langley and tell Conner and Craig to return to California with him or suffer the consequences. He said that he was very pleased to do that.

Two of the warriors, Baribo and Timpani, brought the borrowed canoe forward and prepared to follow Bennet. They removed the war paint and feathers and tried to appear normal again. They found this a bit amusing.

Back at the cave area, Bedard brought the two security dogs in and had the warriors set up the travel security for the two-day trip home.

Tonka was untied from the tree and two rope loops fitted around her neck. Her hands remained tied behind her back and her legs tied together with a short rope so that she could walk but not run. She was led by the neck ropes down the path to the west. She appeared to understand what was happening but was still gagged so she was unable to communicate.

This left Voight and Thompson tied to trees at the cave area. They each had an arrow in a leg and were not in good condition, sagging on their ropes. Bedard returned and confronted the two men. He removed their gags and stood there looking at them.

"Have you anything to say to me?"

They glared at him and remained silent.

These were terrible people, and Bedard had no difficulty killing them.

Bedard travelled at a walk, following the group. When he finally caught up, they were taking a brief rest.

He took the gag out of Tonka's mouth. "We have sent Bennet to Fort Langley and he has agreed to return to San Francisco. We have family members there, so we will be able to ensure that this happens. He has been told that if he does not do as he has been directed, he will be killed. There are not many white men in this part of the world so he would be easy to find again."

Tonka said nothing.

"I have killed Voight and Thompson. I knew them quite well. They were terrible people, killers."

Tonka nodded. "Yes, good."

"Now," Bedard said, "I will remove all of your bonds if you give me your word that you will either return to the Harrison Lake village or come with us in peace. We are going to the Musqueam village called Tsusnahm."

Tonka thought for a moment. "I will go with you in peace. I give you my word."

"You have given your word," Bedard said. "I know that you understand that if you break your word there will be dire consequences."

"I understand. I will not break my word."

Several warriors moved forward and untied her. She only then realized that many of the warriors also spoke English. She looked surprised.

Rugard, one of the warriors who captured her, moved over to her and offered his hand. She took it. They looked at each other and smiled.

"You will like our village and the people there," he said.

"Thank you," she said.

Chief Enthica and the other warriors shook her hand. *This will be good,* Bedard thought.

Team Red's return from Harrison was a big event for the village. Team Yellow met them up the river in full paint and feathers and accompanied them to a special dinner at Chief Roanyon's home. All the members of Team Red participated in a convoluted story of their trip and the various adventures, with much laughter and jeering followed by solemn silence when some of the encountered violence was described.

Tonka, of course, was a special visitor, and she was asked to tell her story, which she immediately warned the group was not a happy one. When she stood up it was obvious that not only was she a big woman but that she was also very fit. She spoke slowly in English and Mot translated.

"I was a warrior," she said, "and a hunter in a very large group of male warriors. There were sometimes over one hundred of us going to battle to protect our nation. We fought neighbouring nations that wanted our land or our water, and once a group that wanted our children."

The group murmured appreciatively.

"Yes," she said, "I know something of your troubles … terrible! We also fought endlessly with the white men and the settlers who were encroaching on our land."

She looked at Bedard solemnly.

"This was definitely a man's world that I was involved in, but I became a very good warrior and an even better hunter, and I was very proud of those accomplishments."

The group had become very interested and listened closely.

"There were only three women warriors, and after ten years of successful work and significant contributions to our nation including leadership roles, we were asked to stay in the villages and make babies and wash the clothes."

The group murmured, not knowing what to make of that.

"Perhaps you can understand that this was very difficult for me." She smiled and several of group laughed lightly with her. "So I ran away to the white men's camps and forts. I learnt how to speak English, but soon found that living as a white man's companion was not a good life. Too many clothes to wash!"

She smiled again. The group again laughed.

"So I moved away again. This time I decided to go to the north. It was easy to just follow a large river. The first river that I followed was called the Snake. This river flows northward, and I was able to borrow a small canoe"—the group laughed knowingly—"and make my way north fairly rapidly.

"I tried to pass by most of the larger villages at night and was easily able to find food and to generally keep to myself. Occasionally, I would chance upon a lone hunter and was surprised to find that our languages were similar and that we could communicate a bit. They were usually startled to find a woman alone in the wilderness, but after hearing the short, mostly true story that I told these hunters and other people I met, they wished me well on my travels.

"After almost three months of travel along the Snake, the river started flowing west and eventually flowed into a larger river heading south that was called the Columbia by some white men that I met there. The countryside was also changing dramatically with more mountains and more white settlers. The native villagers were also different. They were aggressive and definitely not friendly to strangers. I decided to follow the Columbia north. At first, it was fairly easy in the canoe, but soon the current and the rapids forced me to travel overland, which was of course much slower. I had started this voyage at the wrong time of the year. When the snow and cold winds came, I had difficulty finding a place to shelter myself. I had no experience with this harsh climate, and I did not anticipate the change in the weather. It was colder and more uncomfortable than I had ever experienced in my whole life."

The listeners all nodded in appreciation of that.

"I found a stretch of rapids on the Columbia that stayed free of ice, more or less, and took over a small lean-to that must have been used the rest of the year by a few fishermen. The open water attracted quite a few animals, and I managed to collect enough furs to keep me warm. When it was really, really, cold I kept the fire going all the time which worked very well. This was definitely a new experience for me. In the spring, I had difficulty deciding when to leave my now very comfortable home." She smiled. "But when I saw some fishermen coming up the river I decided to move northward. I am sure that they were surprised and perhaps pleased with the improvements to their lean-to that I left for them. When the Columbia turned to the east, I decided to follow a smaller river which I was told would continue quite far north to a warm dry valley very similar to the place where I was brought up farther south.

"At the beginning of the summer, I was in this dry valley with the river quite small and the mountains on either side of the valley quite beautiful. Unfortunately, the villagers were again not very friendly to me. Our languages continued to be similar, and I had quite a bit of experience in communicating with sign language. It was difficult for them to understand why I would travel so far and I felt that, although the area was perfect, they would not be pleased if I decided to stay. I was very sad and disappointed. I then met a group of white trappers who were carrying furs from their northern homes westward to a white man's fort called Fort Langley located on a large river. They were going to follow a well-marked trail through a low pass in the mountains.

"One of the men had stumbled and damaged his leg and was unable to carry the huge pack of furs that each one of the men was carrying. They sized me up and offered me the packing job. I decided that I did not need the job, but if I could negotiate a reasonable pay for the work it would give me a good reserve on which to live easier for a time. So, I negotiated what I felt was a reasonable amount and walked to Fort Langley with an eighty-pound pack of furs on my back."

"I loitered around Fort Langley for a month or so and explored the area. I then found beautiful Harrison Lake surrounded by mountains. The people at the Harrison Lake village also did not like me very much. I think that I was then still very aggressive and generally impolite. I did find a very nice man named Thorn, and we started to live together away from the village."

Here she stopped for a moment, looked for a long time at Bedard, and then crumpled to the ground with great wailing and crying. On her knees, she thumped the ground frantically with her fists and then stretched her arms to the heavens, yelled quite fiercely and then fell forward and became still.

Bedard came forward and Mother and Adrona, along with some of the other villagers, carried Tonka to a comfortable resting area in the building.

Bedard stood before the startled group.

"I think that from Tonka's story tonight we would all agree that she has had a very hard but interesting life. I suspect that in the past two years she was looking for a paradise. Perhaps we are all looking for this paradise."

The group had settled down again now and nodded at Bedard's wise words.

"Tonka has only just realized that she has actually found that paradise. But only tonight, as she told her story, did she realize that the most important part of that paradise is missing from her life at this time. Thorn is not here, and I believe that she now feels that she is entirely and completely to blame for that."

The group was very solemn.

Mother came out and took Bedard aside. "She is better but keeps muttering about Thorn. I am very uncomfortable. Will you come and talk to her? She respects you very much, as we all do."

She smiled, and he gave her a little hug.

Tonka was trying to get up when Bedard arrived at her resting place.

"I must go to Thorn. I am so ashamed of myself. I have been very terrible to him, disrespectful of him. He is a fine person and I love him."

She fell back crying and sobbing and buried her head in her arms, apparently not yet prepared to talk to anyone.

Bedard found Mot and asked him to find Modan.

Modan arrived shortly and Bedard said to him, "This is an unusual situation. Tonka wants to go to the Harrison Lake village and try to get back into Thorn's good graces." Bedard smiled. "She is obviously quite clever and resourceful, and once she sets her mind upon a course of action she will not be distracted. I suspect that she will be successful. However, this gives us at least two minor problems. We must not let her start her journey until tomorrow morning. She will probably want to run non-stop for two days until she arrives at Harrison. Can we lend her a canoe and an extremely strong paddler to go with her?" The three of them laughed lightly.

"It may be difficult to stop her from going on her own," Modan said. "But we will try. We will probably need English translations from time to time during the night." Both Mot and Bedard nodded.

"I have someone in mind to help her. He knows the Harrison Lake dialect, so that might be of some help to her. He does not, however, know very much English."

Mot immediately spoke up. "I will travel with them. Perhaps I can be of some assistance in keeping her calm."

Bedard nodded. "Thank you, Mot. I think that she is well worth saving."

Thirty-Three
February 15, 1858

In the early morning, before the sun came up, Bedard left Adrona and Noua still sleeping and went down to the big tree to meet with Fenciao and Chief Enthica. He'd asked them to accompany him on a short trip to Fort Langley that day. The plan was to check up on Bill Bennet and meet with the two warriors who had followed him. Bedard had decided not to take any of the dogs on the trip and had arranged with Modan to have them fed.

Near the big tree, he also found Tonka, Mot, Komchowa and Komchowa's huge buddy Oricon. Bedard and Oricon were good friends now, of course. Oricon was still involved in the training program's hand-to-hand fighting section. Everyone shook Bedard's hand.

Tonka was in good spirits and gave Bedard a raised eyebrow with a nod at Oricon. She was obviously impressed with this giant of a man volunteering to go with her to Harrison. Their small canoe was already loaded, and the three climbed in with Oricon kneeling on mats near the front. Mot was sitting on the packs just in front of Tonka, who was sitting in the rear. Bedard smiled as he thought that the fore–aft balance looked about equal—Tonka was a big woman!

The plan was that they would travel to Fort Langley and trade canoes with the two warriors there, proceed up the Fraser to the Harrison River and then on to the Harrison Lake Village. It would take them two or three long days. Oricon and Mot would then either buy a canoe or walk back, assuming that Tonka would be able to stay in the village with Thorn.

Bedard, Fenciao and Chief Enthica would follow them at some distance in a canoe and land on the south shore just past the junction of the north and south arms of the Fraser River. They would hide their canoe and proceed by foot to Fort Langley, hopefully arriving in the late afternoon.

Bedard would then find the two warriors, who would now be anticipating his arrival, and find out where Bill Bennet was and whether the two men Bennet was to meet, Conner and Craig, had returned south. He was also hoping to find out the identity of Voight's contact at the fort.

If there were any miners camped in the area, he wanted to meet them in case some of them were on his list. This, of course, could cause him some problems.

He had not decided if he was going to meet anyone inside Fort Langley on this trip. But just in case, he was taking one of several letters of introduction penned by James Douglas.

And finally, Bedard wanted to find a campsite just past Fort Langley where warriors on a training trip to Fort Hope could camp.

On the return trip, he felt that the five men could come down the Fraser River by canoe fairly rapidly with the current, pick up the hidden canoe and arrive in Tsusnahm before noon.

Bedard added his pack to the pile in the canoe and clambered aboard. He was designated the amidships paddler for the first leg, with Chief Enthica up front and Fenciao in the rear. He noted that both men had bows with quivers and rifles with several bullet belts. He was going to have them stop at his cache where he would pick up some weapons. He had not decided what. Komchowa pushed them off and waved.

"Do either of you have pistols today?" Bedard asked. They both nodded.

"One," said Chief Enthica

"Two," said Fenciao." But I may only take one on the trail."

"I have not decided what to take from my cache," said Bedard. "Guns and bullet belts are so heavy."

When they reached his cache landing, Bedard stepped out on the rocky foreshore and tried not to make any marks in the sand by walking on rocks and vegetation. At his first canoe cache he removed two pistols, their holsters and belts and a vest heavily loaded with pistol bullets in the pockets. He decided to only take his back-knife set and not take a rifle or a bow. He also took a small groundsheet roll to add to his pack.

He returned to the canoe with his gear. "Two rifles should be enough. I think that if we get into any trouble it will be at close range where the pistols will work best. Fenciao, like you I have not yet decided whether to take one or two pistols."

"I must look at your back-knife pack," said Chief Enthica. "This seems like a good idea."

Off they went again. The tide was on the rise. In this area, the current was moving upstream so the paddling was fairly easy, and they made good time. Well before noon they crossed the Fraser River beyond the islands and arrived at a well-used landing on the south bank.

The group determined what gear they were going to carry on to Fort Langley. Bedard decided to take both pistols and all of the bullets in the vest. Fenciao elected to take one pistol, his rifle and one of his bullet belts. He replaced half of the rifle bullets in the belt that he had chosen with pistol bullets. Chief Enthica chose to take the bow and quiver, his rifle and one of his bullet belts, and no pistol.

Bedard reviewed the armament. "Let the battle begin!"

The group exchanged grim smiles.

Bedard and Fenciao carried the canoe farther into the forest and found a hiding place.

Fenciao watched as Bedard carefully camouflaged the canoe. He shook his head. "You were teaching us how to do that. That is a very useful skill."

Bedard smiled.

Bedard helped Fenciao pack his pistols in his pack so that they could be removed in a hurry, and they were off on a light run toward Fort Langley.

It had started to rain lightly, and the small group did not encounter anyone on the well-used south trail alongside the river. With the fort visible in the distance, they walked slowly through the small new Kwantlen village that Bedard had seen from the north side of the river a month ago. Chief Enthica and Fenciao said that it was built by a Kwantlen group who had moved there from another village farther west.

Fenciao said that they had moved there because they wanted the protection from their enemies that the fort provided. Bedard knew that there was a similar larger Kwantlen village on the north side of the river.

As his group neared Fort Langley, Bedard recognized the two warriors, Baribo and Timpani, who got up from their resting place and walked toward the fort and then turned south. Bedard's group followed. Soon the two warriors moved off the main trail into the forest, and Bedard caught up to them.

Baribo and Timpani both spoke some English. They reported that after meeting with Bennet just outside of Fort Langley, Conner and Craig had initially travelled south with Bennet, but Conner and Craig had turned back toward Fort Hope on an east–west cross trail to the south of Fort Langley.

Baribo said, "We think that the idea of mining gold and making lots of money was too strong for them, whereas Bennet had been severely frightened and did not want any part of the painted warriors who had threatened to kill him if he did not go south."

Timpani nodded. "We followed them and saw that the two men did not go south, so we ran back to the river and then east and found where the trail that Conner and Craig were on joins the main river trail. We then went up this trail and hid in the forest and waited for them. They both looked like very experienced woodsmen and hunters, but they had only just arrived at Fort Langley. They were very tired from the long two-day walk north from the landing place to the south with their big packs. Baribo thought that they would go off the trail and rest for a few days and then try to obtain some food for the trip on to Fort Hope. Sure enough, we heard them in the distance and saw them move off the trail to the south. They were indeed very experienced woodsmen, and they found a perfect camp area more than a mile south of the trail. We would never have found them if we had not guessed correctly what they were going to do," said Timpani. "Baribo is very clever and it is a pleasure to work with him."

Baribo scuffed the ground in some embarrassment at this praise. "Well, it was Timpani who suggested that we wait until nightfall and then try to steal the rifles, pistols, bullet belts and packs."

Bedard shook his head and the group laughed.

"This was incredibly easy," said Timpani, "because by now the two men were completely worn out, and other than choosing a camp area they did not make any security decisions. I would have slept with my pistols loaded and ready to go, but they just stripped everything off, pulled out a wrap from their packs and went to sleep."

"It was a heavy load," said Timpani. "We had a tough time taking it all back to another hiding place that we found. We were impressed at their strength and persistence in carrying all this gear for two days. We were both smiling when we talked about how to camouflage the stash. When we were finished we thought that even Copco would not be able to find it!"

The group laughed because one of the first warrior training topics that Bedard had focused on was security, which included safety, stealth, invisibility and how to camouflage their bodies and their stashes.

"One of our worries," Timpani said, "was that we might not be able to find the stash again ourselves!" The group laughed again.

"We then hid ourselves and split the sleep time so that we could follow Conner and Craig when they awoke in the morning. We had circled their area and were hiding in trees to the south of them. They were very upset with each other and actually had a knife fight that warned us not to get too close to them because they were obviously very good knife fighters. When they finally got that out of their system, they sat down in their campsite and talked for a long time. We could not hear them, of course.

"They then circled their camp looking for our trail, so we changed our plan and climbed down from the trees and travelled farther south very carefully so as not to leave any trail. We eventually came out on the farmland that was being worked by Fort Langley. We still carried our small packs and our bows and quivers, so we killed a small deer and carried this over to the main north–south trail and slowly made our way northward toward Fort Langley. We passed Conner and Craig going south. They really did not have much choice. They had a bit of money but nothing else. So that worked out very well."

"That was very good work," Bedard said. "They are obviously very dangerous men, but I think that they will come back soon."

The group nodded in agreement.

"We also found out the identity of Bennet's contact at Fort Langley," Baribo said. "We did not get close enough to hear his name, but we can point him out to you. He is in charge of the docks and supervises the loading and unloading of the big boats when they come in."

Perfect, Bedard thought. "Show us the other east–west trail. I want to find a suitable camping place for a large warrior team that will travel toward Fort Hope."

The group of five moved off to the south to the east–west trail and then to the east at a light run. A perfect place was found, and Bedard made a small blaze on a tree trunk so that he could find it again. They then went on to the stash and Baribo and Timpani were pleased that it took Bedard some time to find it.

All of the packs and guns were carefully removed and brought back to a clearing, where the packs were taken apart and pouches of currency and coins removed along with some of the tools, utensils and clothing. The remaining clothes and gear were packed back into the packs and casually tossed into the forest for others to find and use. The guns, bullet belts, equipment and gear that Bedard had decided to take back home were divided up amongst the men. They then travelled west so as to pass by Fort Langley.

It was almost dark when they arrived at the Fraser River and went to the canoe located just to the west of the small village. The rain had stopped, but everything and everybody was damp. They built three small fires and cooked the deer that Baribo and Timpani had killed, and changed some of their clothing and dried off.

Bedard still wanted to visit the small camping area to the east of the fort where the white men had apparently camped for a few days on the way to Fort Hope. They had seen only about six camps earlier in the day. It was dangerous to make a visit to this area at night. But he wanted to leave for home early in the morning, so he decided to take Fenciao and Chief Enthica and just visit each occupied campsite. If he found someone of interest he would then decide what action, if any, to take.

They discussed Bedard's basic plan, and Chief Enthica said that if the two of them were wearing only pistols then he would follow at some distance with a rifle. Baribo and Timpani also wanted to be involved, but Bedard wanted the canoe with all the extra guns and gear guarded, and they agreed to do that.

The five of them created a camping-area search plan with several action alternatives and a security plan for the canoe. Everyone thought that the plans were good, so the group of three moved off with Bedard leading. Fenciao had decided to carry a rifle as well as to wear his pistol strapped to his leg. Chief Enthica followed with one of the new rifles and a small backpack of bullets.

There were still only six camps in evidence just to the east of the fort. Three of them were bunched up and three were spaced farther apart as if some camps groups had moved on recently. All the camps had fires with men sitting around them eating and talking.

Bedard visited the first three camps without incident and did not recognize anyone. But when he approached the fourth camp, all three men rose with pistols in their hands and told Bedard not to approach the fire. Bedard immediately backed off, saying that he was only looking for Bennet, a friend who was said to be in the area yesterday.

The three men did not respond. They could see Fenciao standing behind Bedard. He had dropped his rifle and pulled his pistol up to a firing position. Chief Enthica had his rifle up covering his friends, but he was invisible in the darkness.

One of the men by the campsite yelled and dove to his right. Bedard dropped to the ground with both pistols out. A number of shots were fired, and then it was quiet. Chief Enthica came up with the rifle still at his shoulder. He had taken out two of the men, and Fenciao had hit the third. The three approached carefully, but the three men who had been sitting around the fire were dead.

Bedard identified one of the men as Robert Banner, who was on his list.

A man wearing a white collar indicating that he was a member of a religious order of some sort came down the trail toward them. He was carrying no guns and had his hands in the air. Bedard recognised him as one of the men from one of the previous campsites.

This man told the group that Banner and his two friends had arrived several weeks ago and were waiting for three other men coming from up the south to join them. They had recently decided that these three men were not coming, so they were planning to leave the next day. He said that they had reacted the same way to others who had approached their camp. He told them that he knew Banner, and if he was now dead the world was better off. He introduced himself as Reverend Willy and said that both of the remaining two camps to the east were family groups and would probably not know Bennet. He said that gunshots were relatively common in the camp area because of the liquor, and the men from Fort Langley would not come out to investigate in the darkness.

Bedard tried to be polite and thanked him for the information, but he did not allow Willy to come close to them and told him to go back to his camp, which he did.

Bedard had a meeting with his team, and they decided to take the guns and bullets and any money and coins that they could find and leave everything else.

They soon arrived back at the canoe and the campsite with three rifles, six pistols and a lot of bullets. Baribo and Timpani wondered whether the canoe could transport everything.

Bedard said, "Well, we shall see in the morning!"

To cover the rest of the night the group set up a two hour, two-man security watch taking turns. Then they were off before sun-up the next morning in a slightly overloaded canoe. The trip home, including picking up the second canoe, was uneventful. After reporting the trip highlights to Chief Roanyon, Bedard went off to his room for more sleep.

Thirty-Four
February 16, 1858

David, Dorthea, Elizabeth and her father had been visiting the Mahli and Stsulawh villages for the past week and had arrived back in Tsusnahm in mid-afternoon. Dorthea found Art sitting on the grass with Roger and Bedard watching some of the ongoing warrior training. She dragged them over to the seating area in front of Chief Roanyon's home where the returning group was going to report on their visit.

They were all very excited and had decided that, as the eldest, Art would have the privilege of telling his story first. He was a bit embarrassed initially, saying that the lovely ladies should report their adventures first, but the two women insisted.

"Well, of course I had met Oban here earlier and we had spent some time together. He showed me his workspace and storage area and introduced me to some of the men he calls his advanced hunters, all of whom are marksmen of some note. He had some muskets that he was upgrading and the two of us spent most of two days working on those. We joined Chief Tamburo and Tomala for the late meal on the second day with all the visitors and others from their villages. They are very kind, and they have some very clever people there. My Musqueam is improving, but I have at least two years to go working on it!"

The group laughed and kidded him about that. He had met one of the village teachers and the two had spent part of a day walking along the beaches together.

Art smiled. "Tomala said that she would like to go on a short hunting trip with the two experts, so we set that up. It was most enjoyable. Tomala has only just started using a rifle, but she has a very good eye. She is strong and she listens to her instructor, Oban. I think that she will be very good within a year."

"She is already one of the best archers in this area," Bedard said.

Art nodded. "We also joined Chief Wanso and Amoroa for the late meal with the rest of the visitors a few days later. They have a big group of men and a few women, hunters who own rifles and are marksmen. They told me that they try to go north into the mountain valleys beyond the large, long inlet where the Squamish villages are situated, on week-long hunting trips. They said that this preserved the local game. I told them that that was very wise, and they were pleased with that. It is just like having a nearby farm for deer and moose and other game.

"I believe that you have to protect the animals and perhaps even feed them if the winter weather is harsh. That was a new concept for them, and we talked about how to do that. We have a very large wilderness park near our home in England and the area is well used by hunters. Some years we stop the hunters from entering. We have been doing that for many years because the animal count is down for reasons including disease, weather and over-hunting. We have a permanent feeding program for the animals that is funded by the hunting licences. All in all, I very much enjoyed myself this past week, and we are all looking forward to the shipment of modern rifles in the not too distant future."

Dorthea and Elizabeth looked at each other.

"Well," Dorthea said, "I might as well go next. Tomala and Amoroa, who are the forces behind formal schooling in this nation, introduced me to the teachers in Tsusnahm. There are not many children here, and the teachers are very clever. I decided not to intrude upon the Tsusnahm program until I had visited the much larger program in Mahli and Stsulawh. I did, however, spend a week here with the children listening to the teachers' stories, answering questions about other places in the world and teaching some basic English to the very young children. Being with children is always fun for me.

"When I went west last week and met with Tomala and Amoroa, they had been talking with all the teachers there about how they could make use of my experience as a teacher, including my recent experience teaching in Chief Cobalt's village at Fort Victoria. They had created a list of questions for me. On the first day, the three of us worked through the questions and moved toward what I had initially said would be the development of a curriculum. These two very intelligent people asked excellent questions.

"At first they were concerned that the education process for children over the past three thousand years or so had been undertaken by parents and augmented by stories told by elders. The history of the Musqueam Nation and the ideas that the people have always held closely remain very important. Of course, I was very comfortable with that and said that this was true of every nation of the world. I told them that formal classroom teaching was something new everywhere. I mentioned again that my first teaching experience was with children living in the middle of London who had never been to school before. The next thing that we talked about at length was the fact that there is no Musqueam alphabet and that the English alphabet does not completely include the sounds of this language. The three of us decided this was a definite barrier. Until someone very clever creates the additional symbols that are obviously needed, we will continue to have difficulty writing in Musqueam. We agreed that this could develop into a very important task for the Musqueam Nation. They agreed to talk to their husbands about trying to find someone, not necessarily from the Musqueam Nation, to create the expanded alphabet. I agreed to talk to my father about this challenge."

She stopped for a moment and looked at Bedard, who nodded his head.

"I cannot think of anyone who can do this," Bedard admitted.

"Well," said Dorthea, "we then tried to list what I like to call separate streams of learning and doing. Once we started to work with that idea they really liked it. We ended up with four streams for the younger children just starting school, plus six streams for children with perhaps three to five years of school, with more streams added for those proceeding onwards from there. Tomala and Amoroa feel that learning the English language is important, given the current forecast of many English-speaking people arriving here this year. We decided to start with speech, then add reading and then writing, all on an individual basis.

"The first four streams of learning and doing are the English language, Musqueam stories, which I call Musqueam history, and then music and art, and lastly active participation, which I call exercise and sports. We also prepared a list of other streams including languages, arithmetic, world history, hunting, fishing, dance, cooking, working with wood and many more. Mahli and Stsulawh have a large group of children in their schools already, but even the older children do not have very much basic education other than Musqueam history, so everyone will be more or less proceeding along the same streams. There are also some outstanding exceptions. These are very bright children of all ages who have already shown that their minds are just like sponges and absorb information at incredible rates. I was introduced to a six-year-old who spoke English quite well because her parents spoke several languages at home, and she did not think that knowing several languages was unusual.

"We also talked about what I call slow learners. I said that I had a great deal of experience with this group of children. Tomala and Amoroa were very pleased that I recommended that all children without exception must go to school. I said that some of the time some of the older students can help younger children and that the school could find people to work one on one with a few of the students in the school. I told them some of my stories about slow learners, including a very good story about finding a student with an amazing singing voice. I also agreed with them that the school might initially have to go into the home to work with a child who is very shy or whose parents are reluctant to have their child in a school environment.

"It was a very enjoyable day for me, and we went through all of Tomala and Amoroa's list of questions. That was a very good first day. The next few days were spent visiting all the classrooms where I participated in several activities. The teachers especially liked my vast store of games and activities, including drawing ideas and dance steps. One of the mothers was helping the teacher in one classroom and she joined me in doing some dances. She was very light on her feet and a fast learner. We all enjoyed that, except for her son who seemed a bit embarrassed.

"The books and equipment that I have ordered will help the English stream and the music and art stream. I also hope to start building an education library and start teaching the teachers, perhaps even a teacher's course for older students who are interested in teaching.

"Yesterday, on my last day there, we ended with a meeting of all the teachers. There were a lot of good questions. The area that most interested the teachers was related to the miners and the settlers who are forecasted to come to this area over the next few years. Tomala, Amoroa and I did not have many answers, but we all agreed that educating the children would help the Musqueam Nation deal with the changes that will come."

Dorthea smiled at Elizabeth and gave her a small nod.

Elizabeth sat up straight. "Yes, well, David and I started our adventure in the company of Inchesca and Bella who wanted to come with us to introduce us to the six shamans in the two villages. We met four of these very nice people at lunch with Tomala and Amoroa. We both wish that we could speak this language because the flow of questions and the exchange of ideas was very slow because of the translating required. Mot was translating for us, and Amoroa's two older daughters were helping. We then visited two of Inchesca's and Bella's favourite people, close friends of their mother. These two shamans are sisters who are now bedridden. No one knows their age, but it is over sixty. Incredibly, they both speak quite passable English. They had been briefed by Amoroa on our skills, and they were particularly interested in David's background."

David jumped in. "I was surprised and quite honoured by the questions that they posed to me. They were aware of the security training of the dogs and asked me questions about my experience with animals as a vet. I told them several good stories that they liked, including one where a dog who was an important family friend had severely injured his rear legs. Our team had created a strap-on two-wheeled cart that allowed him to run in the fields with the family and with the other dogs. They had great respect for the village dogs and had constantly encouraged families to train dogs to protect their children."

Elizabeth said, "We then spent most of the week visiting children and adults who were not feeling well. I did not have many medications with me, but we were able to dispense some, mostly painkillers, and suggest several herbs that the shaman had in their inventory. We were also able to identify ailments that we recognised, some with possible solutions and some not. We did recommend something that they were not doing. This was to create a paper record of their visits to each patient and to record any comments that they had each time." Elizabeth looked at Dorthea. "This is definitely a disadvantage for a nation speaking a language that does not have a written form."

"On the fifth day, at the late meal with Chief Wanso and Amoroa and the rest of the visitors, we talked with the six shamans about the advantages of having medical records, including the benefit of being able to refer to the records so as to treat others. Inchesca and Bella said that their mother had often remarked that she wished that she could remember what action she had taken to resolve some of the unique conditions that she had treated many years ago. Tomala said that perhaps each family should have an English scribe to record these and other family events, and Dorthea said that perhaps one of the children taking English in school could do this. And then David had a chance to do surgery on a man who had broken his leg that morning."

"Yes," he said, "this was very exciting for me. I had two tools, a scalpel and a pair of pincers, instead of a choice of thirty tools, and only a small bottle of antiseptic. Elizabeth suggested that I use all of it, and I did. The leg fracture was a simple one, therefore the surgery was very simple, but it taught me a great deal about what I might be facing in the next few years. Afterwards, Elizabeth and I went over our medical order and made a list of several things. In hindsight, it was very exciting to be back in the saddle again."

Elizabeth said, "It was a very interesting visit. All of the shamans were very pleasant to us, and David and I thought that we could easily work with them because we found that in the week we visited we did not have any conflicting ideas. We all want people who are sick to get better. We think that much of the shaman's strength is something that we can easily recognize as the strength of a mind or mind's will."

Bedard said to himself: This has really worked out very well. I am very pleased with everyone.

Thirty-Five
February 19–20, 1858

Bedard looked over his shoulder at the group following him. He could see three men and knew that there were twenty more behind them on the south side river trail. This six- to ten-day expedition to Fort Hope and back was the first trip for their war party. The objective was firstly to test the mettle of the total group in travel mode, the most difficult mode because of the unknown, unpredictable world ahead. And secondly, to show the current group of miners in the Fort Hope area that there were powerful native nations in the area that had to be treated with respect and dignity or suffer the consequences. A third objective was to meet with the chiefs of some of the villages living just north of Fort Hope and share with them the Musqueam vision of the future, and minimize some of the conflict between the natives and the horde of miners that were anticipated.

The footpath that they were following on the south bank of the Fraser River was well used and had been created and maintained by many centuries of native travel as well as by the European traders, and most recently by a few of the early gold miners.

The seven-person spearhead group, including Bedard, Chief Enthica and Mot, was proceeding at a fast running pace with Bedard's four dogs providing security. This group had small front- and backpacks containing personal clothing and specialty war gear. Mot was supported by two warriors with stiff six-foot cords, who were smiling with the pleasure of the run. They all carried rifles, bowie knives and one or two cartridge belts over their shoulders. Two of these men also had bows and quivers. Bedard had his new rapid-fire rifle and his unique compound bow. This was quite a fierce-looking group. They had all decided not to use war paint this time but wore ceremonial feathers in their hair and similar dark-brown American style pullovers.

The second group of nine were the packers, led by Fenciao. They had three heavily loaded draggers, each pulled by two men in harnesses. Fenciao and the other two men carried large professional backpacks as well as two rifles and a cartridge belt, creating a total load of about eighty pounds each. They all moved at a very fast walk.

The third group of eight included Cowen and was led by Roger. It provided security for the second group and also did some of the packing from time to time. Some of the security group travelled off the trail in the bush while others were in front and behind the packers. Most of this group did not have rifles but carried bows and arrows.

This big group was not unusual for this area or for this particular path, but it was unusual for this time of year. Individual miners and a few small groups of two or three miners travelling together for protection had been seen here from time to time late last year and earlier this year. Of course, many native nations used the path but were not so heavily armed, and most often travelled in family groups.

Bedard shared the team's leadership and overall security with everyone in the front group, including Mot. This allowed the front group to be extremely flexible. It would be able to rapidly confront potential problem individuals or groups of adversaries travelling on the same path or living in the areas that the team was traversing, and thereby gain control with this advantage of surprise. It also allowed the whole team to move as one in relative safety at about thirty-five to forty miles per day. If all went well, the trip to Fort Hope would take no more than three days.

This easterly route along the south side of the Fraser River had been scouted by Bedard several times as far as the Fort Langley area. He had chosen the first campsite on a small stream back from the river just past Fort Langley. They would pass the fort with a minimum of fuss in the early darkness of the late winter evening. During the next two days, they would pass only a few small villages.

The main problem that Bedard's team faced was a direct result of the fierce appearance of the spearhead group with the ceremonial feathers and pullovers. Nothing like this had been seen in the area for many years...certainly not in living memory. Most of the peaceful natives would be quite frightened by the group and perhaps do something unpredictable, like trying to fight back against a perceived enemy. Therefore, the general plan was to keep the party hidden until communication had been established.

After leaving the landing across the river from Tsusnahm at daybreak, the war party immediately came up behind a small group of six hunters. The lead dog, JoJo, came back to warn Bedard of the pending confrontation, and all except Bedard and Mot went off the trail. This group of hunters explained to Mot that they were from a village on the south bank of the river. They were off to hunt deer and elk to the east of Fort Langley, since these animals had all but vanished from their immediate area due to overhunting. Chief Enthica, who knew the hunters, came out and socialized for a few minutes until the leading security walkers came up to take over the social responsibility. Bedard, Mot, and the other members of the front group continued onward. This was the normal way the group processed friendly travellers—keeping them secure and amused until the whole team passed by.

Some two hours later they met up with a rowdy group of four English settlers with two native packers coming toward them. Again JoJo came back with the warning and again the group hid, this time leaving Bedard and Chief Enthica to meet them. The settlers and the native packers were at first quite frightened, but both Bedard and Chief Enthica soon put them at ease.

The settlers explained that they were on the way from Fort Langley to a village with a dock near the mouth of the Fraser River where they would be picked up and transported to Fort Victoria and hence back to England. The native packers were transporting their meagre goods and clothing. The settlers told Bedard that they had been at Fort Langley working on the farms located in the plains to the south of the fort for two years, but did not like it so were now retuning home. Baribo and Timpani, who both spoke reasonable English, were delegated to keep them secure until the security walkers and Fenciao took over. This part of the team would then take over this responsibility until the whole war party had passed by. Not much of a problem.

In the early afternoon, the front group stopped short of Fort Langley and scouted the area for a considerable time. They determined that today was indeed a good day to pass by the fort as there was nothing exceptional happening. No boats were at the dock, and the timber crew was working an area far removed from the fort. The Kwantlen who had established a very small village near the water to the west of the fort were still busy building their first longhouse. The women were all engaged in this work and the children were all very young. The plan was to watch from a distance and try to pass by these villagers without their knowledge. If they did see some of the pack team, it was thought that they would not be overly concerned or curious since they were so close to the fort.

Fenciao's special task was to enter the fort and determine first if there were any travellers expected from the east in the next week or so, and then whether any travellers had left the fort going east toward Fort Hope in the past week, and, finally, how many white men were camping on the east side of the fort. With this intelligence, the group would have advance notice of potential encounters.

After Fenciao returned and gave his report, the front group decided that the original plan would work well and set out toward the target campsite, travelling around the fort inland to the south, trying to minimize contact with anyone.

The packers split up into two groups of four, and each group was accompanied by three guards. The packers would keep to those trails, previously identified, that circled around the fort to the south.

Bedard, Mot and the dogs would take up a non-threatening security position in front of the packers and provide initial security at the campsite. It was felt that minor contact would not be a problem so close to the fort. The remaining party of six, including Roger, would follow a short distance behind the packers. Bedard was not very comfortable with this plan. He would have preferred passing far to the south, but this would be difficult for the packers. He also agreed that travelling around the fort was a unique situation that probably would not be encountered on any other trip that they planned to make in the next year.

The day ended successfully with only one encounter. One of the packer groups saw and talked to some farmers as the group was crossing a major trail going south from the fort toward the farm lands.

The entire party was excited to arrive at the campsite and enjoyed a meal and a rest, although the stress was still high due to a "no sound" directive. The security net around the camp was provided by the dogs plus four sentries on three-hour shifts through the night.

In the early evening darkness, Bedard, Roger, Fenciao and Chief Enthica travelled back to Fort Langley on the south side river trail. Although Bedard had previously done this himself, it was a first adventure for this team. Bedard had decided long ago that the dogs were at high risk in certain circumstances, and as this was one of those circumstances they were left guarding the campsite.

The four men had decided to dress like miners. They wore the classic red shirt and were armed with two revolvers tied to their hips, a bowie knife and a rifle. During the training, Bedard had coached the men how to adopt various personalities as part of the disguise program. This time, the men's wide pace gave a swagger to their overall appearance. Although the task before them could be quite dangerous, they were all smiling.

Bedard and Roger walked beside each other on the wide pathway with Fenciao and Chief Enthica following about one hundred feet behind them, almost out of sight in the darkness. Visibility was not good, but at camp the miners were seated around a fire. Bedard thought that he could identify almost anyone who was on his list by the campfire's glow. The campfire would also diminish the miners' ability to see the four men clearly.

They passed two of the four camps and were approaching the third when Bedard stopped suddenly and moved into the light brush at the side of the path, crouching down with his rifle at the ready. The others did the same.

After a few minutes, Roger materialized like a ghost beside Bedard. Bedard put his mouth close to Roger's ear.

"At the next camp there are four places around the fire but only three men. I think that they may have a security man out there somewhere." Two more ghosts appeared, and Roger passed on the message.

Chief Enthica moved up and whispered to Bedard.

"The guard will be located on this side of the path away from the water."

Bedard thought about that for a moment and nodded. He thought to himself, *The chief is really very clever. I am delighted that Mother brought him to my attention.*

Bedard held his hand just over his head with four fingers extended. The other three nodded and moved off silently into the forest. This was a code for one of several standard attack strategies that had evolved during the course of the training program designed to capture a hidden guard. In less than five minutes, Roger and Fenciao had captured, gagged and tied the guard. Then the four men and their captive moved some distance south into the forest so that the team could see whom they had captured.

A small cup of burning leaves allowed Bedard to examine the man in the darkness. His face was not familiar, but he had a tattoo on his shoulder which Bedard thought was an Italian mark.

One of the huge advantages that Bedard's team had was they all spoke a language that none of the miners spoke.

Roger spoke quietly to the man in English. "We do not understand why you were located in the bush away from your camp. We were just walking along toward Fort Langley and did not appreciate the risk that you presented. We are obviously very experienced bushmen and found you easily. I am going to take the gag out of your mouth so that you can answer our simple questions. If you make a loud sound you will immediately die." Roger held up his bowie knife. "Do you want to die?"

The frightened man immediately shook his head.

Bedard spoke in Italian with a southern accent. "We do not want to kill you, but we need to understand the situation here so that we do not make a stupid mistake and perhaps get injured or die for no reason." Bedard translated for the group.

The man was obviously very surprised to hear Italian. His gag was removed.

Roger said in English, "What is your name?"

"Guildo Bono."

"What is your leader's name?"

"There are two men, Don and Wilber Thompson. Tommy Debb and I are hired hands."

Bedard spoke Musqueam. "They are both on my list. We must be very careful. Roger, you and Fenciao check the camp again and come back to report. Be very careful. I think that the three men will have disappeared by now and may be in an attack mode."

Bedard switched back to Italian. "Why were you guarding the camp?"

"The brothers always have a security plan at every camp. I do not know why. I can only guess that they have enemies. I joined them in San Francisco and have been working for them for only two weeks."

Roger returned in a rush. "As you predicted, the camp has been abandoned; all the gear is gone."

Bedard turned back to Bono. "The camp is empty. They have gone. Talk to me."

Bono put his head down and eventually said, "They are always ready to move onwards. The tent is very unusual—it can be torn down and packed in two minutes."

"Where did they go?"

"I do not know. I have been tossed to the wolves!"

Roger moved up his rifle and expertly cocked it.

"No, no! We planned to travel east tomorrow, but I really do not know where they have gone. This is a very unusual situation for them. They travel very lightly, carrying less than forty pounds including guns and ammunition. They are very fit and always travel fast in a run-then-walk style, with security focused ahead of them and not behind."

Roger examined the rifle and the one revolver that was taken from Bono. The Italian had very few bullets, no knives and no ankle gun.

Bedard had Fenciao reinsert the gag and tied Bono to a tree. Bono was moaning and obviously very frightened.

The team moved away so they could talk about the situation.

Chief Enthica said, "They will go east and will have at least half an hour, perhaps more, head start on us. They are obviously very skilled but may stop to rest overnight with a guard to protect them from followers. It is overcast, but it is not going to rain tonight. I do not think that the risk in the extreme darkness is worth the gain. In fact, this may influence our plans to visit Fort Hope and beyond."

"Yes, I agree," said Bedard. "But remember, we were in disguise. They do not know who we are or how many men we have. Arriving in a large native group will stop them from attacking us. We have the advantage in that we now know who they are. This provides us with a small focus for our adventure. A risk of danger to keep everyone alert." He smiled. The others remained deep in thought.

Roger said, "If we keep Bono tied up here overnight, we could send him on his way south tomorrow morning. He has forty dollars, more than enough to get himself back to San Francisco. We are some distance from the riverside camp, so if Don and Wilber come back looking for him, they probably would not find him."

"I am not so sure," Chief Enthica said. "I propose that we take him carefully through the forest closer to our camp because we made an easily followed trail from his guard location to here."

"That is a good idea," Bedard said. "You three move him. I am going to go back to their camp and see what I can find. I will meet you at our campsite."

The four men met at the campsite. Bedard arrived first and quietly told the group about the adventure. Roger reported that Bono had been told of his options and had agreed to travel south as fast as he could go. He did not want to meet up with Don and Wilber Thompson again. Bedard said that the three men had definitely travelled east in full running mode. He had followed their very heavy tracks for over an hour.

The next morning the basic camp was struck, and the party continued on with fundamentally the same structure as the day before. The only large village that Bedard had identified would be passed the next day. The likelihood of encounters with other small parties of travellers was thought to be a minimum.

Fenciao and Chief Enthica travelled west and released Bono, who had been tied up on the ground so that he could sleep during the night. He looked a bit beat up, but he was in very good physical shape and appreciated being released. He set off at a run to the west toward the major trail south. Fenciao and Chief Enthica discretely followed him for an hour, stopped and returned north and then east to eventually catch up with the main group.

The packer group decided that they would try to up the pace of the previous day as an endurance trial. The packers' security group, under the direction of Roger, chose one of their plans to maximise contribution to the packers. The planning group had decided to do some war exercises during the second day.

Bedard was pleased with all of this initiative but he was still a conservative and decided to maintain a small party of three well in front of the packers. He, Mot, Cowen and the dogs went off at a fast run. Mot was not very happy with this arrangement because he would have much preferred to play a role in the war exercises. He was now running with only one stiff six-foot cord attached to Cowen, his favourite leader.

The other five members of the spearhead group, Teddy, Albert, Baribo and Chief Enthica, plus Fenciao, went off ahead of everyone at a very fast pace. The concept was that they would become a war party and undertake some of the war training exercises that they had been using over the past month and attack the main group in the late afternoon.

After about an hour, Bedard stopped his team for a short break. He smiled.

"I wonder if you two would be interested in a small counter move to confuse the war party?"

Mot and Cowen liked the sound of that.

"I propose that we all swing south about a mile to an old path that I found last month that seems to go east. We may need to break trail from time to time. It will be slower than this trail, but it might be fun to mislead the war party. Now, it may be that the path is not as good as I think it is, and the war party may not be deceived, but I think that it would be fun to try. How does that sound to you two?"

"Let's do it," said Mot. Cowen nodded enthusiastically.

"We now need to sell this plan to the packer team," Bedard said.

The three of them moved back down the trail to the west until they encountered the lead security guards and then waited until the remaining group, including the side security guards and Roger, assembled.

Bedard introduced the plan to try to fool the war party. This was immediately accepted by the whole group. Some practical questions were put forward and a more detailed plan was conceived on the spot.

Bedard, Mot and Cowen took off to the east at a fast run, looking for a reasonable path to the south. Once a trail had been found, a simple broken-branch marker was left and the three went down the path to find the east–west trail. Once that trail was found and briefly assessed as acceptable, Cowen went back to the river trail to guide the rest of the party onward.

Bedard and Mot continued to travel eastward on the new trail. Occasionally Bedard used his machete to clear small windfalls or detours around fallen trees. Soon Roger, Cowen and Rugard, one of the security group, caught up to them and the minor trail clearing became easier and faster.

In the meantime, the five members of the war party were enjoying themselves by practicing stealth testing. One person would take a post guard position and the other four would try to sneak up on him undetected. Much fun! And very difficult because all five of these men were older, seasoned hunters and bushmen and took this training and the eventual objectives very seriously.

After a short lunch break, the men decided to "attack" the main party sooner than the late afternoon plan. They conversed for some time on how the attack could be made. The key problem was the dogs. They would be very difficult to fool because all four of the dogs had been providing Bedard with forest security for many years. Another problem was the speed of the first party. It would be difficult to find the group without Bedard and the dogs finding them first and disrupting their attack plan.

It was decided that the weakness at the front of the main group was its reduced numbers. Scanning of treetops would be at a minimum, so the basic plan was to find the group and then sacrifice one member by letting him be "captured." The remaining four would move upward into the high foliage of the many trees along the trail and attack the group near the middle of the packers. It was also decided that the "wealth" to be stolen by the attack group of four would be footgear.

This simple plan pleased everyone. So, the group proceeded westward rapidly in search of the main party, with Albert well out in front as the potential "prisoner" and the others matching his speed as well as searching constantly for reasonable climbing trees.

After about half an hour, Albert came back to talk to the other four warriors.

"No one has come down this trail today," Albert said. They all looked at each other, stunned.

After some thought, Baribo said, "They have played a trick on us."

After more thought, it was Fenciao, the most experienced warrior of this group, who spoke.

"They would not stop and wait for our attack. They cannot fly, they have no boats, so they must have moved south to try to escape our fearsome clutches."

Everyone laughed and then frowned in deep thought.

Chief Enthica, who was known for his intelligence and clever plans, said, "We should travel eastward on this riverside path until we find a southerly path that we can take to intercept the group. We will probably find ourselves behind the packers and also find that they will be expecting us from that direction. The dogs may not all be up front which is the key problem as I see it.

"When we find the group," Chief Enthica continued, "we can then devise a detailed attack plan that we think will be successful. We may also need to sacrifice one or maybe two of us in order to do this. There is no doubt that we can find them fairly quickly. It would be useful if we could surprise them, so we must now travel rapidly, but very silently."

"Perhaps," said Albert, "we should plan to sacrifice one man if they have a rear dog. If we are able to come in from the side, behind the front group and in front of the packers' leading security group, we may avoid the dogs."

"If they did have a rear dog, which one would it be?" Baribo asked.

"Probably JoJo," said Teddy.

Albert nodded. "JoJo. Yes, I agree. I will lead because I know JoJo very well, and I may be able to stop him from immediately reporting our presence, giving us some advantage of surprise with our attack."

All five men felt a great deal better and immediately left at a very fast run eastward on the river trail. It had started to rain very lightly. They had difficulty in finding a southerly trail. They initially took a faint animal trail and then another after the first one veered off to the west. They eventually found the eastbound trail used by the larger group.

They all squatted by the side of the trail and looked at the footprints.

"They are at least an hour to the east," said Albert.

Teddy, also an expert tracker, nodded his head in agreement. "And no signs of a dog here."

"JoJo may be in the bush just off the trail and not right on the trail," said Chief Enthica.

The five of them split up and searched the bush on either side of the trail for signs of JoJo. None were found.

Big John was pleased with that. "Nevertheless, we must continue to be vigilant for signs of a rear-guard dog. They may decide to change the positions of their defences as the day continues."

"I find it very interesting that we are so concerned with the presence of an experienced guard dog. We definitely need more of them," Teddy said.

The others nodded their heads in agreement.

"Yes," said Chief Enthica, "that is a good thought. We should bring it up again at one of our meetings. I know that our villages are training several groups of security dogs, and some of these have been used on previous warrior training trips."

The small group set off to the east at a measured run with Albert, who was aware of his responsibilities, again in the lead. Although the group was generally moving rapidly, Albert slowed the pace down at times when the sight visibility forward was not good due to deadfalls, small hills and turns in the path.

They soon caught up to the rear of the packing group and Albert, who was very hyper by this time, barely avoided contact with the trailing security team.

The attack group stopped to talk again.

"No sign of any dogs yet," Teddy said.

"I think," said Fenciao, "we are more likely to find a game trail to the south of this trail."

The group nodded their agreement, moved off into the forest to the south and soon found a suitable trail. Moving very rapidly in a crouched position, they soon passed the main group of packers who were walking rapidly. They also noted that one of the security guards was off in the forest to the south of the main group.

Chief Enthica called for a meeting and the five men put their heads close together.

Chief Enthica spoke in a whisper. "They will stop for a break soon. Then the security will come back briefly to the main trail before they set up a security net around the group. I think that just as they stop we should attack the whole group from one side while Teddy crosses over to cover us from a security man coming in late from the north."

Soon after, they saw the front security come back and they could hear the packers agreeing to stop. The group of five turned south and immediately attacked. The four packers and their two security guards were of course taken completely by surprise and, as per the agreement, stopped, put down their weapons and sat down at the side of the trail. There was quite a bit of banter and jestful exchanges between the two groups. The attacking group took five pairs of foot coverings and faded back into the forest, knowing that the other group of packers or Bedard and the front runners with the dogs could return at any time.

The war party decided that they'd had enough success and returned to the main trail by the river. They spent the remaining part of the afternoon in two-on-two battles that eventually exhausted them, after which they filed into camp to receive Bedard's congratulations and compliments all around. They returned the foot coverings with a great deal of laughter and accolades from all the warriors.

Thirty-Six
February 21, 1858

The next morning, they reverted to their original three-party groups with Bedard and six warriors going on ahead. There was one large village to pass that day just after the midday break. Once they came closer to the village, they would decide how they would do that.

All of a sudden Hi, who was ahead of the leading group, came back to Bedard with his tail between his legs and refused to move forward. Haus and JoJo also came close to the group and refused to move back into their security positions, in spite of Bedard's signals. Bedard was concerned and baffled. After some discussion, Chief Enthica, one of the front runners, came up with a possible reason for the unusual behaviour.

"Just ahead," he said, "is a large extraordinary rock about one thousand feet south of the trail, about fifty feet high in a large meadow. It is called the Tobol Rock, and the local shamans say that it is an ancient example of the wrath of the large mountain to the south of here. They believe that evil spirits live there and caution travellers to avert their eyes and pass by rapidly. We respect their advice, but I do not remember any unfavourable reports from travellers on this trail. It may be that the dogs feel something that we do not feel."

Bedard remembered the large volcanic mountain he had seen from the lookout tree.

"We are following Don and Wilber Thompson," he said. "But if they were just ahead, the dogs would react completely differently."

"There is a trail that circles the meadow just into the forest," said Fenciao. "We could take a small team and run that trail to ensure that no one is hiding behind the rock."

"Good idea," Bedard said. "You take four warriors and make the circle. We will meet you farther up this trail."

The remaining warriors had caught up to the front runners and the whole party, including the four dogs, walked slowly across the meadow. Looking at the tall rock, Bedard could see that it was very unusual, and he could understand that it would be feared by the local shamans.

Fenciao reported that the area was clear, so the groups moved off again with the dogs back in their security positions. When the lead group stopped short of the village for a midday break, Bedard had a meeting with all the warriors on how to bypass the village.

"This community," Chief Enthica said, "has seen many fishermen and hunters pass through its village in small and large groups over the years. Our group is unusual, but if we send a small group forward first and then follow it with several well-spaced-out groups, I think that there will be no problems."

"Yes," Fenciao said, "I agree with that plan. The only other alternative is to move to the south and try to pass the village without them seeing us. This may result in a serious confrontation if a native hunter meets up with us."

There was some discussion, but most of the warriors agreed with the simple plan.

Four warriors volunteered to travel in the first group. Each of them knew several villagers and could speak their language. Bedard agreed with the plan.

The group passed through the village with a minimum of fuss. Bedard was relieved.

Many of the villagers thought that the head feathers and the brown pullovers were wonderful, and their children's drum corps put on a short performance. The village chief, Chief Chaska, and several of his elders had put on their beautiful ceremonial robes and were introduced to Bedard.

The rest of the afternoon was fun for all the warriors. The groups passed by four small villages that had been alerted to their arrival by a runner from the large village. At each village, the chief and the elders had put on their ceremonial robes, and many of the villagers turned out to welcome the group and be introduced to Bedard. The warrior groups had decided to practice their war chants and put on a bit of a dance, much to the amusement of the villagers.

Bedard was not certain the entertainment was in keeping with the seriousness of the group's objectives but decided not to protest.

At the second small village, Bedard met up with Arentha and Pisano who had returned home the previous month. Bedard stopped and talked to them about the current plans to go north. They were pleased.

The groups arrived at the second campsite location chosen by the advance party in good spirits. At the large village they had been given a large box of dried salmon for the late meal and were looking forward to this treat.

The next day was uneventful. Bedard tried to bring the groups back to what he was now calling warrior status by having small two-man teams travel south and then attack one of the groups. Everyone participated. At the late meal of fresh salmon and deer, the men discussed their day's adventures and Bedard added some critical comments, which produced both frowns and light laughter.

The next day, they planned to pass Fort Hope and find a two- or three-day camping spot well off the trails just before the midday meal so that they could travel back and inspect the Fort Hope area later that day.

They inspected a main trail going east located before Fort Hope, and Bedard changed the plan. The groups proceeded east up this trail and then followed a faint hunting trail northward alongside a small stream leading to a very small beaver lake surrounded by a meadow in the valley beyond. The valley was about a mile long and fairly narrow. The mountains were quite high to the east, and to the west was a heavily forested ridge with the river located on the other side.

The advance party inspected this area and decided that it was easy to secure by placing lookouts in two trees on either side of the pass. The packing groups had dismantled their dragging devices and all of the gear and supplies were carefully transferred into the valley, leaving a minimum trail. Bedard then went back to the main east–west trail with a four-man party and worked on minimizing any traces of their passage.

At the same time, two security trees were chosen, and the dogs were positioned around the campsite. A two-man party traversed the valley looking for other problems.

At the light midday meal, the warriors discussed their campsite in detail. The expert hunters agreed that the valley was not used for hunting game anymore because it was too small and too near larger hunting areas farther to the north and east. Everyone was pleased. The two-man inspection team reported finding two small old camp areas, and a party of four men was sent to examine them and determine when they were last used. The inspection team also reported six very faint animal trails going west over the heavily forested mountain ridge toward the river, and that they had seen two deer at the far end of the valley.

"When we turned off the main trail beside the river," Bedard said, "Don and Wilber Thompson and Tommy Debb were still about one or two days ahead of us. They may have stopped briefly at Fort Hope for supplies. These men have previously demonstrated that they are dangerous and will be prepared to protect themselves, so we need to have a reasonable security plan for our trip to Fort Hope and beyond.

"Today we need to visit Fort Hope and inventory the river bars for about five miles to the north of Fort Hope for miners. We also need to check the river for a distance of about three miles to the south and west because the trail that we were travelling on this morning was not close enough to the river for us to do this. We do not want to confront the miners yet, just locate bars that are being worked and count the number of miners. With this information we will be able to decide what to do tomorrow in our search for these very dangerous men. Be very careful. Chief Enthica knows the chief of the Staulo village just to the north of Hope because his village shared two summer fishing camps with them." Bedard looked at Chief Enthica. "Take your team and go up and over the ridge and visit the village. They may be able to help you do the inventory up the river. We need four warriors to protect our camp today. As usual, we will share these duties. Who's turn is it today?"

Four of the warriors indicated that they would stay.

"I know that I do not have to say this," Bedard said, "but guarding the camp is an important assignment. We have a lot of guns, bullets, bows and arrows and other gear here. To lose this would be a disaster. The dogs will help you. Fenciao, you and your team will lead us out today and go south and west. When you have finished this to your satisfaction, go north, pass by Fort Hope, try not to kill anyone."

Fenciao and his team smiled.

"And then," said Bedard, "continue north and meet us at the village. You may pass us in Fort Hope or on the north trail. Do not say anything to us."

Roger, you and I will be miners and the rest of our team including Mot and Cowen will be carrying our gear and supplies. We will be about an hour behind Fenciao. No feathers, no pullovers! We will buy some supplies at the fort and ask about miners who have recently passed through."

"Very good," said Roger. "We will have two pistols and the red shirts. I think that I will wear the new hat that I borrowed at Fort Langley."

There were murmurs of amusement at that, and Bedard smiled.

"We should also carry a rifle and some bullets. I am going to wear my *old* hat."
Everyone smiled.

"Cowen, the packs should be as authentic as we can make them, and remember: Packers do not smile very much!"

Everyone looked at each other and frowned, then burst into laughter.

The two five-man search teams moved out, carrying small packs and a various collection of pistols, rifles and bows.

Bedard and Roger inspected each other and nodded. Mot and Cowen, each carrying a small backpack, a gun belt and a rifle, would lead four packers who would have half-empty eighty-pound backpacks with waist band, chest strap and head band, and they would carry a bow in one hand. Big John, with a slightly lighter pack, a gun belt and a rifle, would bring up the rear as security.

"You will remember our discussion at the midday meal," Bedard said. "We wish to appear to be well-armed and well-supported miners on the way north to find our fortunes who do not wish to attract any attention. I do not anticipate finding anyone who we are looking for camped at Fort Hope, but we still must be cautious. We will stop just past the fort, and Cowen and I will go back for supplies."

The trip down to the fort was uneventful, and as predicted no one was camped there. Just past the fort at the fringe of the heavy forest, the group stopped and moved off the trail to a small existing campsite. Three of the packers moved into the forest to provide security and two backpacks were prepared for the new supplies.

Inside the fort, Bedard and Cowen found the Hudson's Bay Company store and, with the help of the clerk, selected supplies. Cowen adopted a broken English and wandered around in assumed wonderment, looking at some of the gear and supplies. He picked up several things, including an oil-fired lantern, and asked Bedard what they were. Bedard thought that he was a great actor and told him so after they left with two full packs.

"I think that the clerk is a Kanakas native," said Bedard, "from the Sandwich Islands now known as Hawaii, but I decided not to try his language. Next time."

They smiled.

The clerk had reported that several small two- and three-man groups had passed by in the last week and that there were apparently a few miners on what they called Emory's Creek about twelve miles north who came down for supplies about once a week. Bedard continued to quiz him, but he did not have any more information. Bedard knew that William Yates was in charge of Fort Hope, and he had a letter of introduction penned by James Douglas but decided not to use this yet.

Bedard and his group moved north and soon entered the Staulo village where Chief Enthica and his group were sitting down talking with Chief Tanu, his wife Maria and some of the villagers. They all got up and were introduced to Bedard.

"Chief Tanu and his advisors are having difficulty understanding and believing the future changes to their world that we are reporting," Chief Enthica said.

Bedard shook his head and looked down for a moment. "If I were in his position, I would absolutely not believe this. We can hardly believe it ourselves."

Chief Tanu indicated with a wave of his hand that Bedard and his group should join them in the meeting circle. The local Staulo language was similar to Musqueam, but Bedard was still having trouble with some of the words, so Mot was translating from time to time. Cowen was translating for Roger.

After everyone was settled, Bedard said to the chief, "Do you have a shaman in your village?"

"Yes" He indicated a man seated at his side.

Bedard said, "Do you have any questions that we could try to answer?"

The shaman stood up, looked carefully at each of the fourteen visitors, turned to the south and pointed with his arm to a large mountain that dominated the skyline.

"Lhilheqey still has much snow, so next winter will be cold and long. The villagers have been told that the salmon will not be as plentiful this year, and that we must work hard so that we do not suffer because of this. We hear of terrible battles farther south between the white man and our friends who have lived in that area longer than we have lived here." He stopped and looked carefully at the chief and the other villagers in the circle. "We have heard of this place, California. The white men there have killed almost all the natives that lived there. For several weeks we have been hearing that many white men from California will come this year. We have counted twenty so far this year. This will be a bad year, and I am afraid. I have never been afraid before in my life!"

He crumpled to the ground. Everyone stood up, not knowing what to say, what to do.

Chief Tanu lifted his hands above his head, turned slightly to the left and then to the right. All of the villagers and the visitors sat down. A woman was attending to the shaman.

Chief Tanu looked directly at Bedard. "Our river moves only in one direction, but the people who live along its banks move in both directions. They move in both directions every day. They move in both directions every hour of every day. Copco, you have been on our river for almost two months. We did not know that you were here on the second day." Everyone smiled and some laughed lightly. "But on your fourteenth day we heard of you, and the wonderful story of Noua."

The villagers started a soft clapping and the visitors joined in.

"Then the story of your wonderful dogs, the stories of your incredible bows, and the many stories of evil white men coming to their end. Then we heard the good stories of the arrival of your daughter, the teacher, and the arrival of the medicine lady and her friend who understands the animal world. Then we heard about the experienced gun warrior and the two wooden boat workers. We also heard of the preparations to go north to visit the Haida and find the stolen children. But it was the stories of many white men coming from California this year that we do not understand. What we do not understand we fear."

He sat down.

At that time, a young girl ran to the chief and spoke to him. The chief nodded.

"We have some visitors," he said, and pointed to the south.

On the river four large war canoes were coming fast, followed by several more canoes in the distance. The group moved down to the water and many other villagers joined them.

Chief Tanu said, "I see four chiefs and their wives, and many warriors from our sister Staulo villages to the south."

Just then a small boy who was pointing upstream came running to the chief.

"And more family from the north."

There were three smaller canoes coming downstream from the north.

"Good, we will have a full meeting of the Staulo Nation, and then..." He stopped and turned to look at Bedard. "We will have a party. You have attended many parties at Tsusnahm, but I do not know if we have both shrimp and lake trout."

Bedard and the visitors burst into laughter and clapped their hands. Chief Tanu smiled, very pleased with his knowledge of current activities in Tsusnahm. Three smiling women came in a rush, spoke briefly to Chief Tanu and rushed off again.

"Yes," said Chief Tanu, "we have fresh river trout, but no shrimp yet." He waved at the rapidly approaching canoes. Everyone was smiling.

All seven canoes arrived at the same time and there was much hugging and laughter. Fenciao and his team came up to Bedard.

"We found one bar about three miles south with only two miners. Then on the return trip one of these canoes swooped by the shore and picked us up. Great fun!"

The three following canoes from the south contained a great variety of food. When they arrived and started to unload the boats, the large group on the shore turned and clapped and started singing a song-chant that Bedard thought was very similar to the ones that he had heard several times in Tsusnahm.

Chief Tanu brought Chief Chaska and the other three chiefs from the south with their wives to meet Bedard and Roger again. Everyone was smiling.

Chief Chaska said, "My wife, as you may have noticed when you visited, is a very strong leader in our village, and she insisted that we should join you here. The parties that you have had in Tsusnahm were sometimes larger, but the food that you will be offered tonight will be much better."

Bedard and the warriors all laughed and clapped. Chief Chaska's wife looked a little embarrassed by her husband's bragging.

The chief of the small northern Staulo village, Chief Biyen, was introduced to Bedard and Roger.

"We have heard of you, Copco," he said. "And you, Roger, and we are very pleased to finally meet you. You both look as if you are Musqueam dressed up like white men."

Everyone laughed.

"You are absolutely correct," said Bedard with a smile. Then he turned more serious. "We have enjoyed our trip to this beautiful part of the world, but we are now searching for three very bad white men who have passed through your villages three days ago. They usually travel very fast using a run-walk travelling system."

Chief Biyen turned and spoke to a man behind him, then turned back.

"Yes, they did pass by two days ago, and they may have stopped at what the miners now call Emory's Creek, about eleven miles north from here, where a few others are apparently looking for gold."

Chief Tanu and his advisors started to gather everyone to their meeting area in the centre of the village in front of what Bedard thought was the Chief Tanu's home, a very elaborately decorated longhouse.

Chief Tanu guided Bedard and Roger to their places at the meeting area.

"We are very proud of the history shown on our central building. The legends depicted were first placed there by my great-grandfather and more added when my uncle and then my father were chiefs. I have decided that I am not yet old enough to add my legend to the building."

Maria was walking slowly with the group of men.

"There are now many stories about him, and we think the he is going to have difficulty choosing one or two for the artists."

Chief Tanu smiled down at her. "Perhaps you will have to choose one for me."

Bedard thought that this village was led by a strong family.

The chiefs sat facing the water with some of their villagers seated behind them. Bedard, Roger, Cowen and the other visitors from the Musqueam Nation sat opposite them. Most of the villagers were in attendance, sitting with their friends and family visiting from the local Staulo villages.

Both Chief Tanu and Maria stood up and welcomed everyone. Maria spoke her welcome in Musqueam, much to Bedard's surprise. He noted that there was not much translation going on, only for some of the children in attendance.

"We are particularly honoured," she said, "to have Cowen here with us representing our old friend Chief Cobalt on Vancouver Island."

Cowen nodded his head.

Maria continued. "We also have Fenciao representing Chief Big Bon, one of the living legends on the river." Many of the group assembled clapped. "And we are also very pleased to have Chief Enthica visiting us again. Many of us believe that he is the wisest of all the peoples on the river."

All of the chiefs and many of the villagers stood up and clapped. Chief Enthica smiled and nodded his head. Bedard and Roger looked at each other smiling, remembering Mother's words.

Chief Tanu continued with the introductions.

"We are also very pleased to finally meet Copco and Roger. Copco has many incredible skills and speaks many languages. He has been in our village for two hours and already speaks our language!"

The village group began clapping and started singing a song-chant that Bedard again thought was very similar to the ones that he had heard several times in Tsusnahm.

Bedard got up and he and Mot moved over to Chief Tanu. "Thank you for your kind words. I enjoy learning new languages, and I have a very skilled translator to help me."

Everyone knew Mot, of course, and the clapping intensified.

Chief Tanu said, "Just before our friends and family from the other Staulo villages on this river appeared, I was talking to you about the stories that we have heard about many white men coming from California this year. I said that we did not understand these stories. I also said that what we do not understand, we fear. Can you give us more information, please?"

He sat down.

Bedard rose again. "I am not certain that I can provide you with much information. And what information I do have is not good for you and your families. What is the total number of all the Staulo represented here today?"

It was his wife that answered. "About four hundred people, including two births today." Everyone smiled at that.

"So," said Bedard, "then there are about one hundred men."

She thought for a moment. "Perhaps a few less."

"Well," said Bedard, "I was told today that about twenty white men have passed through this village this year. These are the first of many white men who will pass through your village this year. They search for gold. They think that there is a great deal of gold here along the river and much farther north. The current estimate is that twenty thousand white men will come this year and pass through your villages."

The group exploded. Not many people could understand this number and the concept of looking for gold, but ten minutes later most of them did. The six chiefs walked through the crowd trying to regain order, but the people were standing and sitting in groups and talking in very loud voices.

When Bedard held his hands over his head and started talking again, the noise level immediately dropped. Everyone definitely wanted to hear what he had to say.

"These men will come by boats and by land. The boats will be small at first, but before the end of the year there will be bigger boats holding many more men. The most urgent thing that they will need is food. Many of the men will bring food with them. They will need help carrying their food, cooking pots, clothing, tents and other gear. Some of the men will be sellers of food. Some men will be experienced hunters and your animals will disappear. They will need to cook their food, so all the salmon-drying racks will disappear for firewood.

"They will also bring alcohol. Do not drink the alcohol! It will make you stupid and sick. They will molest your women. And finally, they will take most of your land and you will not be able to do anything about that."

Bedard sat down. There was a deathly silence.

It was Marie who finally stood up. "Is there anything that we can do to keep things the way they are?"

Bedard looked at Fenciao and Chief Enthica. They looked at each other and both of them stood up.

"At the coast," Fenciao said, "in the Musqueam Nation, we have a slightly different situation than you do. This year, almost all of the white men, the gold miners, will pass us by. Bedard has advised us that in several years the white settlers will come, and we will probably lose control over most of our land."

Chief Enthica rose to address the crowd. "We are doing five things. Firstly, we have decided to protect our land as long as we can, and we plan to try to stop white men from stopping on our land. Secondly, we are purchasing guns. We will teach all of our warriors to use both rifles and pistols. It is much easier to learn to shoot a gun well than to learn to shoot an arrow well."

Fenciao nodded. "We have with us today several of the new breach-loading rifles. Some of you have already had a chance to inspect them. They are much better than the old muzzle-loaders that you have. These new rifles are much better for hunting than the bow and arrow."

"This is true," said Chief Enthica. "We also have several new pistols with us today. They are not very good for hunting, but they are very good for killing people."

"And unfortunately," Fenciao said, "all of the white men that will come this year will have one or two pistols, and many will have new rifles. We will give a short shooting demonstration after this meeting."

Bedard stood up, came over and joined Chief Enthica and Fenciao.

"You all know that many of the Musqueam Nation have met the white men who travel in the large sailing ships. These ships have stopped and traded with them often on the coast. Several of you have also met and traded with these people. The Musqueam Nation has had white men living in its villages for short periods of time. Many of our villagers speak English and other foreign languages because they have travelled south to California and west to Hawaii. Several years ago, Musqueam villages started to teach English to their children. They are also teaching English to adults. These villages now have a professional teacher to help them with their school. As some of you already know, the teacher is my daughter, and she also speaks many languages. Speaking English will help the Musqueam Nation deal with the white miners and the white settlers who will surely follow next year."

"And the fourth thing that we are doing," said Chief Enthica, "is planning for more food collection and storage. And finally, we are trying to understand how we can profit from the white men as they pass by. Two white men who are carpenters are working with our woodworkers making simple boats that we plan to sell or rent to these gold miners. We also will have men available to act as packers for them."

"Also," Fenciao said, "you will remember that our village started using children to provide us with village security. I know that you are also using this very simple security system here. With Copco's help, we have started to train our dogs to provide a more complete security system around our villages, especially at night. We have always said that the family dogs we use to hunt and to protect our children are amazingly intelligent. This is working very well, and perhaps you should do this, too. We can help you get this started."

Maria stood up again. "When will the gold miners come?"

"They have started to come already," said Bedard. "But the large groups of gold miners will arrive in about two months' time."

The crowd remained very quiet trying to absorb and understand all this information.

Thirty-Seven
February 21–22, 1858

Chief Tanu stood up. "The report from the cooking chief."

The group stood up and started to clap and smile. Most of them knew who this was, and everyone was looking forward to the feast.

"She says two hours from now. We have time for the shooting demonstration."

Bedard looked at Roger, who was smiling.

"We have gone to our campsite," said Roger, "and brought back your composite bow and the large bag with the crossbow. They have a gun and bow range set up for distances up to six hundred feet. They did not believe me when I asked for targets at nine hundred and twelve hundred feet, so there is now a group on the other side of the river setting up those targets."

The six village chiefs and some of their wives and advisors were settling down together on the riverbank. There was much discussion. Chief Chaska and Chief Tanu broke away from this group and came up to where Bedard and Roger were talking.

"Copco," Chief Chaska said, "you have asked for targets at nine hundred and twelve hundred feet. Are these for bows or rifles?"

Bedard and Roger just smiled.

"You are serious!" said the chief.

Chief Tanu waved over the leader of his small warrior group, Chetan. "You know about the new targets?"

Chetan nodded and smiled. "I know what you are going to ask me. No, I have never used a target at nine hundred feet, let alone twelve hundred feet for either rifle or bow."

The three men turned and looked at Bedard and Roger who continued to smile, saying nothing.

"I have been asked," said Chetan, "and I have agreed to try one of the new rifles at nine hundred feet." He shrugged and laughed.

Chief Enthica did not wish to participate, nor did Mot, Cowen and two of the Musqueam warrior visitors. Bedard, Roger, Fenciao, Baribo and the remaining fourteen warriors were setting up their rifles for the demonstration. The group had also convinced four local marksmen, including Chetan, to try the new rifles. Bedard agreed to shoot first at the nine-hundred-foot target. The target-support group indicated that his shot was a bull's eye. The rest followed, and everyone, including the four local marksmen, shot a bull's eye. The whole audience, including the chiefs, was standing and clapping. That was a good result!

Chetan brought the rifle that he had used back to show to the six chiefs.

"That was fantastic! The sights were very easy to use, and the rifle had hardly any kick. We must get some of these rifles."

Roger had followed Chetan. "Are you going to try twelve hundred feet?"

Chetan did not answer. He looked at his chief. Chief Tanu thought for a moment.

"You have nothing to lose," Chief Tanu said. "Even two feet off the mark would be an incredible shot."

Chetan smiled and returned to the shooting mark with Roger.

For the twelve-hundred-foot target, six of the visiting warriors declined, and only Chetan agreed to shoot with Bedard and Roger.

Bedard and Roger each shot a bull's eye. Chetan's shot was two inches off the mark.

Chetan had shot last, and he had been given some advice by Roger on how to crouch to steady his rifle on his legs, to steady his body with breathing, and to hold his breath to shoot. He was still in the shooting position some minutes after the shot. The whole crowed were on their feet clapping and yelling.

"I think that you should take another shot," Roger said.

Chetan unfolded himself and handed the rifle back to Roger. "No, thank you. That was an incredible experience. That was twice the distance that I have ever shot a rifle!"

Roger handed the rifle back to Chetan. "You keep this one. I have another one that is better."

Chetan clutched the rifle, not knowing what to say.

Chief Tanu came up to him. "That was an incredible shot, Chetan."

"Roger just gave me this rifle," said Chetan. "I don't know whether to laugh or to cry!"

Bedard was just behind Chief Tanu. "I think that we have a convert!"

The four men laughed.

Roger stepped forward. "And now we will have Bedard show you his bows. They are much more interesting."

The crowd, having been well entertained, now saw Mot and Cowen bring a long thin bag and a bigger bag out to Bedard. Fenciao and Chief Enthica, followed by about ten local warriors, also came forward to inspect the bows.

Fenciao, who had now seen three of Bedard's demonstrations, took the bow out of the long thin bag and attached the bowstring carefully. Looking at Bedard with a smile, he described the bows construction and how the energy was stored.

Bedard did his warmup exercises and tested the wind with a bit of straw. At nine hundred feet, he knew that the placement of the arrow would be very good and was pleased when the arrow was reported to have landed in the centre of the six-inch circle. No one else was willing to shoot at that distance. The group was very quiet. Many of the men were shaking their heads, hardly believing what they had just witnessed.

Chief Enthica was standing beside Chetan and asked him if he wished to try the shot using Copco's bow. Chetan approached Bedard and asked to try. Without putting an arrow in place, he drew back the bowstring and then released it.

"Yes, there is no doubt that there is more *energy* in that bow, and because of that the arrow will travel farther, but I am not strong enough to use that bow more than a few times."

He stopped and thought for a few minutes and then took one of Bedard's arrows and measured it against his arm.

"Copco's reach is very long, a good hand longer than mine." He held up his hand, showing the distance from the end of his thumb to the end of his little finger. "This also gives Copco a great advantage for distance and probably for accuracy as well."

Bedard and his group were all smiling, knowing that this was true. Chetan examined the arrowhead.

"The small arrow tip will also help."

Roger nodded. "We now understand why you are a highly respected warrior in this nation." The whole group clapped lightly. Chetan was now a bit embarrassed.

Chief Tanu had joined the group standing around Bedard and had heard the exchange. "We are very pleased to have Chetan's skills, leadership and intelligence." He looked at Bedard. "No, you cannot recruit him."

Bedard's group laughed and clapped. The local group took a few moments to get it and they also laughed. Several hit Chetan on the shoulders and back.

Bedard looked at Chetan. "We will talk."

The group burst into laughter again. Both Chief Tanu and Chetan were now smiling, very pleased with this result. Bedard led the group out to the twelve-hundred-foot marker.

"Now we will see the magic," Chief Enthica said.

The group, which had grown quite large, moved away from the shooting line and sat down on the grass.

"Copco," said Fenciao, "are you going to use the compound bow at the longer distance?"

"No," Bedard said. "It is too windy. I doubt if the arrow will land in the eighteen-inch circle, so there is no purpose in trying that today."

Fenciao carried the larger bag over to Bedard, who removed the bow.

"That is a *crossbow*," Chetan said, using the English word. "I saw two of them about ten years ago in Mahli."

"Yes," said Fenciao, "they said that they had two, but they are stored somewhere and they have been unable to find them yet."

Bedard took the special arrow from Fenciao and walked over to the line. He put the front of the crossbow on the ground and drew back on the lever to cock the unit. He then called Mot over to help him. A few seconds after Bedard got off the shot, the signalled report was that the arrow had struck within the eighteen-inch circle.

"That was a good shot!" said Chetan, and the others agreed.

Bedard and Roger were surprised to hear a bell ringing in the distance.

"Ah yes," said Chief Tanu, "the call to the late meal. We are very modern here."

Bedard's group followed the chief, with Mot and Cowen carrying the two bow bags. They were led into the chief's large longhouse where a meal for all of the visitors and villagers was set out.

The seating arrangement was somewhat similar to what Bedard had previously experienced. The six chiefs and the two wives sat at a higher table. Immediately in front of them, sitting at a lower table facing the same way, were some of the Staulo warriors and staff. Facing these two groups were Bedard, Roger, Fenciao, Chief Enthica and some of the Staulo visitors. Chetan was seated opposite Bedard and Roger. Bedard thought that this was quite clever because the chiefs could hear and participate in the meal conversations quite easily. The remaining villagers and guests were seated behind them in rows. Bedard knew that this worked very well. He was looking forward to this feast.

Bedard's first surprise was when Maria spoke in English.

"We enjoyed the gun and bow demonstrations. We had heard of them, of course, but we know that sometimes stories get a bit twisted as they travel up and down the river."

There were several translators behind the chiefs and squeezed in between the men in front of them. Cowen and Mot were kneeling behind Bedard and Roger. Bedard noticed that many of the Staulo obviously had some English.

Bedard's reply was also in English. "You probably also heard that Chief Tamburo's wife Tomala is now an expert bowman."

"Yes. When I heard that, I approached Chetan for lessons."

There were murmurs of amusement.

"She is progressing very well," Chetan said. "We have heard that other women up and down the river are also practicing. I hope that next winter's competition will include them."

The people at the table smiled and clapped.

"Please excuse me," said Chief Chaska. "My English is not very good yet. I have a question: How do we obtain these new rifles?"

Bedard and Roger both turned and looked at Chief Enthica, who turned and looked at Fenciao who was sitting beside him. Fenciao thought for a moment and then smiled at Chief Chaska.

"We now have about thirty new rifles." He looked at Bedard who nodded. "Most of them have been taken from the evil white men that Copco has found. Some of these men are now dead, and some have been told to return south and not come back again. We hope that they do that. Two of our warriors have purchased new rifles from white men." He again looked at Bedard who looked surprised—he did not know this.

"These rifles were very expensive," Fenciao said. "Thirty blankets each!"

Chief Chaska and many of the Staulo groaned and shook their heads.

"Yes, I agree," said Fenciao. "Luckily, we have made a large order of rifles, school books and medical supplies and equipment with the assistance of Copco's group of businessmen who work in San Francisco. We have heard that they have placed the order with factories and suppliers in the Eastern United States."

"That's true," Bedard said. "We hope that they will cost only five blankets each, plus shipping, say, seven blankets."

Chetan had turned around to look at Chief Tanu, anticipating the question.

"At least forty rifles," he said. "About three hundred blankets."

Another warrior seated in the third row turned to Chief Chaska.

"About the same, perhaps a bit more for our three sister villages."

All of the chiefs were nodding their heads, digesting this information.

"The miners will bring the white men's diseases," said Maria, "so we will need medications. And school books. We must visit the Musqueam Nation soon for their advice."

All of the Staulo were nodding their heads, and they started talking to each other quietly just as the first food arrived.

"Good timing," said Roger, and all agreed.

The feast was very good, and Bedard, who was now an expert at these enormous meals, gave Roger constant advice, some of which he ignored and later regretted.

During the meal, Bedard tried to share his understanding of the impact that the large group of miners would have on this area. This stretch of the river was well known as a valuable fishing area to the native communities for many hundreds of miles around. The natives had been coming here to fish for salmon in the summer season for several thousands of years. There were trails following the river on both sides and numerous fish-drying racks. The total length of the river here was historically assigned to various villages and nations as their fishing area. Disagreements were rare and easily rectified. This was just not an issue.

Bedard felt that this was all about to end. The miners would disrupt the fishing season and life in this village in many ways. The discussion was very difficult because the villagers found it difficult to believe that the miners would demand control over the river and that this would prevent many of them from fishing.

At the end of the meal, Chief Tanu stood up and expressed his pleasure at meeting Copco and Roger, at seeing the rifle and bow demonstrations, and for the advice that the visitors had offered. Bedard stood up and with Mot's help from time to time thanked everyone for the food and entertainment.

Bedard and his group decided to leave some of the packs in the village and returned to their campsite.

At noon the next day, Bedard, Roger, Mot and Cowen were sitting on rocks behind a stand of cedar trees and light bushes on the east side of the Fraser River just downstream from Emory Creek. There were six warriors in a security pattern around them, and four more guarding the main path to the north and south.

Fenciao, Chief Enthica and the other five warriors were down on the river bar watching the miners work. This was something new to all of them.

When their group had arrived, Bedard and Roger positioned themselves on the hillside and saw that the only miners who reacted to the arrival of the native group were at the far end of the bar. One of the three miners stood up with a rifle at the ready. Both Bedard and Roger had long spyglasses and easily determined that the two men who were still panning for gold were Don and Wilber Thompson, and that Tommy Debb was the guard with the rifle.

The other ten miners did not pay much attention, although the newcomers were well armed with rifles and bows but had not assumed an aggressive attitude.

After watching the miners pan at the water's edge, both Fenciao and Chief Enthica went farther down the bar and tried the two pans that Bedard had purchased at Fort Hope. They both had some experience at this, and it was not long before the two remembered that panning for gold was really hard work.

One of the miners, an old gentleman with a long beard who had been sitting on a log nearby, came over to them and offered some advice. He was quite surprised to find that they both spoke reasonable English. He said that all of the gold found north of Fort Hope was in the river bars perhaps one foot down into the fine gravel. The gold-bearing strata varied from one to four feet thick. No gold was found on the riverbanks. The gold was so fine that quicksilver was required to finally separate and isolate the gold from the fine sand.

Roger stood up. "They've gone!"

Bedard put his telescope to his eye. "They have, and it's midday so they've decided to be cautious. We're too late. When we find their campsite they'll be long gone, and it'll be very dangerous to follow them. We'll get them next time. We need to act faster. They're very sensitive to danger."

He looked down at Fenciao and Chief Enthica. "I wonder if gold rush fever will grab our friends on the river bar?"

Roger laughed. "I know that I still have it!"

They moved the rest of the team down onto the bar and had everyone try to pan for gold. Some gold was recovered, but their technique was not very good. Roger participated in the teaching, and everyone had a good time. Both Bedard and Roger talked to some of the miners there. They found, not to their surprise, that the three working the gravel at the far end of the bar were not interested in talking to anyone and stopped anyone who wanted to visit their campsite.

As the darkness came in the late afternoon, the group returned south to Chief Tanu's village and Maria again invited them all to stay for the late meal. There was much bragging about all the gold that they had found, and several of the local warriors were very interested.

After the meal, which was not surprisingly composed of the leftovers from the previous day's feast, Chief Tanu said that they had decided on an early visit to the Musqueam villages and thought that they could make it there in one day using their war canoes. He offered part of their *fleet* to Bedard, who immediately accepted the offer.

Early the next morning, the warrior group and the four dogs arrived at the village with all their gear. The first task was to sort through the gear and leave as much as possible behind. A large group of the villagers was on hand to meet the famous dogs, who were put through a short demonstration to everyone's pleasure and amusement. The collies were as usual quite sensational in one of their famous routines. But the stars of the show were the two mastiffs. No one had ever seen such big dogs, and everyone was amazed to find out how well trained they were. All the dogs loved to pose and enjoyed all the scratches.

Paddling with the river current, the five huge twenty-man war canoes made quick work of the trip down to Tsusnahm. They arrived in late afternoon, and the villagers, being forewarned by the man in the lookout tree, were all out to welcome them.

Thirty-Eight
March 9, 1858

The *Cobalt* moved out of the small harbour of Skedans where it had anchored for two days, trading Hudson Bay Company blankets, bowie knives, machetes, axes, kitchen pots and pans and basic British clothing and material. The clothing and material were much in demand. In return for these goods, the Hudson's Bay Company traders received furs, beautiful carvings in wood and argillite and two large canoes which the *Cobalt* was now towing. The *Cobalt* had spent one evening at the small village of Tanu farther south and was now on the way to the village of Cumshewa for one or two days of further trading before it moved onward to the village of Skidegate.

Cowen and Mot joined Captain Tagore and his translators at both Tanu and Skedans, while Bedard's group of twenty Musqueam warriors on board kept out of sight.

Bedard and Roger had also joined the large meeting on the *Cobalt* with Chief Keyap of Skedans on the first day of trading. Bedard could see that the chief was very old and required considerable help in coming aboard the vessel. Roger had met Chief Keyap many times. The chief was pleased to see him again because Roger had been one of the few white men he had met who not only spoke the Haida language but also lived quietly and peacefully amongst the Haida in Cumshewa for several years. Roger had also demonstrated to this community the Shaolin style of kung fu, including the high kicks, and had completely demolished some of the chief's very tough warrior fighters. Roger was held in great respect by the chief and many in his village.

Bedard was introduced as a kung fu master and was immediately welcomed by Chief Keyap, who said that Roger was the toughest man he had ever met. The chief's advisors who had accompanied him on board the *Cobalt* all knew Roger and had shaken Roger and Bedard's hands in the English fashion, with a great deal of banter with Roger. Roger was very pleased, and Bedard was impressed with the respect shown to his friend.

Chief Keyap told Roger that Chief Loosdallio had died several months ago. "We are sad. He and I were almost brothers. I think of him every day. His son Rondo is now chief. Chief Rondo has a great deal of support in Cumshewa and in all of our villages."

"Chief Loosdallio was very wise," said Roger, "and will be missed by all who knew him. He was a clever man and father. Chief Rondo will lead the village of Cumshewa to more greatness."

The Haida group nodded their heads in agreement.

One of the chief's advisors spoke to him briefly and he turned and spoke to Bedard in Russian.

"Are you the person that we have been hearing about who speaks many languages?"

Bedard was surprised and decide to proceed cautiously, so he replied in Russian.

"Yes, and today I am concentrating on learning the beautiful Haida language, which is probably as old as the Russian language."

One of the chief's advisors translated this into Haida with both Mot and Cowen translating it into English for the benefit of Captain Tagore and his group of traders.

Chief Keyap was very pleased with Bedard's response and responded in Haida. "My Russian is not very good now because the Russians do not come here to trade much anymore. How long have you been speaking Haida?"

Mot replied, "Four days."

The chief was surprised. "You must be very skilled at learning languages. It took me almost ten years to become comfortable speaking Russian."

Bedard said in Haida, "For me, it is much like learning how to prepare a different fish for drying. Once one has done this many times it becomes easier. I also have very good teachers."

One of the chief's advisors again spoke to the chief briefly and the chief turned to Mot.

"We also heard of Mothway several years ago. It is a pleasure meeting you. We do not now have anyone in our village who is blind. My father, Chief Tongaway, became that way some years before he died."

The two men faced each other without speaking for some time.

Then the chief said, "We do not have any Musqueam in our village now."

One of the chief's advisors again spoke to the him briefly, and the chief added, "We believe that most of those who lived here are now in Kitkatla."

The discussion continued in a social way and eventually turned to the goods that the Haida community wanted. This was a significant departure from the method that these people had used for many years. They were very hard to negotiate with, and the trading discussions usually started with what the company had to trade.

Chief Keyap said, "We were very pleased to receive American- and European-designed clothing in recent trading sessions, and the women of our village have made it clear that they want more clothing and material." He waved his hands in the air and some of his advisors appeared embarrassed. "The women in our village have a strong voice, as some of you know." He stopped and looked at Roger who nodded and smiled. "My wife included."

At this all the Haida laughed lightly.

Four of the ship's traders brought out many bolts of medium-weight cotton and pieces of multicolored silk cloth along with several large boxes of everyday clothing. The Haida became very excited and the day's trading discussions started in earnest. This was when the Haida reluctantly traded two of their highly-prized canoes.

The day ended with everyone smiling. As Chief Keyap was leaving with his two key advisors, Roger, Bedard and Mot approached them. Roger addressed the chief.

"Thank you for the information on the Musqueam who were here before. We plan to visit Kitkatla next month and talk to them."

The three Haida men nodded and left the ship.

The next day, the traders from the ship visited the village to exchange the goods that had been traded the previous day.

Early that afternoon, the *Cobalt* moved smoothly west down the fjord toward the village of Cumshewa. Roger was excited because he had not been in the village for more than two years.

Before the *Cobalt* had reached where it would anchor, a huge canoe with about forty paddlers took off from the beach at Cumshewa travelling at an enormous speed.

One of the sailors gave Roger his long glass. Roger smiled.

"That is Chief Rondo in the prow of the canoe. He was my best friend when I was living in his village."

The canoe slowed down and came alongside the *Cobalt* just as it was anchoring. A huge man came up the rope ladder that was sent down to him and bounded onto the deck, sweeping Roger up in his massive arms.

The two men held each other at arm's length, laughing with obvious pleasure.

Chief Rondo spoke in English. "I am very pleased to see you again. I did not think that this would ever happen."

Roger in turn spoke Haida. "I am sorry to hear that your father passed on to the unknown lands."

"Yes," said Chief Rondo, "we are still in mourning for him. You told me that his shoes were very big. I am only now understanding what that means. I married April last year, so I have a very capable *secretary*." They both laughed.

Roger introduced Bedard and Mot.

"Ahhh," said Chief Rondo. "I remember Roger speaking about you and your incredible language skills, and of course your mastery of the Shaolin style of kung fu. We have had many kung fu lessons from Roger, and we still use the basic moves to train our warriors to act and think at the same time." He turned back to Roger. "Your visit is a very good omen for the village of Cumshewa. We will talk."

He turned to Mot. "You are Mothway. We heard of you several years ago. We have one young man who also cannot see. It would be good to have you meet him."

"I would be pleased to do that," Mot said.

"Our trading group will come ashore after the midday meal," said Captain Tagore.

Chief Rondo smiled. "That will be good." He turned to Roger. "Will you come with me?"

"Yes, perhaps we can bring Copco and Mot as well."

"Yes," said Chief Rondo. "Of course."

The four men went down the rope ladder.

Chief Rondo said to Mot, "You have many skills, Mothway."

Mot just smiled, pleased with himself, as climbing rope ladders was a new skill that he had taught himself on this trip. The big canoe moved off smoothly toward the shore.

Chief Rondo noticed the two canoes being towed.

"That is unusual. Probably from Chief Keyap. They are very expensive."

Roger, Bedard and Mot just smiled. Chief Rondo also smiled. "Chief Keyap's wife is not a good trader." The group laughed. "We must be more careful." Everyone smiled again.

The three visitors were led to one of the eight longhouses on the old village site. This house was quite ornate, with six totem poles in front of the arched doorway. Roger noted that four more longhouses had been built along the beachfront to the west since he left two years ago.

Chief Rondo directed Roger's attention. "This is the totem pole that we have just erected to honour my father."

The group stopped to admire it. It gave a very strong feeling and had a large raven at the top.

"It is very powerful," Roger said. "The Toe brothers, no doubt."

The chief nodded, pleased that his friend could remember these skilled village carvers.

"They started the work two years ago, and my father helped design it." He was obviously very proud of his fathers' participation.

The group now entered through the arched doorway and Roger was met in a rush by April with a big hug and a kiss. Chief Rondo put an arm around his wife, and she said to Roger, "You told me to be strong and not let him manage my life. That has been difficult, but since he has started to call me his *secretary,* I think that I am making some progress."

They all laughed, and she kissed her husband and escaped to deal with the upcoming meal.

The group moved forward and were directed to sit down at a curiously curved large table near the cooking fire. Roger was smiling.

"When Roger was here," said Chief Rondo, "he told me that our meetings were dangerous because elders and family representatives at the meetings may have different views on a subject, and someone could easily cross over to harm another person. He recommended adding a barrier between the people. We experimented and found a curved table like this to be the best. This is one of five tables like this that we have, and we carry them through the village and use them for various functions. At council meetings we lower the top surface to about two feet."

Roger nodded. "You were also experimenting with meetings that allowed more villagers to speak. How is that going?"

April arrived at the table and sat down. "We now have one meeting per month where anyone can speak on any subject. It is often difficult to organize, but we have had some very good results with some of the ideas that you left with us. I think that this has helped strengthen our village. It has also attracted other families from the small villages on the west coast to relocate here."

The meal consisted of various fish and shellfish, and it was delicious. Afterwards, Mot was asked to meet with the young man who was blind, and he went off with a woman who was introduced as the mother of the man.

Bedard asked if he could wander around, and one of the chief's older advisors volunteered to go with him.

"You are welcome to join us," said Chief Rondo. "Roger has told us that you are very wise. I think that you would find our discussions interesting, and we would welcome your views."

Roger followed Chief Rondo and April to another building that was both their home and the centre of the village's administration. They sat down on some mats in a corner with three younger village leaders that Roger knew.

After some socializing, April said to Roger, "As I mentioned at *lunch*, the village of Cumshewa has increased in size since you left. A number of families from the small villages on the west coast have asked permission to relocate here. This has been very difficult for us because we have decided to say no to many of these people."

Chief Rondo nodded. "This was relatively easy when my grandfather was chief, but it is becoming more difficult now that we have a more open society."

Bedard and his guide joined the group.

"Good," said Chief Rondo. "We were just starting to discuss what we initially thought was a relatively simple village problem that has now changed into a serious challenge for our community. We have accepted a number of families from the west coast communities and refused others. When my grandfather was chief, it was easy to decide. Now with a larger, more open, community, it is getting more difficult to decide."

Bedard looked at Roger and then back to Chief Rondo. "Why do you refuse to allow a family to join your community?"

Chief Rondo looked at April.

"Firstly," she said, "there are two groups: those who already have a family member living in Cumshewa and those who do not. Initially, those who did not have any family here were not invited to join us. Then this changed and we tried to understand the new family: the skills that they had, the number of children, men and women and the number of aged, the reputation for evil and so on. With this information the council would meet and discuss the family. We used one of Roger's ideas, the black mark. We called it quite simply the no-vote. One no-vote and the request was refused."

"This worked reasonably well," said Chief Rondo, "when the council had seven members. Now there are fifteen members, with three of these members representing groups of new families. All of the council members are men."

April said, "Each of the last ten families that we have considered have received at least one no-vote. Since the vote is confidential we do not know who voted no. We suspect that it is one of the new family representatives. We do not yet know who or why they voted no. Then there are the families who already have a family member living in Cumshewa. We go through the same process of obtaining information from the family. Then we discuss the family at a council meeting but we do not vote. We then ask the family member who already lives here if he or she would like to address the council. Some of these people supported the family request and some did not. After that, the council discussed the family again and voted. All of the last five families have received a no-vote, including two families that my husband and I thought would be excellent additions to our community."

Bedard looked at the three younger village leaders and at the older advisor who accompanied him on his short trip around the community. "This is definitely a difficult situation. Do you have anything to add?"

The three younger men looked at the older man, who then spoke.

"There has been much discussion not only amongst the leaders of our village but also amongst the villagers themselves. Skidegate to the north is also a very large village and has many special problems relating to its size. Many villagers here do not think that our village should become any larger.

"There are some of us"—he looked at the three other men—"who think that a few villagers, possibly only two, do not like the present leadership." He stopped and looked at Chief Rondo. "And are reported to be trying to embarrass Chief Rondo at every opportunity. In the past, villagers who become tiresome to the chief were asked to leave. They did not have much choice—they left. We have not challenged these people yet for we do not have a *strategy*."

Bedard looked at Roger, paused for a moment, and then addressed Chief Rondo.

"In my experience, fifteen people is a large number for a decision-making group. Is there any reasonable way to make it smaller?"

Chief Rondo looked at his wife and nodded. "There are always ways to do something like that," he said. "We have not discussed this. What would be a reasonable number?"

"You have twelve longhouses," Bedard said. "Eleven or twelve might be reasonable, nine or ten would be better."

There was a long pause, and Bedard looked at Roger.

"Yes," said Roger, "this group always thinks before they speak."

Bedard smiled. "Have you talked about changing the system?" he said. "There are many communities, including the three main Musqueam villages, who have moved toward management by representation but retain the chief's decision as final. Some of these chiefs have said that they use this right very infrequently. I like the no-vote, but I like the systems where the chief still has the final decision. After three thousand years, this system still seems to work best in your world. You are a relatively new chief and should be able to change the systems."

There was again a long pause.

"Who is next in line for chief?" Bedard asked.

"Me!" said April. Chief Rondo hugged her and the group laughed.

"We would not usually make that decision until I die," said Chief Rondo, and smiled.

"You should have more women on your council," Bedard said. April laughed and received another hug. The group laughed with her.

"We have actually talked about that many times," said Chief Rondo. "About ten years ago Vera was on my grandfather's council. As I recall, she was a bit Russian in that she did not smile very often. She was very wise and outspoken, too."

The group looked at April and laughed again. April was now a bit embarrassed.

"If you decide to change something," Bedard said, "perhaps the chief could from time to time ask the no-voter to identify himself or herself and explain the reasoning. Then the chief would have the right to accept the reasoning or reject it and cancel that person's vote. It might get more complicated if there were multiple no-votes."

Bedard looked at Chief Rondo. "You have a huge responsibility, not only to the members of this village but also to both past and future villagers. The historic reasons for asking those villagers who do not wish to fit into your village community to leave are still valid ones."

It was very quiet. A man came in and talked to Chief Rondo.

"The trading is underway," said the chief, "and is apparently becoming difficult, so I have been asked to join these efforts. Thank you, Copco, for your words of wisdom."

He and April left together.

The group continued to sit and talk. One of the young men said that there were four women in the village who were approached individually for their advice from time to time.

"Perhaps," he said, "we should get them together and talk."

"Roger and I spent some time in a very large country near Russia called China," said Bedard, "where we learned may things, including the art of kung fu fighting. You are familiar with this." They all smiled at Roger. "I had the opportunity to travel farther to the west of China where there are many different countries with many different languages and dialects. Because I like languages, it was a very exciting time for me. Many of the larger villages had very interesting village management committee systems that included women."

Chief Rondo and April returned. He was frowning; she was smiling.

"We now have enough material to last the year," said April.

Chief Rondo was less pleased. "I now understand why Chief Keyap traded his canoes."

There was general amusement at this comment. April gave her husband a playful nudge in the ribs and even he offered a wry smile.

"We must go now," Roger said, "or we will be left behind."

Outside the longhouse they met up with Mot. He was standing with a man about his own age who had a dog beside him.

"This has been very exciting for me," Mot said. "Bob has a friend who has been trained to protect him. You can see that Wolf—that is his name—has a special handle attached to a harness. Bob holds the handle and Wolf guides him around objects that he would normally bump into. Bob is in the process of training a younger dog, and the four of us went for a walk together. It was fantastic! I was very relaxed knowing that I would not veer off the path or bump into something. He gave me a sketch of the harness. It was apparently made by a German sailor about twenty years ago. Copco, have you ever seen this type of harness?"

Bedard shook his head. "No, I do not recall seeing anything like that, and if I did I may not have understood its use."

Roger took the sketch and knelt down by the dog. "We can do this," he said.

As the group were walking down towards the canoes, Chief Rondo approached Bedard and Roger.

"We were talking about a chief asking villagers to leave the village. You may know that four years ago Chief Taan asked a large group of warriors to leave Skidegate. They, along with their wives and children, moved about five miles west to an old village that still had two longhouses. They subsequently built two more longhouses."

April was walking beside her husband. "Many of the children in that village are Musqueam slaves. At this time we do not think that there are any Musqueam slaves in Skidegate, although there still may be two or three warriors of that same group who were allowed to stay, possibly because their families are very strong."

"Yes, that's true," Chief Rondo said. "We doubt if there are any more Musqueam slaves in any other Haida village here. There may be some children at Kitkatla on the far coast to the east."

Bedard nodded, surprised that Chief Rondo and April would tell him this. "Thank you for that information. We intend to discuss this with Chief Taan, and we intend to visit Kitkatla."

"It was very nice to see you, Roger," said April. "I hope that you will visit again now that peaceful relations have been established up and down the coast."

Towing the two war canoes, the *Cobalt* moved slowly down the sound toward Skidegate in the afternoon's light rain. Bedard, Roger and Cowen were looking at the village through their telescopes.

"They must have their lookout stations manned," said Bedard. "There is quite a bit of action in the village."

Cowen concurred. "They probably knew that we were visiting Cumshewa and Skedans to trade. Skidegate has always been a very complicated and aggressive community."

"There is Chief Taan getting into a canoe with four paddlers," Roger said. "He has a full headdress and an elaborate robe. This is unusual. He has his son with him, and his grandson also, and a young boy. I can't remember the two men's names. There are only two other men. Now the chief's wife has come down to the water and climbed into the canoe."

"Interesting," said Cowen. "Chief Taan is talking to his wife. I wonder if she had been originally included in the group."

Mot was standing nearby. "I wonder why they did not wait until the trading group came to their village."

He turned toward Captain Tagore, who shrugged. "I don't know."

The ship's translators and traders were working with some of the ship's hands to clear an area on the deck and set it up for the surprise meeting. Bedard was amazed to see chairs appearing from storage.

"Captain," said Bedard, "we think that the four of us plus you and three of your senior men might be enough for this unusual meeting. We have always thought that the Haida would know what our objectives were for this trip, and I think that this has been more or less the situation at the last two stops."

Captain Tagore straightened his jacket and roughly combed his hair back with his fingers. "I recognize the two men with him now. One is a senior member of his council, and the other is his personal translator. There are no traders, so I suggest that just the five of us meet his party. I will introduce you."

"It is odd," Roger said, "I cannot think of a reason for the chief to have his son and his grandson with him. I wonder if the young boy is his great grandson. He looks about ten or so. I have met him."

The *Cobalt* came to the anchorage and swung slowly around on the bow anchor until it was parallel with the land, and the second anchor was set from the prow. The canoe arrived and the party climbed slowly up the rope ladders. Chief Taan helped his wife clamber aboard and approached the group of five on the deck.

Captain Tagore welcomed the chief and his wife on board, and Chief Taan introduced the rest of his party. Roger was correct, the young boy was indeed the chief's great-grandson. Both the chief and his wife were smiling greatly.

Roger, of course, did not need an introduction, and the chief and his wife appeared very surprised to see him. He got a big hug from the chief's wife.

The chief's son, grandson, great-grandson and the two older men all knew Roger, and there were English handshakes all around.

Chief Taan addressed Bedard. "We were hoping to meet you. Albert is our best translator and language teacher. I only know a few local languages. My son and his son both know English and Russian, and that has been very useful to our village. But my great-grandson"—the lad was a bit shy and standing behind the chief's wife—"already knows six or seven languages very well, and most of the coastal languages, including Musqueam!"

Bedard was very surprised. The young boy sat in one of the chairs beside Albert and smiled at Bedard.

"Robby," Albert said, "asked to come on some of our local trading trips when he was about four, and we often found him playing with other children in many of the villages that we visited. Just for fun, I asked him some innocent questions in one of these languages and was stunned when he could respond. It was his father who actually found out that Robby could remember almost everything that he heard. Now we have some books in various languages and he *devours* them."

"Impressive," said Bedard.

"Yes," said Albert, "it was quite incredible. We were always on the lookout for a foreigner: some Portuguese on a Spanish boat, or a Chinese man or a Hawaiian. English came very rapidly because his family decided to speak English to him. So he knows English, Russian, French, Spanish, a bit of Portuguese, Italian, Mandarin and Hawaiian. Roger actually worked with him with the Mandarin."

Robby was smiling. Bedard turned to him. "Which European language did you start with?"

Robby looked at Albert. "Albert said that both English and Russian would be difficult to teach and to learn, so we started with French because there was a Frenchman staying in one of the villages on the west coast. I went there for a month and then came back all excited because he knew Spanish too. This was also one of Albert's languages."

Bedard spoke to him in Musqueam, and he replied. Bedard then spoke with an island dialect. Robby looked at Cowen, laughed and replied in the same dialect.

"Cowen is a good teacher too," Robby said.

Cowen shook his head. "Perhaps six hours over four days in two years."

Bedard said something in the Malaysian language.

Robby tilted his head. "I think that that is Malay."

Bedard laughed. "You are correct!"

"I met a sailor last year who was brought up in Singapore," Robby said. "He had some very interesting stories to tell me."

The chief's wife addressed Bedard. "Your Haida is quite good. How long have you been studying it?"

Mot answered. "Five days."

The group looked at Bedard and shook their heads.

Robby asked, "How many languages do you know?"

"I know about forty fairly well, but there are many dialects, as you know, and sometimes these are the most interesting."

Chief Taan turned to Mot. "You are Mothway. We heard of you several years ago. We now have a baby who cannot see. It would be good to have you meet him in a few years. You have no doubt met Bob and Wolf."

Mot nodded.

Then, without warning, the chief's wife spoke up, and the nature of her involvement in the official reception was made clear.

"We do not have anyone from Tsusnahm in our village," she said.

Chief Taan stood up, followed by the rest of the men. The chief's wife, however, remained seated.

"My husband has forbidden anyone from speaking about that event. He has forbidden anyone from speaking about the warriors and their families that he banished from our village. He has forbidden anyone from contacting or helping them in any way. As far as he is concerned, they do not exist anymore. In fact, I think that he would be pleased if they disappeared from our nation."

There was a long pause, and then she stood up. There were handshakes all around, and the visitors left the ship.

As they were leaving, Captain Tagore addressed Chief Tann.

"Our trading group will come to the village early tomorrow morning."

The chief nodded.

The next morning, ten traders made their way across the water in the boat's skiffs with piles of goods to be traded.

Just before the midday meal, the traders returned to the *Cobalt* along with Chief Taan's son in a small canoe. He boarded the ship and met briefly with Bedard, Roger, Mot and Cowen.

"My mother spoke words that we could not speak in front of the chief," he smiled, "but I think that he knew that she would insist on coming with our family to visit you, and I think that he knew that she would speak about the warriors that he banished from our village. While they were away our enemies attacked and we sustained serious losses. Losses that would not have occurred if we had had more warriors."

"The village of Tsusnahm wants their children back," Bedard said.

"My father said for me to tell you that he would not interfere with any professional actions against them." There was a long pause, then he smiled. "My mother thanks you for the gifts of materials and clothing, especially the beautiful silk. When we saw the two big canoes that you are towing, she thought that the other Haida villages had stolen all of it for themselves."

The group laughed and he left the ship.

Thirty-Nine
April 13, 1858

A month later, in the darkness of the night, the *Cobalt* moved rapidly into the sound toward Skidegate towing four twenty-man war canoes full of Musqueam warriors anxious for the action to start. Tow ropes were cut, and the canoes quietly made their way behind the ship as the big vessel passed by Skidegate and anchored. The canoes moved in silence and would put in to shore less than a mile to the west of Skidegate. The nighttime land run to the west was going to be gruelling, more than four miles with an absolute-quiet directive. This was the most important part of the attack. Any prior warning to the warrior village would be disastrous. This group's objective was to surround the warrior village and prevent any escape into the forest to the north.

The *Cobalt* had been in the area, trading under the direction of Captain Tagore with the two villages to the south of Skidegate for a week, so its arrival at Skidegate would not be a surprise for anyone. As it anchored just to the west of Skidegate in the darkness, six more large canoes were launched behind the ship, and the main warrior team paddled quietly westward toward the warrior village for the planned attack from the waterfront just before sunup.

The most difficult part of the attack operations was the need to minimize injury to women and children. It was hoped that the population would be trapped in the four longhouses. The plan was that the attacking forces would have enough time to dig protective trenches in strategic locations. They would also utilize the protection offered by the many sitting logs by the water to minimize their own injuries.

Bedard and a large contingent of Musqueam representatives planned to visit Skidegate at sunup and meet with Chief Taan. They first needed to assess whether the non-interference agreement was still in force. In any case, they hoped that their attack on the warrior village would be complete by then. They also hoped that some Skidegate residents would be involved in the processing of the women and children from the village.

It was probable that some Skidegate residents would try to involve themselves, but Bedard felt that their detailed attack plan would minimize this danger. In any case, the path connecting Skidegate to the warrior village would be blocked with a contingent of Musqueam warriors. It was thought that the Skidegate warrior leaders would try to prevent any involvement by mavericks.

The Musqueam villagers had strongly decreed that killing anyone was to be avoided if possible. This included killing any of the Haida warriors found in the village under attack. The consequences of not killing these hated men were discussed at length and the final plan included trying to capture these men without killing them. Their injuries would be attended to and then they would be subjected to questioning by the leaders of the Musqueam warriors and the Skidegate chief and his advisors. Bedard and several of his key staff including Roger, Cowen and Old Chief Sparrow felt that Chief Taan would deal with these men, who would now have twice embarrassed him, after the Musqueam group had left.

It was this decision to avoid killing anyone that lead to the inclusion of a large contingent of non-combatants on the trip. This group included Chief Roanyon and Old Chief Sparrow, Inchesca and Bella, Elizabeth and David, and twelve Musqueam women, including Mother. It was felt that the impact of the arrival of the two Musqueam chiefs and Mother on Chief Taan would be immense.

Inchesca and Bella were well known to the Skidegate shaman through their mother's work over the years up and down the coast. They felt that the Skidegate shaman held enormous power in the Skidegate village and that the appearance of Inchesca and Bella would have a very strong calming influence on everyone.

Mother thought that the arrival of Elizabeth and David with their medical assistance would astonish the Skidegate villagers and solidify the Musqueam's non-killing policy.

Bedard gave the signal and the two war canoes pushed off from the *Cobalt*. At the prow of each boat stood one of the two chiefs in full robes and feather headdress. The sun had just risen in the east, and the group could see people scurrying around in front of the many longhouses of the large village of Skidegate. The towering totem poles made the village seem quite imposing. The two canoes did not have far to travel, about one thousand feet, so the paddlers took their time. It would be useful to wait for a reception group to form on the land.

As the canoes reached the beach, eight warriors, including Fenciao, jumped out into the shallow water and spread out across the beach in a protective umbrella for the visiting party. These warriors were bare-chested, wore feathers in their hair and bore red and black paint. They all had two pistols strapped to their legs and carried one of the modern rapid-fire rifles at the ready.

The welcoming committee had assembled and villagers were tumbling out of their homes wondering what the commotion was all about. No one had ever seen such an unusual visiting group before, and there was noticeable confusion in the background behind the welcoming group.

Village men grabbed the two canoes and pulled them up on the sand. The two chiefs stepped out followed by Mother, Inchesca and Bella. Then came Cowen and Bedard. This group of seven moved slowly up the sand. Others in the boats remained seated. A third boat with the remainder of the female non-combatants and some warrior paddlers had been launched at the *Cobalt* but had remained there waiting for the signal that all was well.

Chief Taan had by now recognized Old Chief Sparrow and Mother. He turned and raised his hands above his head, pointing to the west and yelling something to what looked like a team of warriors that was being assembled behind him. He turned and proceeded rapidly forward toward the Musqueam group. With a complete lack of ceremony, he hugged Old Chief Sparrow and then Mother, much to their surprise.

"Welcome to our village."

Mother received him warmly. "Chief, I wish to introduce to you the new chief of the village of Tsusnahm, Chief Roanyon."

The two men stood for a moment, looking at each other, and then Chief Taan smiled and moved forward to embrace Chief Roanyon.

"Yes, I met your father once," Chief Taan said. "He was a very fine chief."

"Thank you," said Chief Roanyon. "I have a lot of support in Tsusnahm, and I often remember my wonderful father."

Chief Roanyon turned and introduced the two shamans, Inchesca and Bella. "You will remember their mother who visited you many times in the past."

"Of course!" he said. "Your mother helped us on many occasions. She was a very important person for all of us on this coast. I am very pleased to find that you both are following in her path."

Bedard had returned to the canoes, helped the remaining passengers out onto the beach and signalled the third canoe to come forward.

Chief Roanyon said, "Chief Taan, you know Cowen, I believe, and this is my friend Copco whom you met last month." Cowen was translating.

Chief Taan smiled and nodded his head at Cowen, and then looked at Bedard intently.

"Yes, you are the visitor who knows many languages and has some magic bows." He smiled and shook Bedard's hand in the English fashion. "I hope that we can see some of your bows." Cowen continued translating.

"Yes, of course," said Bedard.

Chief Roanyon then introduced the others in the party, including Elizabeth and David.

The Skidegate chief turned and introduced his wife and the other family leaders, elders and key members of his village in the welcoming party.

"And now, Chief Roanyon, I will send a small party of my best warriors west to help you. They know that you will have men not far down the path from here, and I have warned them to be careful and not get killed." He smiled.

Chief Roanyon nodded. "We will send some of our warriors with them."

Bedard and Cowen were quite relieved. The unusual greeting by the chief of Skidegate was to show the villagers and warriors behind him that these were friends in spite of the appearance of the painted and feathered heavily armed warriors at the water's edge. Bedard moved over to where Fenciao was standing, and they discussed who would go with the Skidegate warriors.

Fenciao had been watching the warrior group assemble behind the welcoming group.

"I know a warrior leader here, his name is Tsaak the Eagle, and it is he who appears to be in charge. I will go and talk to him."

"Very good. Just remember," Bedard said, "we need to be sensitive to possible rebel warriors in the village."

Fenciao grimaced. "We will also talk about that."

Bedard said, "Our plan was to send some of the Tsusnahm women to the village to help with the women and children there. You will recall that we hoped that some of the Skidegate women would go with us."

Fenciao nodded, moved over to the water's edge and talked to all of his men. Then two of them followed Fenciao carefully up towards the assembled Haida warrior group.

Inchesca and Bella had brought Elizabeth and David over to meet the two Skidegate shamans who were part of the welcoming Haida party. Elizabeth called Bedard over to where they were talking.

"Copco, where should we set up our medical area, near the beach or in one of the longhouses?"

Bedard looked up at the sky. "It is not going to rain today, so outside beside one of the longhouses that also could be used for serious cases would be best." The group nodded and Bedard said, "I will arrange for your supplies to be brought to you. Perhaps you could help with this, David."

Bedard and David moved off to the canoes where some of the local men were deep in conversation with two of the Tsusnahm women. They arranged for the two large boxes of medical supplies to be brought up to the area that was now being designated as the medical area.

The combined Haida and Musqueam warrior group left the village, taking with them ten of the Skidegate village women and two of the Musqueam women.

Then two makeshift stretchers carried by four Musqueam warriors arrived in a rush. The stretchers carried one Musqueam warrior and one Haida warrior, both with serious wounds. Elizabeth was surprised but moved forward with her new team to inspect the two injured men.

The Musqueam warriors reported that the village area had been secured by the very well-trained and organized Musqueam group with only ten injured on both sides and two Haida deaths. These two were the most serious injuries.

They said that most of the male residents of the warrior village had been captured in their longhouses and had surrendered with a minimum of fuss. Three Haida warrior leaders had escaped to the north but had been surprised and stopped by the northern group of Musqueam warriors. Unfortunately, these very experienced and ferocious Haida warriors fought on. Two were killed and one, the Haida warrior on the stretcher, had a number of serious gunshot injuries.

It was further reported that at the warrior village the men had been tied up and the women and children were being gathered together when the four Musqueam warriors had left the village in a rush with the two stretchers.

As the Musqueam and Haida party moved away from the water's edge, the remaining Musqueam warriors moved farther apart, covering a larger area.

A call was heard in the distance behind the longhouses. Bedard and Chief Roanyon drew their pistols and moved in front of the Musqueam party. Two of the Musqueam warriors by the water's edge moved in closer with rifles up.

Someone in one of the Musqueam boats fired a rifle and killed a man standing with a rifle in the doorway of one of the longhouses. He tumbled to the ground. Roger climbed out of the boat.

"We need to determine if we are safe, or we should return to the boat."

One Musqueam warrior in the west dropped to the ground with his rifle in firing position and another moved up between two longhouses in a rush. He immediately returned, followed by Baribo and two Musqueam warriors escorting two Haida men with their hands tied.

The remaining Haida party was in a turmoil. Many Haida warriors appeared with bows and a few muskets.

The Skidegate chief was standing with his hands in the air and shouting as loud as he could.

Baribo and his team brought the two prisoners down to the water's edge, where Baribo reported to Bedard, Roger and the three chiefs that three Haida warriors had left the group going west and circled back to Skidegate. His team had followed them but they were unable to prevent the first man from getting into the longhouse before they could react and capture the men.

Chief Taan seized a pistol from one of his warriors and was about to shoot the two prisoners when Bedard grabbed the gun and said that he wanted to talk to them first. This produced a tense situation with the Haida warriors surrounding their chief.

When he had composed himself, the Skidegate chief spoke.

"These are the three warriors from the raiding party of your village who we allowed to remain in our village because their families are very large and influential here. This was obviously my mistake. You, our visitors, have been insulted and many people will pay for this. Now, as my honoured guests, we will go to my home for the early meal."

The wife of the Skidegate chief yelled and rushed off to the west towards a man who had appeared from between the two longhouses. It was Robert leading a very small Musqueam group of six warriors. Their task was to monitor any activity behind the village of Skidegate. Bedard remembered that Robert had heard that his daughter had married the Skidegate chief and that Robert did not know how this was going to play out. Robert, seeing his daughter running toward him, stopped immediately and swept her into his arms.

To be separated from your father for thirty years is a long time, thought Bedard.

Chief Taan watched his wife and said, "I understand this," and moved off toward them.

Robert and Chief Taan talked and eventually shook hands English-style. Bedard was relieved. Chief Roanyon, Bedard and Roger discussed the current status.

"It has gone well," Chief Roanyon said. "The other injured will be here in about an hour, followed by the captured Haida warriors accompanied by some of our warriors. We now need to send the rest of our women to the warrior village."

"Right," said Roger. "We will use a canoe as planned. Perhaps I should go, and take Baribo's warrior group with me to help paddle."

"Yes," said Bedard. "Good plan."

Chief Roanyon nodded, and he and Bedard followed the group to one of the longhouses for the early meal. Mother had remained behind the others and indicated that she also wanted to go with Roger.

Elizabeth came over to Bedard.

"The two men are very lucky. All of the bullets passed through their bodies, so we are in the process of sewing them up. The Haida shamans are very good at this, of course." She smiled. "I think that some of the other injured will not be so lucky, but David has all his surgery tools with him today so we will do our best."

"We think that the other injured will arrive in about an hour," Bedard said. "Would you like to join us for a bit of food?"

Elizabeth turned around to say something just as Inchesca and David arrived. Inchesca suggested that Elizabeth and David should go and have something to eat and that some food would be brought out to the where the wounded were being cared for.

The Musqueam group entered the longhouse, where two Haida women guided them to their seats.

Bedard found himself sitting opposite Chief Taan, who rose and again shook Bedard's hand.

"I have sent our archery team down to the range to make certain that it is perfect and to see if they can create a shooting range longer than one thousand feet. None of our archers practice at distances longer than eight hundred feet, so the team and several of our best archers have been talking about rumours that we have heard that you have demonstrated shooting from thirteen hundred feet. Is this true?"

With Cowen translating, Chief Roanyon said, "You will see this. It is magic!"

Bedard decided that he would try his newly acquired Haida vocabulary.

"Most of the bows that I have were made by a famous English archery craftsman who now lives in New York." Cowen beamed and Chief Roanyon laughed as the Skidegate chief and his wife responded with amazement.

Chief Taan pulled a watch from a pocket and said, "You have been here for less than one hour and you can already speak our language!" The group at the table laughed.

Bedard said in Haida, "I have some very clever teachers."

The Skidegate chief turned to his wife and spoke in English. "Is now the time to show off our English?"

She laughed and shook her head. The whole group laughed again.

Elizabeth and David were sitting beside the chief's wife and had been deep in conversation with the help of one of the Haida translators. Elizabeth turned to Bedard.

"Her English is very good." The translator behind them smiled and nodded his head. The meal was excellent.

Elizabeth and David left first to go back to the hospital. Bedard, the two chiefs and the rest of their group left the building with Chief Taan and his group just as Roger arrived at the beach in a Musqueam canoe full of warriors. Roger got out and reached back for Bedard's two bags of bows.

"I thought you might need these."

The remaining men got out of the canoe. It was obvious that some of them were wounded.

"We took the children directly to the *Cobalt* with Mother and the rest of our women. The small group of warriors who are escorting the lightly wounded village warriors will arrive shortly. We have only ten lightly wounded warriors and will now take them to the hospital."

"Most of the Skidegate warriors have remained in the village guarding the village warriors. The Skidegate women have gathered the remaining children and village women and have apparently been talking about various options that they have."

Roger addressed Chief Taan. "As you know, some of the Skidegate women who came to help have family there, so the options are very difficult."

Chief Taan nodded. "Both of my sisters are at the village."

He looked around him at the group of elders that had followed him out of the longhouse. "They are very wise. They will ensure that the options are very clear. We do not wish to make any more errors."

Everyone agreed.

Chief Taan turned to Bedard and the two Musqueam chiefs. "This was indeed very professional. I thank you for that."

Everyone was very sombre.

Forty
April 13, 1858

Chief Taan raised him arms in a gesture of invitation.

"We now have the opportunity to balance our world with some small pleasures. We must see your bows. Please follow me."

He turned and marched between two longhouses, and turned north up a small rise along a path that followed a small creek. A large group of people followed him. In ten minutes they came to a delightful meadow where a team of archers were waiting under a large tree.

Chief Taan looked down the meadow. "Where have you moved our targets?"

The chief archer, whose name was Tsang, said, "We decided to move the targets to the edge of the lake so that we could have the space to see all of Copco's magic bows in action. This spot is actually thirteen hundred feet from the target." He looked at Bedard and shook his head.

Bedard put down his crossbow bag and walked down the meadow, carrying his second bag of bows to the nine-hundred-foot marker. He removed his longbow and the group examined it. Chief Roanyon, Bedard, Tsang and twenty-two of his archers all shot their arrows and placed them within the six-inch target. Tsang smiled.

Bedard was impressed.

Bedard moved back up the meadow to the eleven-hundred-foot marker and withdrew the three recurve bows. The larger one was also a compound bow, his favourite. Bedard described them in some detail and shot with the larger bow. This arrow also landed within the six-inch target.

Tsang stepped up to the line and released an arrow. The report was that it had landed just inside the eighteen-inch target. He was very pleased.

"That is the longest shot I have ever made!" he said.

No one else shot.

The group then moved back to the thirteen-hundred-foot marker where Chief Roanyon removed the crossbow.

He lifted up the device and Tsang's eyes widened. "That is a *crossbow*. I have had it described to me many times."

Roanyon took the special arrow from Bedard and walked over to the line. He put the front of the crossbow on the ground and drew back on the lever to cock the unit. Bedard came over to help him hold the frame.

The report was that the arrow had struck within the eighteen-inch circle.

"That was a good shot!" said Bedard, and the others agreed.

Chief Taan and Tsang were surrounded by the others as they examined the crossbow. Chief Taan shook his head. "That was hard to believe. I am glad that I was here to see it."

He moved forward and shook both Bedard's and Roanyon's hands.

The group followed Chief Taan south on the trail to the village. As they arrived, they saw a group of warriors milling around by the water. Fenciao detached himself from the group and approached.

"We were demonstrating the new rifles. Roger was shooting ducks flying near that island. Incredible shots!"

Chief Taan's great-grandson Robby came running over and grabbed his grandfather's hand. "Come and see this. This is really *magic!*"

Tsaak was standing with Roger. They were both holding rifles. Tsaak turned and said to Chief Taan and Tsang as they approached, "I have just used this rifle to shoot twice as far as I have ever shot in my life. Roger is hitting birds in flight at more than eight hundred feet!"

Behind them, four Haida men were sitting in the sand, each holding a rifle with their elbows braced on their knees with two Musqueam men instructing each of them. Several translators were in the area assisting. All four shot at about the same time, and the group watching roared with pleasure as two birds were hit.

Two very long tables had been set up for the midday meal in front of the longhouses and everyone slowly moved over to sample the large selection of fish, meat, shellfish, dried berries and greens.

Chief Taan and Tsang stood together with Roger, Bedard and Tsaak, examining some of the new rifles the group had brought with them. The talk turned to revolvers and knives and then to the horde of gold seekers anticipated soon.

The mood as Bedard spoke was subdued.

"There must be about a thousand miners that have already passed through Fort Langley. Some people are predicting twenty thousand miners this year! You will not be impacted here, except for the odd adventurer. Fort Victoria will become a large town before the end of the year. Many of these people will be from California. They do not like natives, and some of them will kill you if you turn your back."

As the midday meal was ending, the magic bows and a selection of arrows and several rifles, pistols and bowie knives were displayed on one of the tables. This drew a crowd.

Tsaak and the bow master's group were talking with the gun master. Roger, Bedard, Chief Taan and his senior translator, Albert, were listening intently.

"I am sorry that I missed the archery," said Tsaak. "The new bows look quite incredible. But I wonder if we should concentrate on guns now."

The gun master nodded. "Rifles will soon be better weapons for hunting. Guns are easier than bows to learn how to use, and perhaps they will last longer. I do not like pistols. They are not very good for hunting. They are best for killing people."

Those words hung in the air between them, but no one wanted to make a comment.

Captain Tagore and his group of traders arrived with three overloaded boats. Chief Roanyon approached Chief Taan. "We have some gifts for you: five rifles with some bullets, a few boxes of European clothing and some material."

The few boxes turned out to be over thirty boxes, and this attracted a swarm of village women to the waterfront. Chief Taan lifted one hand over his head and a group of men came forward with ten bentwood boxes full of wood and argillite carvings.

He then turned to Tsaak and the gun master. "We have received a gift of five new rifles. We can start gun lessons tomorrow." He paused. "Or perhaps tonight!" The group laughed.

The two chiefs shook hands and hugged each other. Chief Taan's wife was standing beside him with her brother Robert.

"This has been a very good day for our village," she said. "I can already see some good changes." She and her husband exchanged smiles.

The remaining visitors then left Skidegate and boarded the *Cobalt*.

The *Cobalt* moved slowly south toward a large island close by to the southwest. As they came closer they could see the small village of Haina. This was the village where Robert's large family now lived, having moved there from a small village on the west coast several years ago.

The large group at the railing of the *Cobalt* could see a welcoming group assembled at the water's edge. The chief and several others could be seen dressed in ceremonial regalia. The group around them were mixed: men, women, children. Some of the women and children were jumping up and down in excited anticipation.

The *Cobalt* anchored, and Robert was taken over to the village in one of the boat's skiffs. He was mobbed by the group even before he had hugged his uncle, who was the chief. Then two more skiffs full of gifts were launched from the *Cobalt*.

Sometime later, Robert came back to the water's edge and waved his hands. As had been arranged, a canoe was launched from the *Cobalt* carrying a large group of dignitaries, including the two chiefs, Mother, Bedard, Roger and ten others.

The meeting was chaotic but very pleasant as everyone was extremely happy to see Robert again and to meet the two chiefs and the other dignitaries. The chief of Haina told Old Chief Sparrow that this was the first time that a chief had visited his village. They apparently had several skilled carvers because there were only three small longhouses but many totem poles, and the longhouses were exquisitely decorated. It was a very beautiful sight.

Bedard and Roger gave a short archery and rifle show followed by a delicious meal where Bedard enjoyed several helpings of his favourite small lake fish.

After the late meal, the visitors boarded the *Cobalt* and started on the long trip east across the sound toward the mainland.

Early in the morning they reached Kitkatla, which was actually located on an island near the coast, and found the village abandoned.

On the beach was a small party of four men, two women, eight children and two young girls. When the *Cobalt* anchored, they came out to the ship and the ten youngsters came aboard. The women were crying. Their canoe returned to the village, and the ship immediately moved off.

Kitkatla had heard of the visit in advance, and the village chief had decided that they had had enough fighting that year. Most of the village families supported this and offered to return the Musqueam slaves that they had. The children told this story to the group, and they were all pleased to be able to leave Kitkatla and return to Tsusnahm. Just as the ship was leaving, a number of gunshots were heard and Cowen who was still on deck caught a bullet in his leg. No one else was hurt. Apparently not all the families in Kitkatla had agreed with this unusual gifting of slaves, but it would be up to Kitkatla to sort that out among themselves.

The return trip was uneventful. The arrival at Tsusnahm was a joyful affair with mothers and surrogate mothers smothering the children with love and kisses. The warriors were welcomed by a complex ceremony created by the elders of the three Musqueam villages based on their memories of similar festivities long past.

Forty-One
April 25, 1858

Bedard did not particularly like attending church. He only went as a courtesy to James and Amelia Douglas. Roger was in the building somewhere. Bedard had not seen him since the previous night. The last hymn was being sung, and Bedard escaped out a side door into the blazing sunlight.

He and Roger had met with Cowen and Aroga for dinner the previous evening. Cowen was recovering satisfactorily from the bullet wound in his left leg under Aroga's care, but Aroga was still not altogether pleased with Bedard for allowing Cowen to participate in the Haida battles. He had not participated and Bedard had told her that, but she still used that term, and he decided not to debate the point. Cowen had certainly made a significant contribution to the success of the venture.

The church was one of the first structures that had been built outside of the fort and it was on a small hill quite near the water and the large wharf there. Pulling into the wharf was a very large old ship named the *Commodore*. Bedard knew this ship and its skipper Jeremiah Nagle from other adventures on this coast.

As he watched the huge ship tie up to the wharf, what struck Bedard as unusual was that the two decks were crowded with men. He was stunned. He turned around to see James and Amelia Douglas emerge from the church and stop in amazement with their mouths open. James brushed past the pastor and ran towards the front gate of Fort Victoria, abandoning Amelia who was still standing on the church's porch with her hand to her mouth.

Bedard's mind went into high gear, recognizing that this was the first boatload of miners to arrive, which was a major problem for him. He immediately moved over to a small tree and sat down in a sailor's squat on his heels with his feet flat on the ground. From this position he could get up rapidly if necessary. He was planning to leave that morning to return to the mainland, so he was wearing his casual clothes and only a forearm knife and a small sock revolver. Squatting near the tree, he looked like a native relaxing and watching the activity along with many other natives and men and women from the fort and the small community that now surrounded Fort Victoria.

One gangplank was lowered to the dock and the men slowly descended, carrying their packs and parcels. Bedard noted that almost all of them also carried one or two rifles.

Bedard scanned their faces thinking that there was bound to be someone on this boat who was on his list. He was thinking furiously and decided that if there was one, there would be more of them in a group, and that the group would have split up so as to try to remain part of the crowd.

Albert Tenner came down the ramp with a large floppy hat covering up most of his red hair. He had a medium-sized backpack and a front pack with one rifle and a bullet belt over his shoulder. This left one hand free to grab the rope railing of the gangplank. Few of the others had bullet belts, and it was this that initially brought Bedard's attention to him. Albert's shirt hung down over his pants to cover what Bedard remembered were his two favourite belt pistols.

Albert and his three brothers posed a serious problem.

Bedard unfolded himself and looked around for Roger. He would certainly need backup very soon.

Bedard followed Albert, who was moving as if he knew where he was going. Most of the miners just milled around the wharf area. Bedard assumed that most of them had more baggage that would be unloaded after all the passengers had disembarked.

Albert went to Second Street and turned north up past some cottages and their white picket fences and past small businesses set well back from the street. Wooden sidewalks had not been built here, and Albert kept close to the side of the road. Suddenly, he turned around and looked back in a very challenging manner.

Bedard had not followed him but had made his way up First Street, which was a little wider and had some wagons travelling on it and pedestrian traffic on one sidewalk. Bedard could monitor Albert's travel up the next street and saw him stop. Bedard continued to walk, and then he turned into a walkway around a big bush. Behind him on First Street, he saw two men wearing identical red shirts, large floppy hats and front and backpacks with bullet belts and carrying rifles.

Not good.

Bedard knew that Albert was ahead of him, so he followed the walkway over to the next street and peered around the corner of a building. He could see Albert walking some distance in front of him.

All of a sudden Bedard sensed a presence behind him, and an arm started to snake around his neck from the left. He immediately dropped his chin to his chest and drove his right arm up vertically. This managed to get his right arm between the attacking arm and his head. With his left arm, he reached over the arm and grabbed a handful of hair. Using the leverage of his left handful of hair, Bedard started a front roll that caught his attacker completely by surprise. As a result, Bedard ended up standing up over the prone attacker.

"Wonderful to see you again, William," he said, and drove a knife into William Tenner's chest.

Bedard then dropped to the ground behind William's body, having seen Albert with a rifle to his shoulder. A bullet slammed into William's body. Bedard heard another gunshot and looked up to see Albert fall to the ground.

Roger's voice in the distance: "Stay down till I find the other two assholes."

"No," called Bedard, "they're long gone. We need to strip these two. That is Albert. He has a waist belt with two pistols and a small sock revolver."

Bedard removed William's utility waist belt and his small sock revolver and found his rifle, bullet belt and two packs in a pile about thirty feet away.

Bedard and Roger slipped on the waist belts, then the two packs and the bullet belts. Roger ended up with three rifles so Bedard took one, and the two went back down the walkway towards the busy First Street, now starting to be crowded with men from the ship. They crossed over the street behind a loaded wagon and cut across to the next street via another board walkway. They started a slow jog across a field toward the fort.

"We'll head for the rear door," Bedard said. "Sergeant Bill will let us in."

Sergeant Bill was surprised to see the two men in full war travel gear but said nothing.

Bedard and Roger went up to their room on the second floor of the staff residence building. They met no one else on the way there. In the room, they started to unpack the packs. All the clothing was too big for them, but they really liked the utility belts and the two wallets full of U.S. and British currency and a bag of gold pieces.

Looking at the utility belts with two guns in fine leather holsters, knives, ropes and other gadgets, Roger said, "I like the look of these. Do you think that we could make use of this type of gear?"

"Try it on," Bedard said, "and see if you like it."

So, Roger punched another hole in the belt so that it fit him better, buckled up the belt and strode around the room swinging this way and that. After a bit, he took it off.

"I'm disappointed. This is too heavy, but I'm going to show it to Aurora and see if she can create something similar. She's very clever with leather."

"I've seen many belts like that," Bedard said. "The one I used for a while had the gun holsters lower down with two ties around my upper leg. I also like knife holsters on my forearm, and on the back of my shoulders. The knife holders on the belt don't work for me. I've several utility belts in storage that I'll show you. I use most of them for travelling in wilderness forests."

Roger had all the gadgets out on the bed and was inspecting them, shaking his head. "Look, a fork and a spoon for god's sake!"

Bedard laughed. "Yes, the Tanner bothers tended to travel first class, as I recall."

"So, these men are on your list?"

Bedard nodded. "It's probable that they were headed somewhere in the village. There's no serious camping gear in their packs. The others will have money packs like this. They're too savvy not to split this up."

"What are we going to do about the other two brothers?" Roger said.

"I don't think that we should look for them," Bedard said. "It might be very dangerous. They're probably not very happy now. I may report this to James Douglas, but I may not. I don't want to make our lives more complicated than they already are. I suggest that we continue on with our plan to leave here today, now. We've very little gear, and we'll take only one rifle each so we'll be able to travel rapidly southeast, avoiding the town before we head northeast towards the coast where the boat is hidden."

"Right," said Roger, "we can take the money and tie up the extra guns and have them shipped to us at Fort Langley or wherever. We'll just leave the clothing in a pile and they can do whatever they wish with it. I'm going to take a set of packs. I like them."

Bedard smiled, thinking that Roger just took charge whenever he saw the opportunity, and that worked well for Bedard. He was very lucky to have met him in China and then again in Tsusnahm. Their friendship had been a very good fit of both their personalities and skills.

The two men left the room soon after and went in search of James Douglas.

James was in the main hall, talking to ten men about how to handle the onslaught of miners.

As soon as he caught sight of Bedard, James said, "We have already found two of the miners dead in the village! This is going to be a disaster!" He turned to the group of men. "You all have your instructions; find your teams and get this show going!"

And with that, all the men trooped out of the room.

"We have left our room in a bit of a mess," Bedard said. "And we wish to apologize for that. There's a pile of old clothes that we do not need and two packages of guns that

I'd like you to send to me somehow, perhaps to Fort Langley for them to hold until I send someone to pick them up. We're leaving now as planned and will see you in the near future." He smiled.

James Douglas squinted his eyes as he looked at Bedard. "You didn't have anything to do with those two men who died, did you?"

Bedard shook his head. "I watched the big show for a while but decided that we needed to be back on the mainland before these men come. Don't forget our discussions about these large groups of people. Not all of them are miners."

"Yes," said James. "We have already confiscated several tons of merchandise that some men brought with them to sell here."

Bedard shook his head. "You'll have your work cut out for you, so we'll say goodbye."

The three men shook hands. Just then Amelia came running in one of the doors and gave both of them a big hug.

"I was pleased to hear that Dorthea was doing so well," she said, "and that she had an English woman friend. Give her our love."

Bedard and Roger made their way through the yard of the fort to the back door where Sergeant Bill let them out.

This time they went towards the water and south behind the church and other buildings near the wharf. The *Commodore* was still unloading and many people were milling about, but the two men melded into the thin edge of the crowd and passed by unnoticed.

They quickly entered light brushland and pastures and proceeded in a medium jog down a series of trails. Soon they came to a small hill that looked out over the fort and its encircling village. Bedard stopped, drew out his small spyglass and swept the area that they had passed through looking for anyone who might be following them.

He passed the spyglass to Roger, who did the same thing and inspected the direct route out of town for some time. Roger returned the spyglass to Bedard without comment, and the two of them turned and continued their way to the northeast and their boat.

Arriving at the waterside just after noon, Bedard called in the two dogs for scratches. Both Liz and Hi were very pleased to see them. Roger had shot a small deer, so Bedard dressed it and built a small fire to cook up a bit of lunch for the four of them. Roger uncovered the boat and the two men dragged it down to the water and set the main mast. Roger prepared it for departure. They did not sweep the area as it was a well-known boat launching spot.

The trip home was fast and uneventful. They had a following wind and managed to hoist both the mainsail and a small but effective spinnaker. Roger, who was skilled at many activities, maneuvered the small boat up the river and into its mooring on the north bank.

The owner of the boat, Tomara, met them there with his son. This really pleased Bedard. It was always great to get unexpected support. The short trip into Tsusnahm with all the gear was easy. The two dogs were sent out to their normal security areas.

Bedard smiled; it was just before dinner. "By God, Roger, we really know how to do this, don't we?"

Roger laughed as he went on toward his room with his gear.

Adrona met Bedard near the fireplace in their building and they had a big hug. Bedard liked big hugs. Adrona smiled and kissed him.

"Good to have you back," she said.

Bedard looked down at her beautiful breasts and hugged her again. "Good to be back. How is Noua?"

She laughed and gave her body a wiggle. "He is fine and is crawling now."

"I will have to see that later," he said. "But right now I must find Chief Roanyon. The first large group of miners are about to descend upon us."

Adrona said, "Large?"

"Yes, about three hundred of them."

Bedard left Adrona standing in the big room looking at him with her hand over her mouth.

He found Mother in her home, and she directed Bedard to the west landing where the fishermen of the village were landing today's catch. Bedard trotted off to the west to find him.

The work was almost done, and the fish were now stored temporarily in one of the fish sheds at the landing in preparation for the gutting and filleting work after dinner.

Chief Roanyon had removed his gloves and cape and was washing up in the river when Bedard arrived.

Bedard shook his hand and started walking back towards Tsusnahm with him.

"The *Commodore* arrived at Fort Victoria today with a load of more than four hundred people. I would guess that three hundred of them are miners."

Chief Roanyon stopped short. "Three hundred miners?"

"Yes, we need to warn Mahli and Stsulawh."

Chief Roanyon started forward in a medium jog. "I will activate a Morse-code signal, but also Young Joey came down from Mahli in mid-afternoon and may still be in town."

Bedard nodded. "That would be useful."

They found Young Joey sitting down to dinner in Mother's home. He was a little embarrassed to have them find that he was still in Tsusnahm, but everyone knew that he liked one of the young girls who worked in Mother's kitchen, actually one of Mother's grandchildren.

Chief Roanyon said, "We will have a letter for you to take to Chief Tamburo after you have finished dinner, so don't eat too much!"

Mother smirked.

Bedard took Mother aside. "Three hundred miners arrived at Victoria today."

She was stunned. She had, of course, been listening to the discussions about the miners and the preparation that had been made to protect the villages, the land and the families from these people, but she had only partially believed that this would happen. It was so much beyond her personal experience.

Bedard and Chief Roanyon went to Bedard's home and retrieved some paper from Bedard's big box kit. They sat down and deliberated on what they should say.

Chief Roanyon said, "We have almost one hundred small boats, and thirty new-design large war canoes in our cove near Fort Victoria, and at least the same in the shipyard." He laughed.

"Chief Cobalt and Cowen have just completed the agreement to provide rowers from Victoria and to return the boats, if so required, pulling other empty boats as before. This is a good deal for them and for us. The three villages here are set to establish security of the shoreline. The other villages on the Lower Fraser have said that they are also ready, but I doubt that. We have not visited Fort Langley in over a month, so we do not know what the current situation is like there. I suspect that it continues to be a disaster. As you know, one month ago there were many white men camped along the river near the fort, and it was pretty ugly."

Bedard drew his hand back over his scalp. "I suggest that we report the simple facts to Chief Tamburo and let him and Chief Wanso get on with their implementation program. I think that the first of the miners will arrive later tonight or tomorrow morning. Hopefully, none on these shores. There may be other big ships docking in Victoria soon."

Chief Roanyon nodded. "I think that you should create the message, and I will see to it that our plans are set in motion."

"Perfect," said Bedard. "Do not forget to eat something!"

Bedard saw with pleasure that Dorthea was at dinner that night. She now spent most of her time at the large schools in either Mahli or Stsulawh. Elizabeth and David were also there, and the three of them were in heated conversation. When Dorthea saw Bedard, she jumped up and gave him a hug, all smiles.

"Oh good," said Elizabeth. "Just in time to help resolve a minor disagreement that we have. Dorthea has, apparently, instructed your man in San Francisco, Mr. Goren, to charge the cost of the medical and school supplies to her account. Did you know that? I think that may cause some concern to the three-village council. They may want to pay their own way, and they may be insulted by this gesture."

Bedard sat down at their table and Roger joined them. Bedard looked around and saw that they were alone, more or less.

"I agree in principle, but in practice our family and associates"—he smiled at Roger—"have received a great deal of direct support and help from this community, and we also wish to pay our own way.

"The two shipments of guns that we have received to date were transported on one of my small ships from New York to San Francisco and then on to Fort Victoria on one of the Hudson's Bay Company ships. This transport cost has not been passed on to the villages, nor has the administration costs of processing all the orders. All of these costs are a small part of the costs of all the other activities that our various regional offices carry out on an ongoing basis. We are pleased to do this. I propose that my daughter negotiate her decision with the three-village council."

Dorthea, Elizabeth and David nodded. "Yes, I will do that," Dorthea said. "Thank you, father."

Bedard and Roger recounted their Fort Victoria adventures, and the others were amazed.

"When will the first miners arrive?" Elizabeth asked.

"Well," Roger said, "a few of them will doubtless leave Fort Victoria tonight, thinking that they can cross the straits at night. Some will succeed, but most of them will turn back and camp overnight on one of the coastal islands. Almost all of them will go to the south arm where some will continue to paddle their canoes and boats up the Fraser

River, past Fort Langley to Fort Hope. Some will decide to walk along the South Trail. A few of them will end up on the North Arm of the Fraser River, and it is these people that the Musqueam will have to deal with. We do not think that that this will be a problem. The communities have discussed this at great length and the plans that they have made are reasonable."

After the late meal, both Roger and Bedard sat in on Chief Roanyon's meeting of the village warriors to plan the disbursement over the waterside area and the positioning of various senior-staff groups. Komchowa was very pleased he was chosen to lead one of these groups, and he stood up and pounded his chest in his signature fashion to everyone's amusement.

Bedard had a chance to join Adrona as she was finishing the late meal clean-up and to play with Noua. Noua was crawling everywhere, and everyone, including Noua, enjoyed this fun.

Shortly after this Bedard and Roger were called out to attend a village meeting. They followed Towaba down to the big tree where Chief Roanyon and his key staff were talking with two warriors from the twin villages and one warrior from the Squamish Nation.

Bedard and Roger again just shook their heads in disbelief at the rapidity that information travelled back and forth between the Musqueam and Squamish villages. It was quite remarkable.

Chief Roanyon turned to Bedard. "We have our first six small boats arriving soon to the South Shore Landing, and one of the larger new war canoes paddled by six natives with a large load and two white men coming up the north arm because the river current is not as strong here, but they are still having difficulty. Our runner from our lookout tree arrived a few moments ago to tell us about this. The Morse code was not set up for some reason. We have decided to encourage the canoe to dock here for a rest, and we will replace the paddlers with six of our own people. I assume that the paddlers are Chief Cobalt's people, and they can quite easily paddle an empty boat or two back to the island for us tomorrow.

"We may send a boat over to the south shore landing if this boat needs packers to Fort Langley. I assume yes. The war canoe can land with some difficulty about three miles north of the South Shore Landing. I want to start our association with Chief Cowpar of Massuxkumiy appropriately. He should provide the packers for this shipment. We will help him if we have to."

Bedard let out a long breath. "And so it starts."

"Do you see any problems?" Chief Roanyon said.

"The south shore landing is still better; the three-mile advantage is not worth the effort."

"I agree," said Chief Roanyon. "We will get a message to that effect to Chief Cobalt."

Much later in the evening, Bedard tumbled into bed with Adrona and Noua. It had been a long day, and it was good to cuddle again.

Forty-Two
May, June 1858

Two weeks after he returned from Fort Victoria, Bedard received a letter from James Douglas saying that he was travelling to Fort Hope next week to see the goldfields first-hand, and wanted Bedard to come with him so that they could talk more about the coming gold rush. So Bedard was dutifully waiting with Roger and three other paddlers at the mouth of the south arm for the *Satellite* to arrive. This was a small steam-powered gunboat that travelled very fast and was perfect for travelling up the Fraser River. It was soon seen slicing through the waves at the river estuary.

"This trip will probably take about five to six days," Bedard said. "So if you come over and camp in about five days I will try to be here."

Roger frowned. "I still do not like the idea of you not having me and the dogs along to protect your back."

"Yes," said Bedard, "I understand. Douglas will have protection, and that might work for me also. I may not go with him to visit the river bars or the forts."

On the appointed day, the ship slowed down and Bedard was able to swing aboard with the assistance of several sailors, and the canoe moved off to the north and home.

Douglas greeted Bedard warmly and introduced him to Captain Provost. They retired to the main wardroom of the small boat, and Bedard noted that there was a group of armed bluejackets on board as he had predicted.

As they discussed various consequences associated with the anticipated hordes of miners due to arrive, it was obvious to Bedard that not very many of Douglas's current fur-trading management team believed in the predictions that Bedard had first made in January and again the previous month. Douglas did not have any authority to do anything on the mainland but he was acting as if he did, and he had the force of character to carry it off. Wilber Abercrombie, Douglas's stalwart advisor, had returned to England as Douglas's emissary to try to obtain the means to cope with this problem.

Douglas told Bedard that he now had reports of small groups of miners prospecting in the Couteau area of the Upper Fraser. On the Thompson River, some miners had been attacked by the natives in December, with some of them killed and the rest driven off. He said that at about the same time there was a similar confrontation farther east where miners travelling north were stopped by the natives. He was obviously very concerned that the natives, having profited from selling furs for many years, would believe that the gold belonged to them and would try to stop all of the miners. He went on to say that the men coming from California had a clear idea of what to do with the natives—just kill them all.

Bedard shook his head.

"There will be a lot of natives and miners killed early in this gold rush, and you will not know much about it because your forces of law and order, officials and the entire apparatus of government have not been assembled yet."

Douglas said that the natives living near Fort Victoria had a large group of canoes of various sizes for sale or rent and were willing to provide paddlers for the miners. He said that some of the miners got lost amongst the islands off the shore and others did not survive the crossing. This was due in part to a lack of knowledge of small canoes, but also as a result of the ferocious storms that lashed the area with little or no notice. He shook his head. There had even been reports that some miners had cobbled together rafts, none of which had survived the passage.

Bedard liked to plan, so he tried to get Douglas, who was very intelligent and astute, to understand the future as he saw it. Douglas had participated with Bedard in these mental games over the years that they had been friends, so he had a small smile on his face when Bedard started prognosticating.

"On the maps that I have there is a long stretch of the Fraser Canyon where foaming rapids will stop everyone but the foolhardy and perhaps even the highly skilled from going farther north. The natives have a walkway along the cliff walls, but this is really treacherous, so the miners, if they wish to go farther north, must use the new brigade trail or other routes over the mountains, and even this will be difficult. The snow blocks these trails for eight months of the year and parts of the trails are reported to be very steep. The natives will use this natural barrier on the Fraser River as a place where they believe that they can successfully stop the miners. Although the natives have guns and know how to use them, they will not be able to stop all of the miners."

They had stopped briefly at Fort Langley to take on more fuel and two native translators. Bedard knew one of them and the three spoke briefly about what was currently happening in and around Fort Langley.

When they were back underway, Bedard continued his analysis.

"The group of fifteen or so men who passed through Fort Langley in March have found gold just south of old Fort Yale at a place they are now calling Hill's Bar. Two of this group recently visited Fort Langley looking for provisions and were forced to travel farther south because there was nothing here. Subsequently, there has been a steady northern flow of men travelling overland from the Washington Territory. It is only fifteen miles to a small village there. Some small boats and canoes have also passed through, going east on the Fraser River. These men will soon swarm all over your forts looking for food and supplies, and the world here will change drastically much sooner than I had previously anticipated."

Douglas nodded. "Yes, we have sent both the *Otter* and the *Beaver* south for a stock of food and supplies. They will arrive back this week. We have already found some American ships carrying supplies into the Fraser River, and last week I announced that American ships are prohibited from carrying weapons, ammunition or alcohol on the Fraser. The miners are required to buy their food and supplies from the Hudson's Bay Company. I don't know how this will be received in London, and I may have to change this later to, say, a ten percent tariff on U.S. goods. It is going to be a difficult period for us from many standpoints. I know that I may need to send officers to Fort Langley to enforce these new regulations."

"Why was Fort Yale abandoned?" asked Bedard.

"Fort Yale was built in 1848 as a stopover point along the new fur-brigade route that goes off to the northeast into the mountains from there. It was abandoned in favour of Fort Hope, fifteen miles farther south. We soon plan to put Fort Yale into use as a third supply centre for the Lower Fraser."

Quite remarkably, the *Satellite* was now approaching Fort Hope, and the boat anchored just as a welcoming committee arrived onto the long finger dock. Douglas and his large group had anticipated staying overnight. The bluejackets marched off down the boarding ramp and turned north to a small meadow where they would put up their tents.

The next morning, a group of six canoes from a local native village arrived to take the group up the river. The currents were strong, but the natives avoided the worst of them, and by the end of the day Douglas had visited seven bars and talked with about two hundred miners who were working hard. He was impressed with the reported gold findings.

After camping overnight, the group pressed onward and arrived at Hill's Bar where Bedard had reported that the first miners had found gold. Thirty white miners were hard at work beside about eighty natives, including some women.

There were a few rockers, but most miners were using pans or wooden bowls. This was very hard work. The rocker box was a very efficient simple wooden device used to process sand and gravel from the benches to extract the very fine gold. The boxes were big and difficult to move, but they were about twice as effective as using the pan.

Two of the white miners who met with Douglas said that the biggest problem they had was the lack of food and supplies. Douglas said that he had taken action on this matter and that food and supplies would soon be plentiful.

Bedard and the translators talked with the natives, who complained that the white miners disrespected them. Bedard said that they just had to protect themselves and that it was going to become worse before it became better.

After talking to Bedard, Douglas went back to the white miners and warned them that British Law would protect both the white miners and the natives equally.

The group returned to Fort Hope, and Bedard and Douglas had dinner with the chief trader William Yates and his family. The next day they all boarded the *Satellite* and returned to Fort Langley. Douglas met with James Murray Yale, who had been the chief factor there for some time. The group toured the area including the farm located on a flat meadow, called Langley Prairie, six miles south of the fort.

Bedard did not participate in this. He decided to meet the chief of the small Kwantlen village to the west of the fort and then to visit the large Kwantlen village across from the fort on the north side of the Fraser River. One of the translators agreed to accompany him. Both chiefs were very pleased to meet him. They had heard of Bedard from their Musqueam friends. The Kwantlen dialect was similar to Musqueam, so Bedard did not have much of a problem communicating with them.

The next day they all boarded the *Satellite* again, and Bedard was met by Roger and the canoe near the south trail landing and travelled back to Tsusnahm.

The months of May and June were hectic for everyone. The new Three Villages Committee had been meeting weekly in Tsusnahm because Tsusnahm had a manpower shortage, and the two large villages decided that they could easily afford the manpower to travel the short distance up the river. The other plus was that Bedard, Roger, and other powerful minds like Chief Enthica, Fenciao, Chief Big Bon, and the highly respected shamans, Inchesca and Bella, were located there and tried to make themselves available for these important meetings. Aunt Betty also tried to attend, and when she did she always had something profound to say.

Squamish representatives always attended these meetings, which were often led by one or two of the senior elders or members of their chiefs' families.

It was difficult for anyone to attend these meetings from the several small south-shore villages, but the Three Villages Committee tried to facilitate this by sending one of the fast twenty-man war canoes over to pick up any one who wanted to attend.

The Morse code communication system had been extended to cover all of these villages, and everyone was not only pleased with the results but were also amazed at the rapidity with which the young children learned the system. Dorthea thought that this had happened because the children enjoyed making an important contribution to their village communities and to their families. The Morse code stations were often high in the trees but links across the water were on the beaches.

Dorthea, Elizabeth and David had expanded their area of influence and tried to make the rounds of all the river delta villages and the many Squamish villages once a month. More school and medical supplies had been ordered and received, and the community transformation was quite remarkable. Almost all of the area's children attended school at least three times a week, and fewer people were home sick than before.

Elizabeth had been forewarned that a few cases of the dreaded smallpox, carried by some of the newcomers, had shown up in Victoria, and she and David had started to vaccinate everyone. This was very new to some of the younger leaders of these communities, but by this time Elizabeth and David had developed a huge positive reputation and not many refused to be protected. The previous smallpox epidemic had occurred about twenty years ago and had decimated the local population.

Dorthea was working very hard to attract and train teaching assistants. There were now several teachers and parents who assisted the teachers in every village, and she also had groups of potential new teachers with whom she was working.

Elizabeth and David had successfully convinced most of the shamans and their assistants to try some of the new approaches to helping the ill, especially some of the treatments that helped reduce serious pain. They were successful at this because they both had attitudes about the world that were similar to those of the shamans. David's remarkable work with the dogs was particularly influential. His ideas regarding aggressive wild forest-animal management and his work on several badly injured deer were greatly enhancing his reputation.

At the same time, the use of dogs for village security had expanded to almost all of these villages, and this helped considerably to contain some of the more adventuresome white visitors.

The ordered rifles had been distributed, and Art Rossland remained in the forefront training warriors how to maintain and repair these modern devices themselves. All of the hunters agreed that rifles were much better than bows and arrows and, after hearing what they initially believed to be farfetched stories about Bedard's dogs herding deer, they were nonetheless all focusing on training their own hunting dogs to do this.

After the first two weeks of May, the number of canoes travelling the north arm of the Fraser River became fewer than one per week, and the lookout trees and the Morse code communication system allowed the villages to minimize their groups of warriors guarding the shoreline.

All of the villages had reviewed their forecasted manpower demands for the coming months based mostly on Bedard's belief that the river mining would seriously interfere with the fishing season north of Hope. In early June, the Musqueam Nation had two four-man fishermen/warrior teams positioned at locations on the Fraser River north of Fort Hope trying to preserve their historic fishing spots. The white miners typically tore down fish-drying racks that had been there for many years to use as dry firewood.

When the first sockeye salmon runs arrived in late June, fishing camps were created with warrior protection for the fishermen. They now had modern rifles and pistols and the skills to use them. One of the strategies that Roger had suggested was to have rifle competitions on the river almost every day. The miners did not bother them.

Although the salmon run was very low that year, the Musqueam fishermen worked very hard and managed to reach quotas that the Three Villages Committee had set for the summer sockeye salmon run. Other native fishermen groups were not as fortunate.

Other major issues that the miners brought with them had minimal impact on the Musqueam Nation. The Musqueam were very fortunate to have few villagers succumb to the impact of alcohol. Those that did were extracted from the influence of the white men as soon as they were identified and sent home to sober up. The problem of women being molested by the miners was not evident because they had already been challenged by some of the white men at the corral, and the villagers had solved this issue with education and better general protection of their women at their summer camps in the mining areas. Visitors to the Musqueam Nation fishing camps were welcomed. These men were surprised to find that several of the fishermen and warriors spoke English and a smattering of other languages.

The other problem for the Musqueam Nation was the incredible attraction of gold wealth. Bedard and Roger had suggested that it would be very profitable for the Musqueam Nation to learn how to mine gold and to establish themselves as miners. Bedard had predicted that all the other local villages, bands and small nations located on the river north of Fort Hope would be doing this but with limited success because of a shortage of skills. The Three Villages Committee ordered gold pans, shovels, quicksilver and one commercial rocker, which they immediately had their boat shop duplicate.

In early June, Bedard and Roger took a small team up the Fraser near where they planned to set up fishing camps and chose a nearby bar to test for gold. The bar tested well and had already attracted about twenty of the early miners who had named it Posey Bar. Bedard's group marked out about forty claims, set up four of their eight rockers and began learning how to become rich. There were a lot of smiles as their gold pouch started to fill, but it was hard work. They started to build a sluice using a small creek that was favourably located. The group soon increased to about fifty miners who were all officially registered with paid-up claim certificates and who worked hard learning the trade. Soon almost all were focusing on working the sluice and were ecstatic with the results that Bedard and Roger reported to them. They started mining another small bar across the river that seemed promising and were soon building another sluice there. They named it Eagle Bar.

Forty-Three
July to September 1858

When the river started to rise in July, both bars were left in the hands of a small team of warriors to protect their equipment and the remaining fishermen. A Morse code link was established between the main camp there and the various fishermen groups. Everything seemed under control.

Bedard visited Hill's Bar and Fort Yale in early July with Roger, Chief Enthica and Fenciao, but they retreated in haste. Both areas were significantly out of control with serious battles with native villages north of Fort Yale reported. Although Bedard's small group was heavily armed and had adopted an aggressive attitude, they all looked like natives and were therefore viewed with contempt by almost all of the miners that they met on the trails.

Bedard was upset because he had not identified many of the men and women on his list. He judged that there were at least ten thousand miners on the river bars from Fort Hope to Fort Yale, and despite the general knowledge that the river would be too high for mining the bars in July and August, more miners were arriving every day.

Back at their base camp near Posey Bar, Bedard expressed his impatience with his lack of progress in identifying these evil men. His powerful team had noticed the change in Bedard's demeanour since they had left Hill's Bar, and they were concerned. This was a very different Bedard than they had ever seen.

"Copco," said Chief Enthica, "we know that the river will fall again in August. At that time all of the miners, including all of the newcomers, will again descend on the river bars or try to travel farther northward. The large town at Fort Yale and the smaller camp at Hill's Bar will continue to be active and unpleasant, but almost all of the miners will be focused on making money mining gold. All of these areas on the river will again become more predictable, and we will be able to focus on your assignment."

Bedard thought about this for a moment and smiled. "Thank you, Chief Little Bon, for your wise advice."

The group was quite relieved to see him smile again.

"Roger," said Bedard, "there is another group of our miners and warriors going home from here today, so we should join them as far as Fort Hope where our canoes are hidden. You and I have been invited north to visit the Squamish Nation, and we should go there now we have the time."

They picked up their packs and gear from the camp and travelled with the larger group in their canoes south to Fort Hope. The traffic on the river and on the main trail was still heavy in both directions.

The group of four camped overnight at a campsite they often used to the east of Fort Hope where Liz and Hi were waiting for them. It was another joyous reunion that both the dogs and the four men enjoyed very much. The next morning, they sorted their packs and left two large packs hidden about a mile south of the camp. After deeming it almost impossible to find the packs again, the four men started out in good spirits to find their canoes and travel home.

"I hope that we can find the canoes," said Fenciao, and everyone laughed.

The hiding place was indeed difficult to find. All of the small creeks looked the same, and they had used this area several times in the past to stash gear and canoes. Bedard finally sat down on the edge of the south shore trail and told the others to leave their packs and gear with him and separate in order to find the canoes.

They were found by Chief Enthica, who decided to do a detailed search at the first place that Bedard had chosen to search. Lo and behold, the canoes were very close to the spot where they had stopped looking. The group laughed and shook their heads, trying to determine who had actually hidden the canoes six weeks ago. Bedard was back in good spirits because he knew that it was not him.

I'm lucky to be supported by such a professional group, he thought.

The trip home was uneventful. They had decided not to stop at Fort Langley because they could see from the river as they passed by that it was a mob scene, with more men going south to the United States than newcomers going east towards Fort Hope.

Arriving at the beach by the big tree in the mid-afternoon, they were met by Chief Roanyon, Chief Big Bon and Old Chief Sparrow in full robes and hats accompanied by a small group of villagers who were not still out fishing, hunting or gathering berries and roots. Adrona gave Bedard a big hug and rushed off, saying that she had work to do. The village had been warned of their arrival by the lookout tree Morse code link, and everyone was beaming. The third shipment of gold pouches had arrived the previous day with a group of the returning village miners, and the current total of all the gold mined was quite incredible.

A reception meal had been cobbled together. The lookout tree staff reported that a large group was anticipated momentarily from Mahli and Stsulawh. Sure enough, Mot announced that the two racing canoes were not far away, and everyone moved over to watch Old Chief Sparrow judge the arrival. Slam, bang, and onto the beach they came with the two chiefs and their wives hanging on for dear life to the front stanchions.

Old Chief Sparrow again signalled a tie, and Chief Tamburo and his wife Tomala and Chief Wanso and Amoroa tumbled out of their boats laughing and debating the results of the race as usual.

The lookout tree Morse code link was flashing madly, and Roger was reading the message out for the group.

"An armada of over twenty canoes of various sizes is coming from the west, to arrive within the next ten minutes."

Mother, Tomala and Amoroa were talking, and Amoroa said, "We had a bit of food sitting around, so we decided to bring that. Then a whole bunch of your friends decided to come too, and we were a bit stretched, but I think that there will be enough."

Mother was very pleased. She loved a party, especially if she was in the middle of it.

Then, to everyone's surprise, a drum roll was heard on the ridge just above the village where four Squamish chiefs could be seen in their ceremonial robes and headgear followed by a mob of villagers chanting their favourite travel song.

The lookout tree staff were flashing madly again, and Roger said that there was another armada of huge Squamish war canoes in the far distance advancing at great speed up the north arm of the river.

Chief Roanyon was laughing so hard he was leaning over, holding his knees to stop from falling.

"I wondered if our friends from the north would join us. They have a very good communication system, and they really like to party, too."

Then, to everyone's pleasure, the young Tsusnahm drummers led by Bedard responded to the incoming group, and the Squamish drummers immediately joined in with the same beat. Everyone clapped in rhythm to the drums.

All the canoes arrived at the same time as the lead party from the north. It was bedlam. Bedard and Roger, standing out of the way near the longhouses, were watching and laughing and clapping. The Squamish group had brought more food in their canoes, and the small reception meal was now a major party!

As evening fell it became very cold, and a light rain turned into an unusual summer snowfall. The children and some of the adults got into a snowball fight, much to everyone's amusement.

Old Chief Sparrow's home was easily the largest longhouse in the village, and this huge mass of people all managed to squeeze in. Many of the people were standing around the edge of the room, and Mother moved some of the curtains back to allow people to sit on the boxes and beds in the small side wall rooms. The noise level was very high as old friends talked.

Mother decided not to have a head table, so Bedard, Roger and all of the chiefs and their wives wandered around the room talking to people. The food was served on six tables that jutted out from the cooking fire, and people helped themselves and sat on the floor in small groups, elbow to elbow.

Chief Big Bon told Bedard and Roger that he had not seen such a big crowd for many years and added that Chief Norman Komchowa liked to bring all of his friends together in the mid-summer high-water period like this.

Chief Roanyon joined the group as he was saying this and nodded.

"My father liked to balance any wealth accumulation by hosting huge parties like this one, that sometimes went on for several days. These parties often included traditional gifts of specific goods to certain families that needed them. He especially liked giving gifts to families that had lost a parent and were having difficulty recovering."

Just as the meal was about to start, Chief Roanyon borrowed a drum and thumped out a rhythm to get everyone's attention.

"This is a wonderful surprise that you all were able to come to visit in the middle of a very difficult year on this very important day. Chief Big Bon has just reminded me of the parties that my father had at this time of the year for the purpose of spreading some of our village's wealth to families in need. The Musqueam Three Villages Committee has just decided that the wealth that we have received from the gold-mining adventure will be shared by the three villages. First a share will be given to Copco and Roger for their leadership. The Tsusnahm, Mahli and Stsulawh shares will be used to support some of our village families, and the balance will go into what Copco calls a reserve fund and what we call a *winter wind*. The gold-mining adventure was very successful. The initial winter-wind amount is now more than the amount we used to purchase all of our rifles this year."

The group was stunned and began clapping and chanting their favourite song.

Bedard and Roger went over to stand beside Chief Roanyon and held up their hands to get everyone's attention.

"We are very pleased with the result of the gold-mining adventure," said Bedard, "and we hope that it will continue to be profitable. We thank you for sharing this wealth with us. We have decided to also place our share in the winter wind to be used to support the medical and school adventures."

The group was very pleased with this and began clapping and chanting again. Everyone was smiling.

How the meal got cooked was a mystery to Bedard, but he managed to eat some delicious clams and some small lake fish that he really liked.

During the course of the evening, the two Squamish chiefs' wives, Joan and Orelotta, cornered Bedard and Roger and insisted that they visit their villages within the next few days. They also introduced Bedard to the two other chiefs and their wives who had accompanied them this time. These people represented two smaller villages, Sun'ahk and Ee'yullmough, to the south and west of Khwaykhway on the south coast of their arm of the ocean. Bedard was of course speaking reasonable Squamish by this time, and the group was very pleased and impressed with his skills.

"I also want to go to your Khwaykhway village this time and visit with the Tsleil'waututh people there," said Bedard.

The next week Bedard and Roger went north with Liz and Hi. Roger was whisked off to visit two of the small northern Squamish villages to help the Squamish Nation implement the new support program that Roger had suggested.

Bedard and the two dogs went east on the ocean arm with two linguist villagers to visit Khwaykhway. It was a beautiful short trip for Bedard amongst the picturesque mountains, many birds and other wildlife. The two villagers made it more interesting for Bedard by coaching him in the Tsleil'waututh language as they were travelling. By the time they arrived at the village beach area, which was some distance from the village itself, Bedard had absorbed a large vocabulary and the two linguists were astonished.

They walked north from the beach to the village where the chief welcomed Bedard and introduced him to four older villagers who spoke this ancient language. It was a very interesting day, which included a midday meal attended by all twelve Tsleil'waututh speakers in the village. Bedard found that the history of this area as shared with him by these very pleasant people was fascinating.

Later in the afternoon, Bedard and his two Squamish paddlers, accompanied by about fifty villagers in canoes, including most of the chief's family and several of his elders, went farther east and then north up another arm of the ocean surrounded by mountains to a very pleasant bay. There Bedard and his two dogs gave a demonstration of herding deer and elk on the mountainside, much to everyone's amazement and pleasure. In less than an hour, five deer and one elk were taken. The hunters in attendance shook their heads and said that this would take a pair of experienced hunters more than a day. The group talked about dog training, not only for hunting but also for village protection. They talked about the gold rush and the settlers that would surely follow. They then had a short rifle competition, with Bedard and two of the villagers doing very well.

Returning to Wh'mullutsthun and the late meal, Bedard was besieged with questions relating to the future, especially by the women who the chief had said, with a great deal of pleasure, were very strong and influential, not only within the village but also at Squamish Nation gatherings. Bedard was impressed, and his two Squamish translators continued to be amazed at Bedard's language skills.

Then, back at Tsusnahm with Roger at the end of the week, Bedard received a message from James Douglas, pleading for him to meet him the next day on the south arm of the Fraser River. This time Bedard brought his team of Roger, Fenciao, Chief Enthica and the four dogs. The four men boarded the *Satellite* and the dogs were left in the two canoes towed behind the vessel.

At their first onboard meeting, Douglas told them that he had been hearing very disturbing reports about the conflicts between the natives and the miners and had now decided that it was time to see for himself what was really happening. He had brought with him twenty marines and fifteen Royal Engineers. He said that peace had been restored in the area above Fort Yale by five large groups of American militia, and treaties had been negotiated with several nations there without the consent of either the British Government or the Company.

Bedard reported that he and his team had been in both Hill's Bar and Fort Yale in early July just after the Fraser River had started to rise and that the two areas were significantly out of control, with serious battles with native villages north of Fort Yale reported.

"It was too dangerous for us to remain there. We found and killed two men with great difficulty, and I still have seventeen names on my list. So we left. We did not even stop at Fort Langley. It was a mob scene."

They continued to talk about the current situation, and Douglas said that there had been a change in government in England and that the Hudson's Bay Company's licence for exclusive trade in New Caledonia, that was to expire next year in 1859, was about to be revoked.

"Furthermore," said Douglas, "I received a personal letter from the new government's colonial secretary offering me the governorship of the new mainland colony, but I would have to give up my direct association with the Company."

Bedard cocked an eyebrow. "And?"

"I have not made up my mind yet." Douglas smiled ruefully. "But I suppose that I do not have many other choices if I still want to remain involved with this part of the world."

At Fort Langley, the *Satellite* stopped to pick up a few passengers and Douglas met with Yale, who told him that the Americans had been very destructive to the Company's properties and farms and that there were hundreds of men camped near the fort on both sides of the river. Many of these men could either not afford the five-dollar mining fee or refused to pay it.

That night the steamer stopped at the mouth of the Harrison River, and Douglas and his group set up camp on the shore. At that time, Bedard told Douglas that he would not travel with them past Fort Hope. Bedard said that he thought that it was too dangerous for him, and Douglas reluctantly agreed.

"You may see us from time to time," Bedard said. "It would be useful if we do not talk."

Douglas smiled and agreed.

Between August fifth and twelfth, the river fell about five feet but rose again, and by the end of August the real fall began. In a few days, two hundred men were at work at Fort Yale Bar and four hundred on Hill's Bar. By the end of September, ten thousand white miners were at work below Yale. Others had migrated north. About five thousand natives were also at work in the river, including about a thousand Musqueam who were mining and fishing.

There was also a large group of Chinese reworking many of the bars to the north of Fort Hope that had been abandoned by the white miners.

Douglas and his group stopped at all of the bars being worked north of Fort Hope, arriving at Fort Yale on September thirteenth. He then spent a week talking to numerous people, including many native chiefs. It was apparent to Douglas how inefficient his few government officials were. He was also very upset with the behaviour of the miners who were killing natives and destroying their villages and fishing areas and desecrating their burial grounds. He was also alarmed at how easily the largely American miners had assembled an armed, well-organized militia on British soil.

By September twentieth Douglas was ready to go home, but before he did he stood on a stump in front of the Company's store in Fort Yale and addressed the miners.

Bedard and his team were hiding in the brush off the main trail in a good place to search the assembled miners for targets and to hear and see Douglas in action.

Listening to Douglas's speech, it was apparent to Bedard that Douglas had already made up his mind to accept the governorship. Douglas said to the miners that he was commanded by the Queen to welcome Americans and all the other nationalities to the territory. He went on to say that the territory was open to settlement and that town lots and farming lands would be laid out at Fort Yale. He finished his speech by wishing them all well. The miners cheered.

Forty-Four
November 1858

After the morning meal, Bedard sat down at the fire with Roger, Fenciao and Chief Enthica. The four dogs formed their usual tight security net around the camp, which was located about a mile to the east of the Fraser River up on the mountainside near Hill's Bar. The team had been roaming the river bars from Hope to Yale and above since early September. Two full months had passed, and it was now the day that they needed to respond to Bedard's question: "Should we continue or go home?"

In the past two months they had found nine men and the two women on Bedard's list, with only six men on the list plus one other man that Bedard had added to the list left to find. This had been difficult and dangerous work.

Bedard's group easily identified the two women on the list. They were working together in Fort Yale and owned five active houses of prostitution. The women were making significantly more money and gold than any of the miners and had a security group protecting them. They were also involved politically in the village, which was good for business.

Before Bedard could take action, however, they were attacked at their residence by one of the large aggressive village groups. One of the women died as a result of the vicious beating she received from these scoundrels. The women's security forces fought off the attacking group, and the surviving woman, fearing for her life, decided to go south by boat the next day. She had planned to travel directly to Fort Victoria but decided instead to save time by travelling south from Fort Langley. Unfortunately, criminals were waiting there to steal the hard-earned gold from small groups of travelers. She and the four-man protection team travelling with her did not survive the dangerous narrow forest trail. If they had asked for advice, they would have waited for a large group.

When he heard this report, Bedard was relieved, because killing women was difficult for him.

Bedard had never before worked with a more skilled team, and he was very pleased. None of the men were married, but they each had a close association with a woman, and Fenciao and Chief Enthica both had several children by previous marriages. Bedard believed that they should have the option to go home.

"Well," Bedard said, "last month I said that I wanted to stay here at least one more month, and you all voted to stay with me. Thank you for that. We were very successful in October and I'm very pleased. You all know that we work well together as a team. This time I want to stay here for about two weeks more, before the snow comes. Our tactics will have to change. We have not seen or heard of the two other Tanner brothers in spite of the fact that they have noticeable red hair. Don and Wilber Thompson and Tommy Debb have also disappeared again. These five men are very skilled and dangerous, and they know that we're looking for them. As we have discussed, I believe that all five have moved north, and I'm not going to follow them there. They remain a very high risk for us because they could return at any time.

"I don't know the two remaining men. I suspect that they've changed their names and will continue to be difficult to find. I would appreciate your support, but this has been an unusual experience for you, and if you wish to return home now that will be perfectly acceptable to me."

Bedard got up and started to move away from the camp. Roger followed him.

Chief Enthica got up and hit Fenciao on the shoulder. "I am going for a quick walk to think."

Fenciao was expecting this. Fenciao preferred to sit and contemplate, while Chief Enthica found it helpful to move while he was thinking. They both had shamans in their close family and often tried to contact them when these difficult questions arose.

Bedard and Roger stopped some distance from the camp on the animal trail that they were following. It was Liz's area, so Bedard called her in for a scratch. She went to Roger first.

Bedard laughed. "I think that she is thanking you for voting to stay with me."

Roger smiled and did not say anything. Liz was quite pleased with all the attention from the two men and held her tail high when Bedard indicated that she should return to her duties.

Bedard got up and moved back toward the camp with Roger following at a distance. When Bedard reached the camp, Fenciao and Chief Enthica were talking. They both turned, smiled and moved forward to shake Bedard's hand.

"We are both in," said Chief Enthica.

Bedard was extremely pleased, and he gave both of them a big thump on the back. This was an unusual expression of pleasure for Bedard, and the two now realized how concerned Bedard had been. Roger, who had been holding back, now came forward and the group made an eight-hand grip like they did when one of their complex operations was successful.

Roger went to the fire and doused it with part of a bag of water that they had brought up for that purpose. Bedard retrieved the packs and arranged the contents. The ground sheets had been rolled up, and Fenciao and Chief Enthica picked up a pack from Bedard and moved into the bush on the faint animal trail to the west. They were all heavily armed with two pistols strapped to their thighs, a bow and quiver over one shoulder, a bullet belt over the other, a rifle in one hand and a machete in the other. The dogs maintained their security net around the four dangerous-looking travellers.

Bedard had decided to visit their main cache to replenish their packs and to make a detailed plan of action for the next few days.

Their main cache was to the east of Hope near a well-used trail up into the mountains that had already received snow this month. Bedard wanted to move the gear and supplies stored there to a new location to the west of Hope near the river. This location would be riskier, but the move was necessary.

Chief Enthica was a friend of Chief Tanu at the Staulo village just to the north of Hope because his small village shared a number of summer fishing stations with them. The warrior training group had visited the village in April. The team planned to hire ten natives from this village to help with the move. They had done this successfully before. Chief Enthica left the group just after noon and would rejoin them early the next morning with the hired hands.

The camp that they used near their cache was just off the main trail. They did not often share it with other groups using the trail because it was too close to Hope. The three men arrived at the camp near the end of the day and it was empty. Fenciao dropped his guns and pack and, taking only his bow and quiver, went at a fast jog farther east up the trail to another campsite to see whether it was also empty, which it was.

Bedard had devised a special security net for the dogs around the camp, which was easy to set up because the dogs had done this many times before.

The sleeping plan would be arranged after the late meal, so the first task was to find a small deer to eat. Fenciao returned and volunteered to do this because he enjoyed working with Liz. Liz was called in and arrived bouncing around like a puppy, wagging her tail enthusiastically because she knew exactly what they were going to do. Fenciao, who was laughing at Liz's antics, moved off into the forest with Liz and soon returned with a deer. Roger cut the deer up and Fenciao started the fire.

Bedard, in the meantime, had visited the cache and found it untouched. He removed some roots, potatoes and dried berries and returned to the campfire.

The four dogs were brought in one at a time for a meal and then the three men had their own.

They were going to move out early the next morning. There was much to be done to prepare the cache for the move, so they planned to go to sleep as soon as it was dark. Sleeping locations were chosen, and the three sat around the fire talking about the work to be done in the following days. No one had passed by on the trail yet that evening, and if the other camp to the east was occupied later in the evening the dogs would inform them of this.

Bedard thought that they could move all the gear and supplies in two trips. Chief Enthica and his team would bring four or five canoes to a loading spot that they had previously chosen.

The most difficult gear to transport were the guns and ammunition that they had confiscated from the men and women that they had disposed of over the past two months. Most of the rifles were new and very valuable. Fenciao wondered if they should try to transport the guns and ammunition that they did not need back to Tsusnahm immediately. They discussed various methods to do this and decided that sending the guns and ammunition back with some of the local natives might be very dangerous. Bedard still thought that was a good idea and wondered if they could get a letter back to Chief Roanyon and have him send several canoes up to meet them near the new cache. They agreed that this was the best idea and that they should include Chief Enthica in this discussion tomorrow and see whether he had any alternative ideas.

Early the next morning, Roger had the fire going and coffee made before the other two straggled out of the forest. Soon after the early meal of gruel and dried berries, Bedard's favourite, they started sorting the cache.

The rifles were bound up in two awkward bundles of fifteen, and the bullets were placed in huge piles of belts and sacks. The large pistols were mostly in holster belts and were also stacked together. The small pistols were collected together and inserted in one pack, leaving a handful that did not fit in. All the bowie knives were tied up and placed in two packs. The remaining supplies were repacked into ten packs, and the remaining empty packs were stuffed in packs. It was quite a pile of gear!

Chief Enthica arrived with a group of twenty natives. The chief was smiling widely and told Bedard that there were many volunteers willing to work for nothing rather than work for the white miners. He felt that this large group might be able to take all the gear and supplies down in one trip.

Bedard, Roger and Fenciao were laughing at Chief Enthica's attempt at explaining the huge crowd of willing workers who were now milling around the obvious loads. All of the loads were claimed, and the large group started down the hill with a massive man nicknamed Bear in the lead. Bear had taken almost all of the bullet belts and the two packs of rifles that weighed about four hundred pounds, and his friends who were following him were razzing him for taking such a small load.

The group now began chanting. Chief Enthica, who was still smiling, told the team that this was an old chant that most of the villages knew in various versions that they used when they were carrying loads on a trail.

Bedard's team cleared the cache area to its natural condition. The four men picked up their personal packs and followed the chanting group down the trail and eventually to the water.

After some discussion, Chief Enthica felt that some of the volunteers would be pleased to take a load down to Tsusnahm. He went on to say that there was a perception amongst many of the younger single men in the village that there were many single women in the three Musqueam villages. They had met some of these women that spring during the early fishing season.

Later in the day when they reached the canoe landing, Chief Enthica addressed the group and immediately got eight volunteers. Bedard spoke to them with Chief Enthica partially translating to ensure that the group of volunteers realized the value of the load and the potential risk of attack. They all scoffed at that, pointed to two of the eight volunteers and said that they were the best riflemen in the village. Someone observed that they were all expert archers and had their bows with them.

Bedard took the two bundles of rifles and undid the ties. He and Fenciao then picked out a number of the best rifles and passed them on to the two rifle experts. They were smiling as they each chose one and loaded it with a measure of familiarity and reported that they did not have such good units but were very pleased to try them out. Roger helped them adjust the sights, after which they amused the rest of the group by shooting at bulrushes in the river.

Bedard looked at Roger, and Roger just shrugged. "No problem."

This was quickly translated, and the whole group clapped while the two rifle experts looked a bit sheepish.

Roger went to the riverbank and sat down so he could rest his arms on his knees as he sighted his rifle across the river. A duck took off from the water, and Roger's shot sent it crashing back lifeless a few yards from the far shore. It was easily one thousand feet away, and the group was stunned.

Chief Enthica clapped his hands. "The show is over. Let's load up so we can finish this adventure today."

The loads were split up appropriately with two of the canoes carrying a load of guns and bullets and the eight volunteers. The remaining six canoes easily carried the remaining gear and the dogs, and they all pushed off into the lazy river current.

Bedard and his team had hidden their two small canoes carefully. Bedard did not want to disturb them, but he wanted the new cache to be close by for convenience when they decided to return south.

It was now well past noon. Bedard decided that the two canoes going farther south would leave early the next morning and might be able to make it to Tsusnahm in one day going with the river current.

The whole group was in good spirits and still talking about Roger's incredible shot. Roger looked at Bedard and smiled, knowing that Bedard had his compound bow with him that had shot well at thirteen hundred feet. Bedard returned the smile.

In due course, Bedard led the group behind a small island on the south shore and into a sliver of water where they pulled onto a pebbly shore. Bedard and his team got out while asking the others to remain in their canoes. The four dogs also jumped out of the boats, and Bedard directed them to form a simple security net around the area. The team passed over the south shore trail and came upon the small stream that Bedard had found on a previous visit. They all walked up the stream about one thousand feet and decided that it was a perfect location for the new cache. Their two canoes were about a mile farther west in a similar cache area off a similar stream.

Roger and Bedard supervised the unloading of the gear and supplies destined for this cache, and Fenciao and Chief Enthica went east and found a campsite that would be perfect for the large group.

All of the canoes went back east on the river and came ashore at the campsite. There was lots to do, including moving the load of guns and ammunition into the camp and hunting for supper. Bedard and Roger soon arrived, and Bedard called in both Hy and Liz who were both bouncing around, much to the amusement of the group. They all shook their heads in disbelief when Fenciao told them that the dogs knew exactly what they were called in to do. Fenciao took three of his friends with him and moved into the forest to the south. In less than an hour, the hunting group returned with three medium-sized deer. The three natives who had accompanied Fenciao told the group how efficient the dogs were in herding the deer past the hunters.

The evening meal for both dogs and men alike went smoothly. Bedard decided that, because they were so close to the main trail and the river, they would post two sentries, working in three-hour shifts through the night. They did not want to lose any of the guns and ammunition.

After preparing a new cache for the remaining goods and equipment, Bedard's team talked into the night about the difficult tasks that they had decided to attempt over the next weeks. Roger felt that the best areas to concentrate on were Hill's Bar and Yale. The numbers of miners located on each of the many other bars on the river was fewer now, but the miners were still well organized and had elected men to help their group keep the mining claims correct and to settle other disputes.

Hill's Bar was also controlled by an elected committee of miners, but it was not very effective. The group of miners was much larger than those working on any of the other bars, still over four hundred but down from a peak of about seven hundred. There was still a very large group of natives mining part of the bar. Several large sluices had been introduced, and there had been several disturbances and claim-jumping incidents recently. Douglas had appointed a magistrate, a constable and a justice of the peace in addition to the gold commissioner there. The camp community on the riverbank some distance away was relatively small with only one saloon. Most of the miners preferred to camp near Hill's Bar.

Yale continued to be a disaster. When Bedard and the team were last there about two weeks ago, it was reported that there were several murders every week. Almost all the miners who were there in July and early August waiting for the river to fall, and those who had been driven from their claims by the aggressive natives, were now back mining the river. The stream of newcomers kept the action in the saloons and gambling halls at a constant level all day and all night.

There was a substantial group who preyed upon the transient population to bully, beat, rob and slay. Bedard had found many of the men that they were looking for in this town. He did not relish going back. It was very dangerous, and although the four-man team was very clever, the dogs were of no use in that kind of environment.

The evening was uneventful, and the two canoes going downstream with the guns and ammunition got off to an early start the next morning after a final serious lecture by Bedard on the risks that they were likely to encounter. They all promised to be cautious and on the lookout for trouble. Bedard and his team went back to the cache and, after again deeming it impossible to find, returned to the canoes. The local natives agreed to paddle Bedard's team farther up the river to a place about ten miles downstream from Hill's Bar where they could access the trail on the east side of the river.

The river bars that they planned to visit were still being worked by small groups of white miners and numerous groups of Chinese miners. A few of the Chinese miners had been on the Lower Fraser for more than six months. Over the past two months, the team had seen more and more of these hard-working people moving up the river to rework the claims on areas of the bars that had been abandoned by the white miners. Almost all the miners on these bars were now using rockers, and many of the experienced Chinese teams had created sluices or had taken over ones that had been abandoned.

Bedard and Roger spoke both Mandarin and Cantonese. Bedard also knew several northern dialects as well as the dialects used in and around Shanghai and Hong Kong. They had previously profited from stopping and speaking to these miners. Some of the Chinese were Americans, of course, but they were all surprised that the two white men spoke their language. After some socializing, the Chinese miners had identified some white miners who had given them a hard time. Some of these racist bullies turned out to be on Bedard's list.

This time the four men, armed to the teeth as usual, stopped at French Bar and planned to go on to the four other bars on the east bank below Hill's Bar. They visited all the Chinese miners, some of whom Bedard and Roger had met before. This show of force initially concerned some of the white miners on the bar until this weird-looking team stopped and started talking in Chinese to a miner. Fenciao and Chief Enthica stopped and talked to the native miners. No serious problems were mentioned, and the team visited all of the white miners.

On Sacramento Bar, they met with a group of ten miners who had constructed a huge sluice that was probably illegal, so they did not want any visitors. Bedard guessed that some of them were Italian and tried to open some sort of communication, which worked well. This group identified another group that was located just downstream across the river at Emory's Bar, one of the earliest bars to be developed. They said that several miners had passed through complaining that a heavily armed group had swept this small bar of all the other miners, including some natives, killing two of the white men in the process. Bedard had planned to visit five of the bars on that side of the river later in the trip and thought that perhaps a slight change in plan might be necessary.

Late in the day, Bedard and his team found the small campsite that they had used several times before. It was well off the main trail, and the four dogs could provide good security throughout the night. It had been a long day and the group decided to review the first day's progress the next morning.

Chief Enthica reminded the group that there was a small native village nearby and that they could probably borrow or rent a canoe to cross the river and go back to inspect Emory's Bar, which was not very far away.

Early the next day, the team was on the west side of the river following game trails south towards Emory's Bar. They had decided that the group controlling the bar would have guards posted north of the bar to protect them from any vengeful miners returning, but that it was unlikely that guards would be posted on the south side. The plan was to find a spot on the mountainside from which to inspect the bar with the two telescopes that they still carried and then, if an attack plan was necessary, the southern approach was favoured unless they also found guards there.

There were indeed two sentries cleverly hidden in the forest some distance to the north of the bar that they easily bypassed, and they found an ideal location to inspect most of the bar. Just as they were setting up to do that, Hy, who was covering their rear, arrived and indicated a major emergency. The team scattered up the forest animal trails to hide, expecting the worst.

In due course, four heavily armed miners came through the forest from the north, also following an animal trail. Bedard decided that these men were not associated with the Emory's Bar group. He signalled the others that he was going to confront this group because they had fairly substantial packs and, except for the lead man, their rifles were slung over their shoulders. This was easily done, much to the surprise of the miners who were now on the ground, one knocked unconscious and each of the other three looking at a rifle in his face.

Bedard deduced from their cries of shock during the attack that they were French, so he and Roger immediately stared quizzing them in French, much to their amazement. Roger translated the conversation to Fenciao and Chief Enthica.

These men were part of a large group of miners who planned to take back Emory's Bar from the usurpers. The main body of this group had travelled south from Yale two days before and had crossed the river to the south of Emory's Bar. Two of the small team had been dropped off earlier. Their job was to kill the two sentries they had passed. The task of the remaining four was to kill the miners who tried to escape to the north after the main attack from the south planned for noon that day.

Bedard and his team moved back somewhat for a team meeting and then quizzed the French miners on the names of the leaders of the group currently in charge of Emory's Bar, and the names of the leaders of the miners in the attack group.

Bedard allowed the French miners to stand up but asked them to leave their rifles on the ground. The man who was knocked unconscious in the initial confrontation had recovered. Bedard had another quick meeting with his group and they decided that they could not determine yet if any of the leaders of either group were men on Bedard's list. They voted to join the attacking group because it seemed like a good thing to do.

It was obvious to the French miners that Bedard and his group were professional fighters of some kind, but they could not understand why two of them spoke French and how the two tough-looking natives fit in.

Bedard quizzed the French miners on exactly where they were going to locate themselves. Their leader said that there was a meadow about half a mile to the north of the bar with a small lake and a stream leading to the river, and that they were going to follow an animal trail that was now just ahead of them, down to the north side of the meadow where some deadfalls would give them protection and a good line of sight.

Bedard had another meeting with his team and addressed the French miners again, saying that they could proceed. He told them that his team would try to protect their uphill flank against some of the miners circling around them. Everyone shook hands and the miners moved off, obviously greatly relieved. Bedard whistled to Liz and the other dogs to allow the miners through the security net.

As the miners left, Fenciao looked at Bedard, dropped his pack and machete and followed the group on another parallel trail. Bedard and Roger moved back to the lookout spot that they had previously found, leaving Chief Enthica in the forest near Fenciao's pack.

Forty-Five
November 1858

Bedard and Roger started their meticulous search of the bar looking at each man. They easily identified the three leaders of the group on the bar, but none of the men looked familiar to Bedard. Most of the miners were working a sluice that was fed by a small stream from the mountainside. Bedard and Roger agreed that this was a problem. The group at the bar probably used the trail to the dam on the stream as a trail going farther up the mountain to hunt deer and moose, and this might be the main route of escape from the upcoming battle.

"I will take Chief Enthica and Fenciao to visit the stream briefly," said Roger. "This could be a major problem if some of those miners escape to the forest on the mountainside above us."

Bedard nodded. "I will work myself down the mountain, looking for a good fighting position. We may have to split our team in two."

Roger looked up at the sun. "We have lots of time."

He returned in about an hour, finding Bedard by following some trail markings that Bedard had created. Bedard's location was perfect for the meadow.

According to Roger there was a small camp on the west bank by the stream and a well-used trail up the mountain that led to a valley through a low pass. He thought that the hunting teams went that way for meat, and he initially felt that the trail would be difficult to monitor during a battle.

Bedard said, "I saw you visiting our friends in the valley."

"Yes. I went down to visit them, thinking that their group would have included in their plan some sort of solution to the mountain trail. They confirmed that their leaders had thought of that but they did not know what the actual plan was. I left with an uncomfortable feeling in my gut. I left Fenciao and Chief Enthica hidden up two trees overlooking the trail. I am still uncomfortable with the situation, so I came back for a conference."

Bedard thought for a moment. "Their group knows the landscape better than we do. They do not know that we exist, so it will be dangerous for us to monitor the mountain path in case they think that we are the enemy. It would be easier for us to stay out of the way and pick off any fleeing miners from here. Fenciao and Chief Enthica should come back. I will send Liz to get them."

Roger smiled and nodded. These dogs were quite incredible.

Roger went up the mountain to intercept Fenciao and Chief Enthica and share the modified plan with them. They both arrived with big smiles and reported how Liz had arrived and obviously wanted them to come down from the trees and follow her.

"I have no idea how she found us," Fenciao said. "Perhaps she smelled us!"

Chief Enthica said, "I now understand why the villages are so excited about having security dogs. It was a remarkable communication that we both understood immediately."

They discussed the problem and the various solutions. Roger left Fenciao and Chief Enthica to establish reasonable positions in the forest and returned to Bedard to report their adventure with Liz. Bedard just smiled.

Shortly after, Fenciao came down, still smiling, and reported that they each had established two fighting positions and so could cover the flank of the mountain easily.

"How did you find us?" Roger asked

Fenciao smiled and shook his head. "You make a terrible trail!"

When Fenciao left, Roger was initially quite upset until he saw that Bedard was smiling too.

"You forget," said Bedard, "Fenciao is a better trapper and hunter than both of us put together."

Roger smiled himself. "Yes, I do keep forgetting that."

Bedard had climbed up into the huge root system of a recent deadfall. He pointed downstream.

"At the top of that next ridge there is a good position that looks down upon the bar. I would like you to go and look at it. Perhaps you can pick off the three group leaders from there when the attack starts. On the way over there, you might visit Fenciao and Chief Enthica to see where they are and then find a few places to retreat to if we find this position gets some action from miners trying to escape by going farther up the hill. It should be fairly easy to cover this hill if we do not shoot at each other."

The actual battle was anticlimactic. Roger killed the three leaders easily from his position on the ridge overlooking the bar, and Bedard killed two unsuspecting miners as they came running out of the forest on the other side of the meadows. Another group who tried to escape along the riverside were confronted and surrendered to the small group on the trail below. Fenciao and Chief Enthica saw no one, and Bedard assumed that the attacking group had been very effective on the trail up the mountain from the bar.

Bedard's team met briefly and decided to go down to the bar to meet the successful miners just in case there was someone on Bedard's list. They followed the faint trail down to the meadow and met up with the group of four who were in the process of securing their prisoners. The group marched down the river trail and onto the bar where Bedard's team was introduced to the leader, Captain Davis.

"We were very fortunate to have the leaders killed so early in the battle," Davis said. "Thank you. I assume that was your work. That was a very good shot from the forest. Without the leadership, the miners were fairly easy to round up." He pointed to the large group sitting on the ground with their hands and legs tied.

He looked at Bedard. "We have met before, I think."

Bedard smiled. "Perhaps on this bar several months ago."

There was a distraction as the group who had been positioned up the mountain arrived at the bar with their prisoners.

Bedard indicated that he wanted to leave, and the four men turned around and walked off the bar to the north with Roger and Fenciao watching their rear in turn. Once in the forest, Bedard quickly led the team up the slope of the mountain to where they had left their packs. The dogs had anticipated their move and adopted a close security net.

JoJo, who was on the river side, immediately indicated a contact and the group froze, listening. They heard the sounds of men running, probably on the lower path. Bedard asked Roger to hide the packs and then come down to the path. Bedard led the way down the mountain. Chief Enthica examined the path and held up five fingers.

Bedard thought for a minute. "They do not have an experienced tracker with them. Otherwise they would have noticed that we had turned off the path to go up the mountain."

Fenciao said, "You assume that they were looking for us?"

Roger had arrived. "So, who do you think Captain Davis is?"

"I don't know," said Bedard. "I have never seen him before that I can remember, but he might have disguised himself, or he might be one of the people on the list who I don't think that I have met yet." He smiled. "In any case, he has sent five people after us. He might even be leading this group."

"What do you think, Chief Enthica?"

Chief Enthica smiled because Bedard usually called him by his social name, which was Chief Little Bon. He had won the archery completion two years ago, and the name that Chief Big Bon had given him had stuck. Chief Enthica was a brilliant strategist, and when Bedard was really stuck he often asked him to devise some clever plan.

All of the group was smiling as Chief Enthica pondered the problem.

"They will stop soon, realizing that we have left the trail, and they will return carefully off the trail up the mountain looking for us. I think that they will realize that they are in trouble and will try to be very clever. They might even separate, with some of them returning after dark down the river in a stolen canoe. If we are very skilful we can hide and allow the dogs to warn us of their pending arrival."

"We need to spread out up the mountain," Roger said. "And if we find one of these men, it will be important to find another. Sounds like bows would be best."

Both Fenciao and Chief Enthica stole off up the mountain. Roger, too, left Bedard. Bedard decided to move down toward the water and found a good position not far off the trail. He called Liz in and sent her to the north in a four-dog screen around the team of men.

Very soon, Haus barked. Haus was well up the mountain so that meant that the miners had returned with one at least, well up the slope. Shortly after, Hy barked and a second miner was identified below the first one. Shortly after that, Liz barked indicating a third miner just above the path.

Bedard moved up the mountain and waited patiently until Roger arrived dragging a man with an arrow in his arm, followed by both Fenciao and Chief Enthica dragging two dead men. Roger sat the wounded man on the ground and leaned him against a tree. Fenciao removed the arrow and dressed the wound.

Nothing was said.

Bedard looked at the man, trying to determine if he was American or from another part of the world. He picked up his bow, put an arrow in it and drew it back pointed at the man. The man closed his eyes.

"Not American," said Roger.

Bedard spoke Musqueam. "Check him for numbers or other marks."

Roger found a mark on his inside right wrist. Bedard inspected it.

"You are a long way from home, sir," Bedard said in Slovakian.

The man was stunned.

Bedard continued. "You need to tell us something about this mining group. If you answer my questions correctly, I will release you if you promise to return to America. Two members of your small group are dead, and the other two will probably die."

The man responded in Slovakian. "If we do not return, they will send others out to find us."

"They will find five dead men," said Bedard, "and will return to the river bar and focus on finding gold. You have the opportunity to return to the river bar and say that the rest of your group are probably dead that and you were lucky to escape after you were captured."

The man reverted to English. "What do you want to know?"

"What is your name?"

"Nicolas Dabchick, I usually use Nick Dabber."

"Who are the other two men?"

Nick thought for a moment. "One is Captain Davis and the other is his friend, Louis."

"How did you come to join his mining group?"

"We met several years ago in California. He is a very clever, experienced miner, and a good boss. I have made a lot of money working with him."

Roger gave Bedard a rifle, a large pistol and a small pistol, and spoke in Musqueam.

"The small pistol was in a custom boot holster."

Bedard noted that all three guns were very new.

"Are these your guns?" he asked.

Nick grimaced. "Yes."

Bedard waited, hoping that Nick would give some more explanation for this professional collection. "What is your responsibly on the river bar?"

Nick continued to look at Bedard and eventually spoke.

"I am responsible for security. I have, or had"—he looked at the two dead men—"a team of two men working with me."

In the meantime, Fenciao had stripped the two men of their guns, including small boot revolvers. Bedard inspected these and chose a rifle. With obvious expertise, he levered a bullet into the chamber and pointed the gun at Nick for a moment and then dropped the muzzle.

Nick took a moment to inspect the four men confronting him and turned back to Bedard.

"The captain thought that he recognized you from somewhere in California. When you left abruptly you gathered up our team and hoped to be able to catch up to you. I told him that we did not have any trackers and that this was a very dangerous plan, but he was insistent. When we did not find you, he said that you had stopped and that we could find you if we came back on the mountainside, so we did." He shrugged his shoulders and winced at the pain from his damaged upper arm.

"You said that you have known Captain Davis for several years," Bedard said. "What was his name when he was in California?"

"I don't remember."

Bedard lifted the rifle and again reverted to Slovakian. "I need you to answer this question. I will give you a count of three and then you are dead. One … two…"

"Yes, yes," Nick said. "He used two names, Davis Woodward and D.R. Williams, D.R. for short."

Roger spoke Musqueam. "D.R. Williams is on your list."

Bedard looked at him and nodded.

Roger spoke to Chief Enthica in Musqueam.

"Take him up into the forest, gag him and tie him to a tree. We will deal with him later."

"Roger," Bedard said, "take Fenciao and Liz and see if you can find the other two men. Be careful. They are obviously more experienced than these three."

He turned to Chief Enthica. "Come back and find me. I will be down by the river."

When Chief Enthica found him, Bedard asked, "How wide is the river here?"

Chief Enthica looked and thought for a moment. "From here to the far side of the water is about nine hundred feet. If we went down to the water's edge, perhaps seven hundred and fifty."

Bedard considered that.

"I originally thought that they would come back in a stolen canoe, but now I think that they will cross over and come back on the east side trail. Can you see the trail from here?"

"I could see it from farther up the slope but not from here."

"So, how far do you think it is from here to the trail?"

Chief Enthica looked at Bedard for a moment, thinking, then he looked across the river.

"About twelve hundred feet. I do not think that our rifles will reach that distance, but perhaps the new ones that we have removed from the men might."

"Roger could probably make that shot." Bedard said. "Perhaps if we exposed ourselves we might get them to come down to the water's edge and get into a shooting match with us."

Just then Roger showed up. "They are on the path on the bank across the river. Fenciao is getting the three rifles that we took from the three men. They might reach across the water."

Bedard and Chief Enthica exchanged amused looks.

"What?" said Roger.

"We were just talking about that," Bedard said. "Chief Enthica estimated that it is about twelve hundred feet from here to the path, but we can't see the path from here."

Roger had his telescope out and was looking across the river. "I think that as the two men pass by on the trail we will be able to see their heads, and that will be enough."

Fenciao arrived with the three rifles. Bedard had removed his bow and was adjusting the string.

"You use the rifles and I will use this."

"They should be here very soon now," said Roger.

The three men inspected the rifles and adjusted the sights for the long shot. They then chose a shooting location and settled down to stabilize their guns.

"You two take the first man," Bedard said, "and we will take the second man."

They all waited patiently until they could see the men coming, as Roger had predicted.

"I will shoot first," said Bedard.

The first man on the path passed a small clearing, and Bedard loosed his arrow. The three guns roared, and the men across the river disappeared.

Bedard said, "We will take Nick back with us to where we hid the canoe and visit that place to see what happened. Nick will make a good shield in case one of them is still alive and able to move."

The team moved up into the forest to collect their packs and other gear. Chief Enthica moved ahead of the group to get Nick and bring him down to the path. The two bodies were stripped of gear and small packs and moved into the brush alongside the trail. The guns and other gear were hidden separately, and they moved off. The dogs were still in their tight security net and would follow the team as they moved north.

They decided to keep the canoe and paddle down the river a few miles to save time and to eventually be able to pick up all of the guns and other gear that they had confiscated. The river current was not very fast at this time of year.

As they walked carefully down the east side trail toward the shooting spot, Nick was leading the way and had guessed why. It was not fun for him, but he was resigned to his fate. The two men were found, both dead. One had an arrow in his neck and was shot in the chest. The other had a head and a chest shot.

Roger said, "The head shot was Fenciao's."

Fenciao shook his head. "I would never aim for the head at that distance. You were just showing off again!"

The four exchanged grim smiles. Nick looked over the river to the west side and shook his head.

Bedard turned both men over and looked at their faces.

"I do not remember meeting either of these men before. If this is D.R. Williams, who is this?"

He looked up at Nick.

"As I said before, he is the Captain's friend, Lewis. In all the years that I have known these two he has always been Lewis. I have never heard his last name. He is a vicious killer. I have seen him kill many people. He never left the captain's side."

Bedard looked at Roger and spoke in Musqueam.

"There was a L. Dawson on the list. This must be him. He is a big man."

Roger nodded. Bedard inspected both men, looking for skin markings.

"Lewis has a similar wrist mark to Nick's. Nick knew that I was going to find the mark. What kind of a game is Nick playing? Chief Enthica, what do you think?"

Without saying anything, Chief Enthica dropped his pack and most of his gear, turned and started to walk northward down the path. The other three men had seen this happen many times before when the chief needed to think over a difficult idea. In a few minutes, Chief Enthica returned.

"Nick must also be a leader of this group of miners."

The group all turned to look at Nick, who was watching from the tree just off the trail that he had been tied to earlier.

Bedard unholstered one of his two pistols, casually walked over to Nick and spoke to him in Slovakian.

"Lewis has a similar wrist mark as yours. Can you tell me about that?"

Nick looked at Bedard and did not say anything.

"You knew I was going to find the mark. You have had some time to think about what you are going to say to me. Answer the question."

Nick looked at the revolver and then at Bedard's face but said nothing. He did not look afraid. Bedard turned, holstered his revolver and returned to the team.

Speaking again in Musqueam, he said, "I wonder if Nick is in fact Lewis Dawson and man next to the captain is merely a professional hired hand, a killer."

Roger and Fenciao stepped over and searched the two bodies. The captain had only the rifle and a bowie knife. The other man had an unusual number of armaments in addition to the rifle and two pistols strapped to his thighs. He had a very long knife on his belt, two sleeve knives, two custom boot revolvers and a rear belt revolver in an unusual custom holster.

"Check his back for knife sheaths," Bedard said.

Roger did this, then ripped off his shirt and removed a four-knife sheath. He spoke English.

"This was made in Hong Kong." He removed the man's boots and found a spring-loaded toe knife in each boot.

Bedard shook his head and went back over to Nick, speaking in English this time. "I believe that you are Nicolas Dabchick, but you have been using the name Lewis Dawson for many years."

Nick paled, and his head dropped.

Bedard turned and returned to his team.

"I think that is a yes. Thank you, Chief Little Bon."

The group smiled. He continued in Musqueam. "I do not think it really matters who this other man is now. Nick is another one of these very clever, evil people. If we released him, he would not return to America. He would try to hunt us down."

Bedard went over to Nick and shot him in the head.

Forty-Six
November 19, 1958

Bedard, Roger, Fenciao and Chief Enthica paddled their way across the wet marsh at high tide, with Liz sitting alert at the prow, toward the south arm of the Fraser River where the Hudson's Bay Company steamship *Beaver* was at anchor. The weather was cold and overcast with a light east wind. Although the team had rain gear, they hoped that the rain would hold off until they had at least reached the ship.

Bedard had received a typically cryptic letter from Douglas the previous week, saying that there was a big show at Fort Langley in a few days where he would officially be made the Governor of the new colony of British Columbia. He would be boarding the Company ship *Beaver* on November 18 at noon accompanied by Mr. Begbie, soon to be the colony's new chief judge.

Begbie had arrived at Fort Victoria on November 15 and wanted to meet with Bedard as soon as possible. Bedard was six feet tall, Douglas was six feet two inches, but Begbie was taller still at six feet four inches, a giant of a man. Bedard had heard of Begbie in England but had never met him personally. He remembered him to be a well-respected, intelligent and fair-minded young barrister who everyone thought was destined to be a judge. He had to smile, thinking that he and Begbie had similar appointments into this wilderness. He was certain that Begbie was perfect for his assignment in this current situation.

Bedard had been invited to the ceremony but had immediately sent a note back to Douglas excusing himself. He had brought his formal suit with him in the canoe, including the top hat as directed by Douglas, but he hoped that he did not have to participate. It was much too exposed a situation. He still had too many enemies in the area.

Bedard was in his normal day-to-day clothing and looked similar to his companions. When the canoe arrived at the *Beaver,* which was lying moored within the mouth of the Fraser River, he was detained by a navy guard until the ship's captain, Captain Mouat, came and vouched for him. It was decided that Liz would stay in the canoe and be towed up the river to Fort Langley behind the *Otter.*

Douglas and others in his party had sailed from Fort Victoria to Point Roberts on the HMS *Satellite.* Then they transferred to the Hudson's Bay Company screw steamer *Otter* and travelled the short distance to the *Beaver* in the Fraser River, arriving there just after Bedard. The *Satellite* had returned to Victoria.

Bedard transferred over to the *Otter* and was immediately met by both Douglas and Begbie. The two men towered over Bedard and he thought, smiling to himself, that it would be interesting for Chief Big Bon to meet these two men. It was very crowded on the ship's deck, so they moved together to the prow in order to get some privacy.

"I have been briefed by the Queen on your assignment here," said Begbie, "and I am not pleased because it would seem to me that there is a high risk of men and women who are not on your list dying."

Bedard was expecting Begbie not to support his assignment, so he had decided to go slowly until he determined what Begbie's actual views were.

"That is somewhat true," Bedard said. "The risk is not high because I and my associates are very experienced professional manhunters. I am a very good planner, and when a target is identified we make plans with various alternatives. So far, the only people killed who were not on the list—and there are eleven—should have been on the list. In any case, there are only four men left on the current list plus one more that I have personally added.

"As you know, when I arrived here on January 1 there were twenty-eight men and two women on the original list. Since then, the Queen has added two more men. The one man that I have added is a gunman hired by two of the men still on the list. I saw the three of them twice earlier in the year but they have subsequently disappeared. The other two still on the list are the brothers of two men who were killed in April in Victoria as the four brothers first arrived from San Francisco.

"It is now very difficult to find the remaining men because there are so many people in this area. It is very easy to hide and very dangerous to search. It is also reasonable to assume that the five men who I have not caught have already travelled beyond Lytton to the Thompson River and the North Fraser River area, and I will not be going up there. I will probably return to England soon and give my report to the Queen early next year."

Judge Begbie nodded. "That is quite a remarkable record. If you find any more of the men on your list, I wish to be informed *before* you take any action."

Bedard looked at Douglas for a moment. "That would be difficult because you will not have an office where I can send a runner." Bedard and Douglas smiled.

Judge Begbie did not smile, however. "I would like you to try to find me, nonetheless." Bedard shrugged.

"I received your note yesterday," Douglas said. "You have decided not to attend the ceremony?"

"I will be there," Bedard said. "But not in tails."

"I am pleased to meet you," Judge Begbie said. "You have done very well on your difficult assignment, and I hope that I can do as well on mine."

They shook hands, smiling.

As they were talking, both vessels proceeded as far as Old Fort Langley where a party of eighteen sappers under the command of Captain Parsons disembarked from the *Otter*. Parsons and his men immediately embarked in the *Recovery* revenue cutter, joining the command of Captain Grant, R.E., who had previously reached this area with a party of the same corps. Both these gallant officers had recently arrived from England with small parties of men under their command. The *Otter*, followed by the *Beaver* and the *Recovery*, proceeded to Fort Langley where preparations were being made for the ceremony on the following day.

The next day it started raining in the morning and rained steadily all day, ruining the plans for the meeting to be held outside. At midday, Douglas, accompanied by Captain Grant and others, disembarked on the wet loamy bank of the Fraser River at the fort and led the procession up the steep bank to the palisade. An eighteen-gun salute from the *Beaver* announced the group as a soaked, dripping British Flag was raised over the main entrance.

The group moved into the fort and eventually entered a large room in the Big House, a building that served as the fort's office and the residence of James Murray Yale, the chief trader, and a few other married couples. About one hundred persons were present, including Bedard and Roger who had spruced themselves up a bit so that they could get into the building but remain in the background, still looking for men on Bedard's list.

Douglas started the ceremonies by delivering to Mr. Begbie Her Majesty's Commission as judge in the Colony of British Columbia.

Mr. Begbie took his Oath of Allegiance and the usual oaths on taking office. He took up her Majesty's Commission appointing Douglas the governor of the new Colony of British Columbia

Governor Douglas, being duly appointed and sworn in, proceeded to issue a proclamation of the act to create the Colony of British Columbia, proclaiming English Law to be the law of the colony. He then revoked of all the exclusive privileges of the Hudson's Bay Company.

In the meantime, Fenciao and Chief Enthica were slowly searching the campground to the east of Fort Langley for groups that responded negatively to their invitations to provide packers or canoes and paddlers. They did not receive any takers for these services because their prices were a little high, but they did find two camps that were particularly belligerent—and they would be visited by the full team later in the day.

In the late afternoon, after the ceremony, Bedard and his team went through the miners' campground again and determined that the two unruly groups did not have anyone that Bedard felt was on his list.

The next day, Governor Douglas left the fort to another salute of seventeen guns. He spoke to a number of the inhabitants who were assembled at the riverside before boarding the *Beaver*. The group cheered as he climbed the gangplank to the steamer.

Bedard and his team had spent the two nights in a reasonably dry tent warmed with a small fire. With Liz's help, they had managed to find several very wet rabbits in the local forest for supper and the early morning meal. The rain had continued through the night and it was very cold. Chief Enthica had pointed out that the snowline on the mountains both to the north and to the south of them had moved down. He reminded them of the shaman's forecast of an early cold winter with lots of snow.

After Governor Douglas and his party had left, Bedard's group had planned to visit the large Kwantlen village across from the fort on the north shore of the Fraser River, but Bedard felt that the weather was going to get worse and decided not to do that, so they paddled directly home instead.

This was a good decision as it started to snow when they were about a mile from the canoe landing. The lookout tree staff had spotted them, and at the Tsusnahm landing by the big tree they were met by Mother and three of her granddaughters, all carrying big fire-warmed blankets. This was a new experience for Bedard who had only rarely seen snow on any of his travels in the last twenty years, and he really appreciated the warm blankets. He was very cold and went immediately to his home and to bed. Adrona came by and warmed him up a bit but had to leave to prepare the late meal for her extended family.

Forty-Seven
November 1858

The next day was clear and slightly warmer. The snow was gradually disappearing from the grassy areas around the village. Bedard got up a bit later than usual and moved north for a short run with the dogs. The forest floor was still covered with a thin layer of snow, and Bedard could see that he was the first villager on this path. Soon Liz, who had rear duty, announced company and Chief Roanyon shortly appeared.

"Welcome back," he said. "I have tried to go for a run every day, but I am not as disciplined as you are."

Bedard said, "What's new?"

"Three babies yesterday, and the last group of our miners and warriors arrived back from Eagle Bar with another large sack of gold. The total is outstanding. I went down to Mahli for two hours and we had a very short Three Villages Committee meeting yesterday afternoon after the midday meal. The Squamish attended, too. We again decided to follow your advice and keep the winter wind account intact until we have a better understanding of our future with the settlers who are bound to come to this large area of reasonably flat land. I also reported that we were having a special celebration today."

Bedard's eyebrows went up and Chief Roanyon said, "The official announcement will probably be made at the midday meal. We also examined, for the first time, the map that has been drawn of the area to the north of the three villages. As you recall, this was to be created by Alfonso and Joseph. It is very detailed and none of us had any difficulty understanding it. The two carpenters, now surveyors—I think that is the term that you used when you introduced this concept to us—were very pleased.

"The group that had been assigned to visit Fort Langley's farm area has not yet returned. We have, however, again discussed the area that we will fence in for the herd of cattle that we have decided to purchase. This was very easy to understand with the map in front of us. I thought of you yesterday when we had the midday meal. It was the small lake trout that you like."

Bedard smiled. They started to slow down in preparation for a turnaround and called in the dogs for scratches.

On the run back toward Tsusnahm, Chief Roanyon continued with his news.

"You will recall that Bobo was assigned to Mot for specialty training, and that is going very well. They added Liz to several of the training sessions and she helped significantly on the overhead-branches training path. Mot is already looking forward to joining a trading trip north next year with Bobo to meet up with Bob and Wolf again in Cumshewa. Art and David returned from a ten-day trip north of the Squamish villages to visit the hunting area where several feeding depots have been established. David said that over a five-day period they saw two hundred and twelve deer visit one of the feed depots. Art, who is a hunter and not a conservative, was very impressed. They plan to visit the same depot in six months for another deer count. David is predicting three or four hundred next time if everyone stays away from that area. And finally, I think that David is making some progress with Elizabeth. We often see them walking hand in hand on the river trails."

"Wouldn't that would be grand?" Bedard said.

"Have you decided when you will be leaving?"

"I have sent a letter to Philip in San Francisco, estimating my arrival on about December first. He has the company's railroad car there, so I won't need to ride a horse for six weeks to reach New York."

At the top of the hill, Bedard again brought the four dogs in for scratches, and then sent them off to their security positions. The two men trotted down the hill, following the stream that was almost overflowing its banks. Bedard was amazed to see that in spite of the snow and cold weather some late-blooming flowers could be seen here and there on the steep slope.

Later in the morning, Bedard and Roger held a meeting with the group of twenty men from Tsusnahm who had been mining for gold at Posey and Eagle Bars. Six of the miners who lived in Stsulawh and Mahli and who were still in the village also attended. They talked about the mining plan for the early spring.

A group of ten of these miners had travelled up to the new town of Lillooet and beyond and reported that the gold was not as easy to find in that area, but the mining was much more profitable. Under Bedard and Roger's guidance, they discussed how much of the gold beyond the forks would be found by digging down to bedrock in the valleys of tributaries to the main rivers rather than the river bars. These miners had joined a group that was sinking exploratory shafts down to bedrock where gold was actually found. They had listened attentively to the two very experienced mining leaders of this group as they described what they saw and why they chose the locations for the shafts.

Roger said that they had made a good start in acquiring the skills to find the gold. Bedard felt that in the spring they should again send a small team north to join other teams of miners who had found gold, and then move off on their own.

The main body of the miners, having exhausted the two bars that they had been working, should move northward and find another bar to work during the spring. Then this group could go farther northward to join the advance group. They discussed the type of tools that they would need and the problem of getting food and supplies. A reasonable road had been recently constructed from the west to Lillooet, and this would improve the packing in of supplies.

At the midday meal, Bedard and Roger were directed to Mother's where a large group had gathered. Adrona and Aurora were cooking with their two young children running around under their feet. As soon as they saw Bedard, both of the scallywags raced over to him and he lifted both of them up in his arms. The group liked that. Fresh salmon was served, and it was delicious.

Near the end of the meal, Art Rossland got up and hit his water glass with his fork.

"I always wanted to do that," he said, and everyone laughed.

"As most of you know, I left England shortly after my wife died. My only daughter had married and had gone off to God knows where." Amused murmurs. He switched to Musqueam. "I was very skilful and eventually found her." Laughter. "And I am now very content and happier than I have ever been at any time in my life." He looked at

Elizabeth and everyone clapped. Bedard thought that Art now spoke Musqueam very well. Mot was nearby and was beaming.

As Art sat down, David got up.

"I also escaped England and was also very skilled to have followed Elizabeth to this beautiful area of the world." Everyone was smiling in anticipation of what he would say next. "I am pleased to report that I have asked Elizabeth to marry me and that she has accepted."

Everyone rose and clapped and started singing the beautiful song that Bedard had heard several times but still did not know. Elizabeth got up and hugged David and then her father.

In a few moments, Elizabeth held up her hand and the singing slowed and stopped.

"The answer to the next question that you all have is as soon as possible. Yesterday we asked Chief Roanyon to marry us. He has agreed to do this at four o'clock today, just as the sun sets in the west."

Mother, Adrona and Aurora looked at each other aghast. Both Bedard and Chief Roanyon saw this and quickly moved over, gathered them up and guided them into a small room nearby. Mother immediately moved into high gear.

"How many?"

Chief Roanyon said, "Two hundred."

The three women gasped.

The men looked at each other, smiling.

Chief Roanyon said, "Only a small group from Stsulawh and Mahli, about eighty or so."

"Possibly half that from the Squamish Nation," Bedard said. "About forty. Chief Roanyon was in Mahli yesterday morning to report this event. Both of these groups should be here within the hour. Then we will have a better idea of how much food they have brought with them. We may have that information now via Morse code. I will go and look now."

Mother said, "We will have to stuff them all in here just like we did at the last big party. That worked very well. We need more wood, and we need to get a group of men to move all of the furniture out again and find the six tables."

Roger, who had just joined the meeting, said, "I can do all those tasks." He disappeared.

Bedard returned laughing. "The Squamish party numbers fifty-two and will be here in ten minutes. Their canoes have just left Khwaykhway and will be here in an hour and a half with food for about one hundred. The Stsulawh and Mahli group have decided to race here and left their beach about five minutes ago. Their total party numbers about ninety. They did not know exactly. The food that follows them will feed about two hundred. So everyone will be here in ten minutes, and we will have more than enough food for everyone."

Mother rushed off, saying that she had to get Old Chief Sparrow into his robes and down to the beach immediately. She stopped and turned.

"I just love these parties."

The group laughed as she scooted off. Adrona and Aurora moved off toward the cooking area. The group that had just finished the midday meal was still bubbling with the news as they followed David and Elizabeth out the front door.

Chief Roanyon turned to Bedard. "I heard you when you said that you planned to be in San Francisco on December first, but it did not register. To get there you would have to leave here next week."

Bedard smiled. "I will be taking the four dogs and a few guns and leaving all the rest behind for you, including all the bows and the two canoes. You have never seen the second canoe." He stopped and smiled because Chief Roanyon was looking very sad. "It is immediately behind the first canoe but about fifty feet back in the brush."

Chief Roanyon said, "Is Dorthea going with you?"

"Yes, I think so, but as of this morning she was still thinking about it."

At that exact moment Dorthea was with Adrona and Aurora at the central cooking area helping with the final cleanup. Roger had a group taking out the furniture. It was a very busy time.

What she had to say weighed on Dorthea, but eventually she just blurted it out.

"I have decided to go back to England with my father."

They all knew that Bedard was leaving soon, but this was a bit of a shock. Adrona started to cry, and the three of them had a group hug. Mothana, who had volunteered to set up the wedding ceremony, came blasting into the building and up to the fireplace. She skidded to a stop when she saw the women crying.

"What?"

"I have just told them that I will be leaving with my father."

"Oh, my goodness! That is not good news. You are such a perfect person!" The four of them started crying.

Mother returned and understood the scene immediately.

"Come now, you people, we need a wedding outfit for Elizabeth, so the four of you need to go with Dorthea and find something suitable in one of her trunks. The seamstresses have been alerted and we can capture Elizabeth after the guests arrive. Now, off you go, all of you. I will finish up here."

And they left.

Old Chief Sparrow was down at the beach just in time to judge the arrival of the two canoes as a tie again. The two chiefs and their wives tumbled out of the huge war canoes and were immediately surrounded by villagers.

Drums were heard in the distance as the two Squamish chiefs and their wives and villagers came down the hill toward the village. Bedard again had the local drummers out, and the whole crowd was smiling and happy and clapping along with them. The four chiefs arrived at the big tree at the same time and were welcomed by David and Elizabeth, who by this time were almost overwhelmed by the attention.

The wedding under the big tree was glorious. The villagers and their visitors made a very large half circle sitting on blankets facing the big tree with the women at the front so that everyone could see the ceremony. This was the first English wedding in this area that anyone could remember, and everyone was interested in seeing how it unfolded. Six of the villagers, three women including Aunt Betty and three men, had been carried out and were carefully seated on chairs or tilted beds and covered with blankets. Children were everywhere, but that was normal. They would disappear and join their parents when the proceedings started.

Mothana had a meeting with Chief Roanyon, David, Art, Bedard, Roger and Fenciao to make certain that everyone understood when and where they were supposed to go and what their duties were.

In due course, the door to Old Chief Sparrow's longhouse opened, all the children were gathered up by their parents and the crowd became silent.

A procession emerged led by Chief Roanyon, followed by the five other chiefs all in their magnificent chief's headgear and robes, closely followed by the six wives all wearing beautiful red and pink English dresses. This was definitely a first for most of these women who were smiling greatly, almost giggling.

The crowd gave a collective *ahhh* of approval and started clapping softly and singing. The drums started in the background.

The procession made its way slowly around the inside of the circle and then down toward the big tree, where they formed a half circle facing north with Chief Roanyon and Mothana in front of them. Ornate embroidered blankets were put on the shoulders of the women to keep them warm. After a few moments, Mother stepped forward and held up her hands. The singing slowed down but continued softly.

Mother addressed the crowd.

"This ceremony will be a bit different than what we have been used to over the past three thousand years." The crowd laughed very quietly with her. "We have been guided into a ceremony that will please you all. It will be based on the British marriage ceremony. For both the Musqueam and the British, marriage is a very important decision. We will also be entertained by the dancers."

The crowd came to life and started clapping and singing again. Mother then moved back to stand beside her husband.

Bedard and Roger, who had snuck out of the longhouse behind the first procession, looked at each other and shrugged. Fenciao who had also slipped out explained that the dancers were the shamans and their assistants.

"There are probably twenty here today because David and Elizabeth have both gone out of their way to embrace the world that the shamans follow. They rarely dance in public. I don't remember seeing them dance more than five times, so this is a very special occasion for them."

The door opened again, and the crowd became silent.

After a short pause, the first out the door were the six Tsusnahm drummers who were playing a marching beat. They were followed by six other children carrying small bouquets of the flowers that Bedard had observed on the hillside. The twelve children were covered in beautiful light-blue silk cloth. They followed the same route around the circle and then, with the assistance of Mothana, lined up in two rows on each side of the path from the longhouse to the small half circle of chiefs and their wives. Everyone was smiling, singing and clapping with the beat of the drums.

The drummers gave three large heavy beats and stopped. The large group became silent in anticipation.

Three beautiful women came out of the door followed by three men. The drummers started up again and the group started to sing and clap. The three women, Dorthea, Adrona and Aurora, wore beautiful light-blue English dresses and carried small bouquets of flowers, and the men, Bedard, Roger and Fenciao, had on light-grey clothing. They came down to the big tree through the two lines of children, then circled the area as the others had done and walked down between the children again and stood on either side of Chief Roanyon. Everyone was smiling. The crowd loved it.

The drummers again gave three large heavy beats and stopped. The large group became very silent in anticipation.

The door which had been closed opened again, and David came out by himself, trying unsuccessfully not to smile. The group started to sing and clap again. David walked down the path between the children and up to Chief Roanyon and Mothana, shook their hands and turned around. Everyone was now quiet looking at the open door.

It was a long wait. The crowd loved the suspense. Then Elizabeth came out the door on her father's arm. They both had great smiles on their faces, and she obviously had been crying a bit. She was wearing a beautiful light-blue dress with a white cap covering the top part of her face. The cap had a long tail to it with six very young children trying to keep it off the ground behind her. The whole crowd stood up and cheered and clapped and then started yet another song that Bedard did not know. Elizabeth and her father proceeded slowly down the path between the children toward David and Chief Roanyon.

As Elizabeth came up to Chief Roanyon, Mothana helped the children move the rear of the dress into position. The small children stepped back one pace and folded their hands in front of them, hardly able to contain themselves, smiling and looking around at the crowd. The drummers and all the children moved over and sat covered with blankets in front of the crowd. Mothana moved back with the group of notables.

Elizabeth and David stood on each side of Chief Roanyon, smiling intensely at each other. The crowd was very quiet. Bedard and Roger looked at each other and smiled.

Chief Roanyon had never done this before. He had a piece of paper scrunched up in his hand on which he had made some notes based on more than two hours of short meetings with everyone who knew anything about weddings, including the two Italian carpenters.

He took the bride and groom by the hand, gently pulled them a little closer to him and started in English in a loud voice so that everyone could hear him.

"One of life's greatest moments is the joining of two hearts. We are gathered here to give recognition to the value and beauty of love and to witness the joining of these two lives." He stopped and looked at them in turn and then continued in Musqueam. "For them, out of the routine of ordinary life, the extraordinary thing happened. They met each other and fell in love and are confirming it with this wedding. A good marriage must be created. It is never being too old to hold hands. It is remembering to say I love you every day."

The group had started to sing again, and Bedard thought that the words fit the music perfectly.

Chief Roanyon turned to David.

"Please repeat after me: I, David, take you, Elizabeth, to be my wife, my partner in life and my one true love. I will cherish our friendship and love you today, tomorrow and forever."

David repeated these words and the couple had tears running down their faces. The singing continued softly in the background.

The chief turned to Elizabeth. "Please repeat after me: I, Elizabeth, take you, David, to be my husband, my partner in life and my one true love. I will cherish our friendship and love you today, tomorrow and forever."

As she repeated these vows, their tears continued to fall.

Chief Roanyon asked David to produce the ring. David reached for a thin rope necklace he was wearing, pulled it over his head and removed a ring that was tied to it and gave it to the chief. Elizabeth had her hand at her mouth in surprise. David was grinning broadly. Only a few of the crowd really understood what was happening.

Chief Roanyon spoke in Musqueam.

"Wedding rings are an unbroken circle of love, signifying to all the union of this couple in marriage."

He took Elizabeth's hand and, holding it, gave the ring back to David who put it on her finger. It fit perfectly. The crowd now understood, and the singing swelled.

With David holding Elizabeth's hand, Chief Roanyon had David repeat after him. "Elizabeth…"

David said, "Elizabeth…"

"This ring is my sacred gift, with my promise that I will always love you, cherish you and honour you all the days of my life."

After David repeated these words, the couple stood looking at each other. The crowd had many translating the English, and the song that they were singing swelled.

Chief Roanyon spoke in a loud voice that could be heard above the singing.

"I now pronounce you man and wife." To the crowd, he said, "I present to you our happy couple: Mr. and Mrs. Anderson."

The two came together in a long kiss and then, as if startled to find the group around them, looked out at them and waved. The group continued the song, and two chairs materialized behind Elizabeth and David and they were urged to sit down. An embroidered blanket arrived for Elizabeth.

Four adult drummers appeared at the side of the space between the wedding party and the crowd, and the dance began.

Bedard found the dance very interesting. It started with two young people holding hands and darting this way and that in a very beautiful fashion to the beat of the drums. When they were on the far side of the circle, four very interesting performers came out wearing furs and full head masks that looked like animals.

The performance continued quite majestically to tell a story about the couple and how they survived in this hostile environment. At the peak of the dance, there were about twenty performers, and the two young people survived all of this together with the help of some of the actors.

Bedard thought that the dance was very professional and obviously reflected the ceremony that they had just witnessed: the voyage of the young couple through life with its many dangers.

It did not last very long, about twenty minutes, after which the performers returned, carrying their masks, and the crowd showed its great pleasure.

At this time, the married couple led the distinguished guests back into the longhouse. The crowd mulled around for a while and entered Old Chief Sparrow's longhouse where it was quite warm.

Most of the food that had been brought to the festivities had been already cooked, and only needed to be warmed up, so the cooks, assisted by several expert visitors, created the meal very rapidly and the crowd helped themselves from the usual six tables. It was all delicious.

David and Elizabeth, who had left by the rear door, arrived again after most of the guests had squeezed themselves in and were guided to two chairs with small tables beside them for their food, which was brought forward by several friends posing as slaves. The crowd was excited, and a flow of friends talked briefly to the couple.

After the meal, a steady stream of people arrived bearing gifts. After two hours of this, the two small rooms behind the wedding couple were full to overflowing, and the couple looked exhausted. Mothana finally shepherded them out of the building, which was still quite crowded, and led them to their quarters. Dorthea arrived to help Elizabeth out of her gown. Then Adrona and Aurora arrived and the five women had their own party. David had been spirited away by Bedard, Roger and Fenciao to another small party. It was quite a day.

The next day, the lookout tree staff reported that the *Cobalt* had passed up the river to Fort Langley and would be returning in two days at about three in the afternoon for Bedard and Dorthea.

Bedard was already almost packed. He had chosen the guns and knives that he was going to take and the only thing that was left on his list was to comb the dogs' fur. This was a long task that took him most of the day.

Dorthea had been working on her list for some time now, even though she had only decided to join her father yesterday. That day, with the help of Adrona, Aurora, Elizabeth and Mothana, with Mother arriving later in the afternoon, she had only six outfits hanging from the line near her rooms. By suppertime it had increased to twelve, and immediately after supper she had it down to eight. Bedard came by and remarked that eight out of two hundred seemed reasonable. Dorthea started crying and Bedard was shushed, and gently pushed out of the longhouse. Mother left to find Modan to arrange for warriors to guard the two doors so that that did not happen again. The ladies thought that this was a great idea, and Dorthea was now laughing.

The next day there was a steady stream of visitors, and Bedard and Roger sat with Dorthea and her friends all day. Bedard had been adamant that the wedding was the last party that he was going to attend in this part of the world. He and Dorthea had also circulated their wishes that presents were not appropriate because they did not have any more room in their luggage. So, the presents offered and accepted were very small tokens of appreciation.

Roger gave him a small rock that he had found. It was black with a white streak. Bedard held it in his hand all day long. Elizabeth ended up with a large handful of beautiful feathers and one very small, very old stone carving from Mother and Old Chief Sparrow. She also had a large collection of artwork from her students.

The next day, just before the midday meal, the two travellers were moving their bags to the front door when Chief Enthica and Fenciao stuck their heads in. They beckoned Bedard and Roger to come out and then showed them two large backpacks, two smaller front packs, two complex belts with two revolvers in holsters and four modern rifles. With a bit of a flourish they added two wide brimmed hats.

Bedard smiled. "The remaining Tanner brothers?"

"Yes," said Chief Enthica. "We heard yesterday from the south shore lookout tree that two men were travelling by canoe unusually slowly and carefully down the south arm keeping to the north side. As soon as they added that they both had bright red hair, Fenciao and I grabbed Teddy, Baribo and Timpani and had a quick meeting. It was obvious who the two men were. They knew of the north shore lookout trees somehow, but not the one on the south shore. They also undoubtedly knew that you two were in this vicinity, but probably did not have enough information. So, it was too dangerous for them to try to find you. We also felt that they would travel to Fort Victoria and depart for San Francisco from there, so they would stop and camp one more night on this side. We took two small canoes, and with the help of the lookout tree found where they had stopped to camp. The rest was very easy. They didn't have a chance against the experts!"

Both Bedard and Roger shook their heads.

"You are indeed experts," Roger said, "because they were intelligent, experienced and very dangerous killers."

The packs yielded some gold plus a huge sheaf of gold vouchers.

"Only two men left on the list," Bedard said. "Don and Wilber Thompson, plus the killer that travels with them, Tommy Deb."

Later in the day, after the midday meal, the two travellers sat with their friends in silence alongside the fireplace. Aurora was quietly crying in Bedard's arms.

"I will remember you every day for the rest of my life," he said.

Roger looked at Chief Enthica and then back at Bedard.

"Chief Little Bon and I might go north in the spring and then visit Hawaii and perhaps Hong Kong and then go farther west as you did. We are still young, and we think that travelling a bit more would be entertaining and educational."

He looked at Dorthea and they smiled at each other.

David was sitting with his arm around Elizabeth. "We are going to stay here as long as we can, but we think that the changes to this world in a few years might influence us to move on, maybe also to Hawaii and China. The world is getting smaller. We understand that Britain is moving to take political control of both Hawaii and Hong Kong."

"I have been away from Britain for four years," Dorthea said. "I am interested to see what changes have been made to my world."

She smiled at Bedard.

He gave her a mischievous smirk. "I think that both Sir Ronald and Dr. Hanson will be waiting."

She hit him with the sweater that she had in her hand.

The canoes that would take them to the *Cobalt* were waiting for them. Modan had called the four dogs down and had attached the lifting harness to each of them so that they could be hoisted into the boat.

Goodbyes were said, and the two clambered into the canoe that would take them out to the boat. Bedard looked around for Adrona but she had disappeared. Aurora was standing at the door with Basso in her arms, and Noua and the twins were waving frantically below her. He waved back.

The small flotilla of canoes moved off. Dorthea was still standing in the canoe, waving at the group on the beach. Bedard was sitting with his head hung down.

"There she is!" said Dorthea.

Bedard stood up and looked back to see Adrona standing on the beach by the water. Neither of them waved. They had said their goodbyes. They both continued to stare at each other until the canoe was out of sight around a bend in the river.

Bedard turned and sat down again, smiling at Dorthea.

20

CPSIA information can be obtained
at www.ICGtesting.com
Printed in the USA
LVHW020048260719
625397LV00006B/21/P

9 780228 814856